Their gazes met and locked.

Something – pheromones, for one thing – buzzed between them with an intensity that nearly buckled her knees.

Or was that the wine she'd consumed doing a number on her?

Perhaps it was both.

Isabella offered him a lighthearted smile. "If you'll excuse me, I think I'll go to bed."

"Sleep tight."

Yeah, right.

She'd set her sights on finding Mr Right – or Señor Right more accurately – but she was afraid that JR Fortune thought he might be that man.

Sure, the city-slicker was handsome – and wealthy.

A very attractive, very appealing man.

But they were as different as night and day.

She'd lost herself and her family roots once, and she wouldn't allow that to happen again.

That's why she was determined to find the right mate.

So what was with her growing attraction to the wrong one?

First published in Great Britain 2010
Harlequin Mills & Boon Limited,
Eton House, 18-24 Paradise Road, Richmond, Surrey TW9 1SR

Triple Trouble © Harlequin Books S.A. 2009
A Real Live Cowboy © Harlequin Books S.A. 2009

Special thanks and acknowledgement are given to Lois Faye Dyer and Judy Duarte for their contributions to THE FORTUNES OF TEXAS: RETURN TO RED ROCK mini-series.

ISBN: 978 0 263 87952 0

23-0310

Harlequin Mills & Boon policy is to use papers that are natural, renewable and recyclable products and made from wood grown in sustainable forests. The logging and manufacturing processes conform to the legal environmental regulations of the country of origin.

Printed and bound in Spain
by Litografia Rosés S.A., Barcelona

TRIPLE TROUBLE

BY
LOIS FAYE DYER

A REAL LIVE COWBOY

BY
JUDY DUARTE

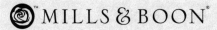

MILLS & BOON

TRIPLE TROUBLE

BY
LOIS FAYE DYER

Lois Faye Dyer lives in a small town on the shore of beautiful Puget Sound in the Pacific Northwest with her two eccentric and loveable cats, Chloe and Evie. She loves to hear from readers and you can write to her c/o Paperbacks Plus, 1618 Bay Street, Port Orchard, WA 98366, USA. Visit her on the web at www.LoisDyer.com and www.SpecialAuthors.com.

For Grant Suh and his proud parents, Steve and Brenda. Welcome to America and our family, Grant – we're so glad you're here.

Chapter One

Nicholas Fortune closed the financial data file on his computer and stretched. Yawning, he pushed his chair away from his desk and stood. His office was on the top floor of the building housing the Fortune Foundation, and outside the big corner windows, the Texas night was moonless, the sky a black dome spangled with the faint glitter of stars.

"Hell of a lot different from L.A.," he mused aloud, his gaze tracing the moving lights of an airplane far above. The view from the window in his last office in a downtown Los Angeles high rise too often had been blurred with smog that usually blotted out the stars. No, Red Rock, Texas, was more than just a few thousand miles from California—it was a whole world away.

All in all, he thought as he gazed into the darkness, he was glad he'd moved here a month ago. He'd grown tired of his job as a financial analyst for the Kline Corporation in L.A. and needed new challenges—working for the family foundation allowed him time to contemplate his next career move. And a nice side benefit was that he got to spend more time with his brother, Darr.

With the exception of the hum of a janitor's vacuum in the hallway outside, the building around him was as silent as the street below. Nicholas turned away from the window and returned to his desk to slide his laptop into its leather carrying case. He was just shrugging into his jacket when his cell phone rang.

He glanced at his watch. The fluorescent dials read eleven-fifteen. He didn't recognize the number and ordinarily would have let the call go to voice mail, but for some reason he thumbed the On button. "Hello?"

"Mr. Fortune? Nicholas Fortune?"

He didn't recognize the male voice. "Yes."

"Ah, excellent." Relief echoed in the man's voice. "I'm sorry to call so late, but I've been trying to locate you for three days and my assistant just found this number. My name is Andrew Sanchez. I'm an attorney for the estate of Stan Kennedy."

Nicholas froze, his fingers tightening on the slim black cell phone. "The *estate* of Stan Kennedy? Did something happen to Stan?"

"I'm sorry to be the bearer of unfortunate news." The caller's voice held regret. "Mr. Kennedy and his wife were killed in a car accident three days ago."

Shock kept Nicholas mute.

"Mr. Fortune?"

"Yeah." Nicholas managed to force words past the thick emotion clogging his throat. "Yeah, I'm here."

"It's my understanding you and Mr. Kennedy were quite close?"

"We were college roommates. I haven't seen Stan in a year or so, but we keep in touch—*kept* in touch by phone and e-mail." *Like brothers,* Nicholas thought. "We were close as brothers in college."

"I see. Well, Mr. Fortune, that probably explains why he named you guardian of his children. The little girls are currently safe and in the care of a foster mother, but the caseworker is anxious to transfer custody to you. The sooner they're in a stable environment the better."

"Whoa, wait a minute." Nicholas shook his head to clear it, convinced he hadn't heard the attorney correctly. "Stan left *me* in charge of his kids?"

"Yes, that's correct." The attorney paused. "You didn't know?"

Nicholas tried to remember exactly what Stan had told him about his will. They'd both agreed to take care of business for the other if anything happened to them. He'd been Stan's best man at his wedding to Amy and he definitely remembered Stan asking him to look after his bride should anything happen. Even though their conversation had taken place while emptying a magnum of champagne, Nicholas knew his word was important to Stan and he hadn't given it lightly.

But *babies?* And not just one—*three.*

"The triplets weren't born when we made a pact to look after each other's estate, should anything ever happen," he told the attorney. *And neither of us thought he and Amy wouldn't live to raise their daughters.* "But I promised Stan I'd take care of his family if he couldn't."

"Excellent." The attorney's voice was full of relief. "Can I expect you at my office tomorrow, then?"

"Tomorrow?" Nick repeated, his voice rough with shock.

"I know it's extremely short notice," Sanchez said apologetically. "But as I said, the caseworker is very concerned that the babies be settled in a permanent situation as soon as possible."

"Uh, yeah, I suppose that makes sense," Nick said. He thrust his fingers through his hair and tried to focus on the calendar that lay open on his desktop. "I've got a meeting I can't cancel in the morning, but I'll catch the first flight out after lunch." Nicholas jotted down the address in Amarillo and hung up. It was several moments before he realized he was sitting on the edge of his desk, staring at the silent phone, still open in his hand.

Grief washed over him, erasing the cold, numbing shock that had struck with the news. He couldn't believe Stan and Amy were gone. The couple met life with a zest few of their friends could match. It was impossible to get his head around the fact that all their vibrant energy had been snuffed out.

He scrubbed his hand down his face and his fingers came away damp.

He sucked in a deep breath and stood. He didn't have time to mourn Stan and Amy. Their deaths had left their three little girls vulnerable, without the protection of parents. Though how the hell Stan and Amy had ever decided he was the best choice to act as substitute dad for the triplets, Nicholas couldn't begin to guess.

In all his thirty-seven years, he'd never spent any length of time around a baby. He had four brothers but no wife, no fiancée or sister, and his mom had died two years ago. The only permanent female in his immediate family was Barbara, the woman his brother Darr had fallen in love with a month earlier. Barbara was pregnant. Did that mean she knew about babies?

Nick hadn't a clue. And for a guy who spent his life dealing with the predictability of numbers, in his career as a financial analyst, being clueless didn't sit well.

But he had no choice.

Despite being totally unqualified for the job, he was flying to Amarillo tomorrow.

And bringing home three babies.

He didn't know a damn thing about kids. Especially not little girls.

He was going to have to learn fast….

Charlene London walked quickly along the Red Rock Airport concourse, nearly running as she hurried to the gate. The flight to Amarillo was already boarding and only a few stragglers like herself waited to be checked through.

Fortunately, the uniformed airline attendant was efficient, and a moment later, Charlene joined the short queue of passengers waiting to board.

For the first time in the last hour, she drew a deep breath and relaxed. The last three weeks had been hectic and difficult. Breaking up with her fiancé after three years had been hard, but quitting her job, packing her apartment and putting everything in storage had been draining. She'd purposely pared her luggage down to a few bags, since she'd be living with her mother in a condo in Amarillo while she looked for a job and an apartment.

And a new life, she told herself. She was determined to put her failed relationship with Barry behind her and get on with her career.

She sipped her latte, mentally updating her résumé while the line moved slowly forward. They entered the plane and her eyes widened at the packed cabin and aisle, still thronged with passengers finding seats and stowing bags in the overhead compartments.

Thank goodness I used my frequent flyer miles to upgrade to first class. She glanced at her ticket and scanned the numbers above the seats, pausing as she found hers.

"Excuse me."

The man rose and stepped into the aisle to let her move past him to reach the window seat.

He smelled wonderful. Charlene didn't recognize

the scent, but it was subtle and clean. Probably incredibly expensive. *And thank goodness he isn't wearing the same cologne as Barry,* she thought with a rush of relief.

She was trying to get away from Barry—and didn't need or want any reminder of her ex-boyfriend. Or fiancé. Or whatever the appropriate term was for the man you'd dated for three whole years, thinking he was the man you'd marry, until you'd discovered that he was…not the man you'd thought he was at all.

Very disheartening.

"Can I put that up for you?"

The deep male voice rumbled, yanking Charlene from her reverie.

"What?" She realized he was holding out his hand, the expression on his very handsome face expectant. He lifted a brow, glanced significantly at her carry-on, then at her. "Oh, yes. Thank you."

He swung the bag up with ease while she slipped into the window seat. She focused on latching her seat belt, stowing her purse under the seat and settling in. It wasn't until the plane backed away from the gate to taxi toward the runaway that she really looked at the man beside her.

He was staring at the inflight magazine but Charlene had the distinct impression he wasn't reading. In profile, his face was all angles with high cheekbones, chiseled lips and a strong jawline. His dark brown hair was short, just shy of a buzz cut, and from her side view, his eyelashes were amazingly long and thick. She wondered idly what color his eyes were.

She didn't wonder long. He glanced up, his gaze meeting hers.

Brown. His eyes were brown. *The kind of eyes a woman could lose herself in,* she thought hazily.

His eyes darkened, lashes half lowering as he studied her.

Charlene's breath caught at the male interest he didn't bother to hide. Her skin heated, her nipples peaking beneath the soft lace of her bra.

Stunned at the depth of her reaction, she couldn't pull her gaze from his.

Despite his preoccupation with what lay ahead of him in Amarillo, Nicholas couldn't ignore the quick surge of interest when he looked up and saw the woman standing in the aisle.

When he stood to let her reach her seat, she brushed by him and the scent of subtle perfume teased his senses. The sleek fall of auburn hair spilled forward as she sat, leaning forward to slide her purse beneath her seat. She tucked the long strands back behind her ear while she settled in and latched her seat belt.

Finally, she glanced sideways at him and he was able to catch a glimpse. Her thick-lashed eyes were green as new spring grass. They widened as she stared at him.

She wasn't just pretty. She was beautiful, he realized. And if the faint flush on her cheeks was any indication, she was feeling the same slam of sexual awareness that had hit him like a fist the moment her gaze had met his.

"Everything okay?" he asked when she continued to stare at him without speaking.

She blinked, and just that quickly the faintly unfocused expression was gone, replaced by a sharp awareness.

"Yes." She lifted one slender-fingered hand in a dismissive gesture. "I had to nearly run to catch the plane. I hate being late."

Nicholas nodded and would have said more, but just then the plane engines throttled up, the sound increasingly louder as the jet hurtled down the runaway and left the tarmac. He glanced at the woman beside him and found her gripping the armrests, eyes closed.

Clearly, she didn't like to fly. Air travel didn't bother Nicholas, but he waited until the plane leveled out and her white-knuckled grip relaxed before he spoke.

"I'm Nicholas." He purposely didn't tell her his last name. The Fortune surname was well-known in Red Rock and being part of a rich, powerful family carried its own problems. He'd learned early that many people associated the name with a preconceived set of expectations.

"Charlene London," she responded as she took a bottle of water from her bag. "Are you flying to Amarillo on business?" she asked, sipping her water.

"Not exactly." He paused, frowning.

Charlene tucked an errant strand of hair behind one ear with an absentminded gesture. *What did that mean?* "I see," she said.

He laughed—a short, wry chuckle. "I don't mean to be vague. My trip is both business and personal."

"Oh." Curious though she was, Charlene was reluctant to grill him. Somewhere in the coach section of the airplane, a baby began to cry.

Nick stiffened and appeared to listen intently until the cries turned to whimpers. Tension eased from his body and he looked at her, his gaze turbulent.

"My college roommate and his wife died a few days ago and I'm guardian of their daughters. I'm going to Amarillo to take custody of three kids. Triplets." He sighed. "Twelve-month-old triplets."

Charlene's eyes widened with shock. She was speechless for a moment. "You're kidding," she finally managed to get out.

"Nope." His expression was part gloom, part stark dread. "I'm not kidding."

"Do you and your wife have children of your own?"

"I'm not married. And I don't have any kids," he added. "The closest I've ever come to having a dependant is my dog, Rufus."

"So you'll be caring for three babies…all by yourself?"

He nodded. "That's about the size of it."

"That's crazy."

"Yeah," he said with conviction. "Insane."

"I'm the oldest of six siblings, two of whom are twins," Charlene said. "If you'd permit a little advice from someone who's been there—you should hire a full-time nanny, and the sooner the better."

Nicholas thought she probably was right—in fact,

the more he considered the idea, the more he was convinced. Before he could ask her more questions, however, the woman walking the crying baby up and down the aisle reached their row.

"Excuse me." Charlene stood.

Nicholas wanted to ask her if she knew anything about hiring nannies, but her abrupt request stopped him. He stepped into the aisle to let her pass him. Her shoulder brushed his chest in the slightest of touches, yet his muscles tensed as if she'd trailed her fingertips over his bare skin.

Nick dragged in a steadying breath, but it only served to flood his senses with the scent of subtle perfume and warm woman.

He nearly groaned aloud. He'd dated a lot of women over the years, but he hadn't reacted to a female with the level of gut-deep, instant lust since he was a teenager. He blinked, frowned and ordered his rebellious body to calm down. He couldn't afford to be distracted just now—he had to focus on dealing with Stan and Amy's little girls.

He dropped back into his seat. He expected Charlene to walk toward the lavatories at the front of the first class section, but instead, she waited until the young mother turned and moved back down the aisle.

"Hi," Charlene smiled at the weary mother. "I bet you're exhausted."

Oh hell. Nick tensed when the woman holding the baby looked like she was going to cry. He hated it when women cried. Fortunately, the woman didn't burst into tears.

"I'm beyond exhausted," the woman murmured, patting the wailing baby on the back soothingly. "And so is she," she added. "I don't think either one of us has slept more than a half hour at a time for days."

"Oh my. My little brother did the same thing," Charlene said, her gaze warm and sympathetic. "He was born several weeks premature and had acid reflux. Poor little guy. It took a while for us to figure out how to handle him so he could fall asleep."

The young mother's eyes widened. "You found a solution? What was it?"

"I'd be glad to show you," Charlene said, holding out her arms.

The woman hesitated, clearly torn about handing her baby to a complete stranger.

"I totally understand if you're not comfortable with having me hold her, after all, we don't know each other," Charlene said reassuringly. "I could try to explain, but it's much easier to demonstrate."

The baby chose that moment to wail even louder than before. The unhappy cry seemed to galvanize the mother, because she eased the tiny little girl off her shoulder and passed her carefully to Charlene.

Nick didn't know much about babies, but every one he'd seen had been cradled or propped against someone's shoulder. Charlene did neither. Instead, she laid the baby facedown on her arm, the little head in the palm of her hand, and gently swayed her back and forth while smoothing her free palm over the tiny back. The baby's arms waved jerkily, slowing in time with her cries that quickly gave way to hic-cupping sobs, then blessed silence.

Nick stared at Charlene. *Damn. She's good. Really good.*

He glanced at the baby's mother and found her ex-pression as surprised as he felt.

"How in the world did you do that?" she whis-pered.

"Experience," Charlene murmured, her fingertips continuing to gently rub in soothing circles over the little girl's back. The pink cotton dress matched the baby's sock-covered feet, now dangling limply on either side of Charlene's arm. "I was twelve when my little brother was born." She glanced down at the baby, fast asleep and seemingly boneless in her arms. "If you tilt her slightly to the right when you hold her, change her diaper or feed her, it helps with acid reflux too. I don't know if your little girl has that problem, but if she does, the pain can make her so uncomfortable that she won't be able to fall asleep or stay asleep."

"Thank you so much." The words carried a wealth of heartfelt appreciation as she carefully took the sleeping baby from Charlene.

"You're welcome," Charlene replied, moving aside to let the mother and child step past her. She watched them move down the aisle and return to their seat in coach.

Nick stood to let Charlene slip into her seat near the window, then dropped into his own.

"Impressive," he told her. "Very impressive."

She shrugged and picked up her water bottle to sip. "Basic stuff, if you've ever helped care for a baby. Unfortunately, most new moms only find out about the little things to make life easier for them and their baby if they talk to someone who's coped hands-on with the problem."

After watching Charlene's easy confidence with the crying baby before she handed the peacefully sleeping child back to her mother, Nicholas knew he'd found the answer to his urgent need for a nanny. "Makes sense. Experience always counts. I need someone with that level of experience. How about you?" he asked.

"How about me…what?"

"Being the nanny for the triplets. I'll pay you double whatever the going rate is," he went on when she shook her head.

"I'm sorry, I really am. But I'll be looking for a job in Amarillo."

"What if I offered you a substantial signing bonus—say, twenty-five thousand dollars?"

Her eyes widened. "That's a very generous offer—and one that guarantees applicants will be standing in line for the position. You'll have your pick of nannies. You don't need me."

"Yes, I do." Nick was convinced. Charlene didn't appear to share his opinion, however. "In fact, I'm so sure you're the only person for the triplets that I'll add another twenty-five thousand dollar bonus if you stay until their aunt is found and comes to get them."

She stared at him for a loaded moment. "Their aunt is taking them?"

Nick was surprised she didn't ask about the money, but if she wanted information about the babies, he'd give it to her. "I don't have permanent custody of the girls, only temporary care until the estate locates Amy's sister, Lana. She's a teacher, and according to Amy, a career volunteer with various organizations overseas, helping children in third world countries. She's also married." Unlike me, he thought. A confirmed bachelor with no plans to marry anytime soon. "So the girls will have two parents instead of only me."

"I see."

For a brief moment, Nick thought Charlene was going to accept his offer. But then she shook her head.

"I'm sorry, especially since I know how difficult it is to care for more than one baby. But I have plans and I've made promises to people. I can't let them down on such short notice."

"You're sure I can't change your mind?"

"No, I'm afraid not."

"Too bad." He pulled a business card and pen from his inner jacket pocket and wrote on the back of the card. "This is my cell phone number, in case you reconsider the offer. I'll be in Amarillo until tomorrow, when I have reservations to fly the girls back to Red Rock."

"You aren't staying in Amarillo very long," she commented as she took the card, tucking it into her purse without reading it.

"No. I want to take the triplets home as soon as possible and get them settled in. I doubt anything will make this easier for them, but I thought the faster I transfer them, the better." He pointed at her purse where his card had disappeared. "Call me if you change your mind."

"I'll keep your card," she replied. "But I don't think it's likely I'll change my mind."

They parted in the terminal, Nicholas heading for the exit and Charlene moving to baggage pickup.

Saying goodbye felt wrong. Charlene had to force herself not to turn around and give him her phone number, ask him to call…plead until he promised to meet her later.

Her level of conviction that Nick was somehow important to her was profound.

This is crazy. She held her chin up and kept walking, but her thoughts continued to tumble, one over the other, refusing to leave Nick even as she physically moved farther away from him.

She'd never felt anything approaching the instant attraction that had flared between them, her nerves shaking with need during that first long exchange of glances. Lust and sexual attraction were far more powerful forces than she'd imagined. The time spent sitting next to Nick during the flight had given her new insight into just how intensely her body could respond to the right man. Those moments were forcing her to reevaluate whether she'd ever truly been deeply moved before—including with Barry, she realized with sudden shock.

Yet she'd become engaged to Barry, she reminded herself in an effort to regain control of her emotions.

Clearly her wisdom in this area wasn't infallible. Besides, a man was the last thing she needed or wanted in her life right now. She definitely didn't need the complication of a man who was about to become an instant father to three little girls.

Still, she'd been impressed with Nicholas's willingness to take on the babies. She couldn't help but compare his heroic, stand-up attitude with her ex's lack of responsibility. She couldn't imagine Barry in Nicholas's situation. She seriously doubted Barry would have agreed to take custody of three children. He was adamantly opposed to becoming a parent. It was one of the issues they couldn't agree on, since she very much wanted children—an issue that, ultimately, had caused her to conclude they were completely mismatched.

Charlene collected her three suitcases and stepped out of the crowd of passengers to pull a jacket from inside the smallest bag. March in chilly Amarillo was a far cry from the warmth of Red Rock, located in southern Texas near San Antonio. Sure enough, when she wheeled her bags outside, she was glad she had the added protection of the coat. She tucked her chin into the shelter of her collar and halted to scan the line of cars crowding the curb.

"Charlene! Over here!" Her mother's voice carried clearly over the hum and chatter of passengers.

Charlene returned Angie's enthusiastic wave and hurried down the walkway.

"Mom, it's so good to see you." Charlene basked

in her mother's warm hug, breathing in the familiar scent of Estée Lauder perfume.

"It's been too long," Angie said, scolding with a loving smile as she stepped back, holding Charlene at arm's length. Her eyes narrowed as she swept a swift glance over her daughter, from her toes to the crown of her head. "You're too skinny."

Charlene laughed. "You always say that, Mom. I've lost inches but not pounds—I've been working out at the gym."

"Well, now that you're home, I'm going to feed you," Angie declared firmly.

They loaded Charlene's bags into the trunk. Moments later, Angie expertly negotiated traffic as they left the airport.

"Are you enjoying being in the condo, or do you think you'll miss having a big yard this summer? You spent hours gardening at the old house, and I know you loved the flowers." Charlene's mother had sold the rambler where she and her siblings had grown up after her parents' divorce three years earlier. Following college graduation and Charlene's move to Red Rock, Angie had insisted she should be the one to travel for visits to her six children, especially Charlene, since her job as a Health Unit Coordinator at the hospital E.R. kept her so busy. As a result, Charlene had only seen her mother's condo on two short weekend trips.

"I love condo life," Angie said with a happy smile. "I still garden, but now I'm planting flowers and herbs in terra cotta pots on the lanai. Of course," she added. "I still have to mow the strip of grass in my backyard, but it's tiny compared to the big lawn at the old house."

Angie's voice rang with contentment. Charlene knew what a difficult time her mother had had after the divorce, and was immeasurably relieved that she appeared to have adjusted so well.

"I'm glad you're enjoying it, Mom." She tucked a strand of hair behind her ear and adjusted her Ray-Bans a little higher on her nose to better block the late afternoon sun. "What are you doing with all your free time, now that you're not mowing grass and pulling weeds?"

"I've been busy at work," Angie began before pausing to clear her throat. "And…I've met someone," she blurted.

Surprised, Charlene looked at her mother and was startled to see a hint of color on her cheeks. "That's great, Mom. Who is he?"

"His name is Lloyd Weber and he's an architect for a firm here in Amarillo. We met playing bridge. I joined the group about six months ago."

"So, you're dating?" Charlene could hardly get her mind around the image of her mother dating. Not that she objected—in fact, she'd urged her mom to get out and about. Angie was fifty-two and loved people and social interaction; Charlene truly believed her mom would be happier in a committed relationship.

"Well, yes—we've been dating for a while." Angie pulled up in front of the condo building and parked.

Her expression reflected concern and a certain trepidation when she unlatched her seat belt and half-turned to meet Charlene's gaze. "I didn't tell you before, because…well, because I wasn't sure whether Lloyd and I were going to become serious. But two weeks ago he moved in with me."

Charlene stared at her mother, stunned. "You're living together?"

"Yes, dear."

"Here in your condo?"

Angie nodded. "His house is being remodeled before he puts it on the market, and he was staying in a bed-and-breakfast. I told him it was silly to spend all that money when we're together nearly all the time anyway. I convinced him to move in here."

"Well, um." Charlene managed to say. "That's great, Mom. If he makes you happy, I'm delighted."

"You're not upset?"

"Mom, of course I'm not upset." Charlene hugged Angie. "I think it's great." She sat back, laughing at the sheer relief on her mother's face. "If he's a great guy who's being good to you and you're happy, then I'm thrilled for you."

"I'm very happy, and he *is* a great guy," Angie said firmly. "Now come on, let's get your things inside so you can meet him."

Charlene followed Angie up the sidewalk, towing a rolling suitcase behind her.

What am I going to do now? The question made her feel totally selfish in light of her mother's transparent happiness. But Charlene's practical side told her the situation required a change of plans. She couldn't stay at the condo with her mother and Lloyd during what was surely the honeymoon stage of their relationship.

She needed a new plan. And fast.

What the hell was I thinking?

Nick strode away from Charlene and didn't look back. The airport wasn't crowded and it was a matter of moments before he reached the exit doors and walked outside. He knew it was the worst possible time to meet a woman who interested him. And Charlene London was too pretty to hire as a nanny.

He was going to have enough problems dealing with the sea change about to happen in his life. He didn't need to move a sexy, gorgeous woman into his house to complicate life even more.

He spotted a uniformed driver holding a sign with his name in big block letters, and changed direction to reach the black Lincoln Town Car. During the drive to Andrew Sanchez's office, he scanned a file with information about Stan and Amy's estate the attorney had asked the driver to give him.

Andrew Sanchez was a rotund, balding man in his mid-fifties. Businesslike and efficient, he still exuded an air of concern and sympathy.

"Do you have family or friends available to help with the triplets?" he asked Nick as they concluded their meeting.

"No, but I'm planning to find a nanny. Until then

I have a housekeeper, and she's agreed to work longer hours until I can find someone."

"You might want to consider two nannies," Mr. Sanchez commented. "Those three little girls are dynamos." He grinned with wry affection. "I'm glad you're a younger man, because just spending an hour with them at their foster home wore me out. You're going to need all the energy you can muster."

Nick nodded. He didn't tell the older man that he had no clue how much energy one little girl required from a caretaker, let alone three of them at once. "You're continuing to search for Amy's sister?"

The attorney nodded. "I've hired a detective agency to look for her. They told me they can't give us a time frame, since she's out of the country, but at least Amy's e-mail files gave us the name of the mission organization in Africa that employed her. It's a place to start hunting." He sighed. "The e-mail records on Amy's computer indicate her sister stopped communicating a month or so ago. Also that Amy had been trying to contact her but had no success."

"Any idea why?"

"Lana and her husband apparently resigned their positions with the relief agency where they were employed. But we don't know where they went after that. And given that the two are working in a remote area of Africa, well…" Sanchez spread his hands and shrugged. "It's anyone's guess where they've gone or how long before they surface. As I said, the detective agency warned me they can't guarantee a time frame for locating the couple."

"Let's hope they find her soon. I have to believe Amy's sister and her husband will be better at caring for three little girls than I am."

"The important thing is that you're willing to try." The attorney shook his head. "The interim foster home where the girls are staying is a good situation, but they can't stay there indefinitely. They'll be much better off with you while we're searching for their aunt."

"I hope you're right." Nick wasn't convinced.

It was after 6:00 p.m. before the attorney and Nick finished going over the will and other documents.

"I took the liberty of booking a room for you in a nearby hotel," Sanchez told him as they pushed back chairs and stood. "I understand the triplets are in bed for the night by 7:00 p.m. I thought you might want to wait until morning to see them."

"I appreciate it." Nicholas held out his hand. "Thanks for everything."

"You're welcome." The attorney's clasp was firm. "Let me know if there's anything else I can do for you. And I'll notify you as soon as I receive any information as to the whereabouts of Amy's sister."

Nick walked to the door. "It seems odd to pick up the girls and leave Amarillo without saying goodbye in some way."

"I know." The attorney nodded. "But their wills were very specific. As the closest living relative, Amy's sister will organize a memorial service so friends can pay their respects when she returns."

"I'm damned sure neither of them ever thought

they'd die together and leave the kids," Nick muttered, almost to himself.

"No one ever does." Sanchez shook his head. "It's a hell of a situation. We'll just have to do the best we can and search diligently for the children's aunt."

"Right." Nick said goodbye and left the office to climb into the town car once more.

The conversation with Andrew Sanchez had driven home the unbelievable fact that Stan and Amy were gone. Nick barely noticed the streets the limo drove down as they headed toward the hotel.

Despite his conviction that Charlene wasn't the best choice for an employee on a purely personal level, he definitely believed her experience made her the perfect woman to care for Stan's daughters. Before he unpacked his bag in the hotel room, he called his office in Red Rock and asked his assistant to run a preliminary employment check on Charlene London.

Just in case, he told himself, *she called and said yes to the job offer.* He knew the fact that she hadn't given him her contact number made the likelihood a million-to-one shot—but he was a man who believed in luck.

And he was going to need a boatload of luck to get through the next few days, or weeks, or however long it took before the triplets' aunt showed up to claim them.

Chapter Two

The following morning, the same limo driver picked Nick up promptly at 9:00 a.m.

"We're here, sir." The driver's voice broke Nick's absorption in memories and he realized they were parked in front of a white rambler with a fenced yard and worn grass. It looked lived-in and comfortable.

"So we are," he muttered.

"Mr. Sanchez told me to wait and drive you all to the airport when you're ready, sir."

"Good, thanks," Nick said absently, focused on what awaited him within the house.

A round young woman in jeans and green T-shirt answered his knock, a little girl perched on her hip.

"Hello, you must be Nick Fortune. I'm Christie

Williams. My husband and I are…were friends of Stan and Amy. We volunteered to be temporary foster parents for the girls. Come in."

She held the door wide and Nick stepped over the threshold into a living room, the green carpet strewn with toys. Two babies sat on the floor in the midst of the confusion of blocks, balls, stuffed animals and brightly colored plastic things that Nick couldn't identify. The girls' black hair and bright blue eyes were carbon copies of the child on Christie's hip, who stared at him with solemn interest.

A woman in a gray business suit rose from the sofa as he entered.

"Mr. Fortune, it's a pleasure to see you." She stepped forward and held out her hand, her grip firm in a brief handshake. "I'm Carol Smith, the caseworker. As you can see, the girls are doing well."

Nick nodded, murmuring an absent acknowledgment, his attention on the two little girls seated on the floor. Both of them eyed him with solemn, big-eyed consideration. They were dressed in tiny little tennis shoes and long pants with attached bibs, one in pale purple, one in pink. He glanced at the baby perched on the foster mother's hip. She wore the same little bibbed pants with tennis shoes, only her outfit was bright yellow.

"They're identical?" He hadn't expected them to look so much alike. If it wasn't for the color of their clothes, he wouldn't be able to tell them apart.

"Yes, they are," Ms. Smith replied. "It's quite rare, actually. In today's world, many multiple births are the result of in vitro procedures and the children are more commonly fraternal twins or triplets. But Jackie, Jenny and Jessie are truly identical."

"I see." *Great. How am I going to tell them apart?*

"Fortunately, Amy had their names engraved on custom-made bracelets for each of them. She and Stan didn't need to use them, of course, but any time the triplets had a babysitter, the bracelets were immensely helpful," the foster mother added. "This is Jackie." She shifted the little girl off her hip and handed her to Nick.

Taken off guard, he automatically took the child, holding her awkwardly in midair with his hands at her waist.

Jackie stared at him, blue eyes solemn as she studied him, her legs dangling. She wriggled, little legs scissoring, and Nick cradled her against his chest to keep from dropping her.

She responded by chortling and grabbing a fistful of his blue polo shirt in one hand and smacking him in the chin with her other. Startled, Nick eyed the little girl who seemed to find it hilarious that she'd found his chin. She babbled a series of nonsensical sounds, and then paused to look expectantly at him.

He looked at the foster mother in confusion. "What did she say?"

The woman laughed, her eyes twinkling. "I have no idea. She'll be perfectly happy if you just respond in some way."

"Oh." Nick looked down into the little face, still clearly awaiting a response. "Uh, yeah. That sounds good," he said, trying his best to sound as if he was agreeing with an actual question.

Jackie responded with delight, waving her arms enthusiastically and babbling once again.

Five minutes of this back and forth and Nick started to feel as if he were getting the hang of baby chat.

"Do they know any real words?" he asked the two women after he'd taken turns holding each of the little girls and had exchanged similar conversations with Jenny and Jessie.

"Not that I've heard," Christie volunteered. "But at twelve months, I wouldn't expect them to, necessarily."

Nick nodded, watching the three as they sat on the floor, playing with large, plastic, red-and-blue blocks. Jenny threw one and the square red toy bounced off his knee. He grinned when she laughed, waving her hands before she grabbed another block. She tossed with more enthusiasm than accuracy and it flew across the room. Clearly disappointed, she frowned at him when he chuckled.

"They're going to be a handful," he murmured, more to himself than to the two women.

"Oh, they certainly will be—and are," Christie agreed. "Have you hired a nanny to help you care for them?"

"Not yet. I called a Red Rock employment agency this morning, but they didn't have anyone on their books. They promised to keep searching and call the minute they find someone." Nick glanced at his watch. "I have reservations for a noon flight."

"You're going to fly the girls back to Red Rock?"

Nick switched his gaze from the girls to Christie. Her facial expression reflected the concern in her question.

"I'd planned to." He didn't miss the quick exchange of worried looks between the foster mother and social worker. "Is there a problem with taking the girls on an airplane?"

"I'm just wondering how you're going to juggle all three of them, let alone their luggage, stroller and the carry-on bags with their things." Carol Smith pointed at the corner of the living room closest to the outer door. The area was filled with luggage, a large leather shoulder bag, toys and three ungainly looking children's car seats. A baby stroller for three was parked to one side.

"All of that belongs to the girls?" Nick rapidly considered the logistics, calculating what needed to be moved, stored, checked at the gate before the flight. "I can load their things into the back of the limo and get a redcap at the airport."

"Well, yes, you can," Christie agreed. "But Jessie has an ear infection and is taking antibiotics plus Tylenol for pain, and I'm not at all sure the pediatrician would approve of her flying. And even if he okayed the trip, you'd still have to take care of all three of them on the flight, all by yourself." She eyed him dubiously.

"Is that an insurmountable problem?" he asked.

"For one person, it certainly could be," Carol Smith put in. "Especially when one of them needs a diaper changed or if they all are hungry at once."

"Is that likely to happen?"

"Yes," the two women said in unison.

"I see." Nick really was beginning to see why the women seemed dubious. Maybe they were right to be apprehensive about his ability to care for these kids. Just transporting three babies was going to be much more complicated than he'd anticipated. On the other hand, he'd organized and directed programs for large companies. How hard could it be to handle three little kids?

"You two have a lot more experience at this than me. Do you have any suggestions?"

"If I were you," Christie said firmly, "I'd rent a car and drive back to Red Rock. And I'd hire someone to make the trip with me, because I can't imagine any possible way you can do this without at least one other person to help."

Nick instantly thought of Charlene and wished fervently that he'd gotten her phone number. But he had no way to contact her, *and besides,* he thought, *she'd sounded definite when she'd turned down his offer of employment as the girls' nanny.*

He ran his hand over his hair, rumpling it. "Unless one of you is prepared to volunteer, I'm afraid I'm on my own."

"Is there a family member who could fly here and drive back to Red Rock with you?"

"Maybe." He considered the idea, realizing that he had no other choice. "But it will take time to locate someone, and they probably couldn't get here until tomorrow at the earliest. I'd like to get the girls home and settled in as soon as possible."

The three adults had identical frowns on their faces as they observed the triplets who were happily unaware of the life decisions being considered.

Nick's cell phone rang, breaking the brief silence. He glanced at the unfamiliar number in his Caller ID and nearly ignored it. Instinct, however, had him answering the call.

"Hello." The female voice was familiar. "This is Charlene London."

While eating dinner with her mother and Lloyd, Charlene had felt distinctly like a fifth wheel.

She liked Lloyd and it was clear the man adored Angie. Her mother also clearly felt the same about the charming, gray-haired architect.

Which delighted Charlene. But it left her with a serious problem. Her plan to live with her mother while she searched for a job and an apartment of her own was no longer plausible. But Angie was sure to object if she abruptly changed her plans, and Charlene strongly suspected Lloyd would feel as if his presence had forced her from the condo. *He really is a nice man,* she thought, smiling as she remembered the besotted look on his face when he'd gazed at Angie over dessert.

She knew any one of her sisters or brothers would welcome her into their homes, but they all led crowded, busy lives. She really didn't want to choose that option, either.

What she really needed was an instant job—and a place to live that wouldn't make her mother or Lloyd feel guilty when she left.

"I could take Nicholas's job offer," she murmured to herself. Having retired to her bedroom early, she donned her pajamas. "But that means going back to Red Rock."

She didn't want to return to Red Rock. She wanted a new start, far enough away so there was no possibility she would run into Barry and his friends while shopping, dining out, running errands, or any of the dozens of activities that made up her normal life.

She slipped into bed and spent an hour trying to read, but her concentration was fractured as she continued to mull over her changed situation.

The antique clock in the hallway chimed midnight. Charlene realized she'd spent the last hour lying in the dark, unsuccessfully trying to sleep. She muttered in disgust and sat up to switch on the bedside lamp. It cast a pool of light over the bed as she tossed back the covers and padded barefoot across the carpet to retrieve Nicholas's card from her purse.

The phone number on the back of the card was written in decisive, black slashes. Charlene flipped the square card over to read the front and gasped, feeling her eyes widen.

"Nicholas Fortune?" She stared at the logo on the business card. "He's a member of the Fortune family?" Stunned, she considered the startling information.

Nicholas's status as part of the prominent family eliminated many of her concerns. There was little likelihood she'd run into Barry if she worked as a live-in nanny for one of the Fortunes. The two men moved in far different circles. Which put a whole new slant on the possibility of going back to Red Rock, she realized.

It also explained why he'd offered a two-part employment bonus. Fifty-thousand dollars was probably small change for one of the Fortunes.

She tucked the card carefully into her purse and turned out the light. Working for Nicholas could turn out to be the opportunity she'd been looking for.

On the other hand, how would she deal with her attraction to him? Would she end up sleeping with him if she lived in his house to care for the babies?

She frowned, fingertips massaging the slight ache at her temples.

Surely she could handle living in close quarters with a handsome, sexy man for a few weeks, she told herself. And, given Nick's good looks and probably wealth, he no doubt had beautiful women by the dozens waiting for him to call.

No, it wasn't likely she needed to worry about Nick making a pass at her. The real question was, could she maintain a purely professional attitude toward him?

When she thought about the bonus he'd offered, she could only conclude she needed to set aside any emotional elements and make a purely practical decision.

The following morning, she waited until she'd showered and broke the news to her mother and Lloyd over breakfast before calling Nicholas.

"Hello."

The deep male tones shivered up her spine, and for a brief second she questioned the wisdom of agreeing to work for a man as attractive as Nicholas Fortune. Then she reminded herself just how badly she needed this job. "If it's not too late, I'd like to take you up on your offer of the nanny position," she said briskly.

"You're hired. How soon can you be ready to leave?"

"Almost immediately—I didn't unpack last night. What time is your flight?"

"Change of plans. I'm not flying the triplets back to Red Rock, we're driving."

"Oh."

"Give me your address and I'll pick you up as soon as I have the car loaded."

Charlotte quickly recited her mother's address and said goodbye. For a moment, she stared at her pink cell phone.

Have I just made a colossal mistake?

At the sound of his deep voice, she'd felt shivers of awareness race up her spine and tingle down her arms to her fingertips.

Then she remembered Barry, and her body instantly calmed as if the reaction to Nicholas had never happened. She wasn't ready to be attracted to another man. All she had to do was remind herself of her poor judgment and disappointment with Barry and she was safe, she realized with relief.

Reassured, she set her nearly full suitcase on top

of the bed and tucked her pajamas into it. A quick trip into the bathroom to collect her toiletries, and she was ready to face her mother and Lloyd.

Squaring her shoulders and drawing a deep breath, she slung her purse over her shoulder, picked up her two bags, and headed downstairs.

Across town, Nick wrestled with the complexities of fastening three car seats into the SUV the rental company had delivered. Fortunately, the vehicle was big enough to have a third seat section and had enough room for an adult to sit between two of the triplets, if necessary.

At last, the babies' car seats were securely locked in place and the bags and boxes filled with the triplets' clothes, toys and food were packed into the back of the SUV. The girls were buckled into their seats, each with a treasured blanket and a favorite stuffed toy in her arms, and their foster mother tearfully kissed them good-bye. Nick had a brand-new appreciation for the details of traveling with three babies when he finally pulled away from the curb.

Fortunately for him, the girls all fell asleep within minutes of driving off.

The motion of the car must lull them to sleep. Good to know.

If they had trouble sleeping at his house, he realized, he could always drive them around his neighborhood.

But he knew figuring out this clue about the babies wasn't enough to make him a reliable substitute parent. If he and the triplets were going to survive until the attorney located Amy's sister, he'd need all the help he could get.

Charlene London was his ace in the hole. He was convinced she had the expertise that he knew damn well he lacked.

He hoped to hell he was right, because he was betting everything on her ability to handle the triplets. If he was wrong, this road trip was going to turn into a nightmare.

Nick's relief at the triplets falling peacefully asleep didn't last long. The girls all woke when he reached the address Charlene had given him and the SUV stopped moving. They immediately began to loudly protest being buckled into their car seats. Charlene said goodbye to her mother and friend in the midst of chaos.

Ten minutes after pulling away from the curb, Nick was no longer convinced he'd found the magic bullet to lull the babies asleep. They cried and fussed nonstop, despite the motion of the SUV.

Several hours of driving south and many miles later, Nicholas turned off the highway into a rest stop and parked. The sun shone brightly, but the afternoon air was still chilly. He left the engine running and the heater on to keep the interior as comfortable as possible for Jenny and Jackie while Charlene changed Jessie's diaper. The little girl lay on the leather seat, kicking her bare legs with obvious delight while Charlene stood in the open V of the door.

Despite the churning little legs, Charlene deftly removed, replaced and snugly fastened a clean disposable nappy.

"I've done my share of tailgating at football games, but this is a new experience," Nick commented as Charlene pulled down Jessie's knit pants and snapped the leg openings closed.

"You're in a whole new world, Nick." She lifted the little girl into her arms, tickling her. Jessie chortled and Charlene laughed. They both looked up to grin at him.

Nick shook his head. Crazy as it seemed, he could swear their faces held identical expressions of feminine wisdom and mystery. "I'm not sure I'm ready for a new world," he murmured as he took the diaper bag from Charlene and returned it to the storage area in the back of the SUV. "I'm getting some coffee," he said, louder this time, so Charlene could hear him. "Want some?"

"Yes, please, I'd love a cup."

Nick crossed the patch of grass between the curb where he'd parked the SUV and the concrete apron surrounding the low-roofed building housing the restrooms. Volunteers manned a small kiosk on one side and offered weary travelers coffee and cookies.

By the time he slid behind the steering wheel again, Charlene had Jessie fastened into her car seat and was buckling her own safety belt. She took the foam cup he held out to her and sipped.

"How bad is it?" he asked, unable to look away from the sight of the pink tip of her tongue as she licked a tiny drop of coffee from the corner of her mouth.

"Not too bad."

He lifted an eyebrow but didn't comment.

"Okay, so it's not Starbucks," she conceded with a chuckle. "But it's coffee and I need the caffeine. I was awake late last night and up early this morning. I really, really need the jolt."

Nick glanced at his watch as they drove away from the rest stop. "The attorney told me the girls are in bed and asleep by seven every night. You're the expert, but I'm guessing it might be a good idea to find a motel earlier rather than later so we can keep them on schedule, if possible."

"I think that's an excellent idea." She glanced over her shoulder at the triplets' drowsy faces. "If we stop earlier, we'll have time to feed them, give them baths, and let them play for a little while before tucking them in for the night."

The motel Nick pulled into was just off the highway. Behind the motel, the tree-lined streets of a small town were laid out in neat blocks, and fairgrounds with an empty grandstand were visible a dozen or so blocks away. Nick was familiar with the motel chain and, as he'd hoped, the staff assured him they could accommodate the needs of three babies.

With quick calculation, he asked for two connecting rooms—one for the girls and Charlene, and one for him. He hoped the babies would sleep through the night.

Not for the first time, he thanked God Charlene had agreed to be the girls' nanny. If he could manage to ignore the fact that she was a beautiful woman, she made the perfect employee.

"If we both carry the girls in first, I can transfer the luggage while you keep an eye on them in the room," he told Charlene when he returned to the SUV. "We're on the ground floor, just inside the lobby and down the hall."

He handed her a key card. "Why don't you carry Jessie, I'll take Jackie and Jenny."

After unhooking the girls and handing Jenny to Nick while he held Jackie, Charlotte lifted Jessie and followed Nick into the motel.

"Our rooms are through there." He led the way toward the hallway on the far side of the lobby.

Distracted by her view of his back, Charlene forgot to reply. Beneath the battered brown leather jacket, powerful shoulder muscles flexed as Jackie and Jenny squirmed in his hold. The jacket ended at his waist and faded Levis fit snugly over his taut backside and down the long length of his legs.

Get a grip, she told herself firmly. *Stop ogling the man's rear and focus on the job—and the babies.*

"Have you got the key?"

Nick's question startled her and she realized he'd halted outside a room.

Feeling her cheeks heat and hoping he hadn't caught her staring at his backside, she quickly slid the key card through the lock slot and opened the door.

"After you." Nick held the door while she carried Jessie inside.

"Nice. Very nice." She halted at the foot of the queen-size bed and glanced around, taking in a round table with three chairs tucked into one corner near the draped window.

Nick swept the room with a quick, assessing gaze. "Yeah, not bad. The connecting room is ours too." He bent and carefully set Jackie on the carpeted floor, then Jenny. Straightening, he took another key card from his back pocket and crossed the room to open the door to the room on the side. "They're exactly the same," he said after briefly looking. He returned and halted next to Jackie, bending to remove a handful of bedspread from her mouth. "Hey," he said gently. "I'm not sure you should be chewing on that."

"She's probably hungry." Charlene set Jessie on her diaper-padded bottom next to Jackie, and handed both girls a small stuffed bear each. Both beamed up at her and Jackie instantly shoved a furry bear leg into her mouth. "Hmmm, make that she's *definitely* hungry."

"I'll bring up the bag with their food before the rest of the luggage. Anything else you need right away?"

"If you could bring up the diaper bag too, that would be great."

He nodded and left the room.

"Well, girls, let's see what we can do to make you comfortable." Charlene laughed when Jessie blew a raspberry before smiling beatifically. "Are you going to be the class clown?" she teased.

Jessie gurgled and tipped sideways before righting herself and reaching for Jackie's bear.

"Oh no you don't, kiddo." Charlene made sure each little girl had their own stuffed animal before calling the front desk. The clerk assured her he would arrange to have three high chairs from the restaurant sent to the room immediately. He also confirmed that Nick had requested three cribs during check-in and that someone would be delivering and setting them up within a half hour.

Satisfied that arrangements were under way, Charlene barely had time to replace the phone in its cradle before Nick returned with the box containing baby paraphernalia and two bags.

For the next two hours, neither she nor Nick had a moment to draw a deep breath. The high chairs were delivered while he was bringing in the luggage. Later, Charlene and Nick spooned food into little mouths, wiped chins and sticky fingers and tried to keep strained carrots from staining their own clothes.

Neither of them wanted to tackle eating dinner in the restaurant downstairs while accompanied by the triplets, so they ordered in. Nick insisted Charlene eat first, and she hurried to chew bites of surprisingly good pasta and chicken while he lay on the carpet, rolling rubber balls to the triplets. By the time Charlene's plate was empty, all three babies were yawning and rubbing their eyes.

The two adults switched places—Nick taking Charlene's chair to eat his steak, Jessie perched on his knee while Jackie played on the floor at his feet.

Charlene toted Jenny into the bathroom and popped her into the tub to scrub the smears of strained plums and carrots from her face and out of her hair.

By the time she had Jenny dried, freshly diapered and tucked into footed white pajamas patterned with little brown monkeys, Nick had finished eating.

"Hey, look at you," he said to Jenny. "What happened to the purple-and-orange face paint?"

Charlene laughed. "She even had it in her hair."

"I think they all do." Nick rubbed his hand over Jessie's black curls and grimaced. "Definitely sticky."

"I'm guessing that's the strained plums," Charlene said. She handed Jenny to him and lifted Jessie into her arms. "Will you watch her and Jackie while I put Jessie in the tub?"

"Sure—but I can bathe her if you'd like a break. I'm sure I can manage."

"No, I'm fine. Besides," she perched Jessie on her hip and started unbuttoning and unsnapping the baby's pants and knit shirt, "I'm already wet from being splashed by Jenny. One of us might as well stay dry."

Nicholas wished she hadn't pointed out that she'd been splashed with bathwater. He'd noticed the wet spots on her T-shirt and the way the damp cotton clung to her curves in interesting places. He was trying damned hard to ignore his body's reaction— and he was losing the battle.

"Uh, yeah. Okay, then. I'll keep these two occupied out here." He perched Jenny on his lap and she settled against him, her lashes half-lowered, apparently content to sit quietly. Nick bent his head, breathing in the scent of baby shampoo from her damp curls.

Something about the baby's warm weight resting trustingly in his arms and the smell of clean soap touched off an onslaught of unexpected emotion, followed quickly by a slam of grief that caught him off guard. The sound of splashing and gurgles from the bathroom, accompanied by Charlene's murmured reply, only heightened the pain in Nick's chest.

Stan and Amy must have fed and bathed the girls every night. Stan probably held Jenny just like this.

How was it possible that Stan and Amy were gone—and their children left alone? In what universe did any of this make sense?

It didn't—none of it, he thought. His arms tightened protectively around the baby.

He was the last person on earth who should be responsible for these kids; but since he was, he'd make damn sure they were cared for—and safe. As safe as he could make them.

Which means I have to rearrange my life.

He was a man who'd avoided the responsibilities of a wife and family until now. He enjoyed the freedom of being single and hadn't planned to change his status anytime soon; but now that surrogate fatherhood had been thrust on him, he would make the most of it.

While Charlene bathed Jessie and Jackie, Nick considered his schedule at work and the logistics of fitting three babies and a nanny into his house and life.

He was still considering the thorny subject when the triplets were asleep in their cribs and he had said good-night to Charlene before disappearing into the far bedroom. He lay awake, staring at the ceiling above his own bed while he formulated a plan.

He'd just drifted off to sleep when one of the babies cried. By the time he staggered into the room next door, all three of them were awake and crying. Charlene stood at one of the cribs, lifting the sobbing little girl into her arms.

"I'll take Jessie into your room to change her diaper and try to get her back to sleep. I think she's running a bit of a fever—probably because of the ear infection. Can you deal with the other two?"

"Sure," Nick mumbled. Charlene disappeared into her room. He patted the nearest baby on the back but she only cried louder. "Damn," he muttered. "Now what do I do?"

He picked her up and she burrowed her face into his shoulder, her wails undiminished. Feeling totally clueless, Nick jiggled her up and down, but the sobbing continued unabated. Willing to try anything, he grabbed her abandoned blanket from the crib mattress and handed it to her. She snatched it and clutched it in one hand, sucking on her thumb. She still cried but the sound diminished because her mouth was closed.

Which left him with the baby still standing in her crib, tears streaming down her face, her cries deafening.

Nick's head began to pound. He leaned over and

snagged the abandoned blanket, caught the little girl with one arm and lifted her to a seat on his hip. Then he lowered the two onto the empty bed, his back against the headboard. He managed to juggle both babies until he could cradle each of them against his chest, their security blankets clutched tightly in their hands. The first baby he'd picked up was crying with less volume, but the second one still made enough noise to wake the dead.

Vaguely remembering a comment his mother had made about singing her boys to sleep when they were little, Nick sang the only tune that came to mind. Bob Seger may not have intended his classic, "Rock And Roll Never Forgets" as a lullaby, but the lyrics seemed to strike a chord with the babies.

The loud sobs slowly abated. Nick felt the solid little bodies relax and gradually sink against his own. When the girls were limp and no longer crying, he tilted his head back to peer cautiously at them.

They were sound asleep.

Thank God. He eyed the cribs, trying to figure out how to lower each of the babies into their bed without waking one or both of them.

He drew a blank.

"Aw, hell," he muttered. He managed to shift one of the little girls onto the bed beside him before sliding lower in the bed until he lay flat. Then he grabbed a pillow, shoved it under his head and pulled the spread up over his legs and hips. "If you can't beat 'em, join 'em."

The sheets were still warm from Charlene's body,

and the scent of her perfume clung to the pillow, teasing his nostrils. He gritted his teeth and tried not to think about lying in her bed as he slid into sleep.

Nick woke the following morning with a kink in his neck and the sound of gleeful chortles accompanying thumps on his head from a tiny fist. He slitted his eyes open. He was nose-to-nose with a tiny face whose bright blue eyes sparkled with mischief below a mop of black curls.

He forced his eyes open farther just in time to see a second little girl as she wriggled out of his grasp and crawled toward the edge of the bed with determined speed. He grabbed a handful of her sleeper just in time to keep her from tumbling headfirst onto the floor.

The quick movement corresponded with a hard yank on his hair.

"Ow." He winced, pried little fingers away from his head and sat up. "You little imp." The tiny wrist bracelet told him this triplet was Jackie. "I'm gonna remember this," he told her.

She grinned, babbled nonsensically and began to crawl swiftly toward the end of the bed.

"Oh no you don't. Come back here." He hauled her back, then threw the spread back and stood, a wiggling little girl tucked beneath each arm. He lowered them each into a separate crib and grinned when they stood on tiptoes, reaching for him. "No way. You're trapped now and I'm not letting you out."

"Good morning."

He glanced over his shoulder. Charlene stood in the open doorway to the adjoining room, hair tousled, eyes sleepy. She was dressed in jeans and a pullover knit shirt, Jessie perched on one hip.

Nick was abruptly aware he was wearing only gray boxers.

"Morning." He gestured at the girls in their cribs. "I'll give you a hand with their breakfast as soon as I'm dressed. I'm going to jump in the shower."

She murmured an acknowledgment as he left the room.

Both adults were sleep-deprived and weary, but the triplets seemed little worse for their middle-of-the-night activity. By the time they were fed, dressed and strapped in their car seats, Nick was beginning to wonder if he should hire four or five nannies instead of one or two.

The trip from Amarillo south to Red Rock was just over five hundred and fifty miles. In normal circumstances, pretriplets, Nick could have driven the route in eight or nine hours with good road conditions and mild weather. But traveling with three babies on board drastically changed the time frame. After numerous stops to change diapers and feed the little girls, they finally reached his home in Red Rock in late afternoon of the second day.

Charlene stepped out of the SUV and stretched, easing muscles weary from sitting for too many hours. The SUV was parked in the driveway of a Spanish-style two-story stucco house on a quiet residential street in one of Red Rock's more affluent neighborhoods. She knew very little about this part of town; her previous apartment had been southeast, across the business district and blocks away.

In fact, she thought as she glanced up and down the broad street, with its large homes and neatly trimmed lawns, she didn't remember ever having been in this part of Red Rock before.

Good, she thought with satisfaction. Her belief that it would be unlikely she might run into Barry or his friends seemed to be accurate.

She turned back to the SUV and leaned inside to unhook Jessie from her seat belt.

"I called my housekeeper this morning," Nick told her as he unbuckled Jackie on the opposite side of the vehicle. "Melissa promised to come by and fill the fridge and pantry with food for the girls. She said she'd wait for the delivery van with the baby furniture too."

Surprised, Charlene's fingers stilled and she stopped unbuckling Jessie's seat belt to look at him across the width of the SUV's interior. "I didn't realize you'd made arrangements—but thank goodness you did."

Nick's gaze met hers and she felt her breath catch, helpless to stop her body's reaction to him.

"We were lucky last night," he said. "The hotel was prepared to accommodate babies. Trust me, there aren't any high chairs or cribs stored in my attic." He lifted Jackie free and grinned. "I'm not sure what we would have done with these three tonight if the store hadn't agreed to deliver and set up their beds today. The only thing I've got that comes close to cribs are a couple of large dog crates in the garage."

Charlene laughed, the sudden mental image of the three little girls sleeping in boxy carriers with gates was too preposterous.

"Exactly," Nick said dryly. He shifted Jackie onto his hip and unhooked Jenny from her seat.

He's much more comfortable with the babies after only a day. Charlene was impressed at how easily he'd managed to extricate Jenny from her seat while holding Jackie.

She quickly gathered the girls' blankets, stuffed animals and various toys from the floor mats where the girls had tossed them and finished unbuckling Jessie to lift her out of the car. She slung a loaded tote bag over her shoulder and bumped the car door closed with one hip.

"I'll unload the bags after we get the girls inside," Nick told her, gesturing her ahead of him to the walkway that curved across the lawn to the front entry. "Ring the doorbell," he said when they reached the door. "Melissa should be here—that's her car parked at the curb."

Charlene did as he asked and heard muted chimes from inside the house. Almost immediately the door opened.

"Hello—there you are." The woman in the doorway was small, her petite form sturdy in khaki pants, pullover white T-shirt and tennis shoes. Her dark hair was frosted with gray and her deep-brown eyes sparkled, animated behind tortoise-shell-framed glasses. "How was the trip?"

"Exhausting," Nick said bluntly. "Melissa, this is Charlene London. Charlene, this is Melissa Kennedy, my housekeeper. Charlene's going to take care of the girls, Melissa."

"Nice to meet you." Melissa's smile held friendly interest. Charlene's murmured response was lost as Jenny wriggled in Nick's arms, her little face screwing up into a prelude to full-blown tears. Nick stepped inside and handed Jackie to the housekeeper before he cuddled Jenny closer.

"Hey, what's wrong?" He carried the sobbing little girl down the hall.

Charlene followed him into the living room, Melissa bringing up the rear with Jackie.

As often happened with the three little girls, when one of them began crying, the other two soon followed. Charlene rubbed Jessie's back in soothing circles and slowly rocked her back and forth. She only cried harder. Melissa murmured to Jackie and gently patted her back, but Jackie's sobs increased until they matched her sisters' in volume.

"Jessie needs a diaper change." Charlene raised her voice to be heard over the combined cries of the three babies.

"Can you and Melissa handle them while I bring in the bags from the car?" Nick asked, looking faintly frazzled.

"Of course," Charlene responded with easy confidence.

Nick didn't look convinced but he didn't argue with her.

"Did the delivery crew set up the cribs, Melissa?" he asked.

"Yes, and the changing tables and dressers too. I put away the diapers and the other supplies in their room, and I had the men carry the high chairs into the kitchen," she replied.

"Good." Nick gently patted Jenny's back with one hand as he strode across the living room toward the stairway, located just inside the front door. "Let's get them upstairs and I'll bring in the diaper bags."

Charlene followed Nick and Melissa up the open stairway, with its wooden railing. The second-floor hallway branched to the right and left. Nick turned left and soon disappeared into the third room, Melissa and Jackie a step behind.

Charlene brought up the rear with Jessie, slowing to glance briefly into the first two rooms as she passed. One held a white, wrought-iron bed, the floor carpeted in light green Berber. The other was a bathroom, fitted in pale wooden cabinets with green marble tops.

The house was lovely but the sparse furnishings clearly stated that this was a bachelor's home. Downstairs in the living room, she'd noted a large plasma television mounted on one wall, with shelves of electronic equipment beneath. CD cases were piled in stacks on the shelves between stereo speakers. A low, oak coffee table sat in front of a dark-brown-leather sofa and a matching club chair and ottoman, angled next to the hearth of a river rock fireplace and chimney. There was no other furniture in the room, leaving an expanse of pale wooden floor gleaming in the late afternoon sunlight that poured through skylights and windows.

She'd glimpsed a dining room through an archway, but again, saw only the minimum of furniture in a table and chairs. She wondered how long Nick had lived in the house, since it appeared to be furnished with only essentials.

She carried Jessie into the bedroom and paused, feeling her eyes widen as she took in the room. It was large, with plenty of space for three white-painted cribs. Two dressers and changing tables matched the cottage-style cribs, and two rocking chairs with deep-rose seat cushions were tucked into a corner. Despite the number of pieces of furniture, the room didn't feel crowded.

Clearly, Nick hadn't skimped on furnishings here.

"I had the men put the third dresser, changing table and rocker in the empty bedroom down the hall," Melissa said to Nick. "I thought it would be too crowded if all of the furniture was in here."

"We might have to move two of the cribs into other rooms. If one of the girls cries, the other two chime in. Maybe they'd sleep better if we split them up." He looked at Charlene. "What do you think?"

"We could leave them together for tonight and see how they do. You can always move them tomorrow, if sharing a room doesn't work out."

Nick nodded decisively. "We'll try it." Gently, he

lowered the now quiet Jenny onto the carpet. "I'll go bring up their bags."

Charlene slipped the canvas tote off her shoulder and lowered it to the floor before kneeling and setting Jessie down next to it. She took a tissue from the bag and wiped the damp tears from Jessie's cheeks before handing the baby her blanket and a stuffed bear.

In Melissa's arms, Jackie's sobs had slowed to the occasional hiccup. She stretched out her arms and babbled imperiously.

Charlene wondered if she could use that combination of regal commands and pleas on Nick. Would he respond with hugs and kisses, as he did with the triplets?

She nearly groaned aloud.

The image of him rising from her bed at the motel, rumpled and sleepy, seemed to have permanently engraved itself on her brain. Try as she might, she couldn't forget how his big, powerful body had looked, clad only in gray boxers, as he'd walked across the room.

Jackie's chattering increased to shriek level and Charlene realized she had no idea how long she'd been standing still, staring unseeingly at the baby. She glanced quickly at Melissa, but the other woman was focused on Jackie, laughing as she jiggled her in her arms.

"I bet the queen of Hollywood divas, whoever she may be this week, doesn't make as much noise as this little girl," Melissa commented as she met

Charlene's gaze. The housekeeper's eyes twinkled with amusement.

Mentally sighing with relief that Melissa appeared oblivious to her distraction, Charlene shoved the memory of Nick's powerful thighs and broad chest into the back of her mind. She ordered the image to stay put—and desperately hoped it would obey.

Chapter Three

Jackie shrieked again and Charlene laughed out loud. "Yes, your royal highness," she said teasingly, retrieving the pink blanket with Jackie's name embroidered across one corner and passing it to Melissa.

"Isn't that clever?" Melissa said admiringly, as Jackie hugged the blanket and beamed at Charlene. "I wondered how Nick planned to tell one baby's things from another." She ran a fingertip gently over the bracelet on Jackie's wrist. "But everything has their names on it, including the little girls themselves."

"I thought their parents came up with a brilliant solution," Charlene agreed. "Though I assume they could tell their daughters apart."

Melissa's face sobered. "Such a terrible thing to have happened, isn't it? How awful to lose both parents at such a young age."

"Yes," Charlene agreed, her heart wrenching as she looked at Jessie and Jenny tugging on their stuffed bears. *So innocent—and thankfully, too young to grasp the enormity of their loss just now.*

Nick strode into the room, pulling two large rolling suitcases and carrying a backpack slung over one shoulder, all stuffed to overflowing with the triplets' clothing and toys. "I put your suitcase in the room across the hall," he told Charlene, shrugging the backpack off his shoulder.

"Thank you," she murmured, delighted to know the lovely room with the white wrought-iron bed and green carpet would be hers during her stay.

In the ensuing bustle of changing diapers and tucking away tiny clothing into dresser drawers, Charlene was too busy to dwell on the triplets' orphaned status.

Melissa was a godsend, helping with the girls as Charlene and Nick fed and bathed them, then tucked all three into bed. The adults returned to the living room and collapsed, Nick in the leather club chair, Charlene and Melissa on the comfortable sofa.

"They're wonderful," Melissa told Nick. "But oh, my goodness." She sighed, a gust of air stirring her normally smooth hair, where one of the triplets had rumpled and dampened it while the little girl splashed in her bath. "Talk about energy. What you two need to do is find a way to collect some of that for yourself. You're going to need it." She looked at Charlene. "Do they sleep through the night?"

"They did last night. I've got my fingers crossed, hoping we'll have another quiet ten hours or so."

"I hope they do too." Melissa pushed herself up off the sofa. "I'd better get home. Ed will be wondering what happened to me."

Nick started to shove up out of the chair but she waved him back. "No, no—don't get up. I can see myself out. You should take advantage of this moment of quiet. Who knows how long it will last?"

"Good point," Nick agreed, settling into the chair, the worn denim of his jeans going taut over muscled thighs as he stretched out his long legs. "We should make the most of this rare minute. It could be the last one of the night."

"Exactly." Melissa grinned at him, eyes twinkling, before she turned to Charlene. "I'll see you in the morning—about eight?"

"Eight works for me. I'm looking forward to it," Charlene replied with heartfelt warmth. After watching Melissa's efficient, comfortable and unflappable handling of the babies over the last couple of hours, Charlene was convinced the housekeeper was going to be an enormous help in caring for the triplets.

"Goodnight, then, you two. I hope you get some sleep. I left my purse and keys in the kitchen. I'll just collect them and let myself out the back," she said. She moved briskly across the living room but stopped in the doorway. "I forgot to tell you, Nick, I left Rufus with

Ed today so you could get the girls settled in before they meet him. I'll bring him back with me tomorrow."

"Good thinking," Nick told her. "Dealing with the triplets was chaotic. Adding an excited hundred-and-twenty-five-pound dog into the mix would have made it crazy."

Melissa chuckled and waved a quick good-night as she disappeared.

A moment later, the sound of her car engine reached the two in the living room.

"I take it you have a *big* dog?"

"Oh, yeah," Nick said dryly. "Rufus is a chocolate Lab. Thankfully, he's very mellow and loves kids, so he should be fine with the triplets."

"As long as he likes them, they'll probably think he's wonderful." Charlene yawned, suddenly exhausted. "I think I'll head upstairs." She unfolded her legs and stood, aware of aching muscles from the long car ride. "I could sleep for at least twelve hours straight. I've never understood how sitting in a car and doing nothing can make me tired."

"It was a long trip," Nicholas agreed, getting out of the chair. He rolled his shoulders and stretched. "Did Melissa show you where everything is— towels, coffee for tomorrow morning, et cetera?"

"Yes, thank you."

"If you need anything, just ask. If I don't already have it in the house, I'll get it." He eyed her, his gaze intent. "I'm damned grateful you agreed to take on the triplets, Charlene. I know it's not an easy job. There's no way I could do it by myself."

"You're doing very well for a man who's never had children of his own," she told him. "And I confess, I'm relieved Melissa will be helping. She's good with the girls and nothing seems to faze her."

"She's pretty unshakeable," Nick said. "I normally work long hours, and she keeps the house together and makes sure there are meals in the fridge."

"How long has she worked for you?" Charlene asked, curious.

"Since a few days after I moved to Red Rock. The employment agency sent over three women and I hired Melissa on the spot."

"Sounds like it was the right decision. Well…" She tugged her white cotton T-shirt into place, suddenly self-conscious. The room was abruptly too intimate in the lamplight and Nick loomed much too large, and much too male. "I'll see you in the morning."

"Sleep well. I have to go to the office for a meeting tomorrow, but I won't leave until Melissa arrives."

She nodded. "Good night."

His answering good-night was a low male rumble. Charlene looked back when she reached the stairway and found him staring after her, his expression brooding. She hurried up the stairs, faintly breathless from the impact of the brief moment her gaze had met his.

He's your employer, she reminded herself as she brushed her teeth in the white-and-green bathroom that opened off her bedroom, *stop lusting after him.*

Apparently, however, the emotional, hormonal part of her was in no mood to listen to the practical, rational command. She fell asleep and dreamed of making love with a man who looked very much like Nick Fortune.

Just as she stretched out her arms, her fingertips mere inches away from the bare chest of her dream lover, a loud wail yanked her awake.

Charlene sat bolt upright, disoriented as she stared in confusion at the dim outlines of bed and dresser in the strange room.

The sound of crying from the triplets' room abruptly scattered the lingering fog of sleep and she tossed back the bedcovers to hurry next door.

"Oh, sweetie," she soothed, lifting Jackie from her crib. "Sh." She patted the little back while the baby's sobs slowed to hiccups. "What's wrong?"

Jessie rolled over in her crib and sat up. In the third crib, Jenny pulled herself to her feet to clasp the rail. Jackie chose that moment to burst into sobs once more and, as if on cue, Jessie and Jenny's faces crumpled. They burst into tears as well.

The combined sound of their crying was deafening and impossible to ignore. Charlene wasn't surprised when Nick staggered into the room.

"What's wrong?" His voice was gravelly with sleep. He wore navy boxers, his broad chest and long legs bare.

Despite the earsplitting noise of three crying babies, Charlene still noticed that Nick looked as good undressed as he did in faded jeans and T-shirts.

"Jackie woke me, then her crying woke the other two." Charlene crossed to the changing table, gently rocking the still sobbing Jackie while she took a fresh diaper from the drawer. "I think she needs a diaper change. Can you pick up Jenny and Jessie— maybe rock them for a few minutes?"

"Sure." Nick shoved his fingers through his hair, further rumpling it, and lifted Jenny from her crib.

The low rumble of his voice as he murmured to the two babies was barely audible as Charlene quickly changed Jackie's diaper. By the time she snapped the little girl's footed sleeper and tossed the damp disposable nappy into the bin, their crying had subsided into silence. She tucked Jackie against her shoulder and turned, stopping abruptly.

Nick sat in the cushioned rocking chair, a little girl against each bare shoulder, their faces turned into the bend of his neck where shoulder met throat. His broad hands nearly covered each little back, fingers splayed to hold them securely. His hair was rumpled, his eyes sleepy.

Charlene didn't think she'd ever seen anything half as sexy as the big man protectively cradling the two sleeping babies. She felt her heart lurch.

Don't go there, she ordered herself. *Do not notice how sexy he is. Remember you swore to avoid men for at least six months after breaking up with Barry. That was only two weeks ago.*

She couldn't remember ever feeling this attracted to her ex-fiancé, but that didn't change the fact that she was determined to never, ever, get involved with her employer.

She moved softly across the room and eased into the empty rocking chair. Jackie stirred, lifting her head from Charlene's shoulder. Charlene quickly smoothed her hand over the baby's silky black curls, gently urging her to lay her head down once more, and set the rocker in motion. Within seconds, Jackie was relaxed, her compact little body feeling boneless where it lay against Charlene.

"Is she asleep?" Nick's murmur rasped, velvet over gravel.

"Yes," Charlene whispered. "What about your two?"

He tipped his head back to peer down at first one, then the other, of the two little girls. "They seem to be." He looked up at her. "Think it's safe to put them back in bed?"

"We can try. Let me put Jackie down and then I'll take one of yours." At his nod, Charlene stood and crossed to Jackie's crib, easing the sleeping baby down onto her back and pulling the light blanket over her before she returned to Nick.

"Which one do you want me to carry?" she whispered.

"Jenny." He leaned forward slightly.

Charlene bent closer to lift the sleeping baby, her hands brushing against his bare skin. He was warm, his skin sleek over the flex of muscles as he shifted to help transfer the little girl to her, and a shiver of awareness shook her. She was aware his head turned abruptly, could feel the intensity of his stare, but she wouldn't, couldn't, allow herself to meet his gaze. Instead, she cradled Jenny in her arms and turned away to carry the little girl to her crib, tucking her in and smoothing the blanket over her sleeping form. Behind her, she heard the soft sounds of Nick tucking Jessie into the third crib.

Nick followed her to the doorway, waiting in the hall as she paused to look back. The room was quiet—no movement visible in any of the three cribs to indicate a restless child.

"I think they're out for the count," Nick murmured behind her.

"Yes, I believe you're right," she whispered, before stepping into the hall and easing the door partially closed. "Let's hope they stay that way for the rest of the night." She gave him a fleeting glance. "Good night."

"Good night."

Once again, she felt his stare as she walked down the hall and into the safety of her room. She closed the door and collapsed against it, the panels cool against her shoulders, left bare by the narrow straps of her camisole pajama top.

There was no way she would ever become involved with her boss. She'd sworn a solemn oath after she'd learned about her father's affair with his secretary that had ultimately destroyed her parents' marriage. She'd never forgiven him, but for the first time, tonight she had an inkling as to what may have caused her father to stray. If he'd felt anything like the sizzling heat that swamped her every time she got close to Nick Fortune, then maybe, just maybe, she should stop being so angry at him. Maybe he'd literally been unable to help himself.

Or not, she thought, still not completely convinced.

But in any event, she had to find a way to insulate herself against the powerful attraction she felt. Especially since it appeared Nick didn't have to do anything, or even say anything, to make her nerves sizzle and her body heat up.

Apparently, he just needed to breathe in her presence.

Groaning, she climbed back into bed and pulled the sheet and blanket over her head.

The triplets were still fast asleep in their cribs upstairs when Charlene tiptoed down the stairs and into the kitchen just before eight the following morning.

Nick glanced over his shoulder and took down another mug from the open cupboard. "Morning," he said. "Coffee's nearly done."

Charlene breathed in the rich scent filling the kitchen and nearly groaned. "Bless you."

Nick's grin flashed, his eyes lit with amusement. He poured the rich brew into their mugs at the same moment that a knock sounded on the back door.

"That'll be Melissa," Nick told Charlene. He grabbed his computer case and crossed the kitchen to pull open the door.

A huge chocolate Labrador retriever leaped over the threshold and planted his paws on Nick's shoulders, whining with excitement, his tail whipping back and forth.

"Ouch." Melissa stepped inside, moving sideways

to avoid getting hit. "That tail of yours is a lethal weapon, Rufus." She waved her hand at the travel coffee mug and leather case in Nick's left hand. "On your way out to work, boss?"

"Yeah." Nick rubbed Rufus's ears. "That's enough. Down, boy." The Lab dropped back onto four paws but continued to wag his tail, pink tongue lolling as he stared adoringly up at Nick. "I'll check with the employment agency today," Nick said, looking over his shoulder at Charlene, "and find out if they've lined up applicants for a second nanny."

"I'll keep my fingers crossed that they have—then maybe we both can start getting more sleep."

Nick grinned, his eyes lit with rueful amusement as his mouth curved upward to reveal a flash of white teeth. Charlene suspected she was staring at him like a hopelessly lovestruck teenager, but she couldn't bring herself to look away.

No man should be that gorgeous.

"I'll tell them we're staggering from sleep deprivation. Maybe they'll take pity on us," he said.

"We can only hope," Charlene said, tearing her gaze away from his smile. Unfortunately, she was immediately snagged by his glossy black hair, thick-lashed brown eyes, tanned skin with a faint beard shadow despite the early hour, handsome features… Were all the Fortune men this blessed by nature? she wondered. If so, heaven help the women who caught their attention—because females didn't stand a chance against all that powerful, charming, handsome male virility. Perhaps she was fortunate that he was her boss and thus off-limits, not to mention he was also clearly far more sophisticated than she. Never mind the fact that he was also not interested in her. Because if he ever turned that undeniable charm on her, she'd give in without a whimper.

It's a pitiful thing when a woman has *no* resistance to a man, she realized with wry acknowledgment.

"So long, boss," Melissa's voice yanked Charlene out of her thoughts. "Have a good day."

"Good luck with the triplets." Nick bent to give Rufus's silky ears one last rub before disappearing through the door.

Charlene echoed Melissa's goodbye before pouring herself another mug of coffee. "The coffee's fresh," she told Melissa. "Want some?"

"Sure, why not." Melissa slid onto a stool at the counter.

Charlene handed her a steaming cup and took a seat opposite her.

"Are the babies still asleep?" Melissa asked.

"Yes." Charlene glanced at the digital clock on the microwave. "They're sleeping in, probably because they were awake several times last night."

"I was telling my Ed about the triplets just this morning—" Melissa began.

Whatever she was about to say was lost as someone rapped sharply on the back door.

Charlene looked inquiringly at Melissa.

"That's probably LouAnn," Melissa said as she left the counter and crossed the room.

Charlene barely had time to wonder who LouAnn

was before Melissa pulled open the door. She felt her eyes widen.

"Good morning, Melissa." The throaty rasp seemed incongruous, coming as it did from a woman who Charlene guessed weighed at best a hundred pounds, maybe a hundred and ten at the most.

"Hi, LouAnn." Melissa gestured her inside. "We're just having coffee. Want some?"

"Of course." LouAnn followed Melissa to the counter, her bright blue gaze full of curiosity and fixed on Charlene. "And who are you, dearie?"

"I'm Charlene, the nanny." Charlene tried not to stare, but the silver-haired woman's attire was eye-popping. She wore a turquoise T-shirt with a bucking horse and rider picked out in silver rhine-stones. The black leggings below the T-shirt clung to her nonexistent curves and hot-pink, high-top tennis shoes covered her feet. Skinny arms poked out of the loose short sleeves of the shirt, and both hands boasted jewelry that dazzled. Charlene was pretty sure the huge diamond on her left hand was real, and more than likely, so was the sapphire on her right. Not to mention the large diamond studs that glittered in her earlobes. She was tan, toned and exuded energy that fairly vibrated the air around her pixie frame.

"Nanny?" LouAnn's penciled eyebrows shot toward the permed silver curls of her immaculate, short hairdo. "Why does Nick need a nanny?"

"Have a seat, LouAnn, and we'll fill you in." Melissa pulled out a chair next to hers and across the island's countertop from Charlene. "Charlene, this is Nick's neighbor, LouAnn Harris."

"Pleased to meetcha." LouAnn hopped onto the tall chair, crossed her legs and beamed at Charlene. "You might as well know you're likely to see a lot of me. I'm a widow. I live alone and my son and daughter live too far away to visit me often, so I tend to get bored. I was delighted when Nick moved in here and hired Melissa—we've known each other for at least twenty years. My, you're young, aren't you?"

"Uh, well…" Charlene looked at Melissa for guidance. The housekeeper grinned, her eyes twinkling. Clearly, she wasn't bothered by the neighbor's bluntness. "I suppose I am, sort of," Charlene replied, taking her cue from Melissa.

LouAnn snorted. "No 'sort of' about it, honey. Compared to me, you're a child. But then, I'm seventy-six, so most everyone *is* younger." She sipped her coffee. "I have to get me a coffeemaker like Nick's. Your coffee is always better than mine, Melissa."

"That might be because I grind the beans. Nick has them sent from the coffee shop he used to go to in L.A.," Melissa explained to Charlene.

"I thought it was the coffeemaker." LouAnn leaned forward and lowered her voice to a raspy whisper. "It looks like it belongs on a space ship."

Charlene laughed, charmed by LouAnn's warm camaraderie.

LouAnn grinned at her, winked, and turned back to Melissa. "Now, tell me why Nick needs a nanny.

I thought he was a confirmed bachelor with no interest in kids."

"He is—and he doesn't, or didn't, pay attention to children," Melissa agreed. "At least, he had no interest in children until recently. It's a sad story, really."

When she finished relaying a condensed version of the situation, LouAnn clucked in sympathy. "How terrible for those poor little girls. And how lucky for them—and Nick—that you were willing to step in and help," she added, reaching across the marble countertop to pat Charlene's hand.

"It was fate," Melissa said firmly. "That's what I think."

"Three little ones—all the same age." LouAnn shook her head. "How are you all coping?"

"Except for a serious lack of sleep, fairly well, I think." Charlene looked at Melissa. "Sometimes it's chaos, of course, but the girls seem to be doing okay. Jessie has an ear infection at the moment, so she's a little cranky. But by and large, they're very sweet little girls."

"I can't wait to see them. How old are they?"

"They're a year—uh-oh." The sound of one of the girls, chattering away upstairs floated down the stairway and into the kitchen. "I think you're about to meet the dynamic trio." Charlene slipped off her chair and headed for the door.

"I'm coming up with you," LouAnn announced, joining Charlene.

Melissa brought up the rear as the three women left the kitchen.

* * *

Nick had a long list of priorities for the day, but as he backed his Porsche out of the garage and drove away, he wasn't focusing on the work waiting for him at the Fortune Foundation. Instead, he was distracted by the memory of Charlene coping with the babies in the middle of the night.

The picture of her in the bedroom, lit only by the glow of a night-light, was seared in his memory. Her auburn hair had been rumpled from sleep, her long legs covered in soft-looking, blue-and-white pajama bottoms. Jackie had clutched the neckline of the brief little white tank top Charlene wore, pulling it down to reveal the upper curve of her breasts.

Even half-asleep, he'd been damn sure she wasn't wearing anything under that top. He felt like a dog for looking, and hoped she hadn't noticed.

He'd known having the beautiful redhead living in his house was bound to cause difficult moments, but he hadn't been prepared to be blindsided by a half-naked woman when he was barely awake.

Which was stupid of me, he thought with disgust. *She's living in my house. I knew she'd be getting out of bed if one of the triplets woke during the night.*

And as long as he was being brutally honest, he had to admit the pajamas she wore hadn't come close to being blatantly suggestive. Nevertheless, Charlene's simple pajama bottoms and tank top would stop traffic on an L.A. freeway.

Maybe he wouldn't have felt as if he'd been hit

by lightning when he saw her in those pajamas if she were a woman with fewer curves.

Or maybe, he thought with self-derision, *if she'd been wearing a sack I'd still have been interested.*

He knew he was completely out of line. He just didn't know how to turn off his body's response to her. Not only was she his employee, she was too damned young for him. His office assistant had telephoned with results of a preemployment background check before he'd left his hotel to drive to the triplets' foster home. The report not only confirmed Charlene had a spotless employment record, it also told him she'd graduated from college only three years earlier.

A brief mental calculation told him that if she'd gone to college immediately after high school, then graduated after four or five years before working for three more years, she most likely was twenty-five or twenty-six years old.

And he was thirty-seven. Too old for her.

Unfortunately, his libido didn't appear to be paying attention to the math.

He'd reached the office while he'd been preoccupied with the situation at home, and swung the Porsche into a parking slot. He left the car and headed for his office, determined to put thoughts of the curvy redhead at home, busy with his new instant family, out of his mind.

He quickly scanned the pink message slips the receptionist had handed him and tossed the stack on his desktop. He rang his brother Darr while he plugged in his laptop and arranged to meet him for lunch at their favorite diner, SusieMae's. Then he closed his office door and tackled an inbox filled with documents and files.

Nick gave the waitress his and Darr's usual lunch order and she bustled off. SusieMae's Café was crowded, but he had a clear view of the door, and saw his brother enter.

Darr swept the comfortable interior with a quick glance, nodding at acquaintances as he crossed the room and slid into the booth across from Nick.

"Where have you been?" he demanded without preamble. "I left two messages on your machine. You never called back."

"You didn't say it was an emergency." Nick shrugged out of his jacket and eyed his brother across the width of the scarred tabletop. "Was it?"

"Not exactly. I wanted to know if you'd talked to Dad or J.R. lately."

"I haven't." Nick took a drink of water. "Why?"

"Because I called and neither one answered. Come to think of it," Darr frowned at Nick, "none of you called me back."

Nick grinned. "Probably because we all assumed you were too busy with Bethany to care if we called you or not."

"Huh," Darr grumbled.

Nick noticed his younger brother didn't deny the charge.

"How's Bethany doing?" he asked. He felt distinctly protective toward the petite, pregnant blonde, especially since Darr was in love with her. When the two married, she'd become Nick's sister-in-law. As far as he was concerned, Bethany Burdett was a welcome addition to their all-male family.

"Good." Darr leaned back to let their waitress set plates and coffee mugs on the tabletop in front of them. "She's good."

Nick didn't miss the softening of his brother's face. He was glad Darr had found a good woman. Bethany made him happy, and he seemed content in a way Nick hadn't seen before.

"You didn't answer my question, where have you been?"

Nick waited until the waitress left before he spoke. "I made a trip to Amarillo. I've been pretty busy since I got back."

"Yeah? What were you doing in Amarillo?" Darr took a bite of his sandwich, eyeing Nick over the top of a double-decker bacon-and-tomato on wheat.

"I picked up Stan's kids." Nick saw Darr's eyes widen. "Three of them," he added, smiling slightly at the shock on his brother's face. "They're all girls—only a year old. Triplets."

Darr choked, set down his sandwich, grabbed his coffee and washed down the bite in record time. "What the hell? Why? What happened?"

Nick lost any amusement he'd felt at his brother's dumfounded expression. "He and Amy were in a car accident—neither one of them made it out alive." Saying the words aloud didn't make the truth any less surreal.

The shock on Darr's face made it clear he was just as stunned as Nick had been at first hearing the news.

"Both of them?" He shook his head in disbelief when Nick nodded. "They were so young. You and Stan are the same age, right?"

Again, Nick nodded. "And Amy was a year younger."

"And you have custody of their babies?" Darr queried,

"Yeah."

"Why?"

"Because Stan's will named me guardian if Amy's sister Lana couldn't take them." Nick took a drink of coffee, hoping to erase the lump of emotion in his throat. He still hadn't come to terms with the abruptness with which Stan and Amy had disappeared from the world. "So they're with me until the attorney locates Lana."

"Where is she?"

"No one knows." Nick stared broodingly at his plate, holding a sandwich and chips. "She and her husband work in Africa and Amy seems to have lost track of them a few months ago."

"Damn." Darr eyed him. "Who's taking care of the kids while you work?"

"I hired a nanny," Nick replied. "And Melissa's working longer hours while I'm at the Foundation during the day."

Darr stared at him. Nick took a bite of his sandwich.

"And?" Darr prompted when Nick didn't elaborate.

"And what?"

"Don't give me that. You're stalling. What else aren't you telling me?"

"The nanny I hired works full-time. Her name is Charlene. She's a redhead and she's great with the triplets."

Darr lowered his coffee mug to the table without taking his gaze from Nick's face. "She's a babe, isn't she."

It wasn't a question. Darr knew him too well to be fooled.

"Yeah. She is." Nick shoved another bite of sandwich into his mouth.

"Full-time," Darr said consideringly. "What hours does she work?"

"She's pretty much on call twenty-four hours a day."

"So…she's living at your house?"

"Yeah."

"Sleeping down the hall from you?"

Nick nodded, saw the glint appear in Darr's eyes and bristled. "Yes, *down the hall.* She has her own bedroom. What the hell did you think, that she was sharing mine?"

Darr shrugged. "It did cross my mind. Face it, Nick, you've never been slow with the ladies. You said she's pretty—and she's living in your house…." He spread his hands. "Sounds like a no-brainer to me."

"Well, it's not," Nick snarled, restraining an urge to wrap his hands around his brother's neck and choke that grin off his face. "She works for me. Have you heard of sexual harassment? She's off-limits."

"Too bad." Darr lifted his coffee mug and drank.

"So," he said, setting the mug down and picking up his sandwich, "just how good-looking is Charlene?"

Too beautiful. Nick bit back the words and shrugged. "Beautiful."

"On a scale of one to ten?"

"She's a fifteen."

Darr's eyes widened. "Damn."

"And she's too young," Nick continued.

"How young?"

"She's twenty-five."

"Thank God." Darr pretended to wipe sweat off his brow in relief. "I thought you were going to tell me she's underage and jailbait."

"Might as well be," Nick growled. "She's twelve years younger than me. That's too damned young."

Darr pursed his lips. "Let me see if I've got this straight. You're cranky because you've got a nanny you can't make a move on because you're her boss and she's younger than you."

"Yeah, pretty much," Nick conceded.

Darr grinned. "Maybe you should fire her. Then you can date her."

"I can't fire her—and I don't want to," Nick ground out. "She's good at her job. If she wasn't helping me take care of the girls, I'd be screwed."

"So hire someone else—and then fire her."

"Yeah, like she's likely to go out with me after I've fired her." Nick rubbed his eyes. They felt as if there was a pound of sand in each of them. If he didn't get some sleep soon, he'd need more than the saline eyedrops he'd been using in a vain attempt to solve the problem. "There's no solution that's work-able. Believe me, I've considered all the angles."

"Where there's a will, there's a way."

"Stop being so damned cheerful," Nick growled.

"Aren't you the one who told me there's always another girl just around the corner? Wait a week and there'll be another corner, another girl. If things don't work out with the redhead, why do you care?"

Because I've never met anyone quite like her.

Nick didn't want to tell Darr that Charlene was unique. He was having a hard enough time accept-ing that he'd met a woman who broke all the rules he'd spent thirty-seven years setting.

"Maybe you're right," he said with a slight shrug, neither agreeing nor disagreeing. "Have you heard anything new about the note Patrick got at the New Year's Eve party? Or about the ones Dad and Cindy received?"

"No." Darr didn't appear thrown by Nick's abrupt change of subject. "That's one of the reasons I wanted to talk to Dad and J.R.—to ask if they've learned anything more."

The Fortune family had gone through a series of mysterious events over the last few months, starting with the cryptic note left in Patrick Fortune's jacket pocket during a New Year's Eve party. The strange message—"One of the Fortunes is not who you think"—baffled the family, even more so when they learned the same message had been left anony-mously with Cindy Fortune and William, Nick and Darr's father.

Patrick had called a family conference at Lily Fortune's home on the Double Crown Ranch in February, on the very day Red Rock had been hit with a freak snowstorm.

Darr hadn't been present at the gathering, since he'd been snowed-in with Bethany in her little house. But Nick had brought him up to speed on everything that happened, including the family's assumption the notes were the precursor to a blackmail demand. So far, however, no such demand had been made. But two subsequent fires—one that burned down the local Red Restaurant, and a second that destroyed a barn at the Double Crown—were suspicious. And potentially connected to the mysterious and vaguely threatening notes.

"Let me know if you reach Dad and J.R.," Nick said. "Meanwhile, I had a message from Ross Fortune when I got back to the office today. We set up a meeting to discuss the notes and fires. Has he contacted you?" Nick and Darr's cousin was a private investigator with an agency in San Antonio. His mother, Cindy, had convinced the family they should hire him to check into the cryptic threats.

"Not yet," Darr said, "but I heard he's in town. The Chief said he called and asked for copies of the department's report on the fire at Red." Darr pushed his empty plate aside and leaned his elbows on the tabletop, his voice lowering. "This isn't for public knowledge, but I'm sure my boss agrees with us— he has serious reservations as to whether the fire was accidental."

"What about the barn that burned at the Double Crown?"

"He didn't want to talk about that one—I suspect he believes I'm too close to the subject, since it happened on Lily's ranch."

"Do you have a gut feeling as to his opinion?"

"Yeah. I'm convinced he believes the Double Crown fire wasn't an accident, either."

"I hope to hell Ross's investigation gets some answers," Nick said grimly. "You or someone else could have died in those fires."

"Bethany damn near did," Darr said darkly, his features hardening. "She was barely conscious when I found her on the bathroom floor at the restaurant. She could have died of smoke inhalation."

"We have to find out who's behind these threats to the family before someone loses their life," Nick said. "I hope Ross is good at his job."

"When are you talking to him?"

"Tomorrow afternoon at one." Nick glanced at his watch. "I have a meeting in a half hour. Gotta get back to the office."

Darr nodded and both men dropped money on top of the check.

"Thanks, guys," their waitress called after them as they left the booth and headed for the exit.

Nick shrugged into his jacket as he stepped outside, a brisk breeze cooling the air, although the sun beamed down, warm against his face.

"Let me know what Ross has to say tomorrow," Darr said, pausing on the sidewalk. "I have the day off, but I'm not sure what Bethany's plans are or if I'll be home, so call my cell phone."

"Sure." Nick stepped off the curb. "Tell Bethany hello from me."

"Will do." Darr headed down the block to his vehicle.

Nick climbed into his Porsche, the powerful engine turning over with a throaty, muted roar when he twisted the key. The low-slung car had only two seats—room for the driver and one passenger.

"Too small," Nick murmured as he backed out of the slot. "I need to get an SUV." Or a minivan. He shuddered. He didn't think he could bring himself to drive a minivan—even for the triplets. Minivans were mommy cars. For a guy who loved fast cars and powerful engines, a minivan was a step too far, vehicle-wise.

He made a mental note to go SUV shopping on his lunch hour tomorrow. Charlene could use it to drive the babies during the week and he'd use it on the weekends if he needed to take the little girls any-where.

If anyone had told him two weeks ago that he'd be contemplating buying a vehicle to transport babies, he would have laughed at the sheer insanity of the idea.

He didn't do kids. Never had. And kids hadn't been part of his plans for the future.

There was some kind of cosmic karma at work here. Nick couldn't help but wonder what fate planned to hit him with next.

Chapter Four

Nick returned to the office, where he forced himself to concentrate on meetings. By the time he reached home that evening, he'd almost convinced himself he'd overreacted that morning.

Surely he'd overestimated the power of his attraction to Charlene.

The neighborhood was quiet, the street lamps casting pools of light in the early darkness when he slotted the car into the garage and got out, tapping the panel next to the inner door to close the garage door smoothly behind him. He unlocked the door leading from the garage into the utility room and passed through, stopping abruptly in the open doorway to the kitchen when he saw Charlene. She

stood at the stove across the room, her back to him
as she poured steaming water from the stainless steel
teakettle into a mug. A box of tea sat on the counter
next to the cup. Her hair was caught up in a ponytail,
leaving her nape bare above a short-sleeved green
T-shirt tucked into the waistband of faded jeans. She
wore thick black socks and she looked comfortable
and relaxed, as if the kitchen were her own.

*Coming home after a long day at work and find-
ing a pretty woman in my kitchen is kind of nice.*

The thought surprised him. He'd never really
understood married friends when they insisted that
walking into a house that wasn't empty was one of
the great things about being married. He liked his
privacy and didn't mind living alone. In fact, he thoroughly appreciated the solitude of his quiet house
after a day spent in meetings.

But finding Charlene in his kitchen, clearly comfortable and making herself at home, felt good.

Of course, he thought wryly, *maybe I'd feel dif-
ferently if she was a girlfriend with marriage on her
mind and not the nanny.* Maybe her employee status
erased the natural wariness of a bachelor when confronted with an unmarried, attractive woman putter-
ing in his kitchen.

Whatever's going on here, Nick thought, *I'm definitely glad to see her.*

Before he could say hello, Rufus bounded in from
the living room, his nails clicking against the tile
floor. Woofing happily, he charged. Nick quickly
lowered his leather computer bag to the tile and

braced himself. The big dog skidded to a halt, reared onto his back legs, planted his front paws on Nick's shoulders and tried to lick his face.

"Hey, stop that." Nick caught Rufus's head in his palms and rubbed his ears.

"Hi." Charlene looked over her shoulder at him. She set the kettle on the range and carried her mug to the island where a notebook lay open beside her laptop computer. "I thought I heard your car pull into the garage. How was your day?"

"Busy," he said, releasing Rufus and bending to pick up his computer bag. The big dog followed Nick to the island and flopped down next to Charlene's chair. "How was yours?"

"Busy."

He laughed at her dry, one-word response. "Yeah, I bet it was. How did it go with the girls?"

"Fine." Charlene spooned sugar into her tea and stirred. "Jackie bonked her chin on a chair rung and has a new little bruise. Jessie smeared oatmeal in her hair and had to have a second bath this morning barely an hour after her first one. And Jenny…" She paused, her eyes narrowing in thought. "Come to think of it, Jenny had a fairly quiet day."

"That doesn't sound possible."

"I know," she laughed. "But she doesn't seem ill, so I'm happy—but surprised—to report that although I've only known them for three days, there's a possibility that maybe one of them has an uneventful day on occasion."

"Well, that's a relief."

"Did you talk to the employment agency today?"

"Yeah, they might have three candidates for me to interview soon. They're running background checks and verifying references for each of the women." Nick turned on the tap and washed his hands, turning to lean against the counter as he dried them. "What did Melissa make for dinner?"

"Lasagne, french bread and salad—she left a plate for you in the fridge and the bread is in the pantry." Charlene set down her mug and shifted to stand.

Nick waved her back. "Stay where you are, I'll get it." The stainless steel, double-door refrigerator was only a step away. He located the plate and salad bowl, took a bottle of dressing from the inner-door shelf and let the door swing closed behind him as he walked back to the counter. He peeled the plastic wrap off the lasagne and slid it into the microwave to heat, tapping the timer before closing the door.

"What do you want to drink?"

He glanced around to see Charlene at the fridge, glass in hand.

"Ice water sounds good, thanks."

He heard the clink of ice and the splash of water behind him as he walked to the island and pulled out one of the low-backed stools. The microwave pinged just as he finished pouring vinegar and oil dressing on his salad and he returned to the counter, grabbing a knife and fork from the cutlery drawer. Charlene set his glass of water down next to his salad bowl and returned to her seat as he carried his steaming plate back to the island. He sat across from Charlene and folded his shirt cuffs back, loosening and tugging off his tie.

"Tell me about the triplets," he said. "How did Melissa survive the day?"

"She said she's going to cancel her gym membership. Evidently, lifting and carrying three babies for eight hours is more fun than weight lifting with her trainer." Charlene laughed. "Seriously, she's great with them, and they seem to like her as much as she likes them."

"I thought they would," Nick commented. "She's good with Rufus, and dealing with him seems to be a lot like having a toddler in the house—he makes messes, demands food regularly, requires massive amounts of attention and sometimes wakes me up in the middle of the night."

"So, what you're saying," Charlene said dryly, arching one eyebrow as she eyed him, "is that three little girls can cause as much havoc as a hundred-and-twenty-five-pound dog?"

"Pretty much," Nick agreed, grinning as she shook her head and frowned at him. The effect was ruined by the small smile that tugged her lips upward at the corners. "As a matter of fact, I can pick him up. I doubt I could juggle all three of the girls at the same time."

"You could, if you had a baby carrier," she said promptly.

"What's a baby carrier?"

"It's sort of a canvas backpack that an adult wears over their shoulders. The child is buckled into it so you can carry them on your chest or your back. Some are made for younger babies, but you can also get one to use for toddlers."

"Ah!" he said, nodding. "Remind me to get one of those. Then, if either of us ever has to take all three of the girls somewhere alone, we won't risk dropping one of them."

"That sounds like an excellent plan," Charlene agreed. "I met your neighbor LouAnn today."

"Did you?" Nick grinned and lifted an eyebrow. "What did you think of her?"

"She's a very interesting woman."

He laughed outright. "Got that right. She's a character. I hope I have that much energy when I'm seventy-something."

"Me too," Charlene agreed, smiling as she remembered LouAnn playing on the floor with the triplets. "She's wonderful with the babies. I'm not sure who had more fun playing peekaboo, her or the girls."

Nick chuckled, the sound sending shivers of awareness through Charlene's midsection. As he ate, they discussed the wisdom of keeping all three girls in the same bedroom.

Charlene sipped her tea, staring with fascination as Nick tipped his head back slightly and drank from the water glass. He'd unbuttoned the top two buttons of his shirt when he removed his tie earlier, and the strong, tanned muscles of his throat moved rhythmically as he swallowed. There was something oddly intimate about sitting in the cozy kitchen with him as he ate and they discussed his children.

"…What do you think?"

"Hmm?" She realized with a start that he'd been speaking while she'd stared at him, mesmerized, and felt embarrassed heat flood her cheeks. "I'm sorry, I didn't catch that. What do I think about…?"

His expression was quizzical. She suspected he noticed her pink cheeks, but she was determined not to become flustered. So she met his gaze with what she hoped was a serene look.

"I asked if you thought it was a good idea to give the girls a week or so together before we decide if they need to sleep in separate bedrooms."

"I think it makes sense to see whether they continue to wake each other, as they did last night." Charlene didn't want to remember the intimacy of the babies' darkened bedroom and the mental image of Nick wearing navy boxers and nothing else. Resolutely, she focused on the other bedrooms she'd seen during the tour of the house Melissa had given her that afternoon. "There's certainly plenty of room if you decide to have them sleep apart. Do you know if their parents had their cribs in separate bedrooms or if they all slept in the same room?"

Nick paused, his expression arrested. "The foster mother had the beds in two small bedrooms but I never thought to ask what the arrangements were at Stan and Amy's." He put down his fork with a thunk. "I should have asked," he said with disgust. "It never even occurred to me."

"If you have a phone number, I can try to reach her tomorrow," Charlene offered, touched by the sheer frustration on his face as he thrust his fingers through his hair and raked it back off his forehead.

"I'd appreciate that. I have her contact information in my desk in the den. Remind me to look it up before I leave for the office in the morning, will you?"

"Of course." Charlene sipped her tea and considered what she knew about the triplets' situation while Nick ate the last few bites of his lasagne. "Did the attorney have any estimate as to how long it might take to locate the babies' aunt?"

"No." Nick rose to carry his empty china and dirty cutlery to the sink. He turned on the tap. "He asked me to let him know if I remembered anything Stan or Amy may have said that would help find her. So far, all I've come up with is going through the photographs."

"Photographs? Does the investigator need a picture?"

"No, he has one." Nick slotted his rinsed dishes and utensils into the rack of the dishwasher and closed the door. "But Amy loved taking photographs— so did Stan—and Amy almost always jotted little notes on the back of the pictures. I'm sure some of the holiday photos they sent included her sister. I'm hoping there might be something in one of Amy's notes that will help locate Lana."

"That's a great idea," Charlene said, encouraged at the possibility of finding a clue.

"I hope it's a productive one, but who knows whether I'll learn anything new." He shrugged. "Still, it's one place we haven't looked yet, and given how little information the investigator has, any small piece might make a difference. When I moved in, I shoved the photo boxes into the back of a closet upstairs. I thought I'd bring one downstairs tomorrow night and start looking."

"I'd be glad to help you search through them," she offered.

"Thanks, but I should warn you, I've never organized the pictures. All the photos I have are tossed in a couple of boxes, and the ones from Stan and Amy are mixed in with all the rest. There might be hundreds of pictures to look at. My mom divided family photos a few years ago and gave me a carton full."

"I'll still volunteer," she said. "Did the attorney search the triplets' house for an address book? I keep a notebook with family and friends' addresses and phone numbers in a drawer by the phone. And in a computer file too," she added as an afterthought.

"Sanchez and the investigator both checked Amy's home computer but didn't find anything helpful. They also looked for an address book at the house," Nick said. "They didn't find one. Whether she carried one with her is unknown because they didn't find her purse at the accident scene. They're assuming it was probably lost or destroyed, if she even had it with her."

"What about old letters from her sister? Didn't Amy keep correspondence?"

"Yes, but the last letter Amy received from Lana was several months ago—just after Thanksgiving. The investigator tried contacting her using the phone number at that residence, but she's no longer living there. The landlord didn't have any forwarding information."

"So, what will he do now? Surely she just didn't disappear?"

"I'm guessing the agency will send someone to Africa to interview the landlord in person, talk to her former employer, et cetera. It's hard to investigate someone's whereabouts from halfway around the world—on another continent," Nick said grimly.

"Yes, I'm sure it is. Who knew it could be so difficult to locate someone?" she murmured. "This is a real wake-up call for me. I should think about what personal files and paperwork to organize in the remote chance I might suddenly disappear. I've never given any thought to the subject before now."

"Most people don't," Nick said, a slightly gravelly edge to his deep voice.

"Of course," she agreed, her tone softening. "It must have been a shock to get that phone call. Had you known each other a long time?"

"Since college." Nick's expression shuttered.

Charlene sensed his withdrawal. His expression didn't invite further questions. Without further comment, she logged off her computer and closed it before picking up her mug and walking to the sink.

"It's late. I think I'll try to get some rest while the triplets are all asleep."

"Not a bad idea." Nick yawned. "I need to let Rufus outside before I come up."

"Good night."

He murmured a response and Charlene left the room. She heard the click of a latch behind her and paused, glancing back. Nick was turned away from her as he held the door open for Rufus. The big dog trotted through and Nick followed, his tall frame silhouetted against the darkness by the kitchen light spilling through the open door.

She was struck by how very alone he looked, standing in the shaft of golden light, facing the black night, before she turned away and climbed the stairs.

He's your boss, she reminded herself firmly. *He's also older, more experienced. There is absolutely no reason for you to assume he's lonely. He's charming and probably wealthy, given his family ties, and no doubt has a little black book filled with the phone numbers of numerous women who'd be happy to keep him company.*

Fortunately, she didn't lie awake thinking about Nick. Being wakened by the triplets several times the night before, combined with her long day, made her tired enough to fall asleep almost the moment her head hit the pillow.

Unfortunately, Charlene wasn't allowed to remain asleep for long.

The first cry woke her just after 1:00 a.m. She tossed back the covers and fumbled for her slippers with her bare toes but couldn't find them. Giving up the search, she hurried across the hall to the triplets' room.

Jessie was standing up in her crib, holding on to the railing with one hand, the other clasping her beloved blanket. Although the room was lit by only the dim glow from the plug-in Winnie The Pooh night-light, Charlene could see the tears overflow and trickle down Jessie's flushed cheeks.

"Sh, sweetie," Charlene murmured, crossing the room and lifting the little girl into her arms. "What's wrong?"

Jessie burrowed her face against Charlene's neck. The heat coming from the little body was palpable.

"You're running a temperature," Charlene murmured, realizing the ear infection was no doubt responsible for the rise in body heat. Jackie and Jenny appeared to be sound asleep. Charlene sent up a quick prayer that they would remain so as she quickly carried Jessie out of the bedroom and into the room next door. Her sobs were quieter now, muffled as her damp face pressed Charlene's bare throat. Charlene rubbed her hand soothingly over the small back.

Earlier that day, Melissa had helped Charlene move a changing table and rocking chair into the empty bedroom next to the triplets' room. The babies still refused to fall asleep unless they were all in the same room—they fretted and worked themselves into a state if the adults tried to separate them. Nevertheless, Charlene was determined to find a solution to their waking each other in the night. If one of them cried, the other two inevitably woke, and the loss of sleep for everyone was a problem that desperately needed solving.

Charlene managed to ease Jessie back, putting an inch or so between them, just enough to unzip her footed pajamas. The pink cotton was damp, as was the diaper beneath.

"Let's change your clothes before we get your medicine," she said, lowering Jessie to the changing table.

The little girl whimpered in complaint and when Charlene stripped off the damp pajamas, Jessie's little mouth opened and she wailed.

In the bedroom next door, one of the other triplets protested and then began to sob. Charlene groaned aloud. The sound was bound to wake Nick.

She took Jessie's temperature with a digital ear thermometer, relieved when it registered only a degree above normal. As she quickly replaced Jessie's wet diaper with a dry one and tucked her into clean pajamas, Charlene fervently wished the employment agency would find a suitable nanny applicant soon. If the triplets had two nannies—herself and another—then maybe Nick wouldn't feel required to get up at night when the babies woke.

And she wouldn't be confronted with seeing him in the pajama bottoms he'd started sleeping in after that first night when he'd staggered into the triplets' bedroom in navy boxers. He might believe he'd found a modest alternative to underwear, but as far as she was concerned, the low-slung flannel pants only made him look sexier.

The low rumble of Nick's voice as he talked to the babies carried through the wall separating the rooms and Charlene was certain both Jackie and Jenny were awake.

"Come on, sweetie," she murmured to Jessie, lifting her.

She left the room and paused in the doorway of the triplets' bedroom. Nick had Jackie in one arm and Jenny in the other. Both babies were sobbing, blankets clutched in tiny fists.

"Jessie's temperature is up again. I'm taking her downstairs to get her medicine out of the fridge." Charlene had to raise her voice to make sure Nick could hear her over the crying babies. His brief nod told her he'd understood, and she headed downstairs, leaving him to cope with the two fractious little girls.

As she pulled open the refrigerator door and took out the prescription bottle, she heard Nick come down the stairs and go into the living room. Jackie and Jenny were still crying, although the volume wasn't quite as loud as before.

Jessie's sobbing had slowed to hiccups and intermittent outbursts. Charlene managed to unscrew the lid from the bottle and fill the eyedropper with the proper dose of pink medicine while balancing the little girl on her hip.

"Open up, sweetie." Fortunately, the medication was strawberry flavored and Jessie's mouth immediately formed an O. Just like a little bird, Charlene thought. Jessie's lips closed around the dispenser and Charlene emptied the pink liquid into her mouth. "Good girl, you like that don't…"

A sudden blast of music from the living room startled Charlene and she jumped, nearly dropping the bottle. Jessie's eyes grew round, her little body stiffening in Charlene's grasp.

"What in the world?"

The volume lowered as quickly as it had blared. The music didn't cease, though, and Charlene wondered why Nick felt a concert by Bob Seger was a good 1:00 a.m. choice for year-old babies.

Jessie, however, seemed to wholly approve of Nick's selection. She kicked her feet and gave Charlene a toothless grin.

"You like that?" Charlene replaced the lid on the bottle and returned it to the refrigerator. Then she took a baby wipe from the container next to the sink and smoothed the cool, damp towelette over tearstained downy cheeks, closed eyes and brow. When she wiped Jessie's mouth and chin, the little girl stuck out her tongue and left a faint pink streak across the baby wipe.

"Feel better?"

Jessie babbled a reply and Charlene nodded gravely. "Excellent. Let's go see how Uncle Nick is doing with your sisters. And let's ask him why he decided to have you all listen to rock 'n' roll before dawn."

She and Jessie reached the archway to the living room. Nick sat on the sofa, Jackie lying across his chest and Jenny sprawled on the soft leather cushion with her head on his thigh. Neither little girl was asleep but they'd stopped crying and appeared to be content. Rufus lay on the floor at Nick's feet, his head on his outstretched paws. He looked up at Charlene and wagged his tail, but didn't get up.

Charlene crossed the room and dropped into the

big armchair. Jessie laid her head on Charlene's shoulder, popped her thumb in her mouth, and was blissfully quiet.

"What did you do to them?" Charlene said, just loud enough to be heard over the music. Bob Seger had finished and she was fairly certain the current song was Tom Cochrane's "Life Is a Highway."

"They love music," Nick said simply. "I should have thought of this earlier."

"But this isn't exactly a lullaby," she said. "Great song, I love it. But not what a year-old baby usually likes."

"Not normal babies, maybe. But Stan and Amy loved music—all kinds of music. We never discussed it, but I'd be willing to bet the triplets have been listening to everything from Seger and Cochrane to Sinatra and Ella Fitzgerald since the day they were born. Probably before they were born," he added with a tired grin. Gently, he lifted Jenny and laid her facedown on her tummy on the sofa cushion beside him. She murmured, stirred, then went still.

"How did you figure it out?" Charlene lowered her voice to a whisper as the state-of-the-art sound system randomly selected tracks from CDs and segued smoothly from Cochrane to Ella Fitzgerald. The chanteuse's mellow tones, smooth as butter, alternately crooned and belted out the lyrics of "A Tisket, A Tasket."

"I remembered my mother telling me she used to sing us to sleep. When the girls woke up at the motel the other night, I sang to them—would have tried a lullaby but I didn't know one, and the only song that came to mind was a Bob Seger favorite." He shrugged and glanced down at Jackie, whose eyes were closed. One tiny fist clutched her blanket while the other held fast to a handful of the cotton pajamas covering his thigh. "I don't have the greatest voice, but it worked—so I thought I'd try the real thing."

"I think you've discovered the magic bullet," Charlene said, smiling at him. "They're sound asleep."

He smiled back, laugh lines crinkling at the corners of his eyes. His hair was rumpled from sleep, his jaw shadowed with beard stubble and his big body sprawled on the sofa with a baby asleep on each side of him. The warm light from the lamp on the end table illuminated half of his face, brushing the arch of his cheekbones and the line of nose and jaw with gold, and threw shadows across the other.

"Sugar," he drawled, his eyes twinkling, "it's a good thing something finally worked. Because after days of little to no sleep, if we were married and these were our kids, I'd seriously consider divorcing you and giving you custody—just so I could have eight hours of uninterrupted sleep."

Charlene burst out laughing.

Jessie stirred, her eyelids lifting. Charlene immediately muffled her laughter, smoothing her palm in circles over the baby's back, and she drifted asleep once more.

When Charlene looked up at Nick, he was watching her through half-closed eyes. Her heartbeat accelerated, her lungs seized as she stared at him. Then his features shifted, erasing whatever she thought she'd glimpsed on his face, and his big body shifted restlessly against the cushions. She could no longer read his expression—was no longer sure the moment had even happened, or if she'd imagined the sudden blaze of sexual awareness she'd felt between them.

"I think it's safe to take them back to their cribs," he said, stroking one big palm over Jackie's back. The little girl didn't stir.

"At least Jackie," Charlene agreed. She glanced down at Jessie, who seemed as deeply asleep as her sister. "And Jessie. What about Jenny?"

"She's out like a light." Nick gently picked up Jackie and stood. "If you'll keep an eye on Jenny, I'll take Jackie up and come back."

Charlene nodded and he headed for the stairs, Jackie cradled in his arms. She turned to watch him go just as Ella reached the end of her song. A heartbeat later, the opening lyrics of Prince's "Little Red Corvette" thumped from the speakers and filled the room.

"I've got to stop watching Nick walk away from me," she muttered to herself. *We have a professional relationship, employer-employee, and ogling the boss's very fine backside is probably taboo. Not to mention embarrassing should he turn around and catch me staring.*

Rufus's tail thumped against the wood floor. Charlene looked down at him and found him eyeing her, pink tongue lolling, ears alert.

She could swear he was laughing.

* * *

The following morning, Charlene wanted nothing more than to hit her alarm clock's Snooze button and roll over for another hour of sleep. But she knew if she didn't shower and have her coffee before the triplets awoke, she wasn't likely to do so until their afternoon nap.

She barely had time to pour a cup of coffee and say good-morning to Nick when he entered the kitchen to fill his travel mug before Melissa arrived. Nick left for the office moments later and the purr of the Porsche's engine had barely trailed away to silence outside when LouAnn knocked on the back door. The triplets awakened soon after, and the day's chaos began. When the babies napped after lunch, Charlene fell into bed and slept dreamlessly.

Just about the time that Charlene was catching her much-needed nap, Ross Fortune arrived in Nick's office for their meeting.

"Ross. Good to see you." Nick shoved his chair back and stood, leaning across the desk to shake his cousin's hand. He hadn't seen Ross since the New Year's Eve party at Red Restaurant. His brown hair was longer, brushing his shoulders. On a less rugged man it might have looked effeminate. On Ross, the long hair had the opposite effect. "Have a seat."

Ross sat in one of the two chrome-and-leather chairs facing Nick's desk and took a small notebook and pen from the inner pocket of his jacket. "I appreciate your cooperation in agreeing to see me today. I know it was short notice."

"No problem." Nick dropped back into his chair, leaning back and linking his fingers across his midriff. "I'm happy to do anything that might help you find out what's going on with the family."

"Good." Ross's brown eyes were shrewd, his gaze direct. "Give me the highlights."

Nick's eyes narrowed. "Someone slipped a note into Patrick's pocket at Red Restaurant during the New Year's party. He called us all together at the Double Crown last month to tell us about it."

"What did the note say?"

"'One of the Fortunes is not who you think,'" Nick quoted, shaking his head. "Makes no sense, at least as far as I can tell. We all thought it was the first contact in a blackmail attempt, but everyone at the meeting insisted they had no idea what it could mean, nor who the blackmailer might be."

"Hmm." Ross glanced at his notes, flipped a couple of pages, and looked back at Nick. "And there have been three more notes?"

Nick nodded. "My dad received one—so did Cindy. That's when your mom suggested we contact you and begin an official investigation." Nick saw Ross's eyes shutter, his face unreadable. He knew Ross and his mother had problems—in fact, as the eldest of Cindy's four children, Ross had pretty much taken over the role of caretaker for his younger siblings. It looked like there were issues between the two that went deeper than a mother-son disagreement. "All three of the original notes said exactly the same thing," he continued. He didn't know Ross well enough to comment or question him about what, if anything, his response to Nick's naming his mother meant. "But then Aunt Lily received a fourth that was more threatening."

"And what did it say?"

"'This one wasn't an accident either,'" Nick quoted, his voice deepening as anger rose. "She got that after the second fire—the one at the Double Crown."

"The first was the restaurant that burned down?"

"Yeah." Nick said grimly. "Darr's fiancée, Bethany, could have easily died in the restaurant fire. And Darr could have died when the barn burned at the Double Crown." He leaned forward, his forearms resting on his desk, and pinned Ross with a level stare. "Whoever the hell is doing this has to be stopped before someone gets hurt."

Ross nodded, his keen gaze fixed on Nick. "There haven't been any other accidents or threats to anyone in the family?"

"Not that I'm aware of," Nick confirmed.

Ross tapped his pen against his notebook, a faint frown veeing his brows downward. "And no one in the family has any idea who might have sent the notes?"

"None."

"Are you aware of any skeletons that might be rattling in someone's closet? Any gossip about a family member having an affair? Anybody gambling? Anyone with a drug or alcohol habit?"

"No." Nick shook his head. "But I've lived in Red Rock for less than two months. Before that I was in L.A. and off the grid on up-to-date family gossip—you might want to ask Aunt Lily. She seems to have her finger on the pulse of what's happening with the Fortunes."

Ross nodded and jotted a note on his pad. "What about the Foundation?" he asked when he finished and looked up at Nick. "Any controversial deals or activity?"

"Not that I know of, although I've only been working here for about six weeks, give or take."

"I understand the Red Restaurant is owned by the Mendozas, and they have a long-standing connection to the Fortunes. Do you have any reason to believe the notes and the fire at the Double Crown might be connected in some way to the Mendozas rather than the Fortunes?"

Nick shook his head. "I'm the wrong person to ask, I'm afraid. My dad might have better information, or Uncle Patrick, or the Mendozas themselves."

Ross nodded and made another note. "I'll be honest with you," he said when he looked back at Nick. "It's time to call in the cops. This has gone beyond possible blackmail. Lives have been endangered and that last note seems to threaten the family with more arson fires."

"I agree," Nick said, nodding abruptly. "But Aunt Lily is dead set against calling in the police. She's adamant about keeping this inside the family."

"The cops can spread a wider net, use forensics on the notes…" Ross stopped, glancing down at his pad before continuing. "If the fire department is investigating the two fires for possible arson, they'll eventually turn their report over to the police."

"I sure as hell hope so," Nick said with feeling. "Nobody in the family wants to upset Lily. It would be good news if the fire chief suspected arson and the department investigators could tie the two fires together, then refer both cases to the police."

"In the meantime, I'll keep digging." Ross stood and so did Nick. "Thanks for your cooperation, Nick."

Nick shook Ross's outstretched hand and walked him to the door. "Anything I can do to help, just ask. I know Darr feels the same."

"Good. I need to talk to him too." Ross took a business card from his pocket. "Would you ask him to give me a call? On my cell phone, not my office number."

"Be glad to."

After Ross disappeared down the hall, Nick placed a call to Darr but got his answering machine. After leaving a brief message to phone him, Nick hung up and walked down the hall to the coffee machine before returning to his desk and the cost analysis file he'd been working on earlier.

It occurred to him that he had more than the Fortunes to worry about now. Charlene and the triplets were living in his house, under his protection.

The possibility that their proximity to him and the rest of the Fortunes might have placed them in danger sent a surge of fierce anger through him.

Ross better solve this mystery—and fast.

But why didn't Lily want the cops brought in? Not

for the first time, Nick wondered if she was trying to protect someone.

Could she be afraid of what the police might uncover?

Much as he cared for Lily, he thought grimly, Charlene and the babies had to be protected. If Ross didn't find answers, and soon, he'd go to the cops himself.

Chapter Five

Later that evening, with dinner over and the little girls tucked into their cribs for the night, Charlene made a pot of decaf coffee and carried a tray with the carafe, two mugs and a plate of Melissa's chocolate-chip cookies into the living room. She set the tray on the coffee table just as Nick's boots sounded on the stairs.

"Here's the first box," he said as he entered the room and dropped the carton on the floor in front of the sofa.

"The *first* one?" Charlene said dubiously, eyeing the box. She wasn't great at estimating size, but the cardboard box looked at least twelve inches deep and two feet square.

"There's another one just like it upstairs." Nick glanced at her, half-smiled and shrugged. "You don't have to do this, Charlene. Much as I appreciate your help, it's going to be boring. I'm sure the official nanny job description doesn't include shuffling through the boss's old photographs."

"I'm sure it doesn't," Charlene said dryly. "But I promised to help and I will." She dropped onto the leather sofa cushion and took a stack of photos from the box.

"I brought down this picture of Stan's family," Nick said, handing her a five-by-eleven photo. A wedding party was frozen in time, smiling and happy. "This is Lana."

He tapped the photo with his forefinger.

Charlene studied the young bridesmaid's facial features, noting the dark hair and athletic build until she was sure she'd recognize the triplets' aunt. Then she gathered a handful of photos and began to skim them.

On the sofa beside her, Nick settled back with a lapful of pictures. He thumbed through a stack of snapshots, paused to squint more closely at one, then tossed them into the reject pile atop the coffee table. Pretty soon the stack teetered and began to slide, glossy photos slithering across the oak table.

"Damn." He grabbed the pile and stood. Rufus lifted his head from his paws and eyed him expectantly. "I'll get an empty box to hold these. Otherwise they'll be all over the floor."

The big dog padded after him as he left the room.

Charlene continued to sort through the jumbled photos on her lap until she reached a colored snapshot of three teenage boys taken on a beach. Behind them, the ocean was bright blue. A younger Nick had an arm slung around the shoulder of one of the other boys, a surfboard lying on the sand beside him. His hair was shaggy, much longer than his current spiky cut, and his lean body was bronzed, white surf shorts hanging low on his hips.

Charlene studied the picture, her lips curving in a smile.

I bet you broke hearts in high school.

Reluctantly, she shuffled the photo to the bottom of her stack and continued to search for Amy's sister. Several photos later, she stopped abruptly. In what was clearly a professional studio portrait, a baby smiled out of the simple frame. A thatch of black hair and dark eyes, combined with the wide grin were inescapably Nick's features.

She trailed her fingertips over the photo, tracing the curve of his smile. Nick had been a darling baby and she couldn't help but wonder what his own children would look like. Would they inherit his charming smile and thick-lashed dark eyes?

What if she and Nick had children—would they be born with her thick auburn mane or with his black hair? And which gene would dominate to create their eye color, his dark brown or her own green?

With a start, Charlene realized she needed to get a grip. *Nick Fortune isn't interested in having babies with you,* she told herself, determinedly slipping the baby photo to the back of the stack. She continued to methodically scan the pictures, searching for Amy's sister while consciously refusing to allow herself to linger over the snapshots of Nick.

By the time he returned and held out a nearly empty carton, she'd finished searching through her stack of pictures and gathered them up, dropping them into the box. With Nick's entries, they made a formidable pile.

"So, how did you happen to buy a house this big?" Charlene asked, desperate to get her mind off her fantasies. "It seems huge for only one person."

"It's a lot of space," Nick admitted, glancing around the big living room as he dropped onto the sofa once more and picked up another handful of photos. "But the previous owners had already bought another house in Dallas and were anxious to move, so I got a great deal. I needed a place to stay in Red Rock, didn't want to rent, and this is a good investment." He scanned the sparsely furnished room once again and frowned. "I keep thinking I should buy some more furniture. I guess I'll get around to it sooner or later, if I decide to stay in Red Rock."

Surprised, Charlene looked at him. "Are you thinking of moving?"

"At some point, probably, but I don't have any definite plans." He thumbed through a small sheaf of photos and tossed them into the reject carton. "I moved here from Los Angeles a month ago to spend time with my brother, Darr."

"But I thought the Fortunes had settled in Red Rock for generations. In fact, I thought the family was a local institution." Charlene tried to remember where she'd heard that, but couldn't recall if some-one had told her when she'd first arrived, or if she'd assumed it because the Fortunes were often referred to as a prominent local family. As it turned out, the three years she'd lived in Red Rock meant she'd been a resident for much longer than Nick.

"Not my branch of the family. I was born in California—grew up in a beachhouse in Malibu. My brother, Darr, moved to Red Rock a while back—then he talked me into moving here to work at the Foundation." Nick gathered a handful of photos from the slowly diminishing pile in the storage box. "How about you? Were you born in Red Rock?"

She shook her head, her hair brushing her shoulders. "No, I lived in Amarillo all my life until college."

"What brought you here?"

"A job offer after I graduated." Charlene didn't want to tell him the move hadn't been her decision. She would have preferred to begin her postcollegiate life in Amarillo. Barry had been the one who chose to accept a job offer in Red Rock, and she'd reluctantly agreed when he'd asked her to move here too.

"When we met on the plane, were you moving back to Amarillo to be closer to your mother?" Nick said.

"Something like that," Charlene replied, not wanting to go into an explanation of her breakup with Barry. "But then she told me she'd met Lloyd and he'd moved in with her—I knew I needed a change of plans."

"And thank God you did." Nick eyed her across the width of leather sofa cushion that separated them.

"I'm sorry your original plan didn't work out, but if it had, you wouldn't be here. And I don't know what I'd do with the triplets without you."

Sincerity rang in his words and a warm glow of satisfaction filled Charlene. "Thanks, Nick. It's always nice to be appreciated."

"Are you planning to go back to Amarillo after I turn the triplets over to Lana and her husband?"

Nick's question wiped the smile from her face.

"I hadn't thought that far ahead. I suppose so." She realized she truly hadn't given a thought to what she'd do after the triplets no longer needed her. Once their aunt took custody, Nick would return to being a bachelor. He certainly wouldn't employ a nanny. She wouldn't have a reason to see him again.

She frowned at the photos in her hand. Why did the prospect of not seeing Nick on a regular basis bother her so much? She barely knew him. In fact... She mentally counted the days since they'd shared an airline flight. Was it really less than a week?

How could she have become so attached to Nick and the triplets in such a short time?

Granted, it had been an intensive few days, but still...

She looked sideways through her lashes at Nick. He was frowning down at a photo with fierce concentration.

"Did you find something?" she asked.

"Maybe." He leaned across the sofa toward her, his forefinger pointing out a woman in the snapshot.

"Amy sent this in a card at Thanksgiving last year. See the girl standing with Lana?"

Charlene bent over the picture, eyes narrowing as she focused. The tangle of jungle was a backdrop for several rough huts surrounding a white wooden building. A woman easily recognizable as Lana stood on the porch steps, her arm around a pregnant young native girl. They both smiled happily into the camera.

"Who is she?"

Nick flipped the photo over but there was only a date—November 15th—scribbled on the back. "Damn. Amy didn't write details." He turned the photo faceup. "I remember talking to Stan and Amy around Thanksgiving, though. Lana had called from Africa and told them she and her husband were thinking of leaving their jobs to take over a privately owned center. Lana wanted to establish a clinic for women and provide prenatal care. Amy asked me if I'd volunteer accounting and financial services for the clinic if Lana could make arrangements with the local government to back the plan. This photo was taken at the center—Amy wanted me to see an example of how young the mothers are that Lana would be helping." He frowned and ran his hand over his hair, rumpling it, as he tried to remember. "I never heard whether Lana and her husband went through with the plan, but since they've dropped out of sight, maybe they did."

"But why wouldn't they have told Amy and Stan where they were going?"

"Stan said Amy hoped her sister wouldn't follow through with the idea because the center was in an isolated area. Maybe there isn't Internet service there—or phones." He looked grim. "Or maybe something happened to them."

"Don't even think it." Charlene fervently hoped nothing had happened to Lana and her husband. The possibility that the triplets might have lost their only remaining blood relative was too awful to even consider. "Is there anything in the photo that might tell you where the private clinic is located?"

They both bent over the snapshot.

"The sign above the porch overhang…I can't read it, can you?" Charlene asked, trying to decipher the faded lettering painted on the rough siding.

"Only a couple of letters. Not enough to know what the word is." Nick studied the photo intently before he gave up. "I'll take it to the office with me tomorrow and ask a friend in the Foundation's publicity department to take a look at it. He has a computer program that scans and enlarges without losing detail. Maybe he can identify the rest of the letters."

"And maybe that will give you the name of the place Lana and her husband have relocated to." Charlene mentally crossed her fingers that the results would be good.

"With any luck, they're one and the same. Although there's no way of knowing until the investigator checks it out." Nick glanced at his watch before he stood, tucking the photo into his shirt pocket. "It's getting late, we'd better call it a night.

At least it's Saturday tomorrow and I don't have to go to work. Although," he added dryly, "I doubt the triplets understand the concept of sleeping in on the weekend."

Charlene rose too, dropping the handful of photos she hadn't yet looked at into the first box. "Do you want to go through the rest of these?" she asked, waving at the box, its pile of photos much smaller. "Or will you wait until the investigator gets back to you about the clinic photo?"

"Might as well keep looking," Nick replied as he stacked the boxes and carried them into the hall.

Charlene followed, snapping off the lamp as she went. Rufus padded after her, leaning his head against her thigh when she stopped at the foot of the stairs. She rubbed his ears and he closed his eyes with a low rumble, leaning more heavily against her.

The muted cry of a baby sounded from upstairs, the whimper carrying easily to the three in the hallway.

Rufus's ears lifted and he swung his head toward the stairway.

Charlene's fingers stilled on Rufus's silky fur and she froze, listening intently. Almost immediately on the heels of the outcry, Willie Nelson's gravelly voice rasped out the opening bars of "Pancho And Lefty."

When she didn't hear another sound from the triplets, Charlene looked across the foyer. Nick stood at the open hall closet door, just as frozen as she. The silence stretched, broken only by the lyrics from Willie. Nick's taut body relaxed. He winked at her and his mouth curved in a heart-stopping grin.

"Looks like it worked." He shut the closet door and strolled toward her.

"Wiring the sound system into the girls room was a brilliant idea. And making it sound-activated was even better. Do you think it will keep them asleep all night?" she asked.

"I have no idea." Nick shrugged. "But it's a good sign the system came on and the girls fell back to sleep just now." He yawned and scrubbed his hand down his face. "I sure as hell hope it works every time they wake up. I could use the sleep—and I'm sure you could too."

"Absolutely," Charlene said with heartfelt conviction.

Rufus nudged her hand, his tail wagging as he rumbled.

"He needs to go out," Nick said. "I'll take him." He snapped his fingers and Rufus left Charlene's side.

"See you in the morning," she called after him as Nick and the big dog headed toward the kitchen.

He looked over his shoulder at her, his eyes darker, unreadable. "Sleep well."

Charlene waited until they disappeared down the hall before she climbed the stairs.

I'm getting way too attached to that man.

Admitting it didn't make the knowledge any less palatable, she realized with annoyance.

The following morning, Nick and Charlene had the girls to themselves, since Melissa didn't work on weekends.

"Let's walk down to the coffee shop," Nick suggested as he lifted Jenny out of her high chair. Elbows stiff and arms straight, he dangled her in front of him while he walked to the sink.

Charlene automatically grabbed a baby wipe from the container on the counter and handed it to him. He set Jenny on the edge of the counter, holding her firmly with one hand while he applied the towelette to the oatmeal smeared over her cheeks and chin.

"I'm sure the girls would love it, but are you sure you're up for it?" Charlene asked, eyeing him dubiously.

"Sure, why not?" he replied, concentrating on washing sticky spots off Jenny's face as she wiggled and squirmed, protesting. Finally, he tossed the towelette in the trash, perched the now clean Jenny on his hip and looked at Charlene. "What? You don't think I can survive taking them on a twenty-minute walk?"

Clearly, he'd read her expression and knew she had reservations about his ability to endure an outing with the three babies. "Have you got earplugs and tranquilizer pills in your pocket?"

"Very funny," he said with amusement, the corners of his mouth curving upward. "You obviously have no faith in me. I survived the drive from Amarillo here to Red Rock, didn't I? I've won my stripes. I can handle a walk to the coffee shop."

Charlene rolled her eyes but couldn't stop the answering smile that tugged at her lips. "All right. But remember, this was your idea."

"We'll take Rufus too."

Charlene didn't comment. A half hour later, after a search for Jackie's blanket and a last-minute change of diaper for Jenny, they finally left the house.

"We're a parade," Nick commented.

He pushed the girls' stroller and Charlene walked beside him, holding Rufus's leash. The dog trotted beside the girls, his wagging tail whacking the stroller's sunshield with each stride. Seated closest to him, Jessie laughed and grabbed for Rufus's tail but missed. Tongue lolling, he veered closer and licked her face. She grimaced and chortled, pounding the stroller tray with delight.

"Rufus, stop that!" Charlene commanded.

"It's just a little dog spit," Nick told her. "It won't hurt her."

"That's such a guy thing to say," she said, frowning at him. "Who knows what he's been eating in the backyard this morning."

"Probably dirt from the rocks he chews on. A little dirt won't hurt Jessie. In fact," he looked sideways at her, "I read an article on the Internet the other day that said kids today are too clean. Too many parents use antibacterial soap to keep kids from catching germs and they don't develop antibodies when they're little. Makes them susceptible later in life."

Charlene was stunned. She didn't know which was more surprising, that Nick was reading child-rearing articles online, or that he thought the girls should eat dirt.

"So you're advocating adding dirt to the girls' diet?"

"No, but I am saying that being licked by Rufus isn't likely to harm Jessie. And she likes it." He pointed at the little girl, squealing with delight when the big dog trotted close enough to enable her to grab a fistful of fur.

Rufus veered away from the stroller, leaving a handful of hair in Jessie's closed fingers.

"Jessie, don't eat that!" Charlene reached down and pried strands of dog fur from the baby's fist just as Jessie was about to shove her hand into her open mouth.

Nick stopped pushing the stroller, waiting while Charlene bent over Jessie and brushed away the remaining strands of brown fur that clung to her fingers.

"Okay, so I can see why we wouldn't want her to eat dog fur," he conceded when Charlene eyed him with exasperation. "Think she'd get fur balls?"

Charlene burst out laughing.

"I think you're getting punch-drunk from lack of sleep," she told him. "I know I am."

"I noticed the girls don't seem to be bothered," he said as they resumed walking.

"That's because they catnap during the day. Probably building up their strength to keep us awake at night," Charlene added darkly. Even though she'd only gotten up once with Jessie, all of the girls had stirred several times during the night and set off the audio system. While she was thankful she hadn't had to go into their room more than once, being wakened by the music still broke her sleep.

"Did your siblings do this when you took care of them?" he asked.

"Sometimes, but certainly not every night, and not on a regular basis," she said. "Usually there was a reason—like they were teething, or they had a cold, or something. But the triplets seem to wake when nothing's wrong. Often, the one that cries first and wakes the others doesn't even have a wet diaper."

"Maybe all the changes they've gone through in the last two weeks have disturbed them to the point that they can't get back to a normal routine."

"Possibly." Charlene glanced sideways at Nick. She couldn't read his eyes, hidden behind aviator sunglasses, but his lips were set in a straight line with no hint of humor. His expression had lost its earlier amusement. "But if that's what's going on, they'll find their balance," she said with quiet reassurance. "Children are resilient."

Rufus chose that moment to bark loudly and bound forward, dragging Charlene with him. Startled, she held on, pulling on his leash in an effort to stop him. He out-muscled her, determined to reach a cat sitting on a lawn several yards ahead. Surprised, the cat leaped into defense mode and raced to a nearby tree, clawing its way up the trunk and out onto a limb before stopping to glare down at Rufus and Charlene.

"Look at the cat's tail," Nick said, grinning as he stopped the stroller on the sidewalk next to Charlene, Rufus and the tree with the cat.

The tabby seemed twice its former size, the fur all

over its body standing on end, including its tail, which looked like a bottle brush. It stuck straight up in the air and seemed to quiver with outrage. Rufus barked again, his ears alert with interest. The cat narrowed its eyes and spat, hissing in fury. "Rufus, I don't think the cat wants to play," Nick said dryly.

The big dog whined, paws dancing against the grass beneath the tree.

"Maybe the cat isn't feeling sociable, but Rufus clearly thinks he's found a friend," Charlene observed.

"Good thing the cat's up there and he's down here," Nick said. "Or Rufus might learn a lesson about unfriendly cats."

Rufus barked and the triplets pounded on the stroller tray, their excited shrieks adding to the noise.

Nick winced and grabbed Rufus's collar, towing him away from the tree while pushing the stroller ahead of them and several feet down the sidewalk.

Still holding the big dog's leash, Charlene gave one quick glance at the tree behind them, where the cat continued to hiss and glower.

"I'm not sure who's more disappointed that the cat wouldn't come down," she said with a laugh when the dog and the triplets had subsided into relative quiet, "Rufus or the girls."

"If sheer noise could tell us, I'd say it's a toss-up." Nick released Rufus's collar and the big Lab ambled along, apparently having given up on the cat.

"Rufus is loud," Charlene agreed. "But I think the

triplets outweigh him when it comes to the length of time they can sustain decibels at an earsplitting level."

"That's because there are three of them and they can pace themselves. Two can keep yelling while the third one breathes," Nick argued. "Rufus has to stop barking to drag in air, and he doesn't have a backup buddy to keep the sound going."

"Who knew chaos could have such a logical analysis?" Charlene said, amused.

"I'm an analyst. It's what I do."

"And you apply the basics of your work to humans? And dogs," she added belatedly when Rufus tugged on her leash.

"Sometimes," Nick acknowledged.

She couldn't see his eyes behind the sunglasses, but she knew there were laugh lines crinkling at the corners.

When they reached the corner coffee shop, Nick tied Rufus's leash to a metal ring set into the wall. Charlene dropped into a chair at one of the little bistro tables, facing the triplets in their stroller.

"Are you okay here?" Nick asked, adjusting the sunshade atop the stroller seat to shade the triplets.

"Absolutely," Charlene replied, laughing at Jessie as she tried unsuccessfully to grab a handful of Rufus's tail.

"What do you want with your coffee?" he asked, grinning as Rufus managed to lick Jackie's face.

"Surprise me." Charlene eased the stroller out of the big dog's reach. Nick disappeared into the shop just as both dog and babies grumbled their disapproval of their forced separation. "Here, you three, have some water."

She handed each little girl a small sippy cup and they went silent, each sucking industriously on the opening in the lids.

"This is a healthy habit to develop, girls," Charlene told them. "Drink lots of water—it's good for you. And don't forget to eat lots of fruits and vegetables."

Three pairs of bright blue eyes watched her, apparently entranced, totally absorbed in what she was saying.

This is the thing about babies, she thought as she smiled at them. *They're fascinated by adults. They pay attention. Too bad they outgrow it later on.*

A small blue sports car zipped past on the street, slowing to wedge into a parking space halfway down the block. A couple got out, doors slamming, and walked toward Charlene.

The sun was at their backs, making it difficult for her to see them clearly, but there was something very familiar about the man. He walked with his arm slung over the woman's shoulders as they strolled nearer, apparently absorbed in each other and their conversation.

It wasn't until they drew nearer that Charlene realized the man was Barry.

Too late to run—and nowhere to hide. She knew precisely the moment when Barry recognized her, because he stopped abruptly, his jaw dropping in surprise.

"Charlene?"

"Hello, Barry," she said coolly, laying a restraining hand on Rufus's collar as he rose to his feet. A low growl rumbled in the dog's throat, his stance protective. "It's all right, Rufus," she soothed.

Barry looked from the dog to the three little girls in the stroller, and then back at Charlene, clearly puzzled.

"I thought you were in Amarillo."

"I was—for a day."

"And now you're back in Red Rock?"

"Obviously."

"With a dog and three kids?" The disbelief coloring his tones was palpable.

Since confirmation seemed unnecessary, Charlene looked at his companion and smiled. "Good morning."

The blonde eyed Charlene with a distinctly antagonistic narrowing of her eyes before she looked back at Barry. He was still staring as if dumfounded at the girls in their stroller. "Good morning," the blonde said finally, her tone cool but polite.

"Where did you get the kids?" Barry demanded.

"In Amarillo."

He glared at her, clearly annoyed by the brevity of her response.

She smiled back at him but didn't elaborate.

"I think I deserve an explanation." His voice held controlled impatience.

"Really?" she said coolly, lifting an eyebrow consideringly. "I can't imagine why."

Barry's face turned a deeper shade of red. Before

he could say anything further, the door to the coffee shop opened and Nick stepped out.

He set down two takeout cups of coffee and a bag on the tabletop. His eyes were still hidden behind the designer shades, but she knew with certainty that he'd swiftly assessed the situation. The two men couldn't have provided a stronger contrast—Nick with his dark hair and eyes, black T-shirt stretched across broad shoulders and chest, faded jeans outlining the powerful muscles of thighs and long legs. Barry's more slender frame seemed almost effeminate compared to Nick's well-toned body, while his blond hair seemed washed out in the bright sunshine, his skin pale next to Nick's California-sun-tanned features.

"I hope you like chocolate doughnuts," Nick said, shifting so he stood on her left and slightly in front of her, effectively placing himself between her and Barry.

The move was subtle but Barry clearly got the message. His face turned even ruddier and he fairly bristled at Nick.

"Who are you?" he demanded.

"Nick Fortune," he said with easy confidence, smiling at the woman with Barry.

Charlene had no trouble understanding why the blonde nearly melted into her hot-pink flip-flops.

"Hello," the woman breathed, clearly dazzled. "I'm Gwen."

"Pleased to meet you, Gwen." Nick smiled at her again and she batted her eyelashes, her smile widening.

Barry stiffened. The blonde met his angry stare

with cool aplomb before she looked back at Nick, ran her fingers through her hair and swept it back over her shoulders.

Well, well, Charlene thought. Instantly annoyed at the flirtatious gesture, she glanced at Nick. She couldn't see his eyes behind the sunglasses, but he seemed to have missed the blonde's invitation. He was turned toward Barry and his big body seemed to radiate menace.

Barry looked at Nick, his frown deepening.

"Fortune?" he said, unable to hide his disbelief. "Not one of the Fortune Foundation family?"

"Guilty, I'm afraid," Nick said.

Gwen seemed to suddenly become aware of the tension in the air. She glanced uneasily at Charlene. Charlene shrugged to indicate she was staying out of what appeared to be a brewing storm.

The blonde frowned and clasped her hands around Barry's arm, just above the elbow. "I'm dying for an ice cream, Barry." Gwen tugged determinedly. "Let's go in."

"I don't…" Barry began, resisting her urging as if he wanted to say more.

The triplets had been surprisingly quiet during the exchange. Jessie chose that moment to bang her sippy cup on the stroller tray, interrupting Barry as she babbled imperiously. Charlene turned to the girls, and out of the corner of her eye saw Gwen draw Barry away. A moment later, she heard the bell on the shop door jingle.

"Well, that was interesting." Nick dropped into the

chair next to her and took the lid off one of the cups. He slid the other coffee across the small tabletop to her and opened the bag. He took out a doughnut and bit into it, waiting until Charlene finished calming Jenny and turned back to pick up her cup before he continued. "So, who was he?"

"My ex-fiancé," she said calmly.

He paused, the doughnut halfway to his mouth, and stared at her. "You're kidding."

"No, I'm not." She frowned at him. "Why would you think I'm kidding about having an ex-fiancé? Do you find it impossible to believe that someone would want to marry me?"

"Hell, no." He frowned back at her. "I'm just surprised you said yes—he looks like a jerk."

"He's not," she denied. Then she considered her response and shrugged. "Okay, maybe he *is* kind of a jerk."

She had the distinct impression that Nick was rolling his eyes behind his sunglasses.

"No kidding." He finished his doughnut in one bite. "How long were you engaged?"

"We weren't actually officially engaged. He never gave me a ring. But we were together for three years."

"Three years, huh?" He took a drink of coffee and studied her over the cup rim. "Where did you two meet?"

"In college." She picked a doughnut from the bag and broke off a bite, popping it into her mouth.

"Let me guess—I bet he was in a drama class with you. Or was it a poetry class?"

She narrowed her eyes at him consideringly. "It was poetry. How did you know that's where we met?"

"Just a wild guess. He looks like the kind of guy who'd pick up girls in poetry class."

"He does?" Charlene considered Barry's blond hair, classically handsome features, a frame that might be called lanky but never muscled, and narrow, scholarly hands, without a callus to be found on the smooth, soft skin. "Hmm, I think I see what you mean."

"You said he was your *ex*-fiancé. What happened?"

"I suppose you could say we drifted apart in the years since college and grew to have different goals for our lives," Charlene said slowly, thinking about his question. The breakup with Barry had been coming for months. Their final argument had followed weeks of escalating bickering over a variety of issues, including whether they should pool their money and buy a house. It had ended with her walking out, their relationship over.

She could hardly believe only a few weeks had passed since they'd officially parted ways. So much had been packed into the last week with Nick and the triplets that it seemed much longer.

She'd dreaded running into Barry. She'd been sure it would be an awkward, emotionally painful encounter. But in fact, she realized, she'd felt very little beyond mild regret and annoyance.

What did that say about the depth of their attachment? Had she really loved him—or had they drifted into a relationship through sheer convenience and habit?

"When did you break up?"

"A few weeks ago."

"So that's why you were leaving Red Rock and flying to Amarillo?"

Charlene nodded. "I was going to stay with my mother while I found a new job and an apartment."

She rubbed her temples with her fingertips, feeling a headache coming on.

"You okay?" Nick asked.

His words interrupted her reverie, yanking her back to the present. She immediately ceased rubbing her temples and picked up her coffee.

"Of course. I'm fine. What was I saying?" She paused to sip her coffee, gaining a moment to recall his earlier question. "Oh, yes—being engaged. Actually, becoming un-engaged." She shrugged. "It's not uncommon for couples to discover they're not well-suited during a long engagement."

"If you say so." Nick looked at her over the rims of his sunglasses, his eyes intent. "Three years is a long time to be engaged."

"We wanted to establish our careers, save money for a house and so on."

"Couldn't you have done that after you were married?" His deep voice held a touch of derision.

"I suppose so, but it seemed wiser to wait until we were more settled." She frowned at him. "I suppose you would have leaped straight into marriage?"

"Damned straight," he said with emphasis. "If I

cared enough about a woman to ask her to marry me, I wouldn't be willing to put off the wedding for three years."

"And if *she* wanted to wait, I'm suppose you'd toss her over your shoulder and haul her off to your cave?"

His mouth quirked and he laughed. "No, I'm not that much of a caveman—although I'd be tempted." He stared at her for a moment. "Charlene," he said bluntly, "your ex-fiancé is a fool. He should have hustled you off to the altar the day you said yes. I'd never make that mistake."

Charlene felt her eyes widen. Her heart threatened to pound its way out of her rib cage. There was something about the intensity of his stare beneath lowered eyelids and the curve of his mouth that was more sensual than amused.

"I don't…" she began. She had to pause and clear her throat, her voice husky with the effort to speak. She lost track of what she'd been going to say when his gaze shifted from her eyes to focus on her mouth, lingering there for a long moment.

His lashes lifted and his gaze met hers. Charlene caught her breath. Focused male desire blazed in his eyes. She felt caught, unable to look away.

Behind him, the door to the coffee shop burst open and a crowd of teenagers poured out onto the sidewalk. Their laughter and raised voices was boisterous and loud, but it wasn't enough to break the web that Charlene felt spun out between her and Nick.

But then one of the boys bumped the back of Nick's

chair and he looked away from her, over his shoulder at the kid.

"Sorry." The teenager raised his hands in apology. "Didn't mean to do that."

"No problem." Nick's voice was clipped.

When he turned back, his face was blank and Charlene could no longer read his eyes.

"Ready to go?" he asked, rising to take his cup and the empty doughnut bag to the trash can.

"Yes, of course." Charlene followed suit.

Despite the distraction of the three babies and an energetic dog on the walk home, Charlene couldn't forget the heat in Nick's eyes. Nor could she ignore her reaction to the sexual tension that still sizzled in the air between them.

She pretended to be unaware, busying herself with Rufus's lead as they entered the house. The dog raced away, disappearing into the kitchen, and she turned to help Nick with the girls.

He bent to unhook Jessie just as Charlene moved. The resultant bumping of shoulders knocked her off balance, and Nick grabbed her, his big hands closing over her biceps to keep her from falling.

"Damn, I'm sorry—are you okay?"

"Yes…I, um…" She couldn't finish the sentence. He stood so close she could see the fine lines fanning at the corners of his eyes and the faint shadow of dark beard along his jawline. Bare inches separated their bodies, and his heat, combined with the subtle scent of aftershave and soap, urged her to close the distance and wrap her arms around him. The need to feel him pressed against her, breast to thigh, was overpowering.

His gaze searched hers, his frown of concern replaced with sensual awareness. His eyes narrowed; his hands tightened on her shoulders and he lowered his head. She waited, breathless, unable to tear her gaze from his.

Rufus bounded back into the room, barking as the babies greeted him with shrieks of delight.

For one brief moment, the two adults remained frozen.

Charlene thought she caught a flicker of frustration in Nick's eyes before he stepped back, releasing her.

"Rufus, down." His voice was deeper, gravelly.

She bent to unlatch Jessie from the stroller.

"Time for the girls' morning snack." Charlene knew she was blatantly using the babies as an excuse, but she needed to put space between herself and Nick.

If this morning was any example of how successfully she could handle her attraction to Nick, she was in big trouble.

Chapter Six

The following day was Sunday and the hours flew by. Caring for the triplets left little time for more personal discussions. Charlene was relieved when Nick seemed more than willing to keep conversation in neutral territory and far away from any deeply personal or potentially intimate subjects.

After Nick left for the office on Monday, Charlene felt tension drain out of her body like air from a punctured balloon. She had an entire day ahead of her to shore up her defenses and come to terms with the desire she'd read in Nick's eyes on Saturday. She wasn't sure it would be long enough.

Not that she hadn't been *trying* to do so every hour

since it happened. She just wasn't having a lot of success.

Improbable as it seemed, Nick was attracted to her.

She couldn't mistake or deny what she'd seen in his eyes. What she didn't know was whether he'd feel the same for any female he'd been thrown into daily contact with. Their situation—sharing a house, sharing the care of the triplets—was tailor-made to promote intimacy.

As she and Melissa cared for the triplets, Charlene pondered the question. By noon, she'd decided that Nick was only reacting as any male would in their situation.

It's not me, she decided. Living in each other's pockets for a week had created a false attraction. Probably like survivors of a shipwreck who are stuck in the same lifeboat together.

Unwelcome though it was, she had to conclude that if she wanted to keep her heart intact, she had to ignore any shivers of longing she might feel for Nick.

The triplets were tucked into their high chairs in the big kitchen while she and Melissa monitored them as they tried to eat lunch. They missed their mouths more often than not, and it was a toss-up as to whether there was more food on the girls' faces, hair and clothes than in their stomachs. The women laughed as much as Jessie and Jenny when Jackie bent over and slurped applesauce directly from her bowl.

When she lifted her head, her mouth, chin, cheeks and the tip of her nose were covered with applesauce.

Jessie and Jenny shrieked and instantly copied Jackie, making smacking noises.

Charlene rolled her eyes and collected the dispenser of wipes from next to the sink and carried them back to the counter, holding the box out for Melissa to extract several before she removed three herself and set the box down within reach.

The phone rang as she and Melissa were removing sticky applesauce and peas from the squirming little girls.

"I'll get that." Melissa tossed stained towelettes in the trash and lifted the phone to her ear. "Fortune residence." She paused, listening. "Yes, she is, just a moment." She handed the phone to Charlene. "It's for you."

Surprised, she mouthed, "Who is it?" but Melissa only shrugged.

"Hello?"

"Charlene? This is Kate."

Hearing her friend and former coworker's voice instantly had Charlene smiling with surprise and delight. The swift exchange of hellos and how are yous made her realize how insulated she'd been over the last week. She hadn't even taken time to let Kate know she was back in town.

"How did you know I was here?" she asked, curious.

"I called your mom and she gave me this number. Meet me for coffee," Kate demanded. "You've got to tell me why you're in Red Rock!"

"I can't—I'm working." She listened as Kate protested. Melissa looked up from wiping Jackie's fingers and lifted an inquiring brow. "No, really, I can't."

"If you want to go out, I can handle things here after the girls go down for their nap," Melissa said.

"Hold on a second, Kate." Charlene covered the mouthpiece with one hand. "Are you sure, Melissa?"

"Absolutely," the housekeeper said firmly. "You haven't been away from the babies since you got here. You should get out of the house. Go meet your friend."

"All right." She confirmed a time with Kate and rang off. "Thanks so much, Melissa. Kate and I used to work together. It'll be so nice to chat and catch up."

"No problem," Melissa assured her.

An hour later, Charlene and Kate sat at a table in the back of the neighborhood coffee shop. The café was nearly empty, the lunch rush over.

"I can't believe you didn't call me. When did you come back to Red Rock?" Kate asked.

"About a week ago, maybe a bit more. Days and nights are just a blur. I've been seriously sleep deprived up until a couple of days ago and I haven't caught up yet."

Kate's dark brows zoomed upward. "Why? What are you doing—or shouldn't I ask?"

"I'm working as a nanny."

Kate stared at her blankly. "A nanny? You left a perfectly good job at the hospital to babysit?"

Charlene chuckled and sipped her iced tea. "Hearing you put it in those terms, it does sound pretty illogical, doesn't it?"

"You think?" Kate rolled her eyes. "Why did you do it?"

Charlene spent the next few moments reciting the sequence of events leading to her accepting Nick's job offer. When she was done, Kate was speechless.

"So, here I am." Charlene waved her hand, indicating the café's interior and the greater world of Red Rock beyond the glass windows. "Back in Red Rock. And working as a nanny."

"I'm not sure where to start," Kate told her. "I've got a dozen questions. Let's get right to the big item on my list." She glanced around the sparsely populated café then leaned forward, elbows on the table, and whispered. "Is Nicholas Fortune as drop-dead gorgeous as rumor says he is?"

Charlene almost choked on her coffee. She leaned toward her friend and whispered back, "Yes. Definitely."

"Ah." Kate's dark eyes twinkled. "I knew there was more to this story than your needing to find a job superquick."

Charlene told her about the bonus offer, grinning as her friend's eyes widened and she gasped.

"Geez, why didn't I meet him first?" Kate groaned. "I'd work as a nanny for that kind of money. That's amazing."

"That's what I thought. I couldn't afford *not* to take the job. And given how desperate I was to get out of my mom and Lloyd's way, the bonus was just icing on an already great cake."

"What are you going to do with all that money—stash it in a 401K?"

"Part of it, probably. I might go back to school for my master's."

"Great idea," Kate said, nodding with enthusiasm. "So nice to have options. Have I mentioned that I'm green with envy?" She added. "Daily contact with the gorgeous Nick Fortune, *and* you're making incredible money for this gig. Life surely couldn't get any better."

Unless Nick is interested in me for more than my babysitting skills. Charlene didn't voice the thought aloud. She didn't want anyone, even Kate, speculating about her feelings for Nick. She didn't doubt they'd remain unspoken by her and unacknowledged by him.

"We should celebrate," Kate went on, obviously unaware of Charlene's lack of comment.

"We are celebrating." Charlene lifted her tea and saluted her friend.

"No, no—we need to celebrate with champagne and a night on the town."

"I'd love to—but I don't have any nights off."

"What? That's not right."

"I'm the triplets' primary caretaker during evenings and overnight. I can take a little time off during the day when Melissa is at the house, but not at night."

"That's got to be illegal. Aren't employers required to give an employee set times for coffee breaks, lunch, dinner, et cetera?"

"I'm sure they do, but this isn't a normal work situation. In fact, the job is only temporary. Once the girls' aunt is found and she arrives to take custody of them, my job will be finished. And I don't mind working long hours."

As she said the words, Charlene realized that when Lana arrived to collect the triplets, she would have to say goodbye—to both the girls and to Nick.

And no amount of bonus money was going to make it easier to walk away.

At the very moment Charlene was joining Kate for coffee at the café, Nick's cell phone rang across town just as he returned to his office after lunch. A quick glance at Caller ID had him grinning.

"Hey, J.R., what's up?" Nick greeted his older brother enthusiastically. The rest of the world might use his given name of William, but to his close friends and family he was always J.R.

"Not much. How's it going in Texasville? Are you wearing a ten-gallon hat yet?"

Nick laughed at his older brother's teasing. "I told you when I left L.A.—I don't think I'm the John Wayne type."

"Too bad," J. R. Fortune drawled. "Women love cowboys."

"Yeah," Nick said wryly. "So I've heard."

"How's the new job?"

"I'm still settling in, but it's going well."

"And what about life in a small town? How's that working for you?"

"A few challenges, but that only makes life more interesting, right?" Nick said, carefully noncommittal.

"What kind of challenges?" J.R.'s tone told Nick

that his attempt at evading his brother's question hadn't worked. J.R. knew him too well.

"Hasn't Darr told you?"

"I haven't talked to Darr. He called and left a message—I returned the call and got his machine. We keep missing each other."

"Then you haven't heard I've become a father."

The statement was met with dead silence.

"Uh, you want to explain that?" J.R. said finally, his voice carefully neutral.

"I'm the guardian of three baby girls—one-year-old triplets."

J.R.'s swift, drawn-out expletive was a testament to his shock. It wasn't often J.R. was caught off guard.

"First of all, they're not mine," Nick said, taking pity on his brother. "Not by blood, anyway—they're Stan and Amy's little girls. I have temporary custody until the estate's attorney locates Amy's sister, then she'll take them."

"Damn."

For the next few moments, Nick and J.R. had a nearly word-for-word repeat of his conversation with Darr.

"You're the last person I'd expect someone to leave their kids to," J.R. said finally. "Especially little girls. And especially three of them at a time. How the hell are you taking care of them, anyway? I can't see you changing diapers. Did you hire staff?"

"My housekeeper went from part-time to full-time, and I hired a nanny."

Something in his voice must have given him away, because J.R. pounced on the comment.

"Yeah? What's she like?"

Irritated, Nick swung around in his chair and glared at the window in front of him. "That's the same question Darr asked me. She's female. She takes care of the kids. What else is there?"

"Yeah, right." J.R.'s drawl held a wealth of disbelief. "If there wasn't something else, you wouldn't care if I asked."

"She's female," Nick repeated. "She has red hair. She's around twenty-five, maybe twenty-six. And she's beautiful." He bit off the words.

"And she's living in your house?"

"Yeah, she lives in the house."

"Okay, okay. Don't be so touchy. Did I ask you if you were sleeping with her?"

"No," Nick growled. "But you were thinking it."

"Well, maybe," J.R. conceded, amusement coloring his tone. "But if our roles were reversed, you'd be wondering the same thing about me."

"I'm her boss," Nick said wearily. "She's a…very nice, very *young* woman."

"Well, that's good. If she's going to take care of your best friend's kids, then she needs to be an up-standing citizen. How does Rufus feel about her?"

"He's crazy about her." Nick half-grinned, remembering the goofy, adoring expression on the big Lab's face when Charlene rubbed his ears and said good-night. "The feeling seems to be mutual."

"She sounds like Mom."

His brother's voice held a deep note of affection. Nick considered the comment. "Yeah, she's a lot like Mom."

Molly Fortune had been a tomboy, and her easy-going, fun-loving nature made her a much-loved member of the sprawling Fortune family. Her death two years earlier had left her husband and sons grief-stricken.

"Then you'd better marry her," J.R. said.

"Marry her?" Nick sat upright. "I said she's beautiful. I didn't say I wanted to marry her. Where'd *that* come from?"

"Any woman that reminds you of Mom has to be serious marriage material."

"Yeah, but I'm not serious about marriage."

"Not in the past," J.R.'s voice held amusement. "That was before you met the beautiful red-haired nanny."

"Doesn't matter. Even if I was the type to consider marriage, Charlene is too young for me—and way too smart."

"I get the age difference thing, although I don't agree with it. But what do you mean, she's too smart?"

"I don't know. I haven't asked her how many college degrees she has, but it wouldn't matter. What she's got doesn't come with a degree."

"What are you talking about?"

"She's very intuitive—she knows a lot about people. I haven't seen anyone yet that doesn't love her at first sight, including my dog." *And that idiot ex-fiancé of hers,* Nick thought. Despite Barry's hostile attitude, Nick was sure he hadn't misread the possessive vibes from Charlene's ex-boyfriend.

"All the more reason to marry her."

"I'm not getting married. I'm not serious about the nanny. Besides," he continued, "I'm her boss. She's strictly off-limits as long as she's working for me." Nick refused to consider the possibility of keeping Charlene in his life permanently. But thinking about how much he wanted her only drove him crazy with frustration.

"Sounds to me like you're blowing smoke," J.R. said. "Who are you trying to convince? Me? Or you."

"Let's change the subject. What's new with you?"

"I'm actually planning a trip to Red Rock—not sure when, but fairly soon. I'm thinking of making a few changes in my life, and since you and Darr like Texas so much, I thought I'd check it out."

"Damn, that's great news. Have you told Darr?"

"No, I haven't been able to reach him, remember?"

"Well, keep trying. If I see him, I'll tell him to call you. It would be great to have you living here."

"No promises," J.R. said. "I'll let you know when I have a firm date to visit. I want to meet your nanny—see if she really *is* anything like Mom. If you're really not interested, maybe I will be."

Nick ground his teeth but let the comment pass. Arguing with J.R. would only convince him that Nick was serious about Charlene.

And I'm not. Not even close.

Some small portion of his brain whispered that he was suffering from serious denial, but Nick refused to listen.

With both Charlene and Nick determined to keep their relationship strictly platonic and each other at arm's length, the next few days went by uneventfully. They focused on the girls while they were awake and retreated to their own rooms when the babies napped or went to sleep in the evening. Since the triplets were now consistently sleeping through the night, there were no more middle-of-the-night encounters in the babies' room.

On Thursday morning, Charlene woke early. It was still dark outside her window, the eastern sky only faintly beginning to brighten with dawn. Unable to fall back to sleep, she tossed and turned for another half hour before throwing back the covers and rising to take a quick shower, dress and apply light makeup. Moving quietly into the hall, she eased open the door to the triplets' room and peeked inside to find the three sleeping soundly. Certain she had an hour or two of uninterrupted quiet before the girls woke and her day began in earnest, she tiptoed down the stairs and into the kitchen.

She halted abruptly just inside the doorway.

The rich smell of brewing coffee filled the room, lit only by the small light over the stove. Nick stood next to the coffeemaker, his hips leaning against the countertop, arms crossed over his bare chest. Faded Levis covered his long legs, his feet bare on the tile floor. The muscled width of his chest was smooth, with only a narrow strip of black hair that started at his belly button and arrowed downward, disappearing beneath the low-slung waistband of his jeans. His shoulders and biceps, chest and abs were California tanned, padded with toned muscles that shifted and flexed when he moved.

He looked up and saw her. His eyelids lowered, shielding his eyes behind the thick screen of black lashes and making it impossible for her to read his expression.

"Morning." His voice was rusty, gravelly with sleep. His dark hair was tousled and damp, as if he'd rubbed it dry with a towel after his morning shower, then ran his fingers through it before heading for the kitchen and caffeine.

"Good morning." Charlene forced her feet to move. She crossed to the island and turned on her laptop. "You're up early."

"I have a meeting in San Antonio this morning." He yawned, dragging his hand over his eyes. "Thought I'd get an early start." He nodded at the coffeemaker. "Coffee should be done soon."

"Great." Charlene walked to the counter and opened an upper cabinet. She took down two pottery mugs and paused, glancing over her shoulder at Nick. "Do you want your travel mug?"

"Sure."

The metal mug with the UCLA logo Nick carried to work each morning was on the top shelf. She stretched, going up on tiptoe, but the mug was just beyond her fingertips. "I need a ladder," she murmured, trying to stretch another half inch.

"Here, I'll get it."

Before Charlene could step back and out of his way, Nick was behind her, bracketing her between his body and the countertop when he reached above her.

She was surrounded by him. The scent of clean soap and the faint tang of his aftershave enveloped her while the warmth of his body narrowed the brief distance between them even more. He leaned forward slightly as he picked up the mug and his bare chest brushed her shoulderblades.

Her breath caught in a faint, audible gasp, and she froze, immobilized as she struggled to deal with an overload of emotions.

Nick heard the quick intake of breath, felt the swift, slight press of her shoulders against his chest as she inhaled. He fought the fierce urge to claim and possess, his muscles locking with the effort. But then her rigidly held body eased slightly against his and his control slipped a notch.

He set the mug down and planted his palms on the countertop, bracketing her between his arms. The faint scent of flowers teased his nostrils and he bent his head until his lips nearly touched her hair, closing his eyes as he breathed in the smell of shampoo and warm woman.

She turned, her shoulder brushing against his chest, faced him, her back to the counter. Her green eyes were dark with awareness when her gaze met his, the curve of her mouth vulnerable. A spray of small freckles dusted the bridge of her nose and the arch of her cheekbones, golden against her fair skin.

Nick clenched his fists against the counter, muscles bunching in his biceps as he fought to keep from touching her. A lock of hair slipped out of the narrow clip holding it away from her face. Tempted beyond reason, Nick lost his battle and gently brushed the strand away from her cheek, tucking it behind her ear.

Her skin was as soft and silky as the bright threads of hair. Lured by the warmth under his hand, he traced his fingertips over the tiny freckles on her cheekbones then followed the smooth curve of her jawline. Her pulse fluttered at the base of her throat and he tested the fast beat with the pad of his thumb, his fingers and palm cupping the curve where shoulder met throat.

His gaze flicked up, met hers. Her green eyes were nearly black, a faint flush heating her throat and coloring her cheeks. Her lips were fuller, slightly parted, her breathing quicker.

The moment spun out, tension thickening the air between them.

"Tell me to step away," he rasped, his voice rougher, deeper than normal.

"I can't," she murmured.

"Why?"

"I don't want to."

"We shouldn't do this." His thumb stroked slowly, compulsively over the fast pound of her pulse point.

She lifted her hands and laid them, palms down, on his chest. Her fingers flexed and he groaned, his fingers tightening reflexively on her shoulder. Her gaze fastened on his mouth and she slid her arms higher around his neck, going up on tiptoe, her body lying flush against his.

Nick lost the struggle. He bent his head, meeting her halfway as her lips sought his.

Determined not to lose control, he pressed his fists against the countertop, resisting the urge to wrap his arms around her and press her close.

Equally determined not to give in to the raging need to devour her mouth, he brushed her lips with his, refusing to deepen the contact when she opened her mouth under his and licked his lower lip.

"You taste like honey and mint," he muttered against her mouth, changing the angle to taste the corner of her mouth. Primal satisfaction seared through him when she gasped and pressed closer.

"Stop teasing and kiss me," she demanded, frustration in her voice. She cupped the back of his head in her palms and refused to let him move away as she crushed her lips against his with pent-up desire.

Nick lost the ability to reason. He wrapped his arms around her and pinned her between his body and the counter behind her. Their mouths fused in a heated exchange.

On some distant level, he knew he had to stop this—

stop *them*—before he lifted her onto the counter and slipped off her clothes. He reached for control, struggled to bring them back from the precipice, until at last their breathing slowed.

He took his mouth from hers, her lips clinging in protest, and rested his forehead against hers while his heartbeat continued to slam inside his chest and thunder in his ears. "You're killing me," he murmured.

She eased away from him, just far enough to look up and search his face. "What do you mean?"

"I've wanted this since I looked up and saw you walking down the plane aisle," he told her.

"Really?" Her face glowed. "Me too."

"Don't tell me that." He groaned when his body leaped in response. "I'm having enough trouble keeping my hands off you. And you're off-limits. You work for me. I don't kiss employees."

"Then maybe I should quit." The bemused smile she gave him held a hint of mischief.

"I wouldn't blame you if you did," he said grimly. "But for God's sake, don't. The girls need you."

Her smile disappeared. Her thick lashes lowered, screening her eyes.

"Of course," she said, her voice cooler, more distant. "For a moment I forgot the circumstances."

She eased back, separating their bodies and putting a bare inch of space between them.

Somehow, Nick felt as if she'd moved across the room.

"I think I'll take my coffee upstairs. I have a few things to do before the girls wake up."

He wanted to drag her back into his arms and kiss her until the cool remoteness dissolved under heat and she was once again pliant and eager. But he knew it was far better that she'd put distance between them. He'd reached the limits of his control. If he spent much longer with her in his arms, he doubted whether he could make himself let her go.

"Right." He shifted away from her, leaning his hips against the counter, arms crossed, while he waited for her to pour her coffee and leave the room.

She didn't look back, her murmured goodbye and "have a good day" spoken over her shoulder, her face half-turned from him.

Then she was gone and he was alone in the kitchen.

He couldn't be sorry he'd kissed her. But now that he knew what she felt like in his arms, what her mouth tasted like under his, he knew keeping their connection strictly employer-employee was going to be damned near impossible.

Frowning blackly, his temper on edge, he filled his coffee mug and headed upstairs to finish dressing before heading for San Antonio.

Once safely in her bedroom, Charlene slumped against the wood panels and closed her eyes to blank out the light.

Stupid. That was so stupid, Charlene.

She never should have given in to the need to discover what it would be like to kiss Nick.

And it was mortifying to admit he would have walked away if she hadn't turned to face him, hadn't been the one to wrap her arms around his neck and instigate that kiss.

She nearly groaned with embarrassment. He was her boss. He'd said he didn't kiss his employees.

And it's against every principle I believe in to have an affair with my boss, she told herself. *So why didn't I stop?*

She'd never been tempted to break her own rules before. What was it about Nick Fortune that blew all her good intentions to dust?

She pushed away from the door and crossed to the bathroom. Running cold water, she pressed a dampened washcloth to her still-flushed cheeks, lowering it after a moment to stare at herself in the mirror.

"Nick is off-limits," she said to her reflection. "From now on, act as if this morning's kiss never happened."

Just how she was going to do that, she had no idea.

She hoped she was a better actress than she suspected, otherwise, Nick would know with one look that she was playing the role of disinterested woman.

And nothing on earth could be further from the truth.

On Saturday evening, two days after their fateful encounter in the kitchen, Andrew Sanchez telephoned. Nick and Charlene were in the upstairs bathroom, taking turns bathing the triplets before tucking them into their pajamas.

Nick left Jackie and Jenny chortling, happily sitting naked atop their damp towels on the bathroom floor, and stepped into the hall just outside the bathroom, covering one ear with his palm as he talked.

When he hung up, Charlene knew by his solemn, faintly grim expression that something had happened. Despite her vow to keep their conversations to business issues only, concern compelled her into speech. "Is something wrong?"

"The attorney in Amarillo found Lana and her husband."

"Oh." Charlene stared at him, torn between relief and dread. "Are they all right?"

"Yes."

"Where were they?"

"At the privately run clinic. The investigator used the information we found in the photo, flew to Africa and tracked her down. She's been out of touch because a river flooded and cut off the clinic from contact with the outside world."

"Are they on their way home?"

"Yes."

"How long before they arrive?"

"Sanchez wasn't sure—probably a few days, maybe a week, at most."

Which meant their time with the triplets was growing short, Charlene realized. Her arms tightened unconsciously, protectively around Jessie's chubby little body.

"I'm going to miss them," she said, her voice husky with emotion.

"Yeah. Me too." Nick's eyes roiled with emotion.

Playing on the floor at his feet, Jackie grabbed a fistful of Nick's jeans just below the knee and pulled herself to her knees. Nick broke eye contact with Charlene and went down on his haunches next to her. Jenny immediately crawled toward him too, babbling imperiously.

"Hey, you two. What are you doing? Are you trying to stand up, Jackie?"

The gentle affection in his voice brought tears to Charlene's eyes. She turned away, Jessie perched on her hip, and leaned over to fiddle with the tub, twisting the release to let the water drain. By the time she turned back, she had her emotions under control once more.

"I'll get Jessie ready for bed. Would you like me to take Jackie or Jenny too?"

"No, I'll bring them." Nick slipped an arm around each baby and lifted them as he stood. The babies gurgled and shrieked as they rose.

"You're a brave man," Charlene said in an effort to lighten the moment. "Neither of them are wearing diapers."

"I like to live dangerously," he replied with a half grin.

Later, when the girls were tucked into bed, Nick and Charlene stood in the hall outside their room.

"I think I'll read for a while before I go to sleep," she murmured.

"Wait." Nick caught her arm as she turned away, stopping her.

The feel of his warm fingers and palm on the skin of her bare arm sent heat shivering through her veins, making her heart beat faster. But the moment she stopped and turned back, he released her.

"Yes?"

"I meant to talk to you about this earlier, but after I spoke with Sanchez, I forgot…." He paused, thrusting a hand through his hair. "I want to take the girls to a party celebrating the reopening of Red. The Mendozas are longtime friends, and most of my family will be there. And I'd like you to come with me."

Charlene's brain stopped functioning. Had Nick just asked her out on a date? Then she realized he'd said he wanted to take the girls. He needed her help.

"Of course," she replied. "When is it?" She calculated swiftly when he told her the date. The opening would be before Amy's sister arrived to take custody.

They said good-night and Charlene headed down the hall to her room. She wanted time to come to terms with the sadness she felt, knowing that her time with the triplets would soon end.

She suspected Nick would miss the babies as much as she would.

Charlene knew the dinner at Red Restaurant wasn't a real date. It was a family affair, a chance for Nick to introduce the triplets to his extended family and friends. Despite sternly lecturing herself that she was accompanying them as an employee only, the evening of the grand reopening found her standing in front of her open closet, torn between choosing a sexy black cocktail dress or a less glamorous gown.

"Oh, get over yourself," she muttered impatiently. She scanned the contents of the closet and took a dress from a hanger. The black-and-white print was less likely to show food stains if one of the triplets tossed dinner at her, and the modest, scooped neckline wouldn't expose too much skin if one of the girls tugged it lower.

She stepped into the dress and pulled it on, zipping the side before standing back to look in the mirror. The dress was comfortable, the fitted waist and full skirt with its just-above-the-knee hem pretty but less figure-revealing than the body-hugging, midthigh hem of her favorite little black dress.

But the one I'm wearing is far more practical for an evening spent with three one-year-olds, she told herself.

She consoled herself by choosing frivolous, black, strappy sandals with three-inch heels before she slipped black pearl studs into her earlobes. Experience told her to skip a necklace, since the triplets delighted in playing and tugging on her jewelry. Instead, she settled for the matching black-and-white pearl ring.

Then she caught up a black clutch evening bag, tucked a few essentials into it, and left the room.

She heard LouAnn's distinctive raspy voice, followed by Nick's quick laugh, and followed the sound to the living room, pausing on the threshold.

LouAnn sat on the ottoman, her skinny frame bent at the waist as she supported Jenny. The little girl was on her toes, wobbling back and forth with a delighted grin.

Jackie and Jessie sat on the carpet, watching Jenny with fascination. All three of the little girls were dressed in matching blue jumpers with white knit blouses beneath, the neat Peter Pan collars edged in blue embroidery. They wore cute little patent-leather Mary Jane shoes with lace trimmed, pristine white socks. Each of them had a white satin bow in their black hair. They looked adorable.

Charlene purposely saved the best part for last. Her gaze found Nick, standing next to the stereo system. He wore black slacks that she was sure must have been tailored for him, a black leather belt and a white dress shirt with the cuffs folded back to reveal the gold Rolex on his wrist.

He looked over his shoulder at LouAnn, smiling as he watched her encourage Jenny. Then he looked past her and saw Charlene. His smile disappeared. His gaze ran from her face to her toes, then back again and something hot flared in his dark eyes.

"There you are," LouAnn said, breaking the spell that held Charlene. "Don't you look nice." She beamed and stood, picking Jenny up.

Charlene forced her gaze away from Nick and smiled at LouAnn. "Thank you."

"And you're right on time," LouAnn continued, waving a hand in the direction of the mantle clock. "You all better scoot or you'll be late."

"She's right." Nick walked toward them, pausing to pick up Jackie and Jessie. "The car's out front." He stopped in front of Charlene. "If you'll take Jackie, I'll collect the girls' diaper bag from the kitchen."

"Of course. Come here, sweetie," Charlene murmured, holding out her arms.

"I'll meet you at the car," Nick said, his face reflecting no emotion beyond casual friendliness.

"I'll carry Jenny out and buckle her in," LouAnn

said, leading the way. "I would have been happy to babysit the girls for you and Nick tonight," she continued as they followed the sidewalk around the front of the house and reached the SUV, parked on the drive in front of the garage. "But Nick said he wanted his family to meet them."

"Mmm hmm," Charlene murmured.

"I must say, I'm impressed by our Nick," LouAnn chattered on as the two women tucked the girls in their car seats and fastened buckles. "He's really stepped up to the plate to take care of these three. Not many confirmed bachelors would have changed their whole life to accommodate babies at the drop of a hat."

Before Charlene could agree with her, Nick joined them. Moments later, the diaper bag was stored away, Jessie was buckled into her car seat, and the SUV was reversing out of the drive to the street.

LouAnn stood in the drive, waving good-bye as they pulled away.

She's right, Charlene thought as the house disappeared in the rearview mirror. *Nick really has reacted in an exceptional way. If I were in desperate need of help, he's the person I'd want on my side.*

And as a woman, he's the man I want in my bed.

The unbidden thought brought a flush of heat to her cheeks. She glanced sideways at Nick. Fortunately, he was looking at the street as he drove, otherwise she was sure he would have known she was picturing him naked.

Chapter Seven

Nick ushered the girls and Charlene into the courtyard of Red and her eyes widened in surprise. Holding Jessie in her arms, she turned in a slow half circle.

"They've restored it just as it was," she exclaimed with delight. The square patio was tucked into the center of the building, edged on all sides with the dark walls of the restaurant. A fountain dominated the middle of the area. Its trickling water splashed against blue-and-white Mexican tiles, greeting diners with soft music. Several fan trees dotted the space, their green ribs draped with strings of tiny white lights. Tables were scattered around the courtyard, the underside of their colored umbrellas sporting more of the small white lights. Before the fire, the courtyard had boasted masses of old bougainvillea; these new plants were smaller, younger, but still colorful with bursts of vivid fuchsia, purple and gold. "This has always been one of my favorite restaurants in Red Rock, and I was hoping the new version would have the same feel."

"They wanted to rebuild as close to the original restaurant as possible," Nick confirmed. "The basic structure is an accurate replica, but some of the furnishings were irreplaceable. A few of the antiques dated as far back as 1845, when President Polk welcomed Texas into the Union." He nodded at the fan trees. "The trees and bougainvillea will need a few years to reach the size of the originals."

"But they will—in time," Charlene said.

"Nicholas!"

Charlene and Nick both turned to find Maria Mendoza moving quickly toward them, her husband José following more slowly.

Nick's face eased into a broad grin.

"How's my best girl?" he teased, bending to kiss the older woman's cheek.

She laughed and shook her head at him, the silver streaks in her black hair gleaming when the strands shifted against her shoulders. "Always the charmer." She beamed at Jackie and Jenny. Perched on Nick's arms, they each clutched a handful of his shirt in a tiny fist as they eyed her with open curiosity. Her gaze moved to Charlene and she lifted an eyebrow, a gleam of speculation in her dark eyes. "And who is this, Nicholas?"

"Charlene London, I'd like you to meet Maria and José Mendoza, the owners of Red and our hosts for the evening."

The adults exchanged pleasantries before Maria nodded at the triplets. "And are these adorable little girls your daughters, Charlene?"

"They're mine." Nick laughed when Maria's eyes widened with surprise. "Temporarily. I'm caring for them until their aunt arrives. Charlene took pity on me and agreed to help."

"They're beautiful," Maria enthused. "Aren't they, José?"

"Yes," the older man agreed, exchanging a very male look with Nick. Over six feet, José towered over his diminutive wife.

"What about your girls? Are they here?" Nick asked, glancing over the crowd.

"All three of our daughters and their husbands are here. Plus Jorge and Jane, of course—and even Roberto," Maria added with a proud smile.

Before Nick could comment, a waitress rushed up and whispered to José. He frowned and touched Maria's arm.

"I'm afraid we're needed in the kitchen—small emergency." He clapped Nick on the shoulder and smiled at Charlene. "Have fun, you two, enjoy your meal. I'm sure we'll see you later."

He ushered Maria away, following in the wake of the harried-looking waitress.

"I hope everything's okay," Charlene commented.

"I'm sure it's nothing José and Maria can't handle,"

Nick said. "Let's go inside and find a table—and some food."

They wound their way through the growing crowd on the patio, but it took them several moments to enter the restaurant. Nick seemed to know everyone present, and all of them wanted to say hello and ask about the triplets.

At last, they crossed the threshold and stepped inside the main dining room. Charlene was happy to see that here too, every effort had apparently been made to replicate the original ambiance and decor. Bright Southwestern blankets were displayed on the walls, together with paintings depicting battles between Mexican General Santa Anna and the Texans. A portrait of Sam Houston dominated one wall, next to a collection of period guns and a tattered flag in a glass case.

Guests sat or moved from table to table, visiting and eating beneath the glow of colorful lanterns hung from the ceiling.

"What a beautiful room," Charlene said. "Filled with beautiful people," she added with a smile.

Nick grinned back. "That's my family—the Fortunes are a handsome lot, aren't we?"

Charlene rolled her eyes. "And modest too."

He laughed out loud and shifted Jenny higher against his shoulder. "Yes, ma'am." He nodded toward an empty table just left of the center of the big room. "Let's grab a seat over there."

No sooner had Nick and Charlene settled the three girls into wooden high chairs and given their order to a waitress than Patrick Fortune and his wife Lacey stopped to say hello.

"It's a blessing you were available to help Nick with the babies, Charlene," Lacey said when introductions had been made all around. "We raised triplets too—three little boys. My goodness, what an experience that was!"

"Oh, yes." Patrick's eyes twinkled and he winked at Charlene. "I remember those days well—looking back, I'm amazed we survived it. Very little sleep, nonstop changing diapers and bottle-feeding—not to mention that the boys had an uncanny ability to synchronize catching colds and earaches." He shook his head. "Taking care of three babies is above and beyond the call of parenting duty."

"But they're worth every moment," his wife said fondly, slipping her arm through the crook of his elbow and laying her head on his shoulder.

"We realized that quite quickly," Charlene assured her. The two women exchanged a look filled with understanding. If all Nick's relatives were as genuinely likeable as the Mendozas and this couple, Charlene thought, she could easily understand why the Fortunes held such a powerful and respected position in the community of Red Rock.

Across the room, Maria Mendoza chatted with her cousin, Isabella, having left José to finish dealing with a minor menu mix-up in the kitchen.

"Nick seems very happy with his new family, doesn't he?" she said, smiling fondly at the gathering of Fortune family members at the table where the three little identical girls held court.

"Yes, he does," Isabella agreed, her gaze following Maria's. "I never would have imagined Nick being comfortable with children, but he's clearly enjoying them."

Just then, one of the little girls tugged the white satin bow from her hair and tossed it at Nick. It bounced off his sleeve and landed in his water glass. The adults at the table burst into laughter.

Maria and Isabella chuckled.

"They're darling little girls," Maria said. She sipped from her champagne glass and eyed Isabella over the rim. "I'm so glad you could be here tonight—I've been meaning to get in touch with you. I'd love to have you sell some of your blankets and tapestries at my knitting shop."

Isabella's eyes widened. "What a lovely compliment, Maria. Especially since I know how carefully you plan your displays at the Stocking Stitch. But are you sure my work will be a good fit?"

"Without a doubt," Maria said promptly. "Your tapestries will be an inspiration for my customers."

Isabella flushed, pleased beyond measure. "I would love to have my work in your shop," she said with heartfelt warmth. "But I can't help but wonder if you're hoping our connection through the Stocking Stitch will bring Roberto and me together."

"Much as I'd love to see that happen, Isabella, I've given up hoping matchmaking efforts might succeed with Roberto," Maria said, her expressive face serious. "I suspect he gave his heart away at some point in the past. I'm afraid he's never gotten over whoever the woman was, and may never do so."

"I'm so sorry, Maria." Isabella instinctively reached out, her hand closing in swift sympathy over Maria's where it clutched her purse.

"No need to apologize, my dear," Maria said, her smile wistful. "If I thought matchmaking for Roberto would work, I'd try. But as it is…" Her voice trailed off and she sighed. "Be that as it may," she said determinedly after a brief moment. "I'm delighted you're agreeable to my proposal. When can you drop by the shop and discuss the details?"

The two women spent several moments arranging a date before Maria was called away by Lily Fortune.

"I need to speak to you in private," Lily murmured. She glanced about the crowded room before catching Maria's arm and walking with her to the relative quiet of a corner.

Intrigued, Maria went willingly.

"What is it?" she asked when they had a small degree of privacy.

"I wanted to ask if you've learned anything new from the investigators about the fire that burned down the restaurant," Lily said softly.

"Not that I'm aware of," Maria said, just as quietly. "But José stays in touch with the fire department and asked the chief to contact us if there are any new developments. I'm assuming he'll be in touch when he has any information. Why? Have you heard something?"

Lily sighed. "I can't help feeling the fires at Red and the Double Crown are related. I received a second anonymous note that said, 'This one wasn't an accident either.'"

"You didn't tell me about the notes." Maria caught her breath. "What did the first one say?"

Lily glanced around, assuring there was no one near enough to hear their whispered conversation. "'One of the Fortunes is not who you think,'" she quoted.

Maria frowned. "That's terribly vague. What do you suppose it means?"

"I have no idea." Lily's face was strained. "At first I thought someone was planning to blackmail the family. But then the fires happened—and the second note arrived." She bit her lip. "I'm afraid someone is going to be seriously hurt."

"We can't let that happen," Maria said with emphasis. "It's a miracle someone wasn't injured already in one of the two fires."

"My family has hired Cindy's son, Ross, to investigate. He wants me to call in the police, but I dread the publicity that would surely follow."

"I can't say I blame you," Maria agreed. "But you mustn't take chances, Lily. You live alone out on the Double Crown. I think you should hire protection."

"You mean an armed guard of some sort?" Lily asked, clearly startled by the suggestion.

"Absolutely," Maria said stoutly. "What if this anonymous person decides to set fire to someone's house next? And with you living alone…well, it's just too dangerous."

Lily shook her head. "No, I refuse to give in to intimidation. I have staff at the ranch and I'll warn them to be more alert for anything that seems unusual. But I'm not going to let this person, whomever it is, terrorize me."

"Then promise me you'll be careful, very careful," Maria admonished.

"I will." Lily smiled at her friend. "And if I'm afraid for any reason to stay alone, I promise I'll show up on your doorstep, bags in hand, and ask to use your guest room."

"José and I will be delighted to have you," Maria said promptly, and enfolded Lily in a warm hug.

As Maria and Lily made plans, Nick and Charlene were scraping tomato and guacamole off Jessie's blue jumper.

"I'll take her to the restroom and sluice the rest of it off her face and hands," Nick said. "Are you okay here with these two?"

Charlene glanced at Jenny and Jackie. They were chortling, waving their white linen napkins and stretching to reach a bowl of guacamole and chips just out of reach.

"We're fine." She laughed and moved the green guacamole across the table, out of Jenny's reach. "If they try to eat the table, I'll call 9-1-1."

Nick grinned, laugh lines crinkling at the corners of his eyes. "You might want to put that on speed dial."

He headed for the bathroom, glancing over his shoulder just before he left the room. Two of Maria's daughters and their husbands were standing next to Charlene, talking animatedly.

There was a lot to be said on occasion for a large family, he thought.

When he left the rest room, Jessie's face and hands scrubbed clean and dried, he'd barely entered the dining room when his cousin, Frannie, stopped him.

"Nick!" She caught him in a warm hug. He returned the affectionate embrace one-armed, keeping Jessie from being sandwiched between them by tucking her higher against his shoulder.

"Hey, Frannie." He smiled down at her. "Are you solo tonight or is Lloyd here?"

"Not only Lloyd, but also Josh and his girlfriend, Lyndsey," she said. "You look better than ever, Nick. What have you been doing with yourself?"

Given that sexual frustration rode him hard nearly every hour of the day, Nick was taken aback at Frannie's comment. "Must be my girls," he said, retrieving his balance with quick aplomb. He chucked Jessie under the chin and she grinned at him. "Is that true, Jessie?"

"Your girls?" Frannie repeated, clearly stunned. "I didn't know you had children, Nick. When did this happen?"

"I'm their temporary guardian. This is Jessie and those…" he pointed across the room "…are Jessie's identical sisters, Jackie and Jenny."

Frannie stared at him, eyes wide. "Tell me how this happened."

By the time Nick repeated his story, Frannie was tickling Jessie's fingers, trying to get her to accept a hug. But Jessie clung to Nick, although she giggled when Frannie made a comical face.

"...And that's the short version of the whole story," Nick concluded. "You've done the parenting thing, Frannie, do you have any expert advice for me?"

Frannie's smile faded. "I'm afraid I'm the last person you'd want advice from, Nick. Neither Lloyd nor I approve of Lyndsey, our son's latest girlfriend. I think Josh is too young to be so involved. I wish they would both date other people and gain more experience before they get serious. But they're so intense about each other."

"If I remember correctly," Nick said gently, "I think you were around Josh's age when you married Lloyd, weren't you?"

"Exactly," Frannie said grimly. "I don't want Josh to make the same mistakes I did." Her gaze swept the big room, stopping abruptly.

Nick half-turned to see what had caught her attention and located Josh, deep in conversation with a pretty young blond girl. She was petite and looked almost fragile.

"I take it that's Lyndsey?"

"Yes." Frannie sighed. She looked at Nick. "Be glad you're only the temporary guardian of the triplets, Nick, and won't be spending their teenage years sleepless and worried about the choices they make."

Someone called her name and she excused herself

to hurry off before Nick could respond. He watched her go, wondering what, exactly, she thought Josh was up to with Lyndsey.

He hoped to God there wasn't a pregnancy involved. After caring for the triplets, he was convinced no teenager should have babies.

Maybe not even twenty-year-olds should have kids.

He looked at Jessie, bent to kiss the top of her silky curls, and shifted her higher against his shoulder.

"No dating for you until you're forty," he told her sternly. "And maybe not even then. Remember, celibacy is a good concept."

She laughed, burbled nonsensically, and bopped him on the chin with a little fist.

Pleased she seemed to understand his lecture, Nick wove his way around diners toward the table where Charlene waited with Jackie and Jenny.

As Nick moved to join Charlene, José Mendoza was deep in conversation with Ross Fortune in one of the smaller, table-filled rooms just off the big main dining room.

"I'm convinced the fire here at the restaurant wasn't an accident," José said forcefully. He glanced around, lowering his voice as he continued. "We installed a state-of-the-art sprinkler system not four months before the fire and the smoke alarms are checked each week. There's no way a fire could have burned out of control and destroyed the building unless someone tampered with the protection systems."

"And used a powerful accelerant," Ross commented, eyes narrowing in thought.

"Probably." José nodded decisively. "Although I can't figure out why anyone would want to burn down the restaurant."

"I'm working on the theory that the two fires might be connected—the one here at Red and the barn out at the Double Crown," Ross said, lowering his voice to keep from being overheard.

José looked taken aback. "What makes you think they're connected?"

Ross scanned the clusters of people, chatting and laughing. "I'd like to show you something." He took a note from his pocket and handed it over.

The older man unfolded the paper, read the single line and frowned. He looked up at Ross. "'This one wasn't an accident either,'" he quoted. "Where did you get this? What does it mean?"

"It's a copy of a note that was slipped into Lily's pocket after the fire at the Double Crown. She doesn't have a clue who put it there, nor who wrote it. But it certainly suggests the two fires are connected." Ross took the note from José and tucked it back into his jacket pocket. "I was hoping you might shed some light as to who might have a grudge against your family and the Fortunes."

José frowned, his eyes narrowing as he considered the question.

"The Mendoza and Fortune families have been close for a long time," he said after a moment. "But I can't imagine anyone would want to hurt my family this way, nor how it could be connected to the Fortunes."

"The two families are more than friends—your daughter, Gloria, married Jack Fortune. Do you know of any disgruntled boyfriends who might want to get back at you because of the marriage?"

"No." José's reply was swift and certain. "I can't think of anyone angry enough about their wedding, nor about any other situation with our families, to plan this sort of revenge."

"No disgruntled employees or business deals gone bad?" Ross prodded.

Once again, José shook his head. "The only mutual ties between our families are our long-standing friendship and the marriage between Gloria and Jack. I don't see how either of those could drive someone to blackmail or arson."

"Which makes me wonder if there might be some other link between your two families. Something we're not seeing," Ross mused.

"What's this about blackmail and arson?" Roberto Mendoza interrupted, joining them. He listened as his father quickly filled him in.

"This is a hell of a situation," he said when José finished his narrative.

"Yeah," Ross agreed.

"How close are you to finding out who did this?" Roberto asked grimly.

"No way of telling." Ross shrugged. "I still have people to interview and leads to follow."

Ross continued to speak but Roberto didn't hear

him. Distracted, his gaze was focused through the archway and across the dining room, his dark face solemn and intent.

Across the busy main room of Red Restaurant, hidden in the shadows, two figures watched the chattering, laughing groups of celebrants. Frowns of dislike twisted each face into matching expressions of irritation.

"Despite all this celebrating, I have it on good authority the Fortunes are concerned and taking the threats seriously."

"They seem to have changed their attitude since the second fire—which was a brilliant move, if I say so myself. If this were a chess game, I'd say we're very close to declaring checkmate." The voice held satisfaction.

"Yes." The response was smug, with a hint of gloating. "The Fortunes think they're so smart and powerful. Well, we'll see who wins in the end."

"I don't doubt the Fortunes will lose this game. Perhaps we should step up the plan? Raise the stakes—rattle the Fortunes even more. We have to make sure our position is secure."

"Are you saying the measures we've taken up to this point haven't been sufficiently threatening?" The words were laced with hostility.

"No, of course not." The response was instant and faintly irritated. "The Fortune family's sense of well-being has clearly been damaged. I'm merely suggesting it might be wise to push them even harder."

"I see your point."

"Excellent." The word oozed satisfaction. "I'm sure if we decide to plan another...incident, we can execute it every bit as well as the prior ones."

"Absolutely." Conviction and a bone-chilling malice underscored the word.

Nick and Charlene left the party early, but even so, the hour was late for the triplets and past their bedtime. The three nodded off in their car seats on the drive home.

By the time Charlene and Nick carried the girls into the house, changed diapers and tucked the babies into their pajamas, the fractious girls were overtired and too awake to fall back to sleep.

"Why don't I take Jessie and Jenny downstairs," Nick said. "I'll turn on the music and walk the floor with them while you rock Jenny up here. When she falls asleep, you can put her in her crib. With luck, one of my two will be asleep by then and we can each deal with one."

"Good plan," Charlene agreed. She was settling into the rocking chair as Nick left the room. A few moments later, Norah Jones's husky voice floated up the stairwell. Charlene contemplated switching on the audio sensor in the bedroom to activate the nearest speaker. But the music was loud enough without the added sound, so she rejected the idea and cuddled Jenny, singing along with Norah Jones.

Jenny squirmed and fussed, unhappy, frustrated, and much too tired to settle. Finally, her eyelashes drifted lower and her breathing slowed. Five minutes later, Jenny's sturdy little body had gone boneless in Charlene's arms.

Rising from the rocker, Charlene carried her across the room and laid her in her crib, tucking her blanket over her. Jenny sighed and curled onto her side, dragging her blanket with her to cuddle the satin binding against her cheek.

Charlene stood over the crib for a moment, struck by the deep sense of contentment the moment held. Then she headed downstairs.

In the living room, Nick walked back and forth with a baby against each shoulder. Jackie and Jessie were still awake, their cheeks stained with tears, but their eyes were half-closed and their blankets hugged close.

"How's it going?" Charlene said softly.

"Another few minutes and they'll be out for the count." Nick tipped his head to look at Jackie, whose face was nearly hidden behind her blanket in the curve of his shoulder. "If you'll take her, I'll walk Jessie for a little longer."

They managed the handoff without rousing either child, and barely a half hour later they had tucked the two sleeping little girls into their cribs, then tiptoed quietly out of the room.

"Well…" Charlene tucked her hair behind one ear and gestured vaguely. "It's been a long day."

"Yeah, it has." Nick shoved his hands in his slacks pockets. "Thanks for helping out with the girls. I really appreciate it."

She couldn't read his face, although instinct told

her there was suppressed emotion behind his polite remote expression.

"I was glad to do it. And it was a pleasure meeting your family—and the Mendozas and all their friends." She smiled, willing him to let whatever he was feeling break through the impassive facade. "I enjoyed myself—and I think the girls did too."

A faint smile curved his mouth, lightening his expression and easing the hard lines of his face. "They would have enjoyed themselves more if we'd let them climb on top of the table and play in the guacamole bowls."

"I'm sure they would," she said wryly. "Fortunately for the rest of the guests, we managed to restrain them."

His smile faded, his eyes hooded as he looked at her with an intensity she felt as surely as if he'd stroked his hand over her skin.

"Well…" she said, suddenly strung with nerves. "I'll see you in the morning, then. Good night."

She reached her bedroom door before he responded.

"Good night."

The simple words held dark undertones that shivered up her spine like a caress. She didn't look back, only slipped quickly inside and closed the door with the distinct impression that she'd just avoided danger.

Living in the same house with Nick Fortune was fraught with temptation. And she was a woman who had little resistance when it came to the undeniably handsome bachelor.

As she'd learned such a short time ago. During that mind-numbing kiss in the kitchen.

Nick hadn't spent his bachelor years avoiding women, she knew. The man could kiss. Just the memory of his mouth on hers made her toes curl and her heart pound.

Since she had very few defenses against Nick, she could only hope his commitment to keep them at arm's length while they worked together held fast.

Because she wasn't at all sure she could withstand him if he crooked his finger and smiled at her to lure her closer.

Chapter Eight

Both Nick and Charlene were hyperaware that their time with the triplets was running out. Much too quickly the days flew by, and all too soon the much-awaited telephone call was received. The babies' aunt and uncle had arrived, checked into a local hotel and wanted to arrange a time to come to the house.

Fortunately, it was Sunday morning and the timing was right. Nick was home, stretched out on the living-room floor while he stacked blocks with the triplets. The girls happily knocked them over as soon as he built a tower, then crawled after the rolling blocks to toss them back at him. Charlene sat on the sofa, smiling at their antics. She jumped nervously when the doorbell rang, her gaze flying to meet Nick's.

"You stay here with the girls. I'll get the door."

Wordlessly, she nodded and Nick left the room. She heard the door open and the quick murmur of voices. A moment later, Nick ushered a man and woman into the living room.

"Charlene, this is Lana Berland and her husband, John," Nick said as they approached. He bent and lifted Jackie into his arms. "This is Jackie. Charlene's holding Jenny—and Jessie is trying to chew the remote control for the stereo system. Jessie, give me that." He bent his knees and scooped the little girl up to perch on his arm. She instantly patted his face and burbled a stream of unintelligible chatter. "Yes, I know, honey, but you can't chew the remote. If you ate it, you'd wind up with plastic rash somewhere."

The three adults, watching him, burst into laughter at the same time, breaking the awkwardness of the moment.

"They're such beautiful babies," Lana said, her eyes welling as she looked at them. "They look so much like their parents. They have Amy's eyes and Stan's black hair."

"Would you like to hold Jessie?" Charlene asked.

"Oh, yes, please." Lana eagerly held out her arms but the little girl clung to Charlene, burying her face against Charlene's neck.

"Perhaps she needs a bit more time to get used to you," Charlene suggested, seeing Lana's stricken expression. "Won't you have a seat?" She gestured at the sofa and perched on the chair with Jessie when Lana sat on the nearby end of the leather couch.

"They're shy with new people," Nick comented, taking a seat on the far end of the sofa with Jackie and Jenny.

"They couldn't remember us," Lana said, glancing at John. "We were back in the States shortly after they were born, but then we left for Africa. We'd planned to return in December to spend Christmas with Stan and Amy this year…" Her voice broke and she faltered.

John sat beside her and took her hand, threading her fingers through his.

"It was a huge shock to hear about Stan and Amy, as I'm sure you understand," he said quietly. "Lana hasn't had time to come to terms with it."

"I understand," Nick said, the bones of his face suddenly more prominent, his jaw tight. "I'm not sure how long it's supposed to take, but a week certainly isn't enough time."

"No," Lana said softly, her eyes filled with compassion and empathy.

"I understand you two were stranded by flooding," Nick said, abruptly changing the conversation. "How long were you cut off?"

Lana and John seemed relieved at Nick's steering the conversation away from the tragedy that had brought them all together. For the next half hour, they chatted companionably about the flooding and the political situation in the area of southern Africa where Lana and John had lived and worked. They also discussed the triplets as Nick and Charlene related episodes that had all four adults laughing.

When Nick told them about the girls' difficulty sleeping through the night and using music to quiet them, Lana clapped her hands with appreciation.

"What a brilliant solution," she said with admiration. "I wouldn't be surprised if Amy and Stan used some of the same music."

"I don't know if they've always been little night owls or if they were upset by the drastic changes in their lives," Nick said. "The court temporarily placed them with a foster mother in Amarillo for several days after the accident before I picked them up and brought them here. It has to be confusing for them—so I guess we shouldn't complain about their not sleeping at first."

"That brings up something John and I wanted to talk to you about," Lana said. She looked at her husband, then back at Nick. "We spent most of the plane ride home discussing how to make the transition with the least impact on the girls."

Charlene saw Nick's body go taut. She doubted Lana or John noticed, but she recognized the telltale signs. She too braced herself.

"As you said, their lives have been terribly disrupted already and by switching their home and caretakers, yet again, we're going to upset their schedules. We thought perhaps the best way might be to ease them into the transition—by having them remain with you for several days, perhaps a week, while John and I visit daily. That would give the girls time to grow accustomed to our being around and allow us to ease into their lives. If the change isn't quite as abrupt, hopefully the stress of transition for the girls will be less when they come to live with us full-time."

Some of the tenseness eased out of Nick's body. "Sounds like a reasonable plan." His gaze met Charlene's for a moment. "I've wondered whether they'll be okay with another sudden shift in their living arrangements. I'm sure Charlene has too."

"Yes, I have," Charlene acknowledged, swept with relief that Lana and John's first concern was for the triplets' welfare. Something cold and scared inside her chest eased and she drew a deep breath. "Will you be taking them back to Amarillo?"

"We haven't had time to make definite plans, but that seems the most reasonable choice. We're temporarily without jobs, or a home—my sister's estate is left to the girls under our guardianship and their house in Amarillo is available, of course." She glanced at her husband and once again, he squeezed her hand comfortingly. "John and I don't have any personal ties there, now that Amy and Stan are gone." She blinked back tears.

"We don't have to decide all the details right this minute, sweetheart," John murmured, slipping an arm around his wife's shoulders.

Jessie chattered, squirming. Charlene shifted her grip on the little girl.

"What is it?" she asked before she realized Jackie and Jenny were also fussing. She glanced at her watch. "It's nearly twelve—time for the girls' lunch." Her gaze met Nick's. "Would you like me to feed them while you discuss arrangements with Lana and John?"

"I think we'll have time to work out details over the next few days. Why don't we all go into the kitchen and make lunch." Nick surged to his feet, bringing Jackie and Jenny with him. "Might as well start getting the girls more comfortable with their aunt and uncle." His lips quirked in a grin. "There's nothing like dodging strained carrots to bring a one-year-old closer to an adult—especially when one of the triplets starts and the other two join in because they think it's hilariously funny. It's a real bonding experience." He lifted an eyebrow at John. "Have any objections to getting applesauce in your hair?"

"None," John said promptly, his eyes twinkling.

"Good." Nick waved the three adults ahead of him. "We need to find something to cover you with, Lana, or the dress you're wearing is going to have food all over it by the time the girls are done eating."

Lana laughed. "Looks like I need an apron."

"Melissa has one in the kitchen—I'll get it for you," Charlene said as they all trooped out of the living room and down the hall.

During the following days, Nick and Charlene had time to get to know Lana and John. Observing their interaction with the triplets put to rest any lingering fears as to how well the couple would cope as parents.

On the last night the triplets would spend at Nick's home, Charlene couldn't fall asleep. She tried reading a new novel, but was too restless to sink into the story. Giving up, she put the book aside and booted up her laptop. Her efforts to focus on updating her resume and making job-search lists were no more successful than her earlier attempts to read.

She found herself staring blankly at the screen. *This is probably the last night I'll spend here,* she thought, her gaze leaving the laptop to move around the comfortable room.

And the last night I'll sleep in Nick's house.

Would she see him again after the triplets left with Lana and John?

Probably not, she acknowledged, her heart twisting with regret and pain. Her job would end when Nick no longer needed her help with the babies.

No more shared laughter with Nick over the babies' antics. No more shared outings, like their walk to the coffee shop or the evening at Red.

And no more unexpected hot kisses with early-morning coffee.

Tears clogged the back of her throat. She'd never know what those kisses might have led to—Nick was clearly determined not to get involved with her. She had to focus on saying goodbye to the triplets— and then move on.

She closed her files, shut down the laptop and moved it to the bedside table before she switched off the lamp. She fluffed her pillow, tugged the sheet higher, and determinedly closed her eyes.

A half hour later, she checked the digital clock for the third time and groaned aloud. The luminescent dial told her the time was twelve-thirty in the a.m.

Frustrated, she stared at the ceiling and tried counting sheep. Their woolly shapes quickly morphed into babies with black curls and sparkling blue eyes. All of them looked exactly like Jackie, Jenny and Jessie.

Muttering, she pulled her pillow over her head and tried not to picture adorable laughing triplets.

The muffled sound of music penetrated the soft down-filled pillow. Clearly, the audio system had activated in the triplets' room.

Perhaps she shouldn't be glad she would have this one last chance to check on them in the dark hours of night, she thought as she left her bedroom and crossed the hall. But somehow, she couldn't regret that one of them had wakened.

The door to their bedroom was ajar and she slipped inside noiselessly, only to halt abruptly.

Nick stood next to Jenny's crib, the little girl cradled against his chest. His head was bent, lips touching the crown of her silky curls as he gently rocked her in his arms.

Charlene's heart caught and tears welled. Clearly, she wasn't the only one having a hard time letting the girls go.

Unwilling to intrude on Nick's privacy, she turned to leave.

His head lifted and he glanced over his shoulder.

She stopped, held by the intensity in his dark eyes, shadowed further by the dim night-light.

"I didn't know you were here," she said softly, whispering so as not to wake the babies. "I heard the music and thought I'd make sure the girls were okay."

Nick nodded and carefully lowered Jenny into her crib. She stirred, curling on her side on the white sheet with its pattern of pink bunnies in flowered hats.

He tucked her blanket closer. She clutched it tightly and sighed, her eyes closed, her limbs sprawling as she fell more deeply asleep.

Nick joined Charlene at the door and motioned her outside, pausing to pull the door nearly closed.

"If I'd known you were here, I wouldn't have interrupted," she whispered.

"Don't worry about it." He ran his hand over his hair, further rumpling it. "I didn't mind checking on Jenny."

"The music didn't put her back to sleep?" Charlene asked, wondering if the little girl was coming down with something.

Nick shrugged, his expression wry. "It might have, but she saw me when I looked in. I thought she might wake the others, so I picked her up."

"Ah." Charlene nodded. She suspected Nick may have had the same reaction she'd had to hearing the music click on and used it as an excuse for a quiet moment with Jenny. "It's hard to believe they'll be gone tomorrow."

"Yeah." His eyes turned somber. "It is."

"I'm going to miss them."

He nodded. "When all this started, I never thought I'd wish I could keep them, but somehow I do."

Charlene fought the onslaught of tears and lost.

Despite her best efforts, her eyes filled, then over-flowed with tears. They spilled down her cheeks.

"Hey," he said softly, moving closer, narrowing the space between them to mere inches. He cupped her face, brushing the pads of his thumbs over the tears dampening her cheeks. "Don't cry."

"I can't help it," she managed to get out past a throat clogged with emotion. "I know I shouldn't have grown so attached, but I couldn't help myself. I didn't plan to," she shrugged helplessly. "It just happened."

Nick cupped her shoulders and gently urged her forward, tucking her against his chest and wrapping his arms around her. "I know," he said soothingly, his chin resting against the crown of her head. "If it's any comfort, I feel the same way. God knows I never thought I'd get used to having three babies around. They cause total chaos—there's food in crazy places I can't reach in my kitchen because they threw it there. I hate changing dirty diapers. And staggering through ten-hour workdays after a couple hours of sleep in the beginning sure as hell wasn't fun. Despite all that, they somehow sneaked under my radar when I wasn't looking. They've grown on me. I actually like the little tyrants."

Charlene accepted the comfort of his embrace without questioning, giving in to the need to be held. His hands moved in soothing circles on her back, the solid warmth of his body supporting her, and her sobs gradually slowed.

She calmed. And was instantly too aware of Nick.

The hall was nearly dark, only faintly lit by cool, silvery moonlight, filtered through the leafy tree outside the window at the far end.

The arms that held her were warm and bare—so was the muscled chest she lay against. Her thighs were pressed against his hair-roughened ones.

She realized with a sudden rush of heat that Nick wasn't wearing the pajama bottoms he'd pulled on in the earlier days when the triplets often got him out of bed in the middle of the night. He was wearing boxers.

Her clothing was just as minimal. The thin tank top she wore over cotton sleep shorts may as well have been made of air for all the barrier it provided between her skin and his.

Her breath hitched. Her heart beat faster, driven by the slow excitement that coiled in her abdomen and spread outward to her fingers and toes. Every inch of her was much too aware that this was Nick who held her—and she wanted him.

She heard his breathing change, felt the subtle tension in the muscled body surrounding her.

"Charlene," his voice rasped, deeper, huskier.

"Yes?" She tilted her head back and looked up at him. His mouth had a sensuous fullness, his eyes slumberous between half-lowered lids.

"You're fired," he said roughly.

"What?" She blinked, disoriented.

"I'm fresh out of self-control. And we can't make love if you're working for me. When we wake up in the morning, you're hired again. But for tonight," he brushed the pad of his thumb over her bottom lip. "It's just us."

"Are you sure about this?" She didn't want a repeat of their moment in the kitchen when she'd been swept away, only to crash, bruised and hurt, when he told her he regretted kissing her.

"I'm sure," he muttered. "The question is, sugar, are you? 'Cause if you aren't, you're fast running out of time to tell me."

Knowing this may very well be the last night she'd spend in his house and perhaps the last time she'd have a chance to be with him, Charlene didn't hesitate. With swift decision, she met his gaze and gave the only answer possible.

"I'm sure."

Instantly he crushed her mouth under his for one fierce kiss, then bent and swung her into his arms.

Like the hallway, his bedroom was lit by silvery moonlight. He set her on her feet, her legs slowly sliding against his, and threaded his hands through her hair, tilting her face up to kiss her again. The kiss scorched her nerve endings, the slow, thorough exploration of her mouth sending shivers of excitement through her. When he finally lifted his lips, her knees were weak. She clutched his biceps for support when he eased back, his hands settling at her waist, thumbs stroking beneath the hem of her tank top.

"You're wearing too many clothes," he rasped, his voice thick with arousal.

She licked her lips. "So are you," she murmured,

her gaze fastened on the sensual twist of his mouth as he smiled briefly.

"I can fix that." His hands moved, carrying her top upward and baring her torso. He pulled the cotton shirt free of her hair and tossed it behind him.

The moonlight fell across his face, highlighting his intent expression as he stared at her, his eyes half-lidded. Charlene's breasts swelled under his gaze, heavy and sensitive. Her knees nearly buckled when he palmed her, stroking his thumbs over the sensitive tips.

She clung tighter, gasping when he bent his head and took her nipple in his mouth. Her head spun as he licked her, the warm, wet cavern of his mouth soothing the tender flesh.

He slipped his hands beneath the waistband of her shorts and pushed them down and off before his arms wrapped around her to pull her flush against him.

"Please. Please, Nick," she murmured, nearly frantic with the need to have him closer.

He muttered what sounded like a curse and, one-handed, shoved his boxers to the floor.

The covers were tossed to the foot of the king-size bed and Nick lowered her to the sheet, following her down.

His weight blanketed her from shoulders to thighs, his big body crowding hers. He levered himself up on his forearms, the hard angles of his hips tight against the softer cove of hers, and bent his head to take her mouth. She shuddered, her hands clutching his shoulders as she welcomed the urgent thrust of his tongue. Taut with excitement, she lifted to press her breasts against his chest, shifting against him, the drag of bare skin against his hard, sleek muscles ratcheting up the tension that gripped her. He kissed her mouth, chin, then trailed his lips down the curve of her throat. The warm weight of his hand settled at her waist. His thumb grazed the small hollow of her belly button. Then his fingers moved higher, over her midriff, until the backs of his fingers brushed the underside of her breast.

The harsh intake of his breath was audible, his hard body going taut.

Impatient, Charlene hooked one leg over his, her calf sliding over the hair-roughened back of his thigh, urging him closer.

His mouth took hers at the same moment his hand closed over her breast and his hips rocked against hers. Heated moments later, Charlene was frantic with need.

He shifted away from her to don protection, then nudged against her center and she wrapped her arms and legs around him, opening herself as he groaned and thrust home.

Charlene came awake slowly, drifting upward through layers of sleep. Heat branded her back, thighs and calves. Something heavy lay across her waist. She shifted, stretching lazily, her toes brushing hair-roughened muscles.

Her eyes popped open and she stared blankly at the bar of early morning light that lay across the end of the bed. For one baffled moment, she tried to understand why her bedspread was now a deep cobalt blue when it had been white and green last night.

Memory washed over her and her eyes widened.

This wasn't her bed—or her bedroom.

It was Nick's. Carefully, she turned her head on the pillow to look over her shoulder at the man sharing the bed.

Nick's body—his bare, naked body—was curled against hers, branding her from shoulderblades to toes. And it was his arm that lay like a possessive bar over her waist, his fingers curled loosely over her ribcage, just below her breast.

A soft smile curved her mouth. There was such an overwhelming sense of rightness—waking with Nick wrapped around her. For several long moments she lay still, basking in the sheer pleasure and the memories of the night they'd spent making love.

Nick was an amazing lover. She should have known he would be by that sizzling first kiss in the kitchen, she thought.

Her gaze drifted lazily past Nick's broad shoulder and landed on the alarm clock.

Her eyes widened.

Good Lord, was that the right time?

The triplets would be awake before long and Lana and John were picking them up today. There were a million and one things to accomplish before they arrived.

With a last lingering look at Nick's sprawled body, Charlene slipped out of his bed. Catching up her top and sleep shorts from where they lay in a heap on the floor, she stole silently out of his room to take a shower in her own bathroom.

"They're here," Nick announced, his voice carrying up the stairs.

Charlene drew a deep breath.

"You okay, honey?" LouAnn's raspy voice held warm concern.

"Yes." Charlene glanced sideways and found the older woman's face soft with compassion.

"It's not easy saying goodbye when you've become attached to little ones," LouAnn said. "I've had to do it a time or two myself." She picked up Jessie, balancing her on one bony hip. "I've never been sorry I had the experience, though, once I had a few weeks to cry my eyes out and get used to them being gone."

Charlene laughed. Granted, it was more of a half laugh, half sob, but LouAnn's blunt and thoroughly practical observation was enough to get her past the emotional moment.

"Thanks, LouAnn."

The older woman winked at her. "Don't worry. I expect you'll be having babies of your own one of these days, soon enough. I've seen Nick look at you, and if ever a man is head-over-heels, it's Nick. I'd bet my last dollar on it."

Charlene didn't reply, busying herself with picking up Jackie and Jenny. She didn't want to think about what Nick did or didn't feel—she'd spent too many hours over the last days agonizing over him. And making love last night had sent her emotions cart-wheeling out of control. She simply couldn't think about Nick now—not if she was going to say goodbye to the triplets with any semblance of dignity.

"There you are." Nick met them halfway up the stairs and lifted Jenny out of her arms. "You should have waited—I'd have carried one of them downstairs."

"Not to worry, we managed." She avoided his gaze and looked over his shoulder at the couple standing in the foyer. "Hello, Lana, John."

"Good morning," they responded.

A mountain of luggage, three diaper bags stuffed to overflowing and boxes with toys poking out of the top filled one corner of the foyer.

Lana held out her arms and Jackie went happily, chattering away as her aunt listened intently and nodded.

The interaction between the two was bittersweet for Charlene—comforting because Jackie clearly felt at home with her aunt, but saddening because she left Charlene's arms so willingly.

"We have some good news," John said.

"What's that?" Nick asked, sitting Jenny on the floor with a stuffed green dragon.

"Do you want to tell them, Lana?" John grinned at his wife.

For the first time since descending the stairs, Charlene noticed Lana wore an air of suppressed excitement.

"Yes, let me." Lana nodded emphatically, beaming at Nick, then Charlene. "We have fabulous news.

John has been offered a job at the Fortune Foundation and we're not going back to Amarillo—we're going to stay right here in Red Rock. And we found the loveliest house not more than a mile or so from here. So the babies won't be going far," she ended with a lilting laugh. "Isn't that wonderful? I was feeling so badly, knowing we were taking them so far away from you both and you wouldn't be able to see them regularly. But now we'll practically be neighbors, so anytime you want to drop in and visit the girls, you can."

Nick looked as stunned as Charlene felt. Then he smiled, a broad grin that lit his face.

"That's great news."

"Yes, absolutely wonderful," Charlene added.

"This deserves a celebration," Nick declared. "Come into the kitchen—there's a bottle of champagne in the fridge. I promise I won't give either of you more than a swallow or two, since you'll be dealing with the triplets today."

They trooped into the kitchen, babies and all, and while Nick took out champagne and Charlene found flutes in the cupboard, Lana and John filled in the details.

"I'll be managing a project to establish an after-school enrichment program for underprivileged kids in San Antonio," John said as Nick handed around flutes with the bubbling gold liquid.

"I'm familiar with it," Nick said. "I worked up projection figures for the costs. The proposal for services was impressive."

"The work is tailor-made for John," Lana put in, clearly elated. "His primary interest has always been in programs that enhance the lives of children."

Nick winked at her and lifted his glass. "With the triplets in your house and heading up the Foundation's new project, I'd say he's hit the jackpot."

Laughter filled the kitchen, glasses were raised, and it was an hour later before Lana glanced at her watch.

"Look at the time, John. I didn't realize it was so late." She stood, balancing Jessie on her hip. "By the time we get the girls' things loaded, drive to the house and unload, it will be nearly time for the girls' naps." She tapped a forefinger on the tip of Jessie's upturned nose. "We don't want to start off on the wrong foot."

"Agreed."

Since the new house was so close, Nick insisted he help transport and unload the triplets' belongings.

Much too soon, Charlene found herself standing at the curb, waving good-bye as the two vehicles drove away down the street.

She went inside, the silence seeming to close about her when she shut the door. She walked into the kitchen to wash the crystal flutes and return them to their shelf. After wiping down the marble countertop, she glanced once more around the kitchen and then headed upstairs.

It was time to pack—and leave.

Chapter Nine

"What are you doing?"

Charlene stiffened, steeling herself before she turned. Nick stood in the open doorway, frowning at her.

"I'm packing." She walked to the closet and slipped the little black cocktail dress off its hanger, folding it as she returned to the bed and the open suitcase.

"I can see that," he said impatiently. "Why?"

She tucked the dress into the bag before she looked at him. "Because it's easier to carry clothes in suitcases, of course."

"Where are you going?"

"I'm not sure yet." She opened a dresser drawer,

removed several T-shirts and laid them on top of the black dress. "Now that the girls are with Lana and John, my job here is finished."

"Yeah, I suppose it is."

Charlene felt her heart drop and realized she'd been holding her breath, hoping he'd tell her to stay. The scowl on his face, however, was convincing evidence that he had no interest in prolonging her time. She forced a smile. "I'll be out of your way in another half hour and you'll have your house to yourself again. I'm sure you'll be glad you can return to peace and quiet," she said as she crossed the room to fetch her toiletries from the bathroom.

"Not likely," he muttered.

"I beg your pardon?" She paused, sure she must have misheard him.

"I hope you've been comfortable here," he gestured at the room, not directly answering her question.

"Oh, yes." She looked about her, knowing she would miss the way the early-morning sun shone through her window each morning, throwing a leafy pattern across the bed from the tree just outside. And she'd miss the well-planned cozy kitchen downstairs, and Nick's state-of-the-art coffeemaker. She drew in a deep breath and managed another vague, polite smile in his direction. She didn't look at him for fear the tears pressing behind her eyes would escape her rigid control and spill over. "You have a lovely home, Nick. Anyone would enjoy spending time here."

"The hell with this," he ground out.

Startled, Charlene switched her gaze from the suitcase to Nick and found him stalking toward her.

"You can't leave." His face was taut. He caught her shoulders in his big hands and held her. "I don't want you to leave."

"You don't?" Charlene was stunned, too afraid to hope, even more afraid that she might leap to conclusions. She needed him to spell out exactly what he meant. "Why?"

"Because I want you to marry me, live with me, have babies with me."

"But…" Charlene's brain spun, trying to absorb this sudden switch. "But you said you never planned to marry. Or have children. You said you couldn't imagine having a family—that you thought Stan and Amy were crazy to pick you to take care of their girls."

"I said a lot of stupid things," Nick said with disgust. "The only reason I was a confirmed bachelor is because I hadn't met you."

"Really?" Charlene's eyes misted. "That's a lovely thing to say."

"I should have said it before." His hands tightened. "I wanted you the day I met you but I told myself all I felt was lust. And you worked for me. I've never crossed the line and slept with an employee." His eyes darkened, his hands stroking down her back to settle at her waist and tug her forward to rest against him. "I couldn't stop myself last night."

"Neither could I," she admitted.

"Darr and J.R. knew I was in love with you. I've known for a while, but it took seeing you packing your suitcase to make me say the words out loud."

"I don't mind." Charlene cupped his face in her palms. "As long as you said it." Her words eased the tension from his face.

He bent his head and brushed his mouth over hers. "Now it's your turn."

Charlene slipped her arms around his neck and went up on tiptoe. "I love you too," she murmured, her lips barely touching his before he leaned back, preventing her from reaching him. Her mouth skimmed his chin.

He bent his head and nuzzled her neck. "That's the best news I heard all day."

"Mmm." Distracted by the movement of his warm mouth against her skin, she was having difficulty following their conversation. She tilted her chin as he nudged aside her shirt. Dazed, she realized she hadn't even felt him unbutton the blue cotton.

He smiled, his mouth branding an amused curve on her skin, and then he lifted his head to look down at her.

"Just remember when we talk about this later—you agreed."

He caught the edges of her shirt. Buttons popped as he ripped it open and stripped it off her shoulders. He shoved the suitcase off the bed and it hit the floor. Charlene barely noticed that the contents spilled out in a fan of color against the pale-green carpet.

His eyes flared with heat as he traced the curve of her breasts in the lacy white bra before he forced his gaze downward and began unsnapping her jeans. His head was bent, his black hair inches from her face, his eyelashes dark fans against his tanned skin as he slid the zipper downward.

"Nick," Charlene breathed.

He glanced up, his fingers going still on her waist-band.

"You're wearing more clothes than I am."

He smiled slowly, closing the distance between them to slick his tongue over her bottom lip. "So take them off," he murmured.

She fumbled with the shirt buttons, breathing rapidly while her heartbeat pounded faster. She reached the button at his waistband and he let go of her jeans to grab his shirt and pull it free.

She reached behind her and unhooked her bra, shrugging her shoulders to let it fall free.

Nick reached for her, pulling her against him, skin-to-skin, and kissed her.

"I feel as if the world is still spinning," Charlene confided an hour later as they sat on her bed, a tray of food between them.

"Why is that?" Nick held out a bite of scone, dripping with butter and jam.

"Mmm." Charlene opened her mouth, chewed and swallowed. "These are heavenly. What did you say the name of the bakery is?"

"Mary Mac's. Hold still." Nick leaned over and licked the corner of her mouth. She tasted raspberry jam when he kissed her.

"Can we have these scones every Sunday?" she asked, caught by the intimacy of the moment.

"Absolutely." Nick grinned at her. "Marry me, babe, and I'll open an account there. You can have scones every day of the week if you want."

She laughed. "You don't have to bribe me. I already said I'd marry you—but the scones are definitely an added inducement," she added.

"Good to know what works," he said. "In case I need to bribe you in the future."

"You won't need bribes," she said softly. "Just ask."

His eyes heated. "You may regret that. I've built up a lot of hunger over the last few weeks."

Charlene's heart skipped, heat moving through her veins. "We've just spent hours in this bed. Aren't you exhausted?"

"Babe, I'm just catching my breath." He waggled his eyebrows at her suggestively and she laughed out loud. He grinned, clearly pleased he'd amused her. "I want to buy you something. What do you want for a wedding present? Diamonds? Rubies?"

"What?" Startled, Charlene searched his face and realized he was serious. "You don't have to buy me expensive things." She wanted to make it clear to Nick that his wealth wasn't why she loved him. But he clearly felt strongly about giving her a gift and she didn't want to disappoint him. She beamed, certain she had the perfect idea.

"There is something I'd love to have," she told him.

"You've got it," he said instantly. "What is it?"

"I would absolutely love it if we could set up a college fund for the triplets," she said earnestly.

He stared at her. "You want me to give the girls money for college?" he said slowly, eyeing her.

"Yes." She nodded emphatically. "Please," she added.

A slow smile curved his mouth. "You're something else, darlin'." He pressed a passionate kiss against her lips. "Any suggestions as to how big the fund should be?"

"No, you're the financial expert." She was still reeling from that kiss. "Oh, wait." She sat bolt upright, excited. "What if we ask the wedding guests to contribute to the girls' college fund in lieu of gifts for us?" She waved her hand at the comfortable, expensive furnishings in his big bedroom. "You have a whole houseful of stuff. What could we possibly need that you don't already have?"

He smiled, his expression tender. "There's nothing I need that I don't already have—now that I have you." He kissed her, wrapping his arms around her and rolling with her on the big bed until she was beneath him. "I think it's a great idea. Let's do it. We'll tell Lana and John this week."

"Good," she managed to say.

She felt surrounded by him—safe, loved, cherished and infinitely desired.

"I love you," she murmured, seeing the instant blaze of heat and fierce emotion in his eyes, just before he covered her mouth with his and the whole world fell away.

* * * * *

A REAL LIVE COWBOY

BY
JUDY DUARTE

Judy Duarte always knew there was a book inside her. Her dream became a reality in March of 2002, when Special Edition released her first book. Since then, she has sold more than twenty more novels.

Her stories have touched the hearts of readers around the world. In July of 2005, Judy won the prestigious Readers' Choice Award for *The Rich Man's Son*.

Judy makes her home near the beach in Southern California. When she's not cooped up in her writing cave, she's spending time with her somewhat enormous but delightfully close family.

You can contact her at JudyDuarte@sbcglobal.net or through her website, www.judyduarte.com.

To Marie Ferrarella, Allison Leigh, Lois Faye
Dyer, RaeAnne Thayne and Kristin Hardy for their
contributions to THE FORTUNES OF TEXAS:
RETURN TO RED ROCK series.
It was a pleasure working with you!
And to Susan Litman, whose keen editorial eye kept us
all on track. It's great having such a supportive editor.
You're the best, Susan!

Chapter One

Isabella Mendoza was late, which was *so* not like her. And to make matters worse, she was the one who'd insisted on meeting early to avoid the lunch-crowd rush.

As she turned into the driveway that led to Red, the popular local restaurant, she groaned as she spotted an all-too-familiar black Cadillac Escalade parked in front.

How was that for luck? Not only did she have to dash into Red and make apologies to her girlfriend and her cousins, but with her luck, she would probably run smack into William Fortune, Jr., better known as J.R. to everyone in town.

Ever since last week, when he'd officially relocated from Los Angeles to Red Rock, Texas, their paths had kept crossing. And to make matters worse, she'd picked up on the wannabe rancher's obvious interest in her. She hadn't encouraged him, even if there were plenty of women in town who would have.

Not only was the man wealthy, but he was good-looking, charming and had the kind of body a woman liked to cuddle up next to. But he definitely wasn't Isabella's type.

She parked her red pickup near the side of the building, slid out of the driver's seat and reached for her purse. After securing the lock, she hurried into the restaurant that had once been an old hacienda.

Just four months ago, an arson fire nearly destroyed Red, which had broken Isabella's heart for more reasons than one. Not only did she have a family connection to the owners, José and Maria Mendoza, but she had a deep love and respect for the Tejana culture and the history reflected in the building.

Over the past few months, José and Maria had worked hard to restore the restaurant just the way it was before the fire, although some of the original artwork and antiques had been irreplaceable.

The hostess offered a friendly smile as Isabella walked through the door.

"I'm meeting friends who are already here," Isabella told her.

Out of the corner of her eye, she spotted the back of a tall, broad-shouldered man as he entered the bar, his movements a shadowlike blur. She hadn't gotten a very good look at him, but she had a feeling it was J.R. There was such a solid presence about the man that it was difficult not to notice him. And she had to confess that whenever they were in the same place at the same time, her gaze tended to meet his more often than she liked.

Not that there was anything *wrong* with J.R. The fair-haired businessman-turned-rancher was actually a good catch, if a woman was into Anglos and men who were at least ten years her senior. But that wasn't Isabella, and she had good reason not to get carried away.

Having been raised by her fair-haired stepfather during most of her childhood and adolescence, she had been denied her Tejana heritage, which was why she embraced it now with all her heart and soul. And when she found her Mr. Right, a Latino, he would appreciate her culture as much as she did.

"Your party is on the patio," the hostess said.

Isabella proceeded through the restaurant, her high heels clicking on the Mexican tile floor.

She especially loved Red's courtyard, where water continuously trickled into an Old World–style fountain and brightly colored umbrellas provided shade. The bougainvillea that bloomed in fuchsia, purple and gold weren't as lush and mature as the ones that had adorned the patio before the fire, but they would grow in time.

The women she was meeting—Jane Gilliam, Sierra Calloway, Gloria Fortune and Christina Rockwell—sat at a table near the blue-and-white tiled fountain.

"I'm so sorry I'm late." Isabella took the empty chair between Jane and Christina. "But I have a good excuse. A local businessman stopped by my studio unexpect-edly. He owns decorator shops in San Antonio and Houston, and he wants to sell some of my blankets and weavings in both of them."

"That's wonderful," Jane said. "We knew something unexpected must have come up."

"Did you cinch the deal?" Sierra asked.

Isabella smiled, feeling a sense of pride. "Yes. And if I get a few more like that, I'll be able to move my studio out of the garage in my father's backyard and find a more professional place to create and show my work."

"I'd really like to see you move to a cute storefront in Red Rock," Jane said. "It would be so nice to have you working in town. And it would be easier for us to meet for lunch."

Yes, it would be. Jane had become Isabella's closest friend. They'd met last year at Fiesta, a ten-day festival held every April to celebrate San Antonio's heritage. Jane mentioned that she worked for Red Rock Readingworks, a children's literacy foundation, and asked Isabella if she would consider giving a presentation on her artistic blankets and tapestries to the children during Cultural Awareness Day. Isabella agreed, and she'd thoroughly enjoyed talking to the kids. But more than that, she and Jane had really hit it off, and their friendship had continued to blossom.

Jane reached for a tortilla chip, the diamond on her left hand sparkling. But the glimmer didn't just stop at the ring. There was a happy glow in Jane's eyes these days, which was not only sweet but ironic.

Just after Christmas, Isabella and several of her unattached friends had met at Red for dinner and margaritas. The conversation turned to men and relationships. Before the end of the evening, they'd each vowed to be married within the next twelve months. Jane, however, was the only one at the table who'd opted out of the "Single No More" pact. Now here she was, engaged to Isabella's cousin Jorge Mendoza, the one-time playboy in the family. A man who also happened to be Christina, Gloria and Sierra's brother.

"So tell me about the businessman," Christina said. "Did he have any romantic potential?"

"Not an ounce." Isabella reached for a chip. "He was in his late fifties and married. I'm beginning to think that you four have snagged all the decent men around here."

"I'm sure there's one or two left," Christina said with a smile. "The right guy will come along when you least expect it."

"I'm sure he will." Isabella returned her cousin's smile, playing the Pollyanna game even though she'd recently begun to wonder if Mr. Right would really come along. She'd gone out on a number of dates since January, but all of the men proved to be disappointments.

"Isabella, I hope you're not putting too much stock in that list you created," Jane said.

Isabella dipped a tortilla chip into the homemade salsa. "I made that list for a reason."

"Which is…?" Sierra prodded.

"To keep focused on what's really important and not fall prey to hormones and impulses. My parents fell in lust and married young. And it was a mistake from the get-go."

The young couple had divorced when Isabella was a toddler, and her mom had remarried and relocated to California, taking Isabella with her.

Gloria placed her elbows on the table and leaned

forward. "I had no idea you made a list. So, let's hear it. What are you looking for in a man?"

Isabella finished munching on the chip in her mouth before answering. "I'm looking for someone down to earth and with a steady job. Someone who's sensitive and caring and isn't afraid of commitment. A guy with a good sense of humor."

"What about his physical appearance?" Gloria asked.

Isabella winced, knowing she shouldn't be too picky, but she was. Her heritage had become so important to her that, in her heart of hearts, she knew the man she would marry would have to be Latino, too.

"Well," she said, "it would be nice if he was handsome, of course, but that's not the top priority for me."

She left it at that. It might sound old-fashioned, but she really wanted a man she could love, a man who would love her back. A man who wasn't afraid of the teamwork it would take to make a marriage last. So making a list had seemed logical, smart even. But, deep inside, she feared that she was being unrealistic, that her requirements might be too hard to fulfill.

Still, the only way to reach the stars was to aim for them. Right?

Footsteps sounded, and Isabella glanced to her right, across the fountain.

When she spotted J.R. Fortune entering the courtyard and carrying two longneck bottles of beer, she tensed. It irked her that she felt a little on edge whenever she ran into him, and today was no different.

Why couldn't he have chosen to eat indoors?

She watched him approach a table at the far corner

of the courtyard, where a man sat with his back to her. J.R. set one of the beers in front of his companion, then took a seat.

Isabella couldn't help wondering who the other man was, and in spite of her resolve to ignore them both, she stole another glance their way, just in time to see William Fortune, Sr. turn toward his eldest son.

That wasn't surprising. The two men weren't just related; they were business associates.

Her dad had told her that immediately after college, J.R. had gone to work with his father at Fortune Forecasting, a successful company that predicted marketplace trends. And before long, J.R.'s leadership skills helped him move up the corporate ladder until he was second in command behind his dad and key to the company's success.

But J.R. had given it all up recently and bought a ranch in the area. Talk about a fish out of water. J.R. might wear denim and spurs—and wear them well—but he was just a city slicker, as far as Isabella was concerned.

So far, he hadn't noticed her, which was for the best. The two of them were ill-suited as a couple, even if he hadn't realized it yet.

Her luck didn't hold, though. The next time she looked his way, he flashed her a charming smile.

"Do I detect a bit of romantic interest in a certain someone?" Gloria asked.

Isabella tore her gaze from the other table and slowly shook her head. "We're just acquaintances. We met at Fiesta last year and keep running into each other. That's all."

"Forgive me for bursting your bubble," Christina said, "but that man is definitely interested in you. I've seen the way he looks at you, the way he acts when he's around you."

"Maybe a bit," Isabella admitted.

"I'd say you're interested, too," Jane added. "You've been craning your neck ever since he walked in. Not that I blame you."

Isabella's cheeks warmed at being found out, but that still didn't mean anything. "All right, let's say I'm a little attracted to him in a physical sense. Who wouldn't be? But trust me, he's not my type."

"Oh, no?" Christina asked. "He's down to earth and he's got a steady job. Sounds like a hot prospect to me."

Isabella couldn't disagree more. The man had given up a lucrative career at the age of forty in hopes of becoming a rancher. How down to earth was that? And as for a steady job, he might have plenty of money, but ranching was just a hobby for him. He'd probably grow tired of it and be back in L.A. by this time next year.

Even so, she didn't want to badmouth the man. The Fortunes and the Mendozas were close friends. And Gloria, who sat across the table from Isabella, was now a Fortune by marriage. So she tempered her response and offered them another reason a relationship with J.R. wouldn't last, even though it might sound superficial, since they might not understand all that was behind it. "My culture is very important to me, and, well, I'm focusing my search on a Latino."

Hooking up with J.R. Fortune might be a coup for

other single women in Red Rock, but in her case, it would be a disaster.

Yet in spite of her resolve to ignore J.R. completely, she couldn't help glancing back at the table where he sat with his father and wondering if her name would come up.

"You didn't need to get up and get those beers," William Fortune, Sr., said. "That waitress would have eventually come back to check on us and remember we'd ordered them."

While they'd eaten an early lunch, J.R. and his father had been discussing his plans for the ranch. But as they'd finished the last of their tacos, a Mexican beer with lime sounded good, and the waitress was nowhere to be found.

"I didn't mind getting them. Besides, I have something to celebrate." J.R. lifted an ice-cold bottle of Corona toward his dad in a toastlike motion.

His dad lifted his longneck in a similar manner. "What's that?"

"I have the deed to my new ranch in hand."

J.R. raised the bottle to his lips and savored a refreshing swallow, as his father did the same.

"By the way," J.R. said, "I've decided on a name for the property."

"Oh, yeah? What's that?"

"Molly's Pride." His voice cracked just a bit as he added, "Mom would have really loved the place."

His dad's eyes grew misty, as they often did whenever anyone brought up Molly Fortune's name. "You're right about that. But then again, she would have loved anything you set your mind to, son."

That was true.

Two years ago, Molly had passed away, leaving a hole in the family, as well as an emptiness in J.R. It wasn't as though he'd spent that much time with his mother, but he valued her opinion and her unwavering support. And she'd always been just a phone call away.

They all missed her, but of his brothers, J.R. suspected that he missed her the most.

His dad took another sip of beer. "Believe it or not, I'm considering a move to Red Rock, too."

The news came as a surprise, although J.R. wasn't sure why it did. Red Rock had been a home away from home to all of them.

"There's something about this town that has always appealed to me," William said. "And now that you, Darr and Nicholas have moved here…"

J.R. understood the draw to Red Rock. When he was a teenager, he would fly out each summer and visit his father's cousin, Ryan, and his wife, Lily, on the Double Crown Ranch. He enjoyed riding horses, listening to country music and playing cowboy for a few weeks each year.

The trips continued when he reached adulthood, although he hadn't found time to visit as often as he would have liked. Then, around his fortieth birthday, he'd begun to feel restless in Los Angeles. And that inexplicable itch grew steadily until he began to question the choices he'd made in life.

Sure, he'd succeeded in business and was well-respected in marketing circles, but he'd eventually gotten bored with the whole corporate scene and realized that there was something missing in his life. Something elusive yet very important.

"There's another reason I feel compelled to move," his dad said.

"What's that?"

"I was talking to my brother Patrick about the fires and those mysterious letters."

During the New Year's Eve party, Patrick was slipped a note that he didn't notice until later. It read, "One of the Fortunes is not who you think." William and their sister, Cindy, received similar letters, and so did Lily, their cousin Ryan's widow.

Then there were the fires, first at Red, which was later deemed arson. At the time, no one had thought the restaurant fire was related to the notes. After all, what did the two families have in common, other than friendship?

But now J.R. wasn't so sure.

After a second fire—at the Double Crown—Lily received a note that said, "This one wasn't an accident, either."

William, Sr., his blond hair now laced with silver, studied his beer, then looked up. "Someone is trying to intimidate the Fortunes, and I'm not going to stand for it. The family will be safer if we all stick together."

J.R. hoped it was just a matter of intimidation. But he understood his father's determination to present a united front.

The waitress finally returned and picked up their empty plates. "Can I get you anything else?"

"Just the check," William said.

When she left them alone again, William asked, "Are you happy you made the move to Red Rock?"

"Yes. I'm just sorry I didn't do it sooner." At the beginning of the year J.R. had come to a New Year's Eve party at Red, where they'd celebrated the Fortune Foundation's fourth year of operation. "The trip I made in January was both nostalgic and therapeutic. And the closer it got to the day of departure, the more I regretted having to return to the rat race in Los Angeles."

"I feel the same way now. I've been tossing around the idea of retiring ever since your mom died. My heart just isn't in the company anymore. I find myself valuing my family more than ever. And most of my family is now here."

"There's definitely something very appealing about the slower pace in Texas."

And for J.R., there was also a certain Latina artisan he'd met last spring, a distant relative of the Mendozas. He'd never been into long-distance relationships, so he hadn't done anything about his attraction back then.

But now that he was here?

J.R. glanced across the fountain at the table where Isabella Mendoza dined. He couldn't help watching her.

With that silky veil of long, dark hair and those big brown eyes, the artisan/interior designer was a stunningly beautiful woman.

Today she wore a turquoise blouse and a handcrafted belt in bright Southwestern shades. The colors she'd chosen to wear with a pair of black denim pants reminded him of the blankets and tapestries she wove.

He'd been intrigued by her from the first time they'd

met, and his attraction had only grown stronger. In fact, if truth be told, his interest in her had played at least a small part in his decision to move to Red Rock. And now that he was a local, he'd set his mind on asking her out.

"She's a lovely woman," William said.

J.R. turned his attention back to his father. "Excuse me?"

"Isabella. She's the one you're looking at, isn't she? The others are all taken, as far as I know."

J.R. grinned. "Yeah. She's the one."

He'd had his eye on her for quite a while and had gotten close to asking her out once, but she'd changed the subject. If he'd had any reason to believe that she didn't share his attraction and interest, he would have dropped it then and there, but he'd caught her watching him too many times to believe it was just a coincidence.

The waitress brought the bill, and J.R. reached for it, but his father snatched it first.

"Lunch is on me, son."

A few minutes later, after receiving his change and leaving a tip, William got to his feet. "Maybe you ought to stop by her table and ask her out."

But J.R. didn't need nudging.

Isabella tried to keep her mind on the conversation going on around her, but she completely lost her focus when she heard approaching footsteps.

She looked up and saw J.R. Fortune heading to their table.

Uh-oh. She sat up a bit straighter, her senses on alert.

Yet the other women turned toward him like flowers to the sun, smiled and opened right up to him.

"Well, if it isn't our newest property owner and resident," Christina said. "Welcome to Red Rock, J.R."

"Thanks," he said. "The house needs a lot of work, but as soon as I can, I'll throw a party for all my family and friends. I can't wait to show off the place."

As Sierra and Gloria added their own welcome-home/I'd-love-to-see-it speeches, Isabella kept her mouth shut. It wasn't that she was trying to be rude, but she just couldn't see J.R. as a permanent fixture in town.

He really should have stayed in Los Angeles, running the family business by day and enjoying the cultural offerings of a big city by night. Ranching was hard work—and not nearly as glamorous as he might think.

Jane pointed to the empty table beside them. "Why don't you pull up a chair and join us?"

"I don't want to interrupt your lunch." He glanced at Isabella, as though waiting for her to give him the go-ahead.

But she couldn't bring herself to do anything other than smile weakly. Sure, he'd caught her looking at him a few times today—and in the past—but never in a coy or flirtatious way. So she hoped he hadn't gotten the impression that she might want to date him.

She just found him interesting, that's all. He was a novelty of sorts, at least here in Red Rock.

Apparently, her lack of enthusiasm at Jane's invitation for him to sit with them didn't bother him in the least, because he grabbed a chair and slid it between Christina and her.

Great. She placed her hand on the menu, fingered the edges, wanting to open it, to focus on the food options, all of which she knew by heart. Instead, she couldn't help thinking about the man who'd wedged in next to her and the scent of a musky aftershave that stirred her senses.

"I can't stay long," he said, "but I have a question I'd like to ask Isabella."

Oh, no. Surely he didn't plan to ask her out in front of her friends. Well, if he did, she would just turn him down in front of them.

"I'm looking for a professional decorator."

At that revelation, she immediately gave him her undivided attention.

His gaze zeroed in on hers. "Would you be interested in giving me a proposal to redecorate the ranch house?"

The old Marshall place? The two-hundred-year-old house that had once been a hacienda? Was he kidding? Her heart spun in her chest, but she didn't dare let him see how eager she was to land the job.

"I…uh…yes," she said. "I'd be interested in drawing up a proposal."

Breathe, she told herself. She couldn't possibly let him suspect she'd be tempted to do the work for free because the exposure and the ability to add it to her professional portfolio would be a real coup.

Her mind raced as her excitement built. She'd give him a competitive price, though. And, being practical, she'd make sure she netted a small profit. The sooner she built up her bank account, the sooner she could move into a real studio and open up a storefront shop. Not that she didn't appreciate working out of the detached garage in her father's backyard, but she needed to establish herself as a professional. And having her own place was the next step in reaching that goal.

"I'm eager to get going," J.R. said. "I want to know exactly what I'm doing with the interior before I give the contractor the go-ahead to get started."

The contractor? Surely he didn't plan to let someone come in and tear out walls or make any structural changes to the building. The Marshall place was a historic landmark. What was he thinking?

Slow down, she warned herself. If he was calling in a decorator first, that meant he would respect the decorator's opinion, giving her or him a say.

She *so* had to land this job, and for a hundred different reasons. She glanced at her friends, saw them glued to the conversation she was having with J.R. They were probably making all kinds of romantic assumptions, but she wouldn't worry about that now.

Taking a breath, she said, "The Marshall house has great potential, J.R. I'm glad you've decided to get a decorator's opinion, and I'd be happy to give you mine."

"I'm sure you're busy," he said, "but do you have time to take a look at the ranch in the next couple of days?"

She *was* busy. She'd been working hard to get ready for this year's Fiesta. Opening day was on the sixteenth and would be here before she knew it. But this job—or rather this potential job—was too important to pass up, so she would make the time.

"What day did you have in mind?" she asked.

"Like I said, I want to get started right away. The kitchen needs to be modernized. My poor housekeeper is doing the best she can under the circumstances, but the appliances have to be replaced. And I don't want to do this in a piecemeal fashion."

The thought of modernizing that old hacienda tied Isabella's stomach in a knot. There were ways to update and make it functional without losing its historic value. But would someone like J.R. go for it?

Hopefully, if she were awarded the job, he would give her free rein.

With every beat of her heart, her confidence grew.

This project, which had at first seemed to be the epitome of a professional challenge, as well as a financial blessing, had taken on an even greater importance. She felt something stir inside her.

Getting involved in refurbishing J.R.'s house would give her an opportunity to preserve Texas history. It was the perfect project for her. And she was the perfect choice—if she could only convince J.R.

"Would tomorrow work for you?" she asked.

"That would be great." His eyes sparked with obvious pleasure, and his smile caused a single dimple to form in his cheek.

For the briefest of moments, she wondered if there might be just a bit more to his enthusiasm than landing a decorator, but she shrugged it off. She was a professional who knew how to keep things on a business level.

"Is nine o'clock too early?" he asked.

She would have agreed to a six o'clock start if it wouldn't have made her sound too eager. "That's fine. I'll see you at nine."

"Good. I hope you'll block off most of the day. It's

going to be a big job—and a costly one. But I have some ideas I'd like to talk over with you, and I want to make sure it's done right."

So much for having free rein.

Still, Isabella would give it her best shot. She needed the job—and she really wanted it.

Even if it meant bumping heads with J.R. Fortune every step of the way.

Chapter Two

The next day, Isabella arrived at J.R.'s ranch at a quarter to nine. Since the old hacienda was located about ten miles from downtown Red Rock, and she wasn't exactly sure how long it would take to get there from her father's house in San Antonio, she'd left earlier than she'd needed to.

As she drove her little red pickup along the graveled drive, kicking up dust, the property was abuzz with activity. Several ranch hands were repairing a stretch of fence along the way, and, next to the barn, a carpenter was busy working with a skill saw and a stack of lumber.

J.R. hadn't been kidding. He *was* eager to whip this property into shape.

And speaking of the new rancher, there he was, talking to a tall, lanky man wearing a leather toolbelt.

In a pair of faded denim jeans, J.R. appeared to fit

right in with both the hands and the construction crew, but his new Stetson and boots shouted, "city slicker."

He glanced up when he heard her pickup approach and grinned, yet he continued to direct the workers.

J.R. may not know much about ranching, but he was definitely a take-charge type, which wasn't surprising. Those white-collar execs usually were.

Still, he was a handsome man, even though he had to be completely out of his league with this sort of thing. But she wouldn't let that slow her down. She was here to study the house, take measurements, sketch out a rough draft of the floor plan and the layout of the outbuildings. All the while, she would let her imagination take flight.

Everything else was secondary.

She slipped out of the driver's seat, reached for both her purse and her briefcase, then stepped out of the vehicle. Normally, she preferred to wear heels whenever possible, but since she had no idea what she'd be getting into today, she'd chosen a pair of moccasin-style boots.

J.R. lifted a finger, indicating he'd be just a minute. She nodded then brushed a hand along the crinkled fabric of her colorful, Southwestern-style skirt, which she'd accessorized with handcrafted silver and turquoise jewelry.

She usually wore her long hair loose, but since it sometimes got in the way when she worked, she'd woven it into a single braid that hung down her back.

As she waited for J.R. to finish instructing the foreman, she studied the exterior of the hacienda, its adobe brick showing under aged, white stucco.

A baroque stone entrance with a Moorish-style arch

led to a solid wooden door, which had to be more than a century old—maybe two—and was remarkable in more ways than one.

The yard, she realized, as she turned to take it all in, would need a gardener. With a good pruning and some tasteful landscaping, the trees and plants would add tremendously to the exterior.

J.R. had been right: the place needed a lot of work. But Isabella couldn't still a burst of excitement at the chance to take part in refurbishing the hacienda.

"I'm sorry to keep you waiting," J.R. said, as he joined her.

She turned and smiled. "It's beautiful."

"I think so, too." He motioned toward the door. "Come on in. I'll show you the interior."

He followed her through the archway that led to the entrance. She opened the door, and they entered. The years, it seemed, rolled back, providing a glimpse of days gone by, of Dons and rancheros, of vaqueros and señoritas.

For the most part, the house was empty, which allowed her to focus on the white plaster walls, the wood-beam ceilings and the distressed-wood floors.

"What do you think?" he asked.

She turned, trying her best to curb her awe and enthusiasm and probably failing. "It's…amazing."

The distinctive structure and layout had great potential, and she again thought of the many positive repercussions of landing the job.

"You're the expert," he said. "What do you think about Spanish tile floors?"

Her jaw dropped, and her eyes opened wide. "Oh, no. This wood needs to stay. Some people pay an arm and a leg to re-create what you already have. All this floor needs is a little polish."

"I was talking about expensive tile, something hand-crafted and imported."

"I'm sure it would be lovely," she said. "*In another home.* Not this one. The original wood flooring needs to stay."

He paused a beat, as though not sure how to handle their first disagreement. Then a slow grin stretched across his face. Flecks of gold glimmered in his hazel irises, turning her heart on edge, and she forced herself to focus on the open space surrounding them and the high-beamed ceilings and thick stone walls. The only furniture in sight was a leather recliner and a side table that sported a hardcover novel and a lamp.

The absence of any of the usual comforts had made her assume he was living elsewhere. But that book and the lamp…

"Where are you staying?" she asked.

"Right here. I found some old furniture in one of the outbuildings, and I brought a few pieces inside. I have a bed and a chest of drawers in the master bedroom. I didn't want to get too carried away until I brought in a decorator."

"If you don't mind," she said, "I'd like to see what else is in that outbuilding. I'd also like to be free to wander the grounds, to make notes and do a few sketches. I won't get in the way of the workers."

"Of course." He placed his hand on her back in a

polite, gracious manner, but his touch sent a rush of heat through her bloodstream.

What was with that?

She shook off the physical reaction as well as she could and allowed him to guide her through an arched doorway.

"I want to introduce you to my housekeeper and cook," he said. "If you need anything, she should be able to help or to answer any questions you might have."

J.R.'s hand slowly dropped, and she missed the contact instantly, even though her skin and spine still hummed from his touch.

She continued through the walkway until she reached the kitchen, where she was met with the aroma of chili and spice. No doubt, it came from whatever was inside a shiny copper kettle simmering on top of the stove, a big, bulky model from the late fifties and early sixties. The white appliance had been cleaned to a glossy shine, its chrome trim sparkling.

A sixty-something woman with salt-and-pepper hair stood at the sink, rinsing vegetables. She turned toward the doorway when Isabella and J.R. entered the room.

"Evie," he said, "I want to introduce you to Isabella Mendoza. She's the decorator I spoke to you about."

Evie, her cheeks plump with a natural blush, smiled. "How do you do?"

"Fine, thank you." Isabella returned her smile. "Something sure smells good."

The matronly woman beamed. "Thank you. I'm making sauce for the chicken."

Isabella took a quick scan of the kitchen, noting that it would need a lot of work to make it more functional, then returned her gaze to the woman who appeared to be doing the best with what she had.

"I'm going to be wandering around the house for a while," Isabella said. "I'll try not to get underfoot."

"Don't worry about that," Evie replied. "I'll be glad to step aside. Mr. Fortune said he wouldn't make any big changes until he'd had a chance to work with the decorator, and my job will be a lot easier once this kitchen is modernized."

"Evie," J.R. said, "I meant to tell you earlier that there would be two for lunch."

"I'll set up a table in the courtyard, unless, of course, you'd like to eat in the office."

"The courtyard might be a nice change." J.R. turned to Isabella and smiled. "Until I purchase a dining set, I've been eating at my desk."

"Every meal?" she asked.

He shrugged. "I've gotten used to working through quite a few meals. Come on, I'll show you the office. I've got the computer set up with an Internet connection. There's also an adding machine, a copier and a fax. You can use whatever you need."

As J.R. led her out of the kitchen and down a hallway, she said, "You've certainly been busy. You've got a crew started on the fencing and repairing the barn. And you've even hired a cook."

"I *have* been busy, but Evie has worked for me for years. When I left Los Angeles, I asked her to come to Texas and help me set up my household."

"She sounds loyal."

"Yes, she is. If her husband hadn't passed away last

year, she wouldn't have made the move with me. But her only family is a couple of stepkids who are closer to their mother than they are to her. I suppose that's only natural, but Evie practically raised them."

"That's too bad," she said.

"I know. Family is important."

Yes, but family dynamics could be very complicated, especially when it came to a yours-mine-and-ours situation. Isabella knew that firsthand.

She'd been raised in California by her Anglo stepdad, and while she'd been treated well and cared for, she'd always felt a bit out of place and out of step. And once her stepfather remarried and started a new family, that feeling of being on the outside looking in had only gotten worse.

But there'd been a happy ending.

Five years ago, when she was finally reunited with her biological father in Red Rock, the entire Mendoza clan had welcomed her with open arms. As a result, she wholeheartedly embraced the Mendozas and the Tejana culture of her roots.

As J.R. led her back to the room he was using as an office, she glanced through a few open doorways, only to see empty rooms with the same plastered walls and wood ceilings. Each room, it seemed, had a fireplace. Wood-burning, she assumed.

"The office is on the left," J.R. said.

Isabella stepped inside, then took a seat across from him at a massive mahogany desk. She scanned the rustic room, which had been decorated with a desk, a bookshelf and modern-style wooden file cabinets.

While obviously expensive and of high quality, the furniture just didn't fit the house.

"I hope you plan on keeping the place much the same as it was," she said.

"To an extent. The contractor said the structure is sound, so I don't see a need to make any major changes."

Before she could respond, a little growl sounded, and she felt a tug on her boot.

"Hey." She glanced down to see a roly-poly Australian shepherd puppy chewing on the leather fringe and bent to pick up the little guy. "Aren't you the cutest little thing. Where did you come from?"

"Sorry about that," J.R. said. "That's Baron, my future cattle dog. Right now, he's kind of a pest."

"He's so sweet."

As if knowing that he'd scored a hit and made a new friend, Baron licked her face.

The only trouble was, when Isabella glanced at J.R. and saw a grin stretch across his face, she got the feeling that he thought he'd scored one, too.

At a quarter to twelve, J.R. headed to the washroom in the barn to clean up for lunch. He was eager to talk to Isabella, to see what kind of plan she'd come up with.

He'd told her that he was soliciting bids and proposals from several decorators, and he certainly could. But what she didn't know was that the job was hers if she wanted it. He would just make sure that it was in the contract that she would have to get his okay on anything major.

After washing up, he headed for the house. Once

inside, he stopped by the kitchen, where Evie was getting ready to serve lunch.

"Have you seen Isabella?" he asked.

"She was in here a few minutes ago, taking measurements and making a sketch. And I have to admit, I'm glad she's here."

Oh, yeah? "Why's that?"

"Because the rascally pup has decided to follow her around rather than tagging along after me and getting under my feet." Evie feigned a scoff, which J.R. knew better than to take seriously. That pup had both of them wrapped around his little paw.

"Can I do anything to help?" he asked.

"No. I've got the table set on the patio. Lunch will be served as soon as you're ready."

"Thanks, Evie."

J.R. went in search of Isabella, finding her in the alcove that led to the courtyard. Baron was sitting a few steps away, scratching his ear.

She had her head bent over a yellow tablet as she made notes to herself. She'd braided her hair today, which was too bad. J.R. liked it better when she wore it long and sleek. A man could fantasize about hair like that.

Actually, he had.

"How's it going?" he asked.

She glanced up and grinned, her dark eyes dancing with ideas and possibilities. "Great."

"Are you ready for a lunch break?"

"I am, if you are." She lowered the notepad to her side. "Each time I've walked near the kitchen, I've taken a whiff of whatever Evie is making. Now I'm starving."

"Evie's the best cook I've ever had." J.R. motioned toward the archway that led to the courtyard. "After you."

She glanced at the puppy. "Come on, Baron. You followed me to every nook and cranny of this big old house. Don't poop out on me now."

The puppy perked up, then trotted along beside her.

J.R. couldn't blame the little guy. He found himself lured by her, too. And as he fell into step behind her, he couldn't keep his eyes off the sway of her hips, the swish of her colorful skirt.

Isabella had an eye for color and style, which had been another thing that had intrigued him since day one.

The courtyard had been swept clean, but it was still a far cry from what it had once been, from what it would someday be again.

Evie had covered the old, glass-topped table with a linen cloth. A vase with several wild roses, which had come from the scraggly bushes near the entrance to the house, added a splash of pink.

"Isn't this a great place to eat?" Isabella asked, as she took in the table, as well as her rustic surroundings.

Someday, it would be, J.R. thought. "It's going to take some work."

"Yes, I know, but in my mind, I can see the finished product." She lifted her hand and flicked her wrist in a would-you-just-look-at-this manner. "Imagine it filled with lush hanging plants, as well as clay pots of bougain-villea."

He envied her imagination, since he couldn't quite get past all the time, work and money that it would take.

"I figure one of the first things that needs to be done is to tear out and replace the fountain."

"I don't think so." She stepped closer to the stone fountain, the gold and orange tile chipped and cracked. "The plumbing needs to be completely replaced, and it will have to be retiled. But this looks like it might be the original, and I'd hate to see it lost."

J.R. held out a wrought-iron chair for Isabella and waited until she took a seat. Then he sat across from her.

Moments later, Evie brought in a tray with two salad plates filled with fresh greens and red and yellow grape tomatoes. Each was topped with a dollop of homemade guacamole dressing and sprinkled with grated cojita cheese.

"Thanks, Evie."

She grinned. "You're welcome." Then she returned to the kitchen.

"What did you think of the rest of the house?" J.R. asked.

"It's fabulous. The artist in me is impressed with the quality of the structure, with the potential. And I hope you'll allow me to be your decorator."

Something told him not to be too easy, too agreeable. It would be best if she didn't suspect he had a game plan at work here. But he didn't want to string her along, either. "The Fortunes and the Mendozas have been friends for a long time, so you've definitely got the edge over anyone else, Isabella. As long as your price isn't outrageous and we have the same vision for the place, I don't see a problem."

She glanced around the sparse, run-down courtyard,

at the fountain that was dry and dusty from age and lack of use. "This was meant to be the center of the home, so it should be the center of the decor."

"Are you suggesting we start here? With the fountain?"

"Yes." She placed her elbows on the table and leaned forward. "I know a Mexican craftsman in San Antonio who would do a wonderful job. He's the one who refurbished the fountain at Red."

"That sounds good to me."

"This place could be a showcase."

He hoped so, although he wasn't interested in impressing anyone. He just wanted his house to be all that it was meant to be. To him, that was important. "I don't know if I told you this or not, but I'm calling the ranch Molly's Pride. After my mother."

"I didn't know her," Isabella said. "But I've heard she was a wonderful woman."

"She was." The eldest of five boys, J.R. had grown up in a loving but rambunctious home. The entire family was incredibly close, but J.R. had shared a special bond with his mom. "My mother was just as comfortable in a formal dining room as she was in a fort my brothers and I built in the backyard."

"It sounds like she was the kind of mom who didn't just love her kids, she enjoyed them, too."

"Yes, she did. She was our biggest champion, but she wasn't a pushover. She made each of us toe the line."

"From what I heard, she had a lot to cheer about when it came to her firstborn."

J.R. had always taken his achievements in stride, and

to hear Isabella mention them, to see her eyeing him with an appreciative grin—or was it merely a polite one?—made him feel a bit…awkward.

Fortunately, Evie chose that time to remove their salads and to replace them with plates bearing grilled chicken with a light covering of spicy tomato sauce, steamed broccoli and rice.

After J.R. and Isabella both thanked her, she slipped back into the kitchen, leaving them alone.

J.R.'s curiosity finally got the better of him. "So what else did you hear about me?"

"That you were the typical eldest son—an over-achiever who excelled in school, that you were a star athlete in football and baseball. That you were social and always on the go."

He shrugged, that sense of awkwardness building and shoving him back in his seat.

Was she talking about him dating a lot? Was she trolling for details?

Or was she just making polite conversation?

It was hard to say, but, either way, he didn't kiss and tell. The truth was that he'd had his share of relation-ships over the years, but nothing serious.

Maybe because, deep inside, he'd been looking for someone like his mom to round out his life and to be the mother of his children. A few of the women he'd dated had come close, but he'd always found them lacking.

He couldn't put his finger on just what he was looking for, but he had a feeling he'd know it when he saw it.

Not that he was looking all that hard. Life was good, and he was happy.

For the most part, anyway.

"To be honest," she said, "I was really surprised to hear that you'd given up your career in Los Angeles and moved to Red Rock."

"Why?"

She took a sip of her water. "This seems like such an abrupt change for such a successful businessman."

"The decision wasn't made lightly."

Four months ago, on New Year's Eve, J.R. returned to Red Rock for a gathering at Red. Emmett Jamison had rented out the entire restaurant for a benefit to celebrate a banner year for the Fortune Foundation, an organization founded in Ryan Fortune's memory. When it was time for J.R. to fly home, he'd wanted to extend his trip, but hadn't been able to.

Then, in February, Patrick Fortune called a family council meeting at the Double Crown to discuss the mysterious letters he and some of the others had received. While in town, J.R. had given in to the urge, called a realtor and begun scouting for parcels. But the only properties that appealed to him were ranches.

Again he went back to L.A., but his heart and his mind were still in Texas.

Next came the fires, the first one at Red and the second at the Double Crown. When arson was suspected, the Fortunes and the Mendozas began to circle the wagons, and J.R. felt drawn to Red Rock more than ever. Two of his brothers were living there now, and he decided it was time to join them.

The realtor kept e-mailing listings to him, and he'd spent a lot of time doing research on the Internet.

One ranch in particular struck his fancy, and he felt compelled to place an offer on it, knowing that a purchase like that would change his entire life. Yet instead of being unsettling, the idea of moving to Texas was energizing. And he couldn't think of a good reason not to follow through on it.

He could be having a midlife crisis, he supposed. And maybe he was reacting to his mother's death. But the reasons didn't seem to matter. Like many of the Fortune men, he was used to doing and getting whatever he wanted.

So, when his offer was accepted, he gave up his position at Fortune Forecasting and moved to Red Rock. It was as simple as that. And even if others might not understand his decision, it had been right for him.

"Are you happy?" she asked, interrupting his thoughts—or maybe picking up on them.

Happy? He'd never given that much thought. He'd always sought contentment in life. Success, peace of mind.

"Are you asking whether I like the rural life?"

"Yes, I suppose I am."

"I definitely love being here. It's all pretty new to me, but I'm a quick study. And I'm surrounding myself with others who have the experience I lack. I've already hired a foreman and several ranch hands, and I've started buying cattle." It all felt *good. Right.*

But if he was perfectly honest with himself, he wasn't what you'd call happy. There was still something missing in his life.

As he glanced across the table at the pretty Tejana artisan, as he watched her close her eyes and savor the taste of her meal in a way that made him hungry for a lot more than lunch, he knew just what it was.

Once at home, Isabella sat at her kitchen table and immediately began working on her vision for J.R.'s home. She pulled out some catalogues and did some online research, too.

It was after midnight when she finally shut down the computer and went to bed, but she was up again at dawn, eager to draw up a proposal J.R. couldn't refuse.

Just after two o'clock in the afternoon, she finally put the finishing touches on her bid, at which time she faxed it to him. Since he was probably outside, overseeing the ranch hands and the construction crew, she had no idea how long it would take for him to even notice the pages in his fax machine, let alone get back to her. So she focused on the pressing job at hand: preparing her blankets and tapestries for this year's Fiesta.

When she first moved to San Antonio, her dad's offer to let her use his garage had been everything she'd been looking for and the answer to a prayer. It might not have been quite as roomy as she would have liked, but rent-free was certainly what she'd call affordable.

In the back of the garage, near the bathroom, she'd created an office area. She'd set up a workshop in the center, and in front, close to the entrance, she'd created a Peg-Board display area for her work.

But as her business grew and her reputation spread, she'd gradually outgrown the garage.

Now, as she went through her tapestries, choosing

the ones to take to the Fiesta next week, her excitement built. April was going to be a busy month. In addition to the ten-day Fiesta, which began on the sixteenth, and a possible job decorating J.R.'s hacienda, her birthday was on the twenty-third.

This year, she'd be turning thirty. Some people struggled when they entered a new decade of life, and Isabella had to admit that it niggled at her a bit. Actually, if she wasn't still single, it probably wouldn't bother her at all.

The door at the studio entrance opened, and the bell her dad had installed for her tinkled, alerting her to either a client, a customer or a visitor.

"I'll be right there." She left the fringe trim she'd been stitching on the worktable, then made her way to the front door.

With her studio in her father's backyard, she didn't have as many customers as she would get if she had a storefront shop. But that time would come.

As she stepped around the paneled Peg-Board that doubled as a barrier separating the front of the workshop from the back, her heart dropped to her stomach when she spotted J.R. standing with his hat in hand, looking far more handsome and appealing than he should.

Her heart jumped and thumped at the sight of him, a teenage, crushlike reaction that made absolutely no sense at all.

"What a surprise," she said, downplaying her wacky pulse rate and willing it to slow down.

"Your fax came through about an hour ago," he said. "After looking it over, I decided to drive out and talk to you."

He could have phoned, but she decided not to point that out.

So why was he here? Had she made an error in the math? Had she projected a cost that he thought was too high?

Too low?

Had he come to negotiate or barter?

She wanted the job badly, so she'd cut the price as much as she could without selling herself and her talent short. Her numbers were competitive already.

"I told you I was eager to get started," he said, "so I wanted to discuss the bid, as well as throw out another idea I had. And if we can reach an agreement this afternoon, I'm prepared to write a check for the deposit."

Wait. What about the other bids? Did he already have some in hand to compare hers to?

She ran her palms along her black denim-clad hips, hiding any trace of moisture that might have gathered. "Why don't you follow me back to my office. We can go over the proposal and the figures."

"All right."

As she led him around the partition, she asked, "Which item concerned you?"

"Overall, I liked your ideas and suggestions. So this is really just a request."

Once at her desk, she pulled up a stool for him. Instead of taking her own seat, she reached for the backrest of the office chair and remained standing, her fingers clutching the faux leather.

He chose to stand, too, which made him appear much taller than she'd remembered. More commanding, more vibrant. He wore a boyish, kiss-the-girls-and-make-them-squirm grin, which made her feel a lot younger than she'd felt just minutes ago.

Maybe she ought to sit down after all.

As she took a seat, he did, too.

"The price is more than fair for all the work you'll be doing," he said.

Why did she expect him to throw in a big *"But..."*?

Or to suggest that they paint the interior some hideous combination of colors?

When he did neither, curiosity got the better of her and she quizzed him. "What's on your mind?"

"For the most part, I like your vision for the place. So the job is yours."

A flood of relief, mingled with pleasure, washed over her. Decorating Molly's Pride would keep her busy for several months. "Is that why you came by? To sign the proposal and to make a deposit?"

"In part, yes. But this is a big job, and it's important to me. I want to make sure it's done right."

Isabella had worked for fussy clients before, but for some reason, she hadn't expected J.R. to be all that particular. "I'm very conscientious. And I can provide references if you'd like them."

"No, that's not necessary."

Feeling way too much like a kid who'd been sent to the principal's office for something she hadn't done, Isabella sat up straight and tossed a long strand of hair behind her shoulder, preparing herself for whatever might be standing in the way of her getting the job.

"I have the feeling that you're going to want to take

a hands-on approach to the decorating," he said, easing into his concern.

He was right. The renovation of a historic building needed to be taken seriously, so she nodded her agreement.

"And for that reason, I hope you'll agree to my request before we lock in too many specifics in the contract."

Feeling more confused than ever, she didn't know if she should lower her guard or raise it higher. "What is it?"

"I'd like you to spend a week at the hacienda."

As she stared at J.R.'s dancing eyes, her tummy zinged and pinged in all kinds of strange ways that had nothing to do with landing the job or even the prospect of adding it to her portfolio, and everything to do with her spending time with J.R. Fortune.

Well, not *with* him, but… "I'm not sure I understand what you're asking."

"I'll give you a five-thousand dollar deposit—non-refundable. But before we sign the actual contract and you jump right into making any major changes, I'd like you to get a real feel for the house and the ranch. That's the reason I suggested we eat lunch in the courtyard yesterday. I wanted you to see it from a guest's perspective. And I'd hoped that you would see all that it was lacking, all that it could be."

That's exactly what she'd done. In her mind's eye, the imaginary plants had begun to grow and unfurl, the flowers had blossomed. She'd almost been able to hear the water gurgling in the refurbished fountain.

"If you actually stayed at the ranch and slept in one of the guestrooms, if you sat near the window in the great room and read a book, I think your work would take on a new dimension."

He had a point, she supposed. But this was the worst possible time for her to leave the studio. "I'm really busy right now, trying to get ready for Fiesta."

"I'd pay extra if you'd hire someone to do that for you."

The man definitely didn't like to take "no" for an answer. "It's not that easy, J.R. I might be able to find someone to watch the studio, but I'm the only one who can finish the last tapestries. I'd have to bring them with me and work on them at your ranch."

"That's all right with me." He flashed her a charming, boyish grin—the kind that made the girls squeal and run, yet secretly want to get caught.

As his gaze strummed over her, sending her mind scurrying to make sense of it all, she couldn't help wondering if he had ulterior motives.

If so, she ought to be leery. So what was with the buzz of excitement?

"I'd like you to immerse yourself in the history that permeates the walls," he added. "There's something special about the place. I think you've felt it, too."

She had. And it surprised her that he'd recognized that the people who'd once filled the hacienda had left something of themselves behind. Not in a ghostlike sense, but with an essence of love and joy.

Of heartache, too, she suspected.

"I think it's important for the decorator to be someone who appreciates the history behind the hacienda, as well as the culture of the people who built it with their blood, sweat and tears."

Isabella couldn't agree more. So how could she say no to that?

"All right," she said. "I'll see you on Friday afternoon."

"Good." He flashed her another charming grin, one that made her senses scatter all over again.

Chapter Three

Isabella arrived at J.R.'s ranch on Friday afternoon, the back of her sporty red pickup filled with her loom, her tapestries and her suitcase. She'd deposited his check yesterday, which made this adventure feel more like the business deal that it was.

As the vehicle kicked up dust along the driveway, she noticed that the fencing had not only been repaired, but had been painted white. And the work on the barn had progressed to the point that it no longer looked like the same weathered structure anymore.

J.R. hadn't been kidding. He was definitely intent on getting things done quickly.

She parked beside J.R.'s Escalade and reached for both her purse and her briefcase before sliding out of the driver's seat. She'd just locked the door when she heard him approach, so she turned to greet him.

As he drew closer, a warm smile crinkled the edges of his eyes, indicating he was happy to see her.

Or was that just her imagination?

"How was the drive out here?"

"Not too bad." She returned his smile, and couldn't help running her gaze over him.

He wore a pair of faded jeans and a white button-down shirt, the cuffs rolled up at the forearms. His hair was damp, as though he'd just showered.

For her? she wondered.

Oh, for Pete's sake. Where had *that* renegade thought come from? J.R. had been working all day, and it was nearing dinner time. Of course he would come out of the house fresh and clean.

"You're just in time. Evie is preparing appetizers and cocktails, which should be ready soon."

Too busy to even think about eating, Isabella had spent the morning packing up her things and the afternoon providing Sarah, the young neighbor who had agreed to look after her studio with a list of instructions. "That sounds good."

J.R. peered into the back of her pickup, then reached for her suitcase. "I'll have one of the men carry the rest of your things inside. Come with me. I'll show you to your room."

She followed him into the house, catching the clean, musky scent of both soap and aftershave.

Even if she could get past the point that he bore absolutely no resemblance to the kind of man she was looking for—she *couldn't* get involved with him. He was a client, she reminded herself. She had a job to do, and staying here was merely part of a business arrangement. Nothing more.

He led her through the house to one of the guestrooms.

Other than an antique bed that was covered with a white goose-down comforter and matching pillows, the room was fairly sparse. An etched-glass vase of pink roses—those same wild ones that had graced their lunch table the other day—sat on the chest of drawers.

The flowers were a nice touch, and she wondered who'd thought about placing them there—J.R. or Evie. She supposed it really didn't matter.

She scanned the room, thinking that it could use a fresh coat of paint, that one of her tapestries might look good on the east wall.

"This is the largest guestroom," J.R. said. "I'm not sure how much space your loom will take up, but you can set it up in a separate room, if you'd like."

He seemed to have thought of everything, and she couldn't help feeling welcome. "Thank you. It might be best if I use two rooms."

Matching nightstands, both antiques, flanked the bed. There was a gardenia-scented candle on one. The other was empty.

"I like this bedroom set," she said. "We'll need to purchase more. Where did you find it?"

"Actually, it was one of the pieces in that outbuilding I told you about. Once you settle in, I can take you there."

She couldn't imagine what other treasures were still on the ranch, just waiting to be discovered. "I'll leave the suitcase on the bed and unpack later. Let's take a look now."

J.R. grinned. "I had a feeling you'd say that. Some of that stuff needs to be hauled to the dump, but there are a few interesting antiques stored in there."

Moments later, Isabella and J.R. strode across the ranch to a set of buildings near the barn.

The sprinklers had been turned on in the pasture. She tried to picture the ranch up and running again, the cattle in the fields, the cowboys hard at work.

J.R. slowed in front of a shabby-looking building. "This is the one." He swung open the door and flipped on a light.

As Isabella stepped inside, she was assailed by the dusty scent of neglect and of years gone by.

She studied the interior, noting an old rocking chair with a broken slat in the backrest, and realized that J.R. had been right. A few of the pieces of furniture weren't usable, while others were just plain old and out of date. Still, there were some lovely antiques, including a dining room set and an armoire.

Against the far wall, she noticed a large canvas draped across a table. "What's over there?"

"Some old paintings. I have no idea whether they have any value."

Isabella wasn't an appraiser by any means, but she wanted to see the artwork for herself and determine whether they'd work as part of the décor.

As she studied each piece, checking out the frames, as well as the paintings themselves, she realized that she could use most of them—in one way or another.

"Why do you suppose all this stuff was packed away?" she asked.

"After Mr. Marshall passed away, his heirs took a few pieces with them. They were going to get rid of the rest, so I told them to leave behind anything they didn't want."

"Well, you certainly scored." She glanced over her shoulder to offer him a smile, only to see that he was standing back, watching her. She suspected that he'd been appraising her, instead of the furniture, although she couldn't be sure.

Again, she wondered if he had something up his sleeve, but she'd be darned if she could read minds.

Of course, when it came to J.R. Fortune, maybe it was just as well that she couldn't.

It was nearly five-thirty when J.R. walked Isabella back to the house. Her clothing was usually both colorful and striking, yet today she'd dressed casually. He'd never seen her in well-worn, comfortable blue jeans before, and they molded her hips every bit as nicely as he would have guessed. Still, true to form, she wore a bright red blouse and silver hoop earrings, adorned with an array of matching beads. Her hair hung in a glossy sheet down her back.

As they continued through the archway into the house, he caught a hint of her perfume—or maybe it was body lotion. He wasn't sure, but the scent, something both floral and exotic, suited her.

Their shoes clicked on the distressed-wood flooring Isabella had insisted should stay. J.R. couldn't see the beauty in it, though. He preferred Mexican tile and suspected they might bump heads over the décor as time wore on. But the important thing was that Isabella was here—close to him and immersed in beautifying the house he loved.

In the great room, Evie had placed a bottle of his favorite Napa Valley chardonnay on ice and left two crystal goblets on an old chest that served as a makeshift coffee table.

Near the hearth, where a slow and steady fire licked the logs and cast a romantic glow, Baron was curled up on his little mat, sound asleep.

Isabella crossed her arms, causing the red cotton fabric to stretch across her breasts and create a slight gap at the buttons. A pretty smile adorned her face. "Will you look at that little guy? He's snoozing as though he doesn't have a care in the world."

J.R. chuckled. "That's because I let him follow me around the ranch today, and now he's completely wiped out."

"How did he do?" she asked. "He's still pretty young."

"He chased a few butterflies, but I'm afraid he's got a lot to learn." J.R. nodded toward the crystal goblets. "Can I get you a glass of wine?"

"Yes, please."

As he poured the chardonnay, Evie entered the room long enough to drop off a plate of crackers, cheese and several small clusters of red and green grapes, as well as a hot artichoke dip.

J.R. thanked Evie, then turned to Isabella. He watched her from behind as she strode toward the fireplace, hips swaying sensually.

He'd been asking various people about her—casually, of course, so that no one would realize just how interested he was. The one who'd given him the biggest insight had been José Mendoza, her father's cousin. José and his wife, Maria, owned Red.

"I heard that you grew up in California, too," he said, as he closed the gap between them. "My family home was in Malibu. Where was yours?"

"Sacramento, Oakland, Santa Barbara. We moved around a lot, at least until I was a teenager. I went to high school in the San Diego area."

"What brought you back to Texas?"

"I'd lost touch with my real dad, so when I finally located him, he invited me to fly out to San Antonio and visit. The Mendozas welcomed me with open arms, and two days after I arrived, I knew that Texas was my home, and that I would never move again."

From what J.R. had gathered, Isabella and her father were very close. So it seemed odd that the man hadn't kept in better touch with her when she was younger. And that she wasn't resentful that he hadn't been in the picture.

"Were there hard feelings between your parents?" he asked.

"I'm not sure of the details. My mom passed away when I was eleven." She reached for a cracker, but didn't take a bite. "My father told me that, in spite of the fiery arguments he and my mom used to have, he loved her— and he adored me. He was heartbroken by the breakup, and when my mom met another man—an Anglo—and moved to California, taking me with her, he was devastated."

"Is that what he told you?"

"Yes. I also found an old letter he'd written to her, and it was very clear that he was really torn up about the divorce."

"Didn't he come to visit you?"

"He would have. I'm sure of it. But while my stepfather was good to me, he was a jealous man and didn't want my mom to remain in contact with my dad or his family. He begged my mom to let him adopt me. She actually approached my dad about it, but Dad told her absolutely not. He loved me and refused to sign over his paternal rights."

J.R. could understand that. If he had a kid, he would be a major part of that child's life.

She took a sip of her wine. "We moved around a lot in the early years. I was young and didn't think anything of it. But in retrospect, I think my stepfather might have done that on purpose so my dad couldn't find us. But I guess I'll never know for sure."

Either way, J.R. concluded, Luis Mendoza had lost touch with his daughter and was obviously glad to have her back in his life.

"When my mom died," Isabella said, "I was devastated. My stepfather took it hard, too, but it didn't take him long to find another woman. An Anglo, like him."

"You say 'Anglo' like it's a bad thing."

"I'm not the least bit prejudiced, if that's what you're thinking. But as much as my stepfather loved my mom, he didn't appreciate her heritage and banished any traces of Tejana culture from our house. He even insisted that she convert to his faith."

The guy sounded both insensitive and controlling, but J.R. kept his thoughts to himself.

"Spanish was my first language," Isabella added. "My parents were both bilingual and wanted me to be, too. They knew I'd learn English once I went to preschool, so that had been their plan. But my stepfather discouraged my mom from speaking Spanish to me at home, and I soon forgot what little I'd learned. Even when I was in high school and needed to take a foreign language, he told me to take French."

"That's too bad."

She took another sip of wine. "Actually, my stepfather was good to me. And after he remarried, so was his wife. Yet I felt like an outsider. When my sisters were born, the entire family was fair-skinned and blue-eyed. So people naturally thought I was the neighbor or the sitter. And whenever we took family photos, I always stood out."

J.R. wanted to tell her that she'd stand out in every photograph—not because of her olive complexion, however. It was her beauty that prompted a double take. But he didn't want to risk showing his hand too soon.

"Don't get me wrong," she said, "I keep in touch with my stepparents. And we all get along much better now. But there's a distance between us, and I'm not just talking about the miles."

"How did you finally hook up with your dad?"

"After feeling especially sad one day, I went through some of my mom's belongings and found that old letter I mentioned, the one my dad had written years ago. There was a return address, and I contacted him."

"Your father must have been glad to hear from you."

"He'd been looking for me for years, so he was

ecstatic." Isabella smiled, and J.R. wondered if she'd ever looked prettier. "I was happy, too. For the first time since losing my mom, I felt loved. *Truly* loved. My father offered me airfare to fly to San Antonio, and I took it. And I'm *so* glad I did. I gained an instant family and felt as though I'd finally come home."

J.R. wondered if that was when she'd taken such a big interest in her heritage. "Thank goodness you went through that box and found that letter."

"You can say that again." She slid him another smile, one that warmed his heart from the inside out.

He lifted his half-empty glass in a toast. "Here's to finding your way back home. And to helping me decorate Molly's Pride."

As the tapping crystal resonated in the room, J.R. couldn't help but feel a growing sense of satisfaction for a job well done. He'd always known how to orchestrate things, to get people to do what he wanted them to without them being any the wiser. And that's what he'd done when he asked Isabella to give him a proposal to decorate his home.

He'd heard something about a bet she'd made with her single friends, a vow to be married before the end of next year. So he'd decided to step up his plan to get to know her better.

Since he was going to be incredibly busy over the next few months and would be virtually ranch-bound, he hadn't wanted to run the risk of some other guy sweeping Isabella off her feet before he had a chance to ask her out. So he'd made up his mind not to leave anything to chance. Isabella was too pretty, too tempting to remain unattached for very long, especially if she was actively looking for a man.

If that were the case, and if she proved to be the woman he thought she was, he'd come to an easy conclusion.

That man may as well be him.

It *had* to be the wine. Though Isabella hadn't downed more than a glass before dinner and another during the meal, as she sat across the table from J.R. and studied him in the candlelight, she felt a definite buzz. A toasty, cozy, can't-help-smiling glow.

Ever since meeting him last spring and running into him several times since the party on New Year's at Red, she'd found herself uneasy around him. But that wasn't the case this evening.

Maybe opening up and telling him about her complicated childhood had temporarily lowered the barrier between them.

Or maybe it was the way the flecks of gold in his hazel eyes glistened in the flame that danced on the wick.

Who knew?

"I hope you saved room for lemon cake," J.R. said.

"I'm full and really ought to pass, but dinner was so good, I'd be foolish to skip dessert."

Evie had outdone herself with the grilled filet mignon, asparagus and twice-baked potatoes. No wonder J.R. had invited the talented cook to follow him to Texas. A woman with her culinary skills would be hard to replace.

"What do you have planned for tomorrow?" he asked.

"I realized that I agreed to hold off on doing anything major, but I did schedule a few of the basics, so I hope you don't mind. I have a painter coming at nine. He's bringing some color samples and will be giving me an estimate."

"That's fine," J.R. said, "as long as I can look over the colors, too."

She hadn't expected him to be quite so hands-on about the project, but it was, after all, his house. He was the boss, and he was paying her well.

"No matter how you look at it," she continued, "the fountain needs to be repaired, so the plumber will be here between ten and twelve."

"I'm okay with that. In fact, I'm looking forward to having the courtyard renovated."

Good. That was a huge relief.

"I have a plasterer coming, too. He can just give us an estimate. I didn't think that was anything you might consider major, since it's a repair that needs to be done."

"That's fine, too."

Good. If the price was right and there were no unexpected problems with the walls, the plastering could be scheduled for Monday.

Feeling a bit braver, she added, "I also asked the tile man to stop by and bring some samples. He's going to try to make it by early afternoon, but he might not arrive until closer to five. So while I'm waiting for everyone to get here, I'm going to work on one of my tapestries."

He didn't respond right away, and she tried her best not to stiffen and prepare for his objection, opting to take a positive stance instead. After all, she couldn't just vacation all week. She wanted to feel as though she'd accomplished something.

As he sat back in his seat, a slow smile stretched across his face. "You don't waste time."

"No one can accuse me of not being conscientious or practical." She returned his smile—and his question. "So how about you? What do you have planned for tomorrow?"

"I have some cutting horses being delivered in the morning. Then, sometime around noon, I'll be getting the first shipment of cattle." His eyes lit up like a child at Christmas, and she couldn't help feeling happy for him, even if she was still convinced that his attempt at ranching would be short-lived.

Evie chose that moment to bring in two slices of lemon bundt cake, a drizzle of glaze across the top. As Isabella reached for her fork, Evie filled their cups with coffee.

"Mmm," Isabella said, nearly praising the woman for the third time this evening, yet not wanting to gush. "This looks wonderful."

"Imagine what Evie could do in a fully stocked, modern kitchen," J.R. said.

Fully stocked, yes. But modern? Isabella would only go so far in compromising her vision for Molly's Pride. Of course, she wasn't going to insist that poor Evie roast beef on a spit in the fireplace or keep her perishables in a container that dangled into the well. She'd have up-to-date appliances, of course. But the focus wouldn't be on those conveniences; it would be on the two-hundred-year-old ranch house, with its white plastered walls and floors made of aged hardwood. The hacienda had a character of its own, and Isabella intended to keep it that way.

"Do you plan to work on Sunday?" J.R. asked.

"I'd like to do some weaving. Why?"

Finished with his cake, J.R. placed his napkin over his plate and leaned back in his seat. "Because I'd like to take you riding."

Her eyes widened, and she couldn't seem to keep the excitement from her voice. "You mean, on horseback?"

He chuckled. "Unless you'd rather walk or take the Jeep I just purchased."

"Oh, no. I love riding. My friend Kathy had horses and would invite me over to ride when I was in high school."

"Then why don't you plan on wrapping up your work by noon on Sunday? We'll take a picnic lunch with us."

Warning bells went off in her head. The ride he was suggesting suddenly sounded way too much like a date, and she didn't want him to get the wrong idea.

"I don't know," she said, trying to tamp down her initial enthusiasm. "I really need to get some work done."

"I think a little fresh air and some beautiful scenery will fuel your creativity."

Would it?

Maybe he hadn't meant the ride to be anything more than a tour of the ranch. And she loved horses.

She bit down lightly on her bottom lip, then studied the table. The candles flickered, and she peered at the wild roses that served as a centerpiece. The romantic ambience was wreaking havoc with her senses, as well as her resolve.

But surely this dinner wasn't a date.

This week's stay at J.R.'s ranch was strictly a business arrangement. She had a job to do, and she intended to do it as quickly and efficiently as she could. She would spend some time on the ranch, getting a feel for the place from a visitor's perspective. She would also organize the workers and outline their tasks for the times when she would be at the Fiesta and wouldn't be able to oversee them. Then it was back to her studio to finish working on the blankets and weavings she intended to sell.

Still, the thought of riding with J.R. on Sunday afternoon was tempting.

How long had it been since she'd gone riding with Kathy—or anyone else?

And he'd asked her to go on Sunday, for goodness sake. Everyone deserved a day of rest. She didn't want to do or say anything she might be sorry for later, even if she wasn't sure which answer—a yes or a no—she might regret more.

"Would it be all right if I let you know later?" she asked.

"Sure. Just give me enough time to order a picnic lunch."

She lifted the linen napkin from her lap and blotted her mouth. Then she pushed back her chair and got to her feet. As she began to pick up the plates, he stopped her. "You're a guest, Isabella. Leave those dishes here. I'll take them into the kitchen."

Their gazes met and locked. Something—pheromones, for one thing—buzzed between them with an intensity that nearly buckled her knees.

Or was it the wine she'd consumed that was doing a number on her?

Perhaps it was both.

She shrugged off the combined effect as best she could. "All right, then. If you insist…"

"I do."

She offered him a lighthearted smile. "Then, if you'll excuse me, I think I'll go to bed."

"Okay. Sleep well."

Yeah, right. Something told her that her mind was going to be swirling with a slew of possibilities in spite of all the obvious problems.

She'd set her sights on finding Mr. Right—Señor Right was more accurate—but she was afraid that J.R. Fortune thought he might be the one.

Sure, the city slicker was handsome—and wealthy. But he was also an Anglo.

A very attractive, very appealing Anglo.

But they were as different as night and day, as ill-suited as two people could be.

She'd lost herself and her family roots once, but she would never allow that to happen again.

That's why she'd made her list.

And that's why she was determined to find the right mate—and however handsome J.R. might be, he could never be that man.

So what was with her growing attraction to Mr. Wrong?

Chapter Four

The next morning passed in a blur. Isabella first met with the painter, who would have to work after the crew came in to replaster the walls. She was very specific about how she wanted him to do the wood trim and white walls. She also let him know about her plan to leave some of the old adobe showing through the plaster, giving it an authentic feel.

She'd asked the painter to use a sponge technique to make the new plaster appear aged in each of the bathrooms. He left the paint samples for her to show J.R., and she gave him a fax number to send his bid for the work.

When the plumber arrived, she took him to the courtyard and showed him the fountain. They discussed the repairs that would need to be done, and she told him to get started as soon as possible. She'd meant what she'd said about the courtyard being the focus of the home, so that was where her decorating project would begin.

The tile man had yet to arrive. She'd asked him to bring some design samples, but she'd been very specific about what she was looking for, using a couple of the projects he'd created for other people as examples.

Before heading for the loom, which she'd set up during her wait between the painter and the plumber, she went into the kitchen for a glass of water.

Baron tagged along. The rascally little pup had been underfoot all morning, but he wasn't a bother. He was both playful and cuddly—everything a happy, healthy puppy ought to be.

Isabella loved animals, especially dogs and cats. Unfortunately, her stepfather had been allergic to dander, and she hadn't been allowed to have any pets when she was a child, so having Baron around was a real treat.

In the kitchen, Evie stood at the stove, stirring something in a pot. She glanced over her shoulder at Isabella's approach.

"Something smells wonderful, Evie."

"I hope you like it. This is a tequila-lime sauce for the chicken and pasta I made."

"It sounds delicious. I'm going to gain ten pounds if I stay her much longer. Did you go to culinary school?"

Evie flushed with pleasure at the praise. "I'm afraid everything I've learned has been a result of trial and error. And believe me, there were plenty of burned pans and disappointing dishes along the way."

"Now I'm *really* impressed."

Evie beamed, then quickly glanced at the sauce simmering in the pan, running a wooden spoon along the edges. "Lunch will be ready in about twenty minutes, but I can get you a snack if you're hungry."

"I can wait. What I came for was a drink of water."

Evie reached into a cupboard, pulled out a glass and handed it to her. "There's also iced tea in the fridge, as well as soda and a variety of juices."

"Thanks, but I'll stick with water." Isabella filled her glass from the jug on the counter and took a nice, long sip. When she finished, she hung out in the kitchen, watching Evie work.

When her mom was alive, Isabella used to enjoy helping with the cooking and baking every chance she got. Of course, those days had ended way too soon, and, as a result, Isabella had never learned to cook any of her mom's dishes. Sadly, none of the recipes had been written down.

Soon after she moved to San Antonio, she'd taken a TexMex class at a cooking school that specialized in foods of the Southwest. She'd love to enroll in another one, but she'd been so busy setting up her new business that she hadn't gotten around to it.

"You know," Isabella said, "I've been meaning to thank you for putting those flowers in my room. It was a nice touch that made me feel special."

"My only job was purchasing the linens, washing them, and making up the bed. J.R. was the one who brought in the roses. He thought the room looked too sparse and bland. He said you were big on colors, and he wanted you to feel at home."

She found it interesting that he'd picked up on the fact that she liked bright colors.

"I'll have to remember to thank J.R. It was really thoughtful of him." She felt that all-too-familiar twinge of suspicion and again wondered about his motives. But, then again, he hadn't made any moves to suggest that he was interested in anything more than a client/decorator relationship.

Maybe her imagination was playing tricks on her.

"J.R. is a good man," Evie added. "One of the best. I can't believe that he's still single. He's not only handsome and wealthy, but he's goodhearted, too."

There were a lot of reasons a forty-year-old-man was still single, Isabella thought. And she wondered what J.R.'s were. Something told her he wasn't nearly as fine a person as Evie thought.

"How long have you worked for him?" Isabella asked.

"Only a couple of years, but I've known him almost twenty. My husband George and I used to own a little bistro in Malibu called the Silver Spoon. J.R. was one of our regulars. When George died, leaving me with some big medical bills, I had to sell the place. J.R. had been overseas on a business trip at the time, but when he returned and learned about my situation, he offered me a job in his kitchen. Needless to say, I took it. Then, when he decided to make the move to Texas, he asked me to join him. There's no way I would have refused."

"He must be a great employer."

"He's the best." Evie's eyes lit up. "He's also pro-vided me with a sense of belonging, which is something I lost when my husband passed away. I really don't have a family, per se. So he's sort of become the son I never had."

"Family is important," Isabella said, repeating the truism J.R. had mentioned earlier.

And he'd been right.

Isabella's stepfather hadn't allowed her to have a relationship with the Mendozas, which was horribly unfair. She was having a difficult time forgiving him for that, no matter how good he'd been to her while she was growing up.

She supposed that was part of her stepfather's personality, though. Stan Reynolds had always been loving toward her mother, but he'd been controlling, too, and had clearly ruled the roost.

No way would Isabella let a man have that much say over her life.

"I must admit," Evie said, "I was surprised when J.R. told me he was moving to Texas. Not many men would give up a high-paying position like the one he once held and make a life-altering move the way he did."

Like Stan, her stepfather, Isabella thought. He'd get a wild notion and decide to move, whether anyone else wanted to or not.

"J.R. is certainly one of the most determined men I've ever met," Evie said.

Well, he definitely had the financial resources to make things happen.

Stan hadn't been anywhere near that wealthy, but he'd insisted on having things his way. As a result, while she was living with him, Isabella had nearly lost the essence of the person she was truly meant to be.

Evie chuckled. "I really have to hand it to him. When J.R. Fortune makes up his mind about something he wants, he goes after it. And this ranch is proof."

That it was. But Isabella still suspected he'd get tired of it all, and that this place—house, cattle and all—would be for sale within the year.

Yet she couldn't disregard the spark of excitement she'd seen in his eyes when he talked about the cattle and the horses coming.

Sometimes, she realized, when she'd caught him looking at her, she'd seen a similar spark in his eyes.

J. R. had plenty to keep him busy all day, so in spite of wanting to draw out breakfast and linger over a second cup of coffee, he'd left Isabella to do whatever needed to be done inside the house.

His first chore had been to meet the ranch foreman he'd hired last week. Well, make that both foremen.

His first interview had been with Toby Damon, a young man who'd grown up on a ranch not far from here. Toby had recently graduated from college with a degree in animal husbandry, and he'd returned to the ranch to work with his father, Frank.

Frank Damon had been a foreman on the Rocking S for years and had sacrificed to send his son to college. He'd hoped the boy would pursue a business degree and land an important white-collar job, but Toby loved the world he'd grown up in.

So his first job offer had come from his dad's employer. Things went along just fine for about six months, but then the crap hit the fan.

During Toby's interview with J.R., J.R. had taken a liking to the kid right from the start and had been impressed by his education. Yet Toby had also been upfront about the circumstances of his previous employment, which J.R. had appreciated.

But J.R. hadn't just bought the story outright. He'd made a few phone calls and was assured that Toby had been telling him the truth.

The older rancher's trophy wife had come on to Toby right after his return from school, suggesting that they engage in a discreet affair.

"It's not like she wasn't pretty," Toby had told J.R. "She was about five years older than me and had a body that would put a Hooters waitress to shame. But she was married. And she was my boss' wife. No way was I interested, and I told her so. At first, she wouldn't take no for an answer, and things got really uncomfortable. But finally, when she realized I wasn't going to buckle, she got mad. And she told her husband that I'd made a play for her."

"What did he do?"

"He fired me."

"You had a solid claim of sexual harassment. You could have sued," J.R. had told him.

"I know, but I didn't want to make trouble for my dad. He'd worked there for years, and I just couldn't risk him losing his job."

More than one of J.R.'s contacts had told him as much. From what he'd heard, Debbie Grimes wasn't just hot to look at, she was hot to trot, too.

Yesterday, J.R. had learned that Toby's dad had

resigned his position, too. Disgusted by the false alle-
gations Debbie had made against Toby, Frank said he'd
just make do until he landed another job.

Realizing that Frank was a man of principle, too,
J.R. had hired him on the spot.

It was a win-win situation for all of them.

If J.R. wanted his ranch to thrive, he knew that, with
his limited experience in ranching, he would need to hire
men with the knowledge he lacked, men he could trust
to be loyal and ethical.

After washing up in the barn, J.R. went into the house
for lunch. He popped his head in the kitchen door, just
to see if he could spot Isabella, but she wasn't there.

"I can serve lunch whenever you want me to," Evie
told him.

"I'm ready."

"All right, but since the plumber is working on the
fountain, I thought you would rather eat in the house. I
set a table in the great room, if that's okay."

"It's fine. Thanks, Evie."

"Oh," the older woman said. "Isabella is in the guestroom, weaving."

"Thanks for the tip." A smile stole across J.R.'s lips.
Evie, who'd worked for him long enough to know that
he didn't usually take such an active role when enter-
taining the women he invited home—such as planning
menus and picking flowers for the centerpiece—had
connected the dots before Isabella had even stepped on
the property.

Moments later, J.R. turned into the doorway that led
to Isabella's workroom, where Baron lay on the floor,

chewing on a braided and knotted piece of purple and yellow yarn. The pup glanced up at J.R., then resumed his chomping.

But it wasn't the puppy that had caught his interest. It was Isabella, with her hair sluicing down her back like a satin curtain.

He leaned against the doorjamb, watching her work.

Before long, as though she'd sensed his presence, she glanced over her shoulder. "Oh, hi. I didn't hear you."

"You seemed so intent on what you were doing, I didn't want to disturb you."

She glanced at the face of the silver bangle watch on her wrist. "I guess it's lunchtime."

"Yes, it is. Evie set a table in the great room."

He could have excused himself at that point, but he couldn't seem to tear his gaze away from the lovely Latina artisan.

As she moved about the room wearing a turquoise blouse and a pair of black jeans, he realized that her very presence added a splash of color to the house. He couldn't help thinking that, if he and Isabella were to become romantically involved, she would bring some fresh color to his world, too.

Up until a year ago, he'd been happy and perfectly content with the life he'd created for himself. He'd worked hard and played hard. And he'd enjoyed being a dyed-in-the-wool bachelor. But things had begun to change, and after he'd moved to Texas, he'd told himself that he would consider settling down if he ever found the right woman.

And now that Isabella was here, now that he'd gotten

to know her better, he suspected that she just might be that woman.

All he had to do was convince her.

That night, dinner was served in the dining room, where Evie had placed several candles to add a warm glow to the antique table that, up until two hours ago, had been gathering dust in the outbuilding. But thanks to a couple of ranch hands, it had been brought inside and polished to a high sheen.

Now, Isabella sat across from J.R., who'd poured them each a glass of red wine, as they ate another delicious meal. The food, as usual, was sumptuous, and mealtime had become something to look forward to.

The country-western background music, courtesy of a Bose stereo that had been plugged into an outlet and placed on the floor, made the atmosphere even more homey—and a little romantic.

"So," J.R. said, as he took a sip from his goblet. "How did things go this afternoon? Did the tile man ever show up?"

"Yes, finally. He left some samples for you to choose from. We can look at them after dinner."

"Good." J.R. took a roll from the linen-covered bread basket. "How about the fountain? Did the plumber run into any unexpected problems?"

"No. He expects to finish his work tomorrow. And then, assuming we choose something that's in stock, the tile man can start work on Monday morning." Isabella glanced across the table and watched J.R. spread a slab of fresh butter on his roll.

"I'm going to be pretty fussy about that fountain," he said, "so I don't want to choose something just because it's in stock."

And she *wasn't* going to be particular?

A prickle of irritation rose to the surface, and she did her best to tamp it down. "Why don't you wait and see the samples he brought. It's all high quality with old-world charm. I think you'll be able to find something you like."

"Did you see anything *you* liked?" he asked, as though her opinion might actually matter after all.

"As a matter of fact, I saw several. And one in particular."

"Then maybe we *will* be able to decide on the tile tonight." He flashed her a boyish grin that mocked her initial reaction to his male control.

Maybe he wasn't all that bossy. Maybe it was just a case of knowing how to handle him.

"Have you contacted an electrician yet?" J.R. asked.

"No, I haven't. I was under the impression that the previous owner had the house rewired last year."

"Yes, but I'd like to have a stereo system set up so that I can pipe music into the courtyard. If you can bring someone in, I'd appreciate it." He reached for his glass of wine, and fingered the stem. "I'm not a big entertainer, but I'll definitely host a party or two on occasion, and I like music."

She glanced at the Bose stereo on the floor. Had J.R. been the one to add the background music? She'd just assumed that Evie had done so, since he'd been pretty scarce all afternoon.

Not that it mattered, she supposed, but the candlelight, as well as the music, had cast a romantic aura on their dinner.

She couldn't help thinking that J.R. intended to ask her out or make some kind of sexual overture before the night was through. And if he did, she would just have to put him in his place.

Yet the conversation didn't drift in that direction. As a result, she began to lower her guard, settling into an easy groove. Getting more comfortable.

"So," Isabella said, opting to continue the dinner conversation. "How was *your* day?"

"It was great." His eyes took on that amazing, boyish sparkle again. "The first herd of cattle arrived this morning. Now they're grazing in the south pasture. And we unloaded the cutting horses late this afternoon."

"I'd like to see them."

"They're in the barn. I'll show them to you tomorrow. Are you still up for a ride?"

Her pulse spiked a tad in anticipation, yet she glanced at the window. Outside, a branch scratched against the glass. The wind, it seemed, had kicked up this evening. Was a storm brewing?

"I'd love to go horseback riding with you," she said. "But do you think the weather will cooperate?"

"Frank, my new foreman, said it might rain a little tonight, but they're not predicting anything major. By tomorrow morning it should be clear."

"Good. And since I got a lot more weaving done today than I thought I would, my whole day is free. We can go anytime you like."

"How about eight? Is that too early?"

"No. Not at all."

He took another sip of wine, and she couldn't help looking at him, assessing him. Many women would find him attractive, with that thick head of blond hair and a roguish grin that dimpled a single cheek. No doubt, many had.

No one had to tell her he was a ladies' man. The only way a bachelor as handsome and as wealthy as J.R. Fortune had remained single until his fortieth birthday was because he wanted it that way.

Actually, his bachelorhood bothered her a bit, although she wasn't sure why.

Maybe because she had a problem with men who wouldn't commit.

Shouldn't he be happily married with a few kids by now?

Again, she suspected that his life was just the way he wanted it—unencumbered and free.

Where were all the marriage-minded men now that she'd decided to do some serious looking?

"I really like this song," he said, drawing her from her musing.

She listened carefully, catching the melody of a hit by Faith Hill, a love song called "Breathe."

"I like it, too." The very first time she'd listened to the sexy words, the heady, sensual beat, she'd decided it was the kind of song a couple could make love to.

J.R.'s gaze locked on hers, and she found herself completely caught up in awareness, in attraction.

It was the song, she told herself. The candles, the roses and the wine, too.

Yet it was even more than that. Whether she wanted to admit it or not, it was the handsome man sitting across from her, his allure so real she could almost touch it.

J.R. slid back his chair and got to his feet. A heated intensity blazed in his eyes, and for the life of her, she couldn't tear away her gaze.

He reached out his hand, as though inviting her to join him without saying a word.

She wanted to tell him no, to set him straight about their business relationship. Yet, for some wild and crazy reason, she took the hand he'd offered and let him slowly draw her to her feet.

Mesmerized—by the song, by the words, by the heat in his gaze—she found herself slipping into his arms and swaying to the music. Their bodies melded, their hearts beat in time. As their scents mingled, a slow and steady rush whizzed through Isabella, rivaling the one Faith sang about.

When the song ended, J.R. continued to hold her, to move slowly to a silent beat.

She wasn't sure where this was going, wasn't sure what she would do about it. And while she should have pushed away, ending it before it got completely out of hand, she couldn't bring herself to do it. Not yet. It felt too good. So she held on tight until he finally—and, maybe, reluctantly?—released her.

Unable to help herself, she tilted her face, her gaze seeking his.

Passion simmered in his eyes.

Oh, wow. He was about to kiss her, which should have scared the daylights out of her, since it would definitely complicate any plans she had for her future, as well as the business arrangement they'd entered.

Yet instead of uttering any kind of objection, her heart pounded to beat the band, and her hormones blared out of control.

Yes, he was definitely going to kiss her; she was sure of it.

But he didn't.

In a surprise move, he reached out and touched her hair, letting a silky strand sluice through his fingers.

"Thanks for the dance," he said.

Her heart was now pounding so hard she could hear it thunder in her ears.

She wouldn't have allowed him to kiss her, although she'd been sorely tempted.

Liar, a small voice whispered.

If she'd truly planned to push him away, then why was she standing here like a love-struck adolescent, drowning in a sea of disappointment?

Chapter Five

J.R. woke early on Sunday morning and made his way to the kitchen, where Evie had brewed a fresh pot of coffee and baked a batch of cranberry-orange muffins.

It had taken everything he had not to kiss Isabella senseless last night, but he knew she had reservations about getting involved with him, although he wasn't exactly sure why. She clearly wanted him as badly as he wanted her—there were some things a man just knew.

So he'd drawn out the dance and the near-kiss, a decision that had nearly backfired on him, since he hadn't realized how hard it would be for him to refrain.

In truth, it had just about killed him to settle for anything less than a sweet, gentle assault of her lips and mouth, but that had been a part of his plan. He'd wanted to set off a longing in Isabella that would make her want to progress to a physical level so badly that she'd stop fighting herself.

Trouble was, it had set off a longing in him that had kept him up for hours last night and had awoken him before dawn, eager to start the day.

"Good morning," Evie said, handing him a steaming mug of fresh-brewed coffee. "How did things go last night?"

He smiled. "As well as I'd hoped." It's not as though he'd discussed details with Evie either before or after dinner, but he'd inadvertently clued her in prior to Isabella's arrival by telling her that he wanted to make his new decorator feel welcome.

Evie had worked for him long enough to be able to fill in the blanks, especially when J.R. started picking roses for the guestroom and lighting candles.

And no. He hadn't gone to that much trouble to impress a woman in California—nor had he needed to—but Isabella was different from anyone he'd ever dated in the past.

"Is the picnic lunch ready to go?" he asked.

"Yes, it's all packed. I even found an old basket in one of the cupboards that you can carry it in. If you're anything like my husband, George, you'll probably scoff at carrying your lunch in anything other than a brown paper bag, but the basket is sweet. And it will definitely please Isabella." Evie smiled. "I had a little fun decorating it, too. No one appreciates romance more than I do."

J.R. tossed her grin right back at her, trusting that she'd done him proud. He'd no more than taken another sip of coffee when Isabella stepped into the kitchen, wearing a breezy smile that made her eyes dance.

A pair of stylish jeans molded over her hips, and a tailored yellow blouse she'd tucked in showed off a small waist. Her hair had been swept into a twist on the back of her head and was held in place with a bulky silver clip.

Too bad, he thought. He'd been having some Lady Godiva fantasies last night when he thought of Isabella on horseback, and her long, flowing hair had been a big part of them.

A renewed smile, triggered by Isabella's entrance and the renewal of his fantasy, spread across J.R.'s face.

"You were right about the rain," Isabella said. "It only sprinkled a bit last night. The ground is damp, but the sky is clear and sunny."

"It's going to be a nice day for a ride." He took a mug from the cupboard and poured her some coffee.

"Thank you." She took the cup with both hands and lifted it to her nose. Then she closed her eyes, as though savoring the aroma of the fresh morning brew.

There were plenty of things he could be doing right now, but none of them were as intriguing as standing here, watching her.

"You know," she said. "I'd meant to show you the paint and tile samples last night."

She didn't have to say why she hadn't. The kiss they'd nearly shared had left them both unbalanced.

As their gazes met, her cheeks flushed, convincing him he'd been right. But with Evie in the room, he decided to let the memory drop, at least for the moment.

"We can look the samples over after our ride," he said.

"Good idea." Isabella reached for the creamer and poured a bit into her cup. Then she added a spoonful of sugar.

He nodded toward the counter, where a plate of warm muffins awaited. "Why don't you have a bit to eat while I see to the horses."

"All right, but I won't be long. If you want to wait for me, I'll eat quickly."

J.R. leaned against the kitchen counter. "Take your time."

Five minutes later, with the picnic basket Evie had packed in one hand, J.R. walked Isabella out to the barn.

Just outside the newly repaired door, Frank and Toby stood, each drinking coffee—no doubt from the pot they kept in their quarters.

"Hey, boss." Frank smiled and tipped his hat to Isabella. "Good mornin', ma'am."

J.R. placed his hand on the small of Isabella's back as he introduced her to his key employees. He supposed the possessive touch was his way of letting the men know he'd laid his claim on her—at least, in a way.

Or maybe he just wanted to touch her again, now that they'd shared a sensual dance and had held each other close.

Isabella offered the men a pretty smile. "It's nice to meet you."

"Toby and I saddled those horses for you. That buckskin mare was a good choice. And so was the chestnut gelding."

"Thanks, Frank."

"You're welcome. Toby and I are heading into Red Rock this morning. A couple of the cowboys from our old spread are going to meet with us for breakfast. They're good men, and I heard they might be looking for work."

"We can certainly use a few more hands. Have them come talk to me tomorrow morning."

Frank nodded. "I'll do that, boss. Thanks."

As the men headed toward the ranch pickup, J.R. again placed his hand on Isabella's back and guided her toward the barn. "Come on. Let's go."

They found the horses saddled and waiting. After leading them through the newly repaired door, J.R. sensed that Isabella might have trouble mounting.

"Need a boost?" he asked.

"Yes. Do you mind?"

"Not at all." J.R. clasped his hands together, making a step for her foot.

She took the reins in one hand and gripped the saddle horn with the other. As she mounted, he relished the scent of her, something distinctly feminine that hinted of exotic flowers.

Once she was atop the mare, he climbed into the saddle, and they both took off. As they approached the nearest corral, where they'd turned out the cutting horses yesterday, he pointed them out.

"They're beautiful," Isabella said.

J.R. wouldn't go that far. But the horses were sure-footed and well-trained. Purchasing them had made him feel as though he really was a rancher, as though his dream was finally coming together.

"Let's head this way." J.R. urged the gelding to the right, and Isabella followed.

They rode to the pasture, where the first cattle now grazed. He had another load coming on Tuesday, so the men Frank had told him about would come in handy, if he ended up hiring them.

"Are you glad you made such a big change in your life?" Isabella asked.

"Absolutely." As he studied the herd in the field, his heart swelled with pride. "Now, that's what I call beautiful."

"Beef cows?" she asked. "Not the horses?"

"Yep." He slid her a glance. "Do you think I'm crazy?"

She laughed. "At times? Yes, it's crossed my mind. You had it all in Los Angeles."

"No," he said. "I came close to having it all in L.A. But this is the real thing."

And, when it came to women, to partners who could weather the storms of life, as his parents had, he had a feeling Isabella was the real thing, too.

After checking on the cattle, they rode along the property line of his ranch, and he pointed out where his ranch ended and his closest neighbor's began.

Birds chirped in the treetops, and a pleasant breeze rustled the leaves. By the time they'd ridden along the creek to the lake, it was growing close to eleven.

"Why don't we stop here and have lunch," he said.

"Sounds good to me."

The sun had dried most of the dampness from the ground, yet J.R. searched for a perfect spot, settling on a grassy knoll. When he opened the basket Evie had packed, he found a red vinyl tablecloth, which he spread on the ground in lieu of a blanket. "Let's sit on this. That way we won't get muddy."

Before long, the horses were grazing in the new green grass, and J.R. had a feast set before them: fried chicken, potato salad, fresh strawberries and chocolate cupcakes.

"Evie's worth her weight in gold," Isabella said. "I hope you're paying her well."

"I am, but she's more than an employee." Evie had become nearly as supportive as his mother had been— and just as easy to talk to. She'd lost her husband about the same time J.R.'s mom had died, so they'd shared their grief and helped each other work through it.

J.R. and Isabella ate in silence for a while. Then he asked, "Who did you hire to look after your studio?"

"Her name is Sarah. She's the daughter of one of my dad's neighbors. She comes by the studio and hangs out sometimes. She's young and just out of high school, but she has a real interest in art. So I've been encouraging her to take some classes at the local junior college."

"It sounds like a perfect setup."

"Well…" Isabella lifted one of the red napkins, dabbed it at her mouth then wiped her hands. "I'm kind of like a worried mama with my business. I find myself calling to check up on her all the time."

"I'm sure she'll do fine."

"Either way, I'm going to have to spend a lot of time burning up the highway. It's tough to be in two places at once, but I really need to be a presence at the Fiesta. Hopefully, by the time it starts next week, I'll have everything lined up here and won't need to spend every minute at the ranch."

"I understand. And while I'm in a hurry to get things done, feel free to put some things off until you *can* spend every minute here."

She shot him a *what*-did-you-say? glance.

He shrugged a single shoulder and slipped her a crooked grin. "You're different than any woman I've ever met."

"How so?"

He'd like to tell himself that Isabella was just another pretty face, just another potential relationship, but he didn't buy that.

The more time he spent with her, the more drawn to her he felt. This could be the real thing.

"You have an exotic beauty that captivates me. And I'm in awe of your artistic ability. I'm intrigued by you, and I'd like to get to know you better."

She seemed a bit stymied by what he'd admitted. And maybe he'd confessed too soon. But he wasn't the only one dealing with interest and attraction, and the sooner they both admitted it, the better.

When they finished eating and it was time to head back to the ranch, J.R. packed the remnants of their lunch into the basket. Then they walked to the horses that were grazing in the sweet grass nearby.

The mare lifted her head as Isabella approached and snorted, as if saying, "Aw, do we have to?"

J.R. felt the same way. They'd shared an idyllic morning, and he hated to see it end.

She reached for the reins, as well as the saddle

horn, then glanced over her shoulder. "Can you give me a boost?"

"Sure." He threaded his fingers together to provide a step for her, but as she placed her foot into his hands, her other leg seemed to give way and she stumbled, falling against him.

Thrown off balance by the unexpected shift in weight, J.R. lost his footing, and the two of them tumbled onto the rain-softened ground.

He rolled to his side, bracing himself on his elbow, and raised up to look her over, hoping she hadn't gotten hurt. When her eyes met his, a belly laugh erupted from deep inside her, and he couldn't help laughing himself.

"I stepped in a gopher hole," she said. "Did I hurt you?"

"Just my pride. I was trying to be gallant."

Her hair had come out of the clip. At least, part of it had. The other half was tangled in it. He brushed a loose strand away from her brow.

Her laughter ceased, and a serious expression stole over her face, chasing away any sign of playfulness. Something simmered in her eyes. That same something that told him she'd been expecting him to kiss her last night, that she'd actually wanted him to.

But right this moment, any careful planning he'd done in the past no longer mattered. Not when he had an overwhelming urge to kiss her.

As he should have done last night.

Isabella hadn't expected to fall into J.R.'s arms, to roll onto her back and find him hovering over her with desire brewing in his eyes.

That kiss they'd nearly shared last night was going to take place today, even if she had to make the first move.

Perhaps her senses had been jarred silly. But right now, neither her list nor her good sense seemed to matter.

Just one kiss, she told herself. What would it hurt? A kiss was a great way to judge whether a couple had any chemistry at all.

Perhaps it would be disappointing. After all, there had to be a reason a man as handsome and as wealthy as J.R. Fortune was still single at the age of forty.

Being a lousy lover was certainly a possibility.

But as he brushed his lips across hers, as he nipped playfully at her mouth, baiting her, urging her on, her lips parted, and all bets were off.

The kiss deepened, and something raw, something dangerously compelling took over, as need exploded into a heady rush.

He slid his tongue inside her mouth, exploring, seeking, tasting.

Unable and unwilling to put a stop to the sweet assault, she kissed him back with all she had, combing her fingers through his hair, gripping him with a quiet desperation.

Never had she felt such need, such desire.

Why? she asked. Why with a man who wasn't her type?

And J.R. Fortune was *so* not her type.

Was she crazy? She pushed against his chest, and his heartbeat pulsed against her fingers.

So much for him being a lousy lover. If that one little kiss had the power to turn her senses inside out and make her consider having sex in a field of wildflowers, what effect would foreplay have on her? Or the act itself?

Oh, for Pete's sake. What in the world was she thinking? Her uncontrollable reaction was enough to scare the dickens out of her.

In their carefree youth, her young parents had shared a passionate, ill-fated relationship, and look where following their hormones had gotten them—married to the wrong person.

Divorced with a two-year-old child.

And speaking of children, J.R. wasn't the man with whom she wanted to create a family, the man with whom she wanted to grow old.

"I'm sorry," she said. "I can't. This wasn't…"

"Don't tell me it wasn't good for you." His smile told her that he would know the truth from a lie.

Still, she couldn't help but deny the effects. Or, at least, put them in perspective.

"Okay, as far as kisses go, it was pretty good. But it wasn't what you thought it was." She rolled to the side, scrambled to her knees and stood.

"What did I think it was?" He remained sprawled out on the grass, braced up on his elbow. He continued to grin, as though he knew something she didn't.

She reached for the silver clip that was now tangled in her hair. "Well, I'm not exactly sure what you thought. But, for the record, I'm not interested in having a romantic relationship."

He still didn't appear to be in any hurry to rise. "Actually, we hit that kiss out of the ballpark. And since you were an active participant, I'm surprised that you want to fight the feeling."

Why had she let her hormones rule her head?

She tore her gaze away from him and tried to open the hair clip and tug it free from the tangled strands, but the more she worked at it, the more stuck and knotted it became.

Ironically, that's the kind of situation in which she'd just found herself: the harder she tried to get free, the more convoluted the whole mess seemed.

"Okay," she finally said. "You're a great kisser. And since it's been a long time since I've kissed anyone, it was easy to lose my head. But that doesn't mean I want to get involved with you."

"Why not?"

She couldn't tell him the real reason without risking her job or hurting his feelings.

How would he respond if she told him her actual reservations—that she didn't want to get involved with him because he was a city slicker? That he not only belonged in California, but that he would surely return there when his whim to be a rancher faded?

Giving the clip another tug and feeling a sting of pain at her scalp, she took a deep breath and gave him another answer, one that was both logical and reasonable. "I don't mix business with pleasure. And since you're my client, I'd like to keep our arrangement strictly business."

When she gave the clip another unsuccessful tug, she groaned, and J.R. got to his feet.

He strode toward her, that amused grin still splashed across his face. "Let me help."

She didn't want his help. She didn't want anything except to go back to the ranch and pretend that this had never happened.

Without much effort, J.R. managed to take the clip out of her hair and hand it to her with a bemused smile. "You look especially pretty when you're flustered."

She didn't feel one bit pretty. Her hair, which was half up and half down, was now a tangled mess. And her clothes were damp and dirty, especially her knees, hips and back, all of which had touched the rain-soaked ground.

"I'm not really flustered," she said, willing the words to be true. "It's just the adrenaline that kicked in during the fall. I'll be fine as soon as I climb on my horse."

But something told her she wouldn't be fine for a long, long time.

The adrenaline—or whatever the heck it really was—hadn't kicked in until J.R. had hovered over her with a heated expression that stole her breath away, until they'd kissed and her world had spun out of control.

A world that was still spinning like crazy.

J.R. and Isabella tiptoed around that kiss for the rest of the day and evening. Then, after a quiet dinner, she reminded him that they hadn't yet looked over the paint and tile samples that had been left at the house.

After the table had been cleared, she laid them out for him to see.

J.R. furrowed his brow and lifted one of the paint samples. "They're all white. What kind of color choice is this?"

"Actually, the one you have in your hand is called Eggshell." She pointed to another. "And this one is Sweet Cream."

He returned the card to the table. "Don't you think we need some color on the walls?"

Not if they were going to maintain an authentic feel to the house. She placed her hands on her hips, annoyed that he was questioning her sense of style. "I'm going to add color by way of the fabrics, wall coverings and decorator items."

No way would she agree to paint those beautiful, old plaster walls any color but white.

They appeared to be at an impasse until he shrugged. "It's not as though I wanted you to choose something red or purple for the walls. It's just that these will be boring."

"I'll use plenty of color in the house," she said. "Didn't you read my proposal?"

"Yes, but I thought some of those items would be left to negotiation, after your week here is up."

"What's wrong with white walls and splashes of color throughout?"

He seemed to ponder that for a while, then shrugged. "Okay, you're the expert."

She hadn't expected him to put up a fight about having plain plaster walls, but at least he'd yielded, which was a good sign.

"So we can go with white walls?" she asked.

He scrunched his face. "All right. But I can't tell a difference between these samples. Not really. You go ahead and pick whichever one you want."

She hated to feel smug about winning something so simple, so she stifled a grin and laid out the tiles that Ernesto Ramos had left with her yesterday.

Of all the samples Ernesto had brought, Isabella had

chosen four. She placed her favorite down first, followed by the others in order of her preference.

J.R. pointed to the last one. "This is nice."

"I think so, too," she said, although that particular tile design had been her last choice. She placed her index finger on her bottom lip, as though really giving it a lot of thought. Then she pointed to her favorite, which had a white background with a blue and yellow design. "How about this one? It has a lot of old-world charm."

"I don't know…"

"What's wrong with it?" she asked.

"There's nothing *wrong* with it. It's just that I like the other one better. I can see red flowers in the courtyard, and this one has red in the design."

He had a point, she supposed. It was, after all, his house, his fountain. And ultimately his choice. But there was something about this particular project that made her want to take a more active role in the décor.

Or was it that she just didn't want to yield to J. R. Fortune?

Unwilling to ponder that thought, she reminded herself again that it was his house, and that he was the client. "All right. Can I tell Ernesto that we'd like this one?"

J.R. nodded, and the choice had been made.

Yet that still didn't help her sleep any better that night than the one before.

Bright and early on Monday morning, Isabella drove back to San Antonio to check on Sarah Weatherford, the eighteen-year-old woman who was looking after her studio.

Sarah, a petite redhead with green eyes and a scatter

of freckles across her nose, lived in the house across the street from Isabella's father. The young woman had been going through a difficult time, thanks to a boyfriend who'd dumped her for a college coed he'd met on campus.

The breakup alone would have been tough for anyone to deal with, but Sarah, who'd struggled with learning disabilities for years, had taken it especially hard because she'd always considered college to be out of her reach.

Yet in spite of just limping through high school, she'd excelled in art classes. When she heard that an artisan had opened a studio in the neighborhood, she'd come by to visit and to introduce herself to Isabella.

Sarah had been impressed with the weavings and in awe of Isabella's talent. In time, Isabella had been able to talk Sarah into enrolling in an art course at the junior college.

The class had done wonders for Sarah's self-esteem, and so had Isabella's request for Sarah to watch over the studio in her absence.

After arriving at her father's house in San Antonio, Isabella met with Sarah and discussed her plans for the upcoming week—preparing for Fiesta. Then she checked messages and returned phone calls. She saved the best for last, calling her friend, Jane Gilliam, who would soon marry Isabella's cousin, Jorge Mendoza.

She dialed the Red Rock Readingworks, then waited for Jane to get on the line.

"Can you sneak away for lunch?" Jane asked.

"I'd love to."

"Great. I have a meeting this morning, but it should be over by noon. I'll see you at Red."

Isabella always enjoyed her time with Jane, but she especially looked forward to talking to her today. She needed someone to confide in, someone she could trust to listen, to understand and to offer advice. This "thing" with J.R. had gotten way too complicated, and she could use her friend's perspective.

As was her habit, Isabella arrived at the restaurant early, hoping to snag a table in the courtyard. Unfortunately, they were all occupied, and she had to take one in the main dining room.

She'd no more than settled into her chair when the busboy served two glasses of water, chips and salsa.

Jane arrived moments later and took the seat across from her. The women chatted a few minutes about the meeting Jane had just left.

"So how are things going with the new decorating project?" Jane asked.

"Actually?" Isabella tried to smile, but it fell flat. "It's…a bit troubling."

"Why?"

Isabella snagged a chip and popped it into her mouth, the crunch doing little to ease the tension she'd been feeling ever since J.R. had kissed her. "I think J.R. is interested in more than decorating his home."

Jane leaned forward, her eyes sparking. "Really? Lucky you."

Isabella shook her head. "No, I'm *not* lucky. J.R. is the last guy I'd date. He's not my type."

"You mean there isn't any chemistry?"

She sighed. "I wish there weren't, but I let him kiss me yesterday, hoping to prove a point to myself. And, *unfortunately,* our chemistry level is off the charts."

"What's wrong with that?" Jane leaned back in her seat with a grin that looked suspiciously smug. "Chemistry is definitely important and should be high on your list."

Isabella had left it off the list completely. "I thought if a man had all the other qualities, the chemistry would be a given."

"That's not always the case."

"Okay, so I was a little naive. But J.R. still isn't my type."

Jane reached for a chip and dipped it into the salsa. But instead of eating it, she held it upright like the pointer a professor used during a lecture. "If I recall some of those things on your list, J.R. definitely ought to be in the running."

"I wanted a man with a steady job and his feet planted firmly on the ground. Leaving L.A. and launching a new career at J.R.'s age reeks of midlife crisis."

Jane leaned forward, that chip still raised. "The guy is wealthy, Isabella. I'd consider that stable and dependable. What more could you want?"

"Okay, he might dress like a successful Texas rancher, but he's used to traveling in much more sophisticated circles. And I'm not."

"You're no slouch in a social setting. And with your business taking off the way it is, you'd better get used to moving in those dreaded circles."

Isabella fingered her napkin, rolling the corner, as she pondered the truth of Jane's statement. Then she glanced across the table. "You're my best friend. You're supposed to let me vent and tell me that I'm right."

A knowing smile spread across Jane's face. "Even if I think you're wrong?"

"Ever since you fell head over heels for Jorge, you've had stars in your eyes. But love has nothing to do with this. I'm just terribly attracted to J.R. for some reason. And to make matters worse, he's forty and has never been married. That clearly means he's a perpetual bachelor at heart and afraid to commit."

"No, it doesn't. Look at Jorge. Now there was a perpetual bachelor. But he fell in love with me, and let me tell you, the man is definitely committed, and I couldn't be happier."

Isabella slumped in her seat, something her stepdad used to pester her about. Something she rarely did anymore.

"Do you know what I think?" Jane asked.

"What?"

"I think you're the one who's afraid to commit."

Isabella had to chew on that for a while.

"Maybe you should burn that perfect-mate list," Jane added.

The waiter chose that moment to take their orders.

"I'll have the TexMex salad," Isabella said.

Jane chose a chicken tostada.

After the waiter left, Isabella relented. "Okay, I admit that I'm probably being foolish. But there's still something holding me back."

"What's that?"

"I'm not attracted to Anglos, remember?"

"Apparently, you're attracted to *this* one."

Isabella blew out a sigh. Jane wasn't helping at all. "Okay. So it's really not the Anglo thing. It's just that my heritage is an important part of me, and I want someone who can appreciate my Tejana roots, someone who will share my traditions. I'm not sure a man who isn't Latino will do that."

"It depends on the man," Jane said. "I'll bet J.R. can. After all, he's letting you decorate his house, so he's definitely going with your style."

"I don't know about that. He hasn't given me a lot of freedom, and we don't always see eye to eye. If truth be told, I suspect that he awarded me this job to keep me close to him. Why else would he insist that I spend the week there?"

"Maybe he's falling for you and wants an opportunity to see what develops. If so, I think you should feel flattered."

Actually, if that had been J.R.'s motivation, it was a bit too much like her stepfather's attempt to keep her mom all to himself, to cut her off from the Mendozas.

Isabella placed her elbows on the table, leaned forward and spoke quietly. "I think he's enamored with an image of me, although I have no clue what image that is."

Jane smiled. "Every woman deserves to be held in high esteem by the man she loves."

"But that's just it," Isabella said. "I *don't* love him."

"Why don't you give him a chance to change your mind?"

Isabella couldn't do that. What if he were able to sweep her off her feet? Then what?

Or what if she did let things progress and he decided to sell the ranch and head back to Los Angeles? No way would she consider either a move or a long-distance relationship. Not when she'd finally found herself—in Texas.

"Maybe you should just let things ride and see what happens," Jane said.

But Isabella wasn't so sure. What if she lost herself all over again?

Chapter Six

On Wednesday, as the sun began to sink low in the sky, J.R. used his arm to wipe the sweat off his brow. He'd been working with Toby and Frank since just after noon on a stretch of fence in the south pasture. He had a second shipment of cattle coming tomorrow morning, and this is where they would graze.

Baron crouched in the grass, his tail wagging as he sniffed and growled at something—a bug, no doubt. At five months old, he was really too small to be of any help, but J.R. had grown attached to the little guy and liked having him around. Besides, he was going to be a ranch dog, so he might as well get used to riding with the hands.

Had Isabella not taken off for San Antonio on Monday, J.R. might have left Baron in the house with her. She'd really taken to the pup, which seemed like a good sign.

Too bad she didn't claim the same affection for J.R.

Actually, he suspected that she was feeling a hell of a lot more than she admitted. He'd seen it in her eyes—both before and after that kiss.

In all of his adult years and even before that, he'd rarely been attracted to a woman who didn't find him appealing and didn't at least consider having a relationship of one kind or another. On the contrary, it was usually J.R. who put the brakes on.

So why was Isabella holding back?

A lesser man might have let her go, telling himself there were other fish in the sea, but when J.R. set his sights on something, he didn't let anything stand in his way.

And now that he'd kissed Isabella, now that he'd experienced her passionate response, he was even more determined than ever to pursue her.

He wasn't entirely sure what he was feeling for her, but it was definitely more than just a little attraction. Not that he'd call it love, but he'd never been involved with a woman who turned him every which way but loose. Isabella, though, was coming pretty damn close.

"Well," Frank said, lifting his hat long enough to wipe his forehead with a red handkerchief, "looks like we got 'er done. This ought to hold 'em."

J.R. studied the repaired fencing and nodded his approval. There was nothing like a good workout that produced not only results, but plenty of sweat.

"I'll load up the pickup," Frank said. "And then we can head back to the ranch."

Toby, who'd been overseeing work on the well and had joined Frank and J.R. after they'd gotten started on the fence, had ridden one of the horses out to the pasture. "Baron and I'll meet you there."

"Do you think he can keep up with you?" J.R. asked. "He's still pretty young."

"It's not that far. If he tuckers out, I'll pick him up and let him ride with me."

Everyone, it seemed, had grown fond of that rascally pup, and Toby was no exception.

Baron growled again, then bravely barked and snapped at the grasshopper he'd found. He'd been napping for the past hour, so he was probably raring to go.

"Go ahead," J.R. said.

Toby helped load the tools and extra fencing material into the bed of the truck, which was parked along the county road, next to where they'd been working. Then he mounted his horse and called Baron.

The pup wagged his tail and followed Toby's gelding through the field and toward the barn.

J.R. and Frank slipped between the barbed-wire strands and climbed into J.R.'s pickup. They'd just reached the house when Isabella pulled up.

"I'll take care of putting away these tools," Frank said.

"Thanks. I appreciate that." J.R. watched as Isabella slid out of the driver's seat, wearing a lime-green blouse and a pair of white slacks. Her hair hung down her back, long and silky, just the way he liked it.

When she'd left on Monday morning, she'd said she would be back, and he'd known she would. Still, things had been pretty awkward between them after the kiss, so seeing her again was a pleasant surprise.

"How were things at the studio?" he asked.

"It's been pretty quiet. Sarah assured me that she has everything under control."

"That's got to be comforting." J.R. knew that if he were to leave the ranch, Frank and Toby could handle anything that came their way. And that if there were any questions, they'd call and run things by him for approval.

Isabella swept a strand of hair behind her shoulder. "It's a bit of a relief, I suppose. But I tend to be a control freak, and it's hard for me to let go, although I guess I'll have to get used to that. If my business continues to grow, I'll have to rely on others to help out."

If she began hanging out at the ranch more, she'd also need to leave Sarah in charge more often.

Isabella nodded toward the house. "How did the plastering go today?"

"I have no idea." J.R. held up his dirty hands. "I've been working on the south fence all afternoon."

She reached for her purse and shut the driver's-side door. "I'm going to check and make sure the workers did what I asked them to do."

"I'll come in with you," he said. "I'd like to see what they've done, too."

He'd also decided that he would have to keep an eye on Isabella. He liked her overall plans for the house and had refused to consider another decorator, but he didn't want to give her too much freedom.

A few antiques were fine—and so were some of the leftover paintings and artwork. But Isabella seemed intent on maintaining the original hacienda aura, and while he could appreciate her vision, he didn't want to end up residing in a living history museum, which just might happen if he left her on her own.

"Where's Baron?" she asked. "I've missed that little guy."

J.R. tossed her a smile. "Baron's with Toby. He's been learning how to be a ranch dog. Before you know it, he'll be herding cattle for us."

"That's hard to imagine," Isabella said, as the two of them started for the house.

They didn't get more than a few steps, when they heard Toby shouting, "Boss!"

There was a tinge of panic in his voice, as he rode up to J.R., holding the puppy in his arms.

"Baron got hurt," Toby said. *"Bad."*

J.R.'s heart dropped to his gut. Damn. He should have insisted that the pup ride back in the truck. "What happened?"

"When I stopped at the gate, he nipped at the gelding's hoof. Ol' Smokey wasn't in the mood for games and kicked him in the head. Baron was knocked out. He came to, but he's loopy."

J.R. reached for the limp puppy. A wave of fear and concern swept over him. The wound had turned the white fur on his head bloodred.

Baron whimpered as he was transferred from Toby's arms to J.R.'s.

"I hope we don't need to put him down," Toby said.

J.R. felt the same way. He knew that putting an animal out of its misery was a real—and sad—part of ranch life, but he sure hoped it wouldn't be necessary with Baron. And it wasn't just because the pup had good bloodlines. J.R. had grown attached to the little guy—apparently even more than he realized.

"I'll take him to the vet," J.R. said. "It's not quite five, so will you give Dr. Eldridge a call and tell him we're on our way?"

Toby climbed off his horse. "I'll do it right now. You know where the office is, right?"

"Yes, I do. Ethan, the doctor, is an old friend of mine."

A couple of weeks before, J.R. had stopped by Ethan's office and told him he'd moved to Red Rock and would be using his services someday. He just hadn't expected the doctor's first patient to be Baron.

"If he's a mobile vet," Isabella said, "maybe we should call him out here."

"It'll be faster if we take Baron to him." J.R. just hoped Ethan wasn't away from the office and on a call. But if he was, he'd have a veterinary technician on duty who might be able to help.

As J.R. started for his truck, Isabella placed her hand on his forearm, momentarily stopping him. Her whiskey-brown eyes were filled with compassion. "I'm going with you. Do you want me to hold him? Or should I drive?"

Surprised that she'd offered, yet appreciative, J.R. thanked her then added, "If you don't mind holding him, I'll ask Evie to bring out a towel."

"There's no time for that." Isabella reached for the dog, gently taking him into her arms. "Since you know where you're going, you drive."

J.R. nodded, then rushed toward the truck. After they climbed into the cab, he started the engine and put the transmission into gear. He glanced in his rearview mirror long enough to back up the vehicle and turn around. Then they were off.

Once they were on the county road and headed toward Red Rock, he stole a look at Isabella, who held the pup in her arms. Blood from Baron's head had stained her blouse, yet she didn't seem to mind.

Had Molly Fortune been alive and at the ranch just minutes ago, she wouldn't have given her clothing a second thought, either. She would have put a hurt child or an injured animal first.

He was suddenly struck by their similarities. Of course, when it came to appearance, Isabella didn't resemble Molly in the least. But the fact that they shared some of the same admirable character qualities was hard to ignore.

J.R. still wasn't sure exactly what he was feeling for Isabella. But at that very moment, he realized that whatever it was had grown beyond mere sexual attraction.

Isabella glanced down at the puppy she held in her arms, his body as flaccid as a wrung-out dishrag. Yet he raised his head slightly, and his eyes opened. He whimpered before settling back into her arms. It broke her heart to see him hurt and in pain.

"How's he doing?" J.R. asked, as he focused on the road ahead.

"I'm not sure. The bleeding stopped, so that's good." She placed two fingers on Baron's chest, feeling for a pulse. It seemed to be steady, but what did she know? She had very little knowledge of first aid of any kind— human or canine.

"Thanks for coming with me," J.R. said, his gaze snagging hers and making her feel like some kind of teammate.

Strangely, right at this moment, she'd fallen easily into that role. "I knew you'd need someone to hold him while you drove."

J.R. glanced at her chest, where a splotch of red had smeared with brown. "I'm afraid you might never get that bloodstain out."

She'd thought about that, but only after she'd taken the puppy in her arms. Yet that didn't seem to matter in the scheme of things. Clothing was replaceable, and while some people might believe that animals were, too, Isabella wasn't one of them. So she shrugged and offered him a wistful grin. "I'll try soaking it when I get home."

J.R. returned his attention to the road, and ten minutes later, they arrived at the veterinarian's office.

Dr. Ethan Eldridge, a tall, tanned man in his late thirties or early forties, had been expecting them, thanks to Toby's phone call, and met them in the waiting room. "I was just about to lock up and head home, so I'm glad you caught me."

The vet led them to an exam room, and Isabella carefully laid the puppy on the small, stainless-steel examining table. Baron lifted his head slightly and looked at Isabella, his eyes glassy.

She couldn't help remembering how spunky he'd been, how he would growl as he chewed on the knotted yarn she'd made him. How he'd tag after her from room to room. How he'd lick her face whenever she picked him up. Seeing him this way brought tears to her eyes.

As the doctor examined the puppy they'd both grown to care about, Isabella and J.R. stood back, watching.

The vet tech, a young woman in her early twenties, came in. Moments later, she and the doctor took Baron back for an X ray.

"Now I know how my parents felt the night I got hurt during a high school football game," J.R. said.

Isabella turned to him, saw him standing with his brow furrowed, his arms crossed. She tried to imagine him as a teenager, a football player. She assumed he'd been popular, especially with the girls.

"What happened?" she asked, wanting to know what he'd been like when he was younger.

"I was a running back, going out for a swing pass, and took a hard hit from both the safety and a defensive end. I was knocked unconscious, and they had to carry me off the field."

"Head injuries are scary," Isabella said.

"That's what my mom always used to say. She was a real trooper whenever my brothers or I needed stitches or a cast. But a little concussion sure shook her up."

Isabella could see why it would and flashed him a knowing smile. "It sounds to me as though she was a typical mom."

"In some ways, I guess she was, but she was also unique. Special." His mind seemed to drift into memory mode, as he glanced down at the floor. Then his gaze lifted, meeting hers. "You remind me of her."

"I do? In what way?"

He shrugged, as though he hadn't really given it a

whole lot of thought. Or maybe because he didn't want to discuss their similarities.

The door swung open, and Dr. Eldridge returned alone. Isabella braced herself, afraid they were about to hear a grim prognosis.

"The good news is that there isn't a skull fracture," Dr. Eldridge said.

"And the bad news?" J.R. asked.

"Baron has a serious concussion, and I'd like to keep him overnight for observation."

"But he'll be okay?" J.R.'s brow furrowed again, his worry and concern for the puppy obvious.

As Isabella took note of this tender side of J.R. and how much he cared for the little dog, it touched her in a way she hadn't expected.

"I don't foresee any reason why he won't be back to his playful self in the next couple of days," Dr. Eldridge said. "We'll keep him quiet and sedated this evening. If all goes well, he can go home tomorrow."

J.R. thanked the doctor, taking time to introduce him to Isabella. Then J.R. asked about the vet's wife, Susan.

Isabella quickly put two and two together, realizing that she'd met Susan on several occasions. Susan Fortune Eldridge was J.R.'s cousin; their fathers had been brothers.

Susan, who had a PhD in psychology, once worked for a national hotline that specialized in troubled teens. Now she was employed by the Fortune Foundation, doing the same kind of outreach at a local level.

"Susan's doing great," Ethan said. "You'll have to come out to the ranch and visit one day soon."

"I'd like that." J.R. turned to Isabella. "Ethan owns a gentleman's ranch."

"I'm afraid I was raised in the city," she said. "So I'm not exactly sure what that is."

"It's smaller than a working ranch, but still sizable in acreage. It's a great place to get in some fishing and hunting. Or you can enjoy the wildlife."

Ethan saw them out, then locked up the office behind them.

As Isabella and J.R. headed for his pickup, she said, "I know this is the best place for Baron right now, but it doesn't feel right going home without him."

Home? The word had rolled off her tongue, but rather than own up to the slip, she let it slide, hoping J.R. hadn't noticed.

It was an easy mistake, she told herself. She'd stayed at the ranch over the weekend and had easily settled in. Too easily, actually, since J.R.'s ranch would never be home to her.

He opened the passenger-side door for her, and she slid into the seat. As he circled the pickup and got behind the wheel, she glanced down at her blouse, at the smudge of dirt and blood. The garment was new, and the stain probably wouldn't come out, but it didn't really matter. She was glad that Baron would be okay.

"Thank goodness we didn't have to put him down," J.R. said. "I was afraid that's what Ethan was going to recommend, and it would have been a tough decision to make."

Isabella knew just what J.R. meant. Losing that puppy would have been sad. Yet ranchers had to face the harsh realities whenever animals were seriously injured or sick. Putting an animal out of its misery was a fact of life for them, something they took in stride.

And that, she realized, was one more reason to believe that J.R. was a city slicker at heart.

Before he knew it, J.R. would grow tired of ranching and head back to Los Angeles—where he belonged.

The drive home was quiet, and even though J.R. and Isabella were both relieved to know that Baron would pull through, they were sorry to leave the puppy behind.

By the time they arrived back at the ranch, it was getting dark.

"Well," Isabella said as J.R. parked the pickup and shut off the ignition, "I'd better get inside and check out the plaster."

"Aren't you hungry?" he asked.

"Actually, I worked through lunch, so I'm starved."

As J.R. led Isabella to the door, he couldn't help thinking about the way she'd jumped right in when Baron got hurt, going the extra distance. She was becoming a part of the ranch. She belonged here; she just hadn't realized it yet.

When they entered the house, they found Frank and Toby waiting in the kitchen with Evie.

Toby, who'd been leaning against the refrigerator, pushed off and crossed the room to meet them, his face a mask of worry. "How's Baron? Is he…? Did he…?"

"He's going to be fine," J.R. said. "Dr. Eldridge just wanted him to stay overnight for observation."

"I never should have kept him with me." Toby's blue

eyes glistened with regret. "It's my fault that he got hurt. And I want you to know how sorry I am."

"Hey," J.R. said. "Baron is just a puppy, but he's a cattle dog. There's a lot he needs to learn. And I suspect he'll know better than to get too close to a horse's hooves from now on."

"We held off on eating dinner until you got back," Evie said. "Everything is still warm, so if you'll give me a minute or two, I'll get it on the table."

"Do you need any help?" Frank asked her.

J.R. shot a glance at his foreman. What had provoked him to make an offer like that? Not that J.R. didn't appreciate the fact that Frank was being polite, it just seemed…well, odd, that's all.

"Thanks," Evie told the cowboy. "I've got it all under control."

As she grabbed two pot holders and carried a ceramic baking dish toward the dining room, Frank watched her go, his interest in the cook going a bit above and beyond.

True to her word, Evie had the food on the table in a matter of minutes. And before long, the five of them dined on meat loaf, baked potatoes and a garden salad with buttermilk ranch dressing.

Evie might be a fabulous cook, and Isabella might assume that J.R.'s relationship with her was strictly business—that of employer/employee—but that wasn't the case. Before Isabella's weekend visit, Evie and J.R. had eaten all their meals together. But when the older woman had concluded that J.R. had romance on his mind, she'd made sure that he and Isabella had eaten in private.

Now that J.R. had begun hiring ranch hands, everyone would eat together.

Still, J.R. looked forward to getting Isabella alone again in the courtyard one day soon. He envisioned a quiet, romantic dinner for two. When he was able to pull that off, he would go all out with candles, music, wine…

"This is the best meat loaf I've had in ages," Frank said, lifting his napkin and blotting his mouth. "You're a great cook."

Evie, whose cheeks bore a natural rosy hue, flushed a deeper shade of pink. "Thank you, Frank. It's fun to cook for people who enjoy eating."

J.R. leaned back in his seat, watching as the cook and the foreman snuck glances at each other. There was something simmering between the two, and it was kind of nice to see.

He didn't know much about Frank, just that the man had lost his wife to cancer about fifteen or twenty years ago and had never remarried. He'd had to raise Toby, their only child, alone. So, for that reason, the father and son were especially close.

J.R. couldn't help but feel as though he needed to watch over Evie, to make sure she didn't get hurt. She'd been devastated when she lost her husband, and even more so when her stepchildren had all but shut her out of their lives. And the kindhearted woman didn't need any more disappointments.

Frank seemed like a reliable guy, though, and the references he'd provided had checked out. J.R. also prided himself on being a good judge of character, and both Frank and his son clearly were men of exemplary character.

As J.R. glanced across the table, catching Isabella's eye, he tossed her a smile. He'd trusted his instincts with Isabella, too. And hers was a sterling character, as well, wrapped in a bright whirl of Southwestern colors.

When they'd all finished dinner, Evie excused herself and went to bring out dessert—big slices of double-fudge cake that had them all oohing and aahing.

"You're going to have to roll me out of here," Isabella said, clearly joking about how good the cake was.

But J.R. had no intention of her rolling anywhere, other than into his bed, which was obviously not going to happen anytime soon.

As Evie began to pick up the dessert plates, and Frank jumped in to help, J.R. said, "Now might be a good time to check out the plaster work."

"You'll see that the crew got a lot done today," Evie said, pausing in the doorway that led to the kitchen. "But they didn't finish. This room is just one of several they'll have to plaster tomorrow."

After the table was cleared, Toby and Frank excused themselves to go to the bunkhouse, and J.R. and Isabella began a slow tour of the house, checking out the walls.

The new application of plaster looked good to him, although he wasn't entirely sold on the adobe brick that showed through in spots.

"What do you think?" he asked.

"They did a nice job." Isabella carefully studied the walls and the texture. "This is exactly what I asked them to do."

As they entered the guestroom in which Isabella had

slept, a room he thought of as hers, they continued to study the workmanship.

Rather, *she* continued to peruse the room. He was more intent on studying her.

As she reached the foot of the bed, she placed her hand on the comforter and turned toward the vase, where the roses had fully bloomed.

"Are Frank and Toby the first hands you've hired?"

"Yes."

"Where did you find them?"

He wasn't sure why she'd asked, why she cared, but he had no reason to keep it a secret. "Toby answered an ad I placed in the paper. And during our interview, he mentioned that his father was out of work. I asked to meet with him, too. Why?"

"It's just the mother hen in me, I suppose." She fingered the top of the antique dresser. "Frank seemed... Well, I got the feeling that he was interested in Evie. Maybe even romantically."

So J.R. hadn't been the only one to catch the I'm-sweet-on-you glances. "I noticed that, too."

"It's really touching," Isabella said. "I mean, assuming the interest is mutual."

So Isabella *did* have a romantic side. Otherwise, she wouldn't be impressed by Frank's interest in Evie. That was a good sign, J.R. supposed.

"I conducted a pretty thorough background check on both men, so if you're concerned about Evie, I think it's fair to say that she'd be in good hands if anything developed between them."

Was that it? Was Isabella concerned that she wouldn't be in good hands with J.R.?

As their gazes met, something hot and fluid rushed between them, something even she would be hard-pressed to ignore or to downplay.

He cupped her cheek with one hand, and his thumb caressed her skin. He continued to take in every bit of her pretty face, yet in his peripheral vision, he spotted the bed in the background, the goose-down comforter that promised to be a lot softer than a grassy field.

What he wouldn't give to take her in his arms, to kiss her senseless. To lay her on that bed and make love to her until dawn.

She stepped back, breaking the mesmerizing spell that seemed to hold them both captive.

He spotted the hesitation in her eyes, a sign that she was questioning her desire for him. But he wouldn't push. Not yet.

"I really need to get to bed," she said, taking a step back. "I have a meeting tomorrow morning with a guy who wants to display my blankets and tapestries in his stores, so I'll be leaving early for that. And then, in the evening, I have to attend my step-sister's birthday party. So I won't be able to stay here tomorrow night. I hope you're okay with that."

Actually, he wasn't okay with it. He had a feeling she was trying to put some distance between them, and he wanted her to stay at the ranch, like she'd agreed to. But she had a job to do, a career to build. And family was important.

"I understand," he said. "Will you be back on Wednesday?"

"Yes, of course. We have an agreement." She took another step back, her gaze still on him. "You're right, you know."

"Right about what?"

"When you said that staying here, sleeping under your roof, would provide me with a better perception of the house. It's working."

So she wasn't running scared? She was actually looking forward to coming back to the ranch?

Her body language wasn't very convincing, though. Yet her eager response to his kiss and the passion that simmered in her eyes was.

Isabella Mendoza was a contradiction—a lovely one, and J.R. couldn't seem to get enough of her.

"I'm afraid you won't see much of me over the next few days," she added. "I have a lot to do to get ready for Fiesta. Opening day is on the sixteenth."

"When does the art show begin?"

"On the sixteenth. But even if it didn't, I wouldn't miss opening day for anything."

Oh, yeah?

Then neither would J.R.

Chapter Seven

Opening day of Fiesta was always exciting. The festivities officially began at nine o'clock in front of the Alamo, with singing, dancing and pageantry.

One of the highlights was the cutting off of an official's necktie to signify the casual dress and the party atmosphere for the next ten days of the festival. But nothing was more exciting than the breaking of the *cascarones* as the crowd proclaimed *"Viva Fiesta!"*

Cascarones, Isabella had learned when she moved back to San Antonio as an adult, was a Mexican tradition. At various celebrations, people broke decorated, confetti-filled eggshells over the heads of friends and loved ones for good luck and good cheer.

So, two days ago, Isabella and Sarah had made a dozen of them. First, they poked two small holes at each end. Then they blew on one side, forcing the egg white and the yolk out the other. Afterward, they rinsed them out. When the eggs had dried thoroughly, they decorated each shell with bright paint and glitter. Next, using a paper funnel, they filled the shells with confetti and sealed the hole shut with a piece of tissue and glue.

Isabella would never forget the first time she'd witnessed the opening day ceremony and the breaking of the *cascarones*. She'd been in awe of the military band, the flamenco dancers, the mariachis—the sheer pageantry of it all. She hadn't wanted to miss a single exhibit, program or presentation.

She'd admired the local artists who'd exhibited their work—the incredible paintings, miniatures, pottery and other crafts. She'd eagerly looked forward to the next Fiesta, so she could show off her blankets and tapestries, too.

Her only regret had been that she'd missed out on so many Fiestas during the years she'd lived in California.

As she and Sarah stood in the center of the plaza, holding a basket filled with their colorful *cascarones,* she couldn't quell her excitement.

She'd dressed for the occasion in a bright, Southwestern skirt and a matching red blouse. She also wore some of the silver jewelry she'd purchased at last year's Fiesta.

"Good morning," a male voice boomed over the din of the crowd.

Isabella turned to see J.R. heading her way, with Toby at his side. Toby had dressed the part of the cowboy he truly was, but her focus was on the wannabe rancher.

J.R. looked sharp in his new boots and Stetson,

although she suspected he'd be more at home in tailor-made suits and designer shoes. Still, she couldn't help casting a lingering gaze his way.

As he closed the gap between them, she ignored her rising pulse rate and asked about Baron.

"Other than the stitches on his head, you'd never know he'd had a run-in with a horse."

"That's good." She offered him a smile, yet struggled with the excitement she felt at seeing him again.

J.R.'s presence always set her senses on edge. At least, that's the excuse she made for the buzz that rippled through her when she saw him approach.

Since she'd finished out the week at Molly's Pride, she'd returned a time or two to check up on the workers and to line them out, but she hadn't been able to devote the time she'd wanted to spend on his project. A part of her wanted to move back into his guestroom so she could oversee the progress of the workers. J.R. had been right about living there in the midst of the renovations. It had given her a better perspective.

"How are things going?" she asked. "Has the tile man finished yet?"

"Yes. The fountain is now full of water and in good working condition."

"I can't wait to see it." And if truth be told, she couldn't wait to return to the ranch, to roll up her sleeves and get busy renovating and decorating the old hacienda. "What about the electrician? Did he finish wiring for the stereo?"

"He sure did. And as you suggested, I purchased some hanging plants that hide the speakers completely.

The courtyard is really coming together. When Fiesta is over I'd like you to join me for dinner. You'll be surprised by the difference."

Since they'd been skating around that kiss for the past two weeks, she really should nix anything even remotely romantic, like a dinner in his courtyard. But her enthusiasm for the project and her curiosity got the better of her. Besides, she had her heart under control now. The preparation for Fiesta had provided a nice buffer. "I'd love to see it."

The announcer called out, drawing their attention to the festivities.

"Last year was the first time I ever attended Fiesta," J.R. said. "But I missed opening day."

"Well, you're just in time for the breaking of the *cascarones.*" She proceeded to explain the history behind them, as well as the meaning. She lifted her basket, showing him the ones she and Sarah had made. "We have extras in case we run into someone who doesn't have any."

Toby, who stood to J.R.'s left, kept sneaking glances at Sarah, whose lightly freckled cheeks bore a faint flush that suggested she was all too aware of his interest in her.

Sensing their shyness and curiosity, Isabella made the introductions.

"Sarah is my assistant," she added.

Toby lifted his hat respectfully, and the petite redhead flushed an even deeper shade of pink.

There was something about a cowboy that appealed to a lot of women, Isabella thought. And she had to admit that she was no different. But try as he might, J.R. just wasn't the real McCoy.

Too bad, she thought. She almost wished that he were.

As the crowd began to smash *cascarones* on the heads of friends and loved ones, Isabella reached into her basket and chose a red egg. She lifted it toward J.R. "You might want to remove that fancy hat."

"Why?" he asked.

"Because I'm going to officially wish you good luck and good cheer."

J.R. did as she asked, and rising up on tiptoe, she broke the egg against his head, baptizing him with confetti.

"Viva Fiesta!" she shouted.

He grinned, oblivious to the colorful sprinkles of paper littering his blond hair and forehead. "Thanks for the good wishes." He glanced at the eggs in her basket. "You said that you brought extras. Can you spare one of those?"

"Of course." She watched as he chose a blue egg with red and yellow zigzags down the middle. Then he broke it on top her head.

"Viva Fiesta!" he said.

Isabella pegged Sarah with an egg, then took another and gave Toby the same chance to remove his hat as she'd given J.R.

The young man, with his short-cropped, wheat-colored hair, wasn't exactly what you'd call handsome, but he was pleasant-looking. And he had a polite way about him.

Sarah, it seemed, had noticed that, too.

Isabella was glad. Interest in a new man would be a welcome diversion and just might help to heal her broken heart.

"Did you set up your blankets and tapestries in the same spot as last year?" J.R. asked.

"Pretty close," she said. "My dad volunteered to sit with my exhibit. He knows how much the opening ceremony means to me and encouraged me to take part. But since he plays in a band and needs to meet with the other musicians, I have to get back to relieve him."

"If it's okay with you," J.R. said, "I'd like to see what you've made this year. I'm sure I could use one or two at the house."

"I'll show you what I have." She led the way to her exhibit. "But you might find something you like better from one of the other artisans, so don't feel obligated to purchase one of mine."

When they reached the booth where Luis Mendoza waited, J.R. reached out his hand in greeting to José Mendoza's cousin. "It's good to see you again."

"How have you been?" Luis asked, taking J.R.'s hand and giving it a firm shake. "Busy with the new ranch, I suspect. I'd like to see it some time. Isabella told me it's really going to be something when you finish renovating and redecorating the house."

"You're welcome to stop by anytime," J.R. said.

The men chatted a while, then Isabella's father excused himself to find the other members of his mariachi band.

As J.R. looked at the tapestry Isabella had created during the winter months, he fingered it gently. "This is beautiful."

"I'm glad you like it."

"It would look nice hanging in the great room."

She smiled, pleased that he thought so, too. "I'll put it away so no one thinks it's for sale."

While she folded the tapestry he liked, J.R. perused her blankets. As he did, she watched his movements, his facial expressions. His words and tone indicated sincerity, yet she was still wary of him, just as she would be with any of the tourists who found her traditions "quaint."

She checked her emotions each time she felt herself drawn to his one-dimpled grin, melting a little when he glanced her way.

One day, she reminded herself for the umpteenth time, J.R. would grow tired of playing cowboy and go back to his sophisticated lifestyle in Los Angeles. So why let down her guard when she ought to be raising it? Why even consider getting involved with him any more than she already had?

Focus on the list, she told herself. Listen to logic, not your heart. Don't grow weak just because of that kiss in the grass.

She'd had a good reason for making a list of qualities for a perfect mate in the first place, so she took the time now to consider each trait she was looking for.

Someone down to earth with a steady job.

That was important, and Isabella didn't care what Jane had said. Leaving a lucrative career and moving halfway across the country to try his hand at something he'd never done before wasn't a sign of someone dependable and solid.

Someone sensitive and caring.

Okay, so J.R. had displayed a tender heart, especially when it came to Baron.

Someone able to make a commitment.

Come on, now. What made her think he'd settle down with her, when he'd obviously had countless women in the past, none of whom had rocked his single world enough to make him consider marriage?

A guy with a good sense of humor.

She again thought of the day they'd fallen into each other's arms on the grass, how they'd laughed over the mishap. Then he'd kissed her until she'd nearly melted right into the field of wildflowers.

True, their chemistry couldn't be discounted. Her vivid memories of a heated kiss proved that.

She also had to admit that J.R. was handsome, but looks weren't a top priority for her. The most important thing of all was that she could fall deeply and madly in love with a man, trusting that he would love her back, just as much. She wanted and needed someone who wasn't afraid of the teamwork it would take to make a marriage last.

A giggle erupted, and Isabella stopped her musing long enough to see that Sarah and Toby had managed to push through that awkward stage and had moved on to innocent flirtation.

Her gaze returned to J.R., who'd also caught the flushed cheeks, giggles and shy smiles.

He stepped closer to Isabella and whispered, "For the record, Toby's a good kid."

"So is Sarah."

They were talking about the younger couple, yet their gazes locked on each other. That heart-thumping, soul-stirring rush that rose up whenever their eyes met surged again—this time stronger than ever.

"Romance is definitely in the air," J.R. said, apparently alluding to Frank and Evie, and now Toby and Sarah.

Isabella just hoped it wasn't contagious.

For the next few days, Isabella found her resolve to avoid J.R. slowly weakening. Each morning, he showed up at Fiesta, bringing her coffee—just the way she liked it—and a muffin or a sweet roll.

"I thought you needed to be at the ranch," she'd said yesterday, as she took the blueberry scone he'd handed her.

"Frank is a natural-born cattleman with years of experience. He'll be okay without me for a while."

"Still," Isabella said, "I'm surprised you're back again."

"Don't be. There's an artist down the way who works with metal. I like some of the sculptures he's created, and he told me he had the perfect piece for me. He promised to bring it from home today. If I like it—and I have a feeling I will—I'm going to buy it."

Twenty minutes later, J.R. returned with a rustic sculpture made of barbed wire, spurs and who knew what else—the key to a John Deere tractor perhaps?

"What are you going to do with that?" she'd asked.

"I thought it would look great in my office."

She'd crossed her arms and arched a skeptical brow. As it was, the furniture in that one particular room was modern, and all the equipment—the fax, the copier, the computer—was state-of-the-art. Of course, she couldn't very well expect him to go back to the stone age in that respect. And she supposed he ought to be able to do whatever he wanted in the office.

"Interesting," she said, knowing she would never have a piece like that in her house.

The next morning, as she went up on tiptoe, trying to hang up one of her favorite tapestries in the front of her exhibit, she heard J.R.'s voice as he approached.

"Come on," he said. "This is going to be a lot easier on you if you try to keep up."

Who was he talking to? A small child? She glanced over her shoulder and saw that he had Baron on a leash. Other than a shaved spot on the head where Dr. Eldridge had sutured his wound, the puppy appeared to have completely recovered from his run-in with Ol' Smokey.

Isabella set the tapestry back on the table, then went to greet the rascally pup. She knelt on the ground and scratched his head. "Hey, buddy. How're you doing?"

He wiggled, and his tail wagged like crazy, as he gave her a hearty and affectionate lick.

J.R., who was juggling a small white paper sack and a cardboard carrier that held what appeared to be hot coffee, dropped the leash beside her. "Can you hold onto him while I set this down?"

"I'd be glad to." Isabella took the strap in hand, then glanced up at J.R. and smiled. "He looks great."

"He sure does." J.R. placed the box and the sack on the table.

Isabella had begun to expect J.R. to stop by with treats, so she'd gone without breakfast this morning. "What did you pick up this time?"

"Churros." He handed her a heat-insulated cup of coffee, which he'd again prepared with a splash of cream and sweetener.

"You're going to spoil me," she said.

He tossed her a bright-eyed grin, which made her wonder if that had been his plan all along. Then he reached into the sack, pulled out one of the doughnut-like treats and offered it to her.

She took it, noting that it was still warm from the vendor's stove. "I love these things."

"Me, too."

The guy had been racking up points, whether that was his intention or not, and she couldn't help but lower her guard just a bit.

He hadn't been coming on strong at all, which is what she'd expected. As a result, she was growing more comfortable in his presence, knowing that she was in full control.

If he asked her out, maybe it wouldn't hurt to agree. It's not as if she had to sleep with him.

Of course, he was a wonderful kisser, which meant his lovemaking skills were probably amazing. And it had been so long since she'd...

J.R. took a sip of his coffee, then scanned the immediate area. "Where's Sarah?"

"Fussing with her hair and lipstick." Isabella smiled. "Did you know that Toby asked her out? And that he's meeting her here today?"

"Yes. That's why we came in separate cars. He's taking her to the Fiesta carnival at the Alamodome."

An actual date, Isabella thought. How long had it been since she'd gone out with a guy she found attractive?

Too long, she decided.

A day at the carnival sounded like a lot of fun. Too bad

she had to man her exhibit. Still, if Sarah watched it for her one day, she might be able to steal an afternoon away.

Isabella slid a glance at J.R., then scolded herself for letting her thoughts stray. He probably wasn't the Tilt-a-Whirl type anyway. Still, if he asked…?

She just might say yes.

When he didn't, she banished her silly romantic fantasies by bringing up their decorating project and the renovations to his house. "By the way, I have pictures of the furniture I'd like your permission to purchase and sample fabric for the window coverings."

"When did you find time for that?"

"Last night. The design center I normally use stayed open late for me." She bit into her churro and savored the sugar-and-cinnamon taste of the deep-fried treat.

J.R. took another sip of coffee. "I've been busy in the evenings, too. Last night, I ordered a fifty-two-inch plasma TV."

Before she could comment or question where he planned to put a television that massive, Sarah arrived, her hair combed and curled. Mascara enhanced her eyes, and a light coat of blush covered her freckled cheeks. The young woman looked prettier than Isabella had ever seen her—happier, too.

When was the last time Isabella had fussed over a man? When had she experienced the excitement of a special date?

"You look great," Isabella told Sarah.

"Thanks." The younger woman beamed.

Had J.R. not been standing there, the two might have

lapsed into typical girl talk: Is there too much curl in my hair? Do these jeans make my butt look big?

As it was, they turned toward the crowd perusing the art exhibits, noting a boy and a girl who were carrying a cardboard box as they approached Isabella's booth.

"What do you have there?" J.R. asked.

"They're kittens," the boys said. "Four of them. Me and my sister found them. Their mom got hit by a car, so we took 'em home. Our dad said we could have one, but we have to get rid of the rest."

Isabella handed Baron's leash back to J.R. so she could get a better look. She reached for an orange tabby, picked it up and drew it to her cheek. She'd always wanted a pet and had seriously considered getting one to keep her company. Since she didn't particularly like living alone, she thought a watchdog might be a good idea. But dogs needed a lot of care.

Cats, on the other hand, didn't require as much time.

Should she consider a kitten?

"They're really cute," Sarah said. "How much do you want for them?"

"Aw, heck," the boy said. "We don't want to make money on 'em, lady. We just want to find them good homes."

Sarah eased closer to Isabella and studied the little orange tabby she was cuddling. "Maybe you should treat yourself to an early birthday present."

Should she?

"When is your birthday?" J.R. asked.

Isabella pondered her response. To be honest, she

was struggling a bit over turning thirty and wanted the day to pass quietly, without any fanfare.

"Is it a secret?" he asked.

"No. As far as I'm concerned, it's just another day." And it was. She didn't want him to get any ideas. If he bought her a present, it would make their relationship even more…awkward than it already was. "For the record, it's on the twenty-third."

"But it's not an ordinary day," Sarah said. "It's one of the biggies, and I think you should celebrate."

Isabella gave her a please-don't-even-go-there look, although it was too late. She could already see the wheels and cogs turning in J.R.'s head.

J.R. couldn't help smiling at Isabella's discomfort over her upcoming birthday. At least, the age thing was his best guess.

If the birthday was a "biggie," she was probably turning thirty. Apparently, that bothered her, but he couldn't see why it would.

"Don't stress about getting older," he said. "You're still a *pollo primavera*."

She scrunched her face at his attempt at Spanish and laughed. "Are you trying to call me a *spring chicken?*"

"Did I say it wrong?"

She laughed. "I'm not fluent in Spanish by any means, but I think that's one of the idioms that doesn't translate very well."

Suddenly realizing the two kids were waiting for her to make a decision, she slowly turned and reluctantly placed the kitten back in the box. "I'm sorry, you guys.

As sweet as this little thing is and as much as I'd love to take it home with me, I can't."

She crossed her arms and watched the kids walk away, their shoulders slumped.

Isabella's seemed to slump a bit, too.

"Why didn't you take the cat?" he asked.

"Because I live in a small apartment, not on a ranch." Her gaze followed the children, her expression almost wistful. "Besides, I need a pet like I need a hole in the head."

He'd seen her with Baron, seen the way the pup had taken to her, too. The puppy had followed her through the house, and when she'd worked on her loom, he'd curled up at her feet, just wanting to be near her.

"Why don't you think you need a pet?" he asked.

"They require time and attention, and I'm very busy." She shrugged a single shoulder. "But the kitten was cute, wasn't it?"

J.R. was actually a dog person, but he supposed that little orange tabby was okay—for a cat.

Sarah broke into a grin, and when J.R. looked up and saw Toby approach, he realized why.

While he didn't envy the young couple their nervousness, he did envy their excitement and the newness of a budding romance.

"Hey," Toby said.

Sarah glanced down at the ground. When she looked up and smiled, her cheeks bore a rosy tint. "Hi."

"Are you ready to go?" he asked.

"I guess so." She glanced at Isabella, then at J.R and back to Toby. "I mean, yes. I'm ready."

"Have fun," Isabella said.

As the couple walked away, it took everything J.R. had not to slip his hand into Isabella's, to draw her to his side. To tell her that he wanted to go to the carnival, too. That not only did he want to work with her on the renovations of the house, but he also wanted to play and have fun with her.

But he couldn't very well admit that yet. Not when she'd made it clear that she wasn't ready.

Of course, he sensed that her resolve was weakening. It wouldn't be much longer.

She turned to him, her lips parted.

Damn, she was a beautiful woman. And he realized that a lot of what he'd done since the beginning of the year had been done, in large part, because of her.

Sure, he'd wanted a ranch of his own for years. And he was glad he'd made the purchase, no matter how this thing with Isabella turned out.

But the actual move, relocating to Texas from California, had also been motivated, at least in part, by his desire to be close to her. He'd wanted to pursue a relationship with her that wouldn't leave them at a disadvantage because of the distance between them.

J.R. considered himself a patient man, but that patience was wearing thin and he was ready to put more of his plan into action.

If Isabella was still reluctant about their becoming romantically involved, he'd just wear her down.

He was used to getting what he wanted—and he wanted her. The more he'd gotten to know her, the more he was convinced that she was the woman for him.

"Well," he said, giving Baron's leash a gentle tug. "I need to go. I've got a few things to take care of while I'm in town."

Before he could walk away, an elderly couple wandering through the exhibits stopped to look at one of the blankets Isabella had displayed.

"See, honey?" the silver-haired woman said. "This is the one I told you about. I love the colors and the design."

The man reached for his credit card.

As Baron got to his feet and lunged forward, tugging on the leash, J.R. said, "I'll leave you to your customers."

"Okay. Thanks for the coffee and churros. I'll see you tomorrow."

The fact that she'd come to expect him was a good sign, and a smile stretched across his face.

As soon as he was out of her sight, he reached for his cell phone and asked the operator to patch him through to Red. When someone answered, he asked to speak to either José or Maria Mendoza.

Maria's voice came over the line as she introduced herself. "How can I help?"

"This is J.R., Maria. I'd like to reserve your back room for a birthday party on the twenty-third. It's a surprise."

After checking the date, Maria came back on the line and told him he was in luck. The room was available.

"How many people are you expecting?" she asked.

"Well, the dinner party is to celebrate Isabella's thirtieth birthday, so I'll be including the Mendozas and the Fortunes."

They chatted for a moment or two about the menu, then Maria asked if he had any special requests.

"Actually," he admitted. "I have several."

He went on to explain what he wanted and let her know to add it to his bill.

When the call ended and he put away his cell phone, he and Baron moved through the throng of Fiesta shoppers, as he looked for the kids peddling the kittens.

Hopefully, the orange tabby was still available.

J.R. glanced at the pup. "You aren't going to give that little cat a hard time, are you?"

He hoped not. Because if he had his way, Isabella and the kitten would be happily moving into the ranch before the month's end.

Chapter Eight

On the day of Isabella's party, J.R. arrived at the restaurant early, just to make sure everything was on track. The florist had come through, bringing a bouquet of red roses for each table. And everything else had been set up just as he'd ordered—food, music, entertainment.

As he made his way through the throng of family and friends, he greeted each of them, welcoming them and thanking them for coming.

He was glad to see how many had showed up, although certainly not as many as on New Year's Eve, when everyone had been in town for the holidays. His father was here, sitting next to Uncle Patrick and Aunt Lacey. J.R. had hoped Aunt Lily would make it, but she'd been feeling under the weather and had remained at the Double Crown.

From what he'd heard, his aunt, Cindy Fortune, was

back in town, but he hadn't extended a personal invitation to her. If she showed up at the restaurant, so be it. But if not, he certainly wouldn't be disappointed.

Cindy had always been a wild child. As a young woman, she'd run off and had become a showgirl, something that had been an embarrassment for the family. And in the course of her life, she was married four times, although none of the unions had lasted. She had managed to have four children, two with her second husband, and one each with husbands three and four.

Her kids, J.R.'s cousins, had turned out pretty well, considering the various upheavals in their lives that had been caused by their mother's flair for the dramatic.

Cindy's only daughter, Frannie, was here—alone. Apparently, Josh, her seventeen-year-old son, was on a date with his steady girlfriend tonight. There was no telling where Frannie's husband, Lloyd Fredericks, was, and J.R. didn't ask. Instead, he gave the lovely, stylishly dressed blonde a hug.

"It's good to see you," he told his cousin. And it was, but it was also sad to note how subdued the once fun-loving and spirited woman had grown over the years.

"I haven't had a chance to welcome you to Red Rock," Frannie said. "I'm glad you made the move."

After a little small talk, J.R. went on to greet the other guests.

The Red Rock Mendozas were here—Maria and José, of course, and four of their five children, nearly all of whom were either married or engaged. Roberto, who lived in Denver, was the only one who'd been unable to attend.

Isabella's four half siblings were here, and J.R. made a point of thanking each of them for coming.

As he continued to make the rounds, he stopped to chat briefly with Jorge Mendoza and Jane Gilliam. Jane was a friend of Isabella's, and Jorge was a cousin of hers. The happy couple were looking forward to their wedding next month.

J.R.'s brother Darr arrived with his fiancée, Bethany.

"How's it going?" J.R. asked Darr.

His brother slipped an arm around a very pregnant Bethany and drew her close. "Great. How about you?"

"So far, so good." J.R. slid him a slow smile. After this evening, he hoped to be able to proclaim his complete happiness, too.

Nicholas, another one of J.R.'s brothers, was here with Charlene London, his future wife.

Damn, J.R. thought. Romantic relationships were springing up all over Red Rock. Hopefully, he would find that romance was also in the cards for him and Isabella.

Their relationship had grown since opening day of Fiesta, although he hadn't tried to kiss her again.

He did, however, plan to make up for that tonight, when the crowd dissipated and they were alone. So, needless to say, he was looking forward to her arrival and to getting the party underway.

Initially, he'd thought about bringing her himself, once the guests had gathered. But he'd worried that she might turn down his offer to take her to Red for dinner. So Luis, her father, had been assigned to get her to the restaurant at seven.

She would be expecting a quiet evening with her

father, but she was in for a big surprise. She'd also be wearing red—if she agreed to the request Luis had made on J.R.'s behalf.

It was all part of J.R.'s master plan, although the birthday party had been an unexpected twist.

Things were certainly falling into place—the party, their budding relationship.

"She's coming!" someone called from the doorway.

The guests grew still, awaiting her arrival.

J.R.'s pulse pounded with anticipation, although party excitement had nothing to do with it. He always found his senses on high alert whenever Isabella entered a room.

As she swept through the doorway wearing a bright red dress, complementing her womanly curves, he studied her in rapt silence as those around him shouted, "Surprise!"

Her lips parted, and her eyes widened as she took in her surroundings and realized that someone had planned a party and that she was the guest of honor.

She looked at her father, who was smiling broadly.

"Who...planned all this?" she asked, her pretty brow furrowed.

Luis pointed to J.R., who took that moment to close the gap between them.

"Are you surprised?" he asked.

"Floored is more like it."

There wasn't time for any additional chitchat because her friends and family began to swarm around her, wishing her a happy birthday.

J.R. stepped back, allowing this portion of the evening to be hers alone.

As the party wound down, he would steal a few moments of his own.

Isabella couldn't believe all the trouble J.R. must have gone to in an effort to surprise her, and while she hadn't wanted any of the usual birthday fanfare, she couldn't help feeling both happy and honored that he'd pulled it all together—and in such a short time.

From the first day she'd returned to Red Rock to visit the Mendoza side of the family, she'd been welcomed with open arms. And tonight she'd felt even more loved, more accepted.

She greeted her family and friends, thanking each one for coming. She paused when J.R.'s voice came over a microphone.

"Excuse me," he said. "Can I have your attention?"

Isabella turned and faced the center of the room where the handsome rancher stood next to a portable dance floor, a mike in hand. For some reason, dressed in black jeans and a Western jacket, a white shirt and bolo tie, he didn't look at all like a city slicker tonight.

A hush fell over the crowd, as they waited for him to continue.

"I'd like to thank you all for coming this evening and sharing in a very special occasion—Isabella Mendoza's birthday. As part of the welcome, I'd like to invite her brother, Javier Mendoza, to sing a song to this very special lady. If I had the talent and the voice that Javier has, I'd be singing those words myself, each one from my heart."

Isabella's oldest half brother made his way to the

center of the room, stepped behind the keyboard and adjusted the microphone. Then he began to play and sing "Lady in Red."

It was Javier's voice singing the words, but as Isabella sought J.R., as their gazes met and locked, she realized that the lyrics were indeed coming from his heart.

As Javier continued to play and sing, J.R. approached Isabella and held out his hand.

Her heart flip-flopped in her chest, yet she let him lead her to the dance floor.

At this very moment, any reservations she'd ever had about him—about *them*—flew by the wayside as she stepped into his arms and began to sway to the music. Tonight her heart took the lead.

J.R. might not consider himself a singer, but he definitely knew how to dance.

"I can't believe you did this for me," she said.

He drew her closer. "Like Sarah said, this birthday is a biggie, Isabella. I thought you ought to have a proper celebration."

Charmed by his thoughtfulness and more than a little enamored with the romantic gesture of the song, Isabella leaned into him, relishing the feel of his arms around her, the beat of his heart against hers.

As they continued to move to the sexy beat of the music, she savored the musky scent of his aftershave and the feel of his cheek against hers.

When the last note ended, when the song was through, a rousing cheer erupted, followed by claps and whistles.

"Enjoy the evening and your guests," J.R. said, releasing her from his embrace. "I'll talk to you later."

As he turned and walked away, her knees wobbled. She hadn't realized how much she'd depended on his body as support, but she did her best to shake off the effects of their arousing embrace.

Ten minutes later, dinner was served in the main dining room, where red roses graced each linen-draped, candlelit table. Isabella had assumed that J.R. would sit with her, but he chose another seat, leaving her to be with her father and siblings.

What was with that?

The contradiction unbalanced her. Was he giving her space? Respecting her wishes not to get involved with him? Or had she been misreading his interest all along?

Yet throughout the night, his eyes were always on her, and she found herself constantly wondering where he was, what he was doing.

After dinner, she was lavished with cards and gifts— a bottle of wine, a basket of soaps and lotions, a CD of her favorite Tejana music—and she thanked everyone for their kindness and generosity.

As chocolate cake was served, and the party began to wind down, J.R. finally approached her again. This time he carried a small, colorfully wrapped present with a fancy red bow.

"What's this?" she asked.

"A little something from me."

"You've done enough for me already." She swept her arm in Vanna White style, indicating the party. "You didn't need to get me a present."

"I know. But I wanted to. Open it."

She took the package and carefully removed the ribbon and paper. Then she lifted the lid and peered inside. On a piece of cotton sat an elegant, hand-crafted, silver-and-onyx necklace. She gasped at the beauty, the artwork. She pulled it out of the box, letting it dangle from the fingers of one hand as she fondled the black, glossy, inlaid gem with the other. "It's beautiful, J.R."

"It was handcrafted by one of the artisans at Fiesta. I saw it there the other day, and it reminded me of something you'd wear, something you'd like."

"I don't know what to say." The fact that he'd purchased something culturally appealing to her made her wonder if he really *did* understand where she was coming from. "Thank you."

"You're welcome." He took the piece from her and reached to unhook the clasp. "Here, let me."

She turned and drew the veil of her hair aside. As he placed the intricately designed necklace on her chest and drew the chain behind her neck, his hands lingered on her bare shoulders and sent a sizzle spiraling through her bloodstream. Her heart went topsy-turvy, as she fingered the black stone.

His hands slowly slid down her arms, and she struggled not to turn, to gaze into his eyes. She was losing the strength and the will to fight him off, to challenge the feelings that were growing by leaps and bounds.

She turned, and their eyes met. Something blazed between them—not only heat and arousal, but emotion as well—fusing them in an unexpected bond.

"I have something else for you," he said. "Come with me to my car."

"You've given me too much already," she said.

J.R. chuckled. "Don't thank me for this one, yet. You might insist that I keep it myself."

Curiosity urged her to follow.

As they strode through the restaurant and out the front door, she expected him to take her hand. In fact, if truth be told, she *wanted* him to.

But he didn't, and she fought off a wave of disappointment. Still she continued to walk by his side.

They headed toward his SUV, where Toby stood near the back end.

Toby hadn't been at the party. At least, she didn't remember seeing him. So what was he doing out here?

"What's going on?" she asked.

"Your other gift needed a sitter," J.R. said.

The explanation made no sense.

She watched Toby take a cardboard box from the back of the vehicle and pass it to J.R. Crossing her arms, she waited as he reached into the box and pulled out what appeared to be the same orange tabby kitten she'd seen at Fiesta.

He handed her the little ball of fur. "Take it home and see if you enjoy having a pet. If you think you can't take care of a kitten, let me know. I'll give it a home on the ranch."

"But I don't have any food for it," she said, stroking its little head.

"I've got everything you need right here—kitten chow, toys, a litter box."

Isabella cuddled the kitty, trying to decide whether she should accept J.R.'s gift or not.

"Is this the same kitten those kids had?" she asked.

He nodded. "I knew it was a struggle for you to give it back, which made me think you really wanted it. So I followed the kids and told them I'd take it. If I was wrong, and you're sure you don't want a cat, I'll take it home with me."

She wasn't sure if she should be impressed that he'd somehow sensed how badly she'd always wanted a pet, or angry that he'd been so presumptuous. Still, she continued to cuddle the kitten.

"I have to admit that she and Baron had their moments, but they seem to be getting used to each other now. So taking her back to the ranch won't be a big problem. But why don't you give it a try?"

She stroked the kitten again. "I worried about leaving a pet home all day while I worked. But I guess I can take her to the studio with me."

J.R. smiled then turned to his hired hand and nodded toward the white pickup that belonged to Isabella's father. "Toby, will you put the kitten supplies into the bed of that truck?"

"You got it, boss." Toby took a bigger box and a sack out of the back of J.R.'s vehicle, then did as he was instructed.

"Sarah's waiting inside," J.R. said.

Toby beamed before dashing into the restaurant.

As J.R. returned his attention to Isabella, that bond, that buzz—whatever it was that surged between them—was in overdrive.

In the light of a silvery moon, his thoughtfulness, as well as his musky, leathery scent turned her heart and her mind inside out. She no longer wanted to wait for him to make the first move.

She held the kitten to her chest with one hand and, with the other, reached up and cupped his cheek, felt the light bristle of his beard, the warmth of his skin.

Regret might rear its head tomorrow, or even later tonight, but that didn't matter right now. Mindful of the kitten, she drew his lips to hers and kissed him—softly, at first. But as their breaths mingled, as their tongues touched, the kiss deepened.

She'd never experienced desire like this before, and she feared she never would again.

If she were willing to let her body run rampant over her mind, if she could just set aside her list for a few hours…

Give in, something deep within her urged. *Let go.*

But she couldn't quite do that yet. Not tonight.

An important decision like that shouldn't be made in the heat of the moment. If she chose to have a sexual relationship with J.R., she wanted to do so with a clear head, and she definitely wasn't thinking rationally right now. So she released her hold and broke the kiss.

"I'd be more than happy to drive you home," he said, not indicating which home he was talking about—hers or his. And in a sense, it really didn't matter.

"I think it's best if I go with my father," she said.

"Are you sure?"

No, she wasn't. Did she dare consider dating a man whose lifestyle and culture were so different from her own?

She'd feel much better about all this if she made that decision in the morning light. "Can we talk more about this tomorrow?"

"Fair enough," he said. "I want you to be comfortable with whatever you decide. You call the shots."

Footsteps sounded as her father approached. "Am I interrupting anything?"

"No, Papa." Her fear of a relationship with J.R. had already done that.

"Good night," J.R. said. "I'll talk to you in the morning."

She thanked him again, then watched as he climbed into his SUV.

As she got into her father's pickup, she had an almost overwhelming compulsion to run back to J.R., to tell him she'd had a change of heart.

Instead she watched him leave.

As her father started the engine and began the drive back to San Antonio, she realized that she would be kicking herself all the way home.

J.R. returned to the restaurant long enough to pay the bill. He told José he'd continue to pick up the bar tab for those who remained, although he suspected that most of them had wound down and were ready to leave.

Once he'd gotten into the Escalade, he started the engine and turned on the radio. Then he began the drive back to the ranch.

He hadn't thought a kiss could be any better than the one he and Isabella had shared the day they'd picnicked, but he'd been wrong. If he'd ever had any doubts about

Isabella being the woman he wanted to spend the rest of his life with, they'd disappeared just minutes ago.

Things were coming together just the way he wanted them to. If he knew her as well as he thought he did, she was now ruing her decision to ride home with her father instead of him.

As a grin began to form, his cell phone rang.

For a moment, he wondered if it was her, calling him to tell him she'd changed her mind.

But it was his father's voice that sounded over the line. "Son, I meant to talk to you about something after Isabella's party, but you left before I got the chance."

"What's up?"

"Patrick and I were talking, and we think we should take a more active stance against those threats."

Concern overtook J.R.'s romantic thoughts. At least, for the moment. "What do you plan to do?"

"There's not a lot we *can* do until we find out who's making those threats and what they have against the Fortunes and the Mendozas. But Patrick and I have finally convinced Lily that she needs more protection on the Double Crown than just ranch hands. I'm on my way to tell Lily that I'm going to move in and stay with her until the culprit is caught."

J.R. was worried about his widowed aunt, too. When Uncle Ryan died four years ago of a brain tumor, Lily had been the love of his life. And now Lily was alone.

"To make matters worse," William said, "Cindy was involved in a car accident this afternoon."

Cindy Fortune had always marched to the beat of her own drummer. Divorced three times and widowed once, she'd never lacked a sexual relationship. Now seventy years old, with brassy blond hair and a flirtatious eye, she was still a fine-looking woman who could turn a man's head.

J.R. had never been too close to her, but then again, not many people in the family had been. Not only did she have a flair for the dramatic, she was also self-centered and, at times, self-destructive.

"What happened?" J.R. asked.

"Her car ran off the road."

"Was she badly injured?"

"From what I understand, she suffered a serious concussion and lacerations. She's been hospitalized, but she should pull through."

"I'm glad to hear that." J.R. wondered if alcohol had been involved.

"Here's the thing," his father said. "Neither Patrick nor I think it was an accident. Not with the arson fires and the threats we've been getting."

J.R. had to admit that his father had a point.

"I don't think anyone in the Fortune or the Mendoza family is entirely safe," his father added. "So keep an eye on Isabella. I realize that she's only a second cousin to the Red Rock Mendozas, but who knows what—or who—the guilty parties are really after."

If anything happened to Isabella, J.R. didn't know what he'd do, and the force of his emotion surprised him. "Don't worry, Dad. I'll look out for her."

J.R. slowed his vehicle until it came to a full stop. When it was safe, he made a U-turn and headed back to San Antonio.

He was going to look out for Isabella—whether she wanted him to or not.

At the same time, in a private hospital bed in Red Rock, pain exploded in Cindy Fortune's head, and she moaned. Her mind was a swirl of shadows and fog, and she struggled to sort through what had happened to her.

A car crash, she thought. That much she could piece together. And she'd been hurt. If the pain was any clue, her injuries were serious.

Oh, God, she thought, willing the sledgehammer in her brain to stop long enough for her to piece things together.

She'd returned to Red Rock in an attempt to reconcile with her only daughter. Of her four children, Frannie was the one she was closest to, although, if truth be told, they'd had a slew of problems and disagreements over the years.

They'd met for lunch today, and things had gone… Well, they hadn't gone all that well, but Frannie had at least seemed willing to give their mother-daughter relationship another chance.

But the car? The crash?

Oh, yes. It was coming back to her…

After leaving the restaurant, she'd been driving along, when, somehow, she'd lost control and had run off the road.

That's all she remembered, though—barreling through the guardrail and down an incline.

As she lay trapped in the driver's seat, she'd welcomed the loss of consciousness, because it had kept the pain at bay. And now she was in a hospital; she knew that much.

"Miss Fortune?" a male voice asked.

Cindy, who'd never kept the last names of any of her husbands, turned toward the sound and the blurred form of a man standing at her bedside, a man wearing a uniform and a badge.

"Yes?" she asked, blinking her eyes and trying to focus.

"Do you know anyone who might want to hurt you?" the officer asked.

Truthfully? In her seventy years on earth, she'd made the usual number of enemies along the way, but no one in particular came to mind. "Why do you ask?"

"Because your brakes have been tampered with."

Cindy tried to make sense of the shocking news. Was he suggesting that someone had tried to kill her?

The note she'd received a couple of months ago pressed through the clutter in her mind.

One of the Fortunes is not who you think, it had read.

She hadn't been the only one to receive that same cryptic message. Patrick and William, her brothers, had received similar, unsigned letters. And so had her sister-in-law, Lily.

To make matters more suspicious, there had been two different arson fires—first at Red, then at the Double Crown Ranch since then.

Try as she might, Cindy couldn't quite comprehend what had happened and what it might mean. Nor could she will herself to stay lucid long enough to tell the police officer that there could be a correlation.

As another wave of darkness rolled back and forth across her mind, as she drifted in and out of consciousness, she quit fighting to stay awake.

What was the use?

But as the fog briefly lifted, she had one lucid moment and was haunted by one irrefutable thought.

I deserve it, she told herself. *I deserve to be punished for what I did....*

Chapter Nine

"That was some party," Isabella's father said on the drive home. "It must have cost J.R. a small fortune. I didn't realize the two of you had gotten so close."

"It's complicated," Isabella said. But if the truth were known, she was now beginning to wonder if it was all very simple. Maybe she was the one who was complicating the issue by dragging her feet.

J.R. definitely cared for her. He was also very generous and thoughtful. And to top it all off, the chemistry between them was explosive.

So why was she riding home with her dad when she could have been with J.R.?

Fortunately, her father must have realized that she didn't want to go into detail because he didn't press for more.

Twenty minutes later, he dropped her off at her place, a small one-bedroom apartment located in a quiet San Antonio neighborhood. He helped her carry in all her gifts, including the kitten and the pet supplies J.R. had given her.

Then he kissed her goodnight and went home.

Now here she was, alone. Well, except for the kitten she'd decided to call Rusty.

She kicked off her shoes, plopped onto the sofa and watched Rusty check out his surroundings. "So, what do you think, little guy?"

When a knock sounded at the door, a shiver of goose bumps feathered up and down her arms.

That was odd. It was too late for visitors. She glanced at the clock on the cable box—10:47 p.m.—then looked at Rusty, who was oblivious to the unexpected nocturnal visitor. But what did she expect from a cat?

Too bad she hadn't chosen a dog for a pet when she'd first moved in—a great big Rottweiler named Killer.

The knock sounded again, this time louder and more insistent. Not that she'd planned to ignore it, but deep inside she'd hoped whoever was standing outside would suddenly realize that this was the wrong place.

Isabella went to the door, but she didn't open it. Instead, she lowered her voice in a don't-mess-with-me way. *"Who's there?"*

"It's me, Isabella. J.R."

A wave of relief swept through her, followed by a pang of curiosity. Why was he here? Was he having second thoughts about letting her call the shots?

If so, maybe she ought to be glad that he'd had a change of heart.

Or should she?

Darn those conflicting thoughts and desires, she thought, as she opened the door for him.

As he stepped inside, the small, cozy living room seemed to shrink in his masculine presence. He took off his hat and held it a bit sheepishly. "I'm sorry for barging in on you like this, but I just learned that Cindy Fortune was involved in a suspicious accident this afternoon, and I wasn't comfortable knowing you were home alone."

An eerie shudder of concern settled over her. "What happened?"

"My dad just spoke to the police, and it seems that someone cut her brake line. She crashed through a guardrail and rolled down a slope."

Isabella had never met the woman, but she frowned, saddened by the news. "Who would do such a thing?"

"We don't know. But because of the fires and the notes that people in our families have been getting, everyone is growing more and more uneasy."

She tried to sort through what he was telling her, what those cryptic notes and the fires had really meant. "When I heard about those notes, I assumed they were some kind of prank."

"So did everyone else."

"The fires were a lot more worrisome. But messing with someone's brakes? That's scary, J.R. Is your aunt going to be all right?"

"Yes, but she could have died." He motioned to the sofa. "Why don't we sit down while we talk about this?"

"All right." She sat, and he took a seat beside her.

"My father is on his way out to the Double Crown.

He's going to stay with Lily." J.R. placed his hat on the armrest, then turned to face her. His concern was palpable, and the intensity in his gaze reached somewhere deep inside of her. "I'd like to either stay with you or take you back to my ranch."

She was touched by his offer of protection, yet she wasn't convinced that she really needed it. Was there a threat? Who could possibly want to hurt one of the Fortunes or the Mendozas?

Of course, those threats had taken a dangerous turn, so someone definitely harbored some ill will toward their families.

She turned to J.R., her knee brushing against his. "You don't think it's safe for me to be alone?"

"I'm not sure what any of this means, and I don't know who's behind it or why. So until Cindy comes to and we can learn who might have tampered with her brakes, it's impossible to know who's safe and who isn't." He took her hand, his thumb caressing her skin.

His presence in her home and the intimate gesture were enough to jolt her through and through, and she didn't know what to think—of him, of his news.

She really wasn't frightened by the threat, yet having someone in the house tonight did make her feel a lot better.

"To be honest," he added, "I don't think I could stand it if anything happened to you, Isabella."

The sincerity of his words, of his expression, touched her very soul, and she gave his hand an appreciative squeeze.

"So," he said, "do you want me to sleep on your

sofa? Or do you want to pack some things and come home with me?"

"It doesn't sound as though you're giving me much choice." Yet on the other hand, it didn't seem to matter. If truth be told, she wanted to be with him tonight—threat or no threat.

"I can take you to your father's house, if you'd feel more comfortable there."

She ought to feel more comfortable staying with her dad than with J.R., who was little more than a stranger, but she didn't.

"Do you want to stay here with me?" she asked. "It's a long drive back to your ranch."

"I'm okay with that."

She glanced at the sofa, which she'd purchased because it was smaller than most and wouldn't over-whelm the ten-by-eleven-foot living room. "I'm afraid you might not be very comfortable, though."

There were other options, and they both knew it.

Still, he shrugged. "Don't worry about me. I'll be fine."

She stood, deciding to get a pillow and blanket. Of course, she had a queen-size bed that would be a whole lot more comfortable for him than a sofa his feet would hang over.

"Do you think it would be too difficult for you to sleep in my room with me?"

A boyish grin tugged at his lips. "It shouldn't be a problem. I'm a gentleman."

Did she want him to be one tonight?

A part of her didn't, but she couldn't allow her thoughts to continue in that vein. "We're both adults."

Which meant what—exactly? That they could ignore any adolescent yearnings and do the right thing?

Or that it didn't matter what happened while they shared her bed?

She reached out her hand, and as he took it, she pulled him up to a standing position. "I haven't had a sleepover in a long time. But to be honest, after hearing about your aunt, I'm not sure how well I'd sleep if you left me here alone. I appreciate you driving all the way out here, as well as your offer to stay. I certainly can't insist that you sleep on the sofa and end up with a crick in your neck and back tomorrow."

"If it makes you feel better, I can sleep on top of the covers, and you can sleep under them."

And if she wanted more than that?

Oh, for Pete's sake. What was with her?

He stood before her now, all male, all lean—and willing to sleep wherever she wanted him to.

She placed her hand on his lapel, gripped the fabric of the expensive Western jacket he wore, felt the solid beat of his heart, the warmth and the male essence that bubbled up from deep within him.

For a couple of long, drawn-out seconds, she struggled with her conscience, with whether this man and this moment were right. But her reservations didn't last long.

She met his gaze, and the connection they'd shared for the past few weeks surged with undeniable force.

Could she do it? Could she set aside her list for one night? Could she allow her feminine needs to dictate her actions and just let go?

She wasn't sure, but just considering the possibility warmed her from the inside out.

As if sensing her indecision, he offered her a genuine smile. "As I said, you don't have to be afraid that I'll do anything you don't want me to do. You're still calling all the shots—and that means whether one of us sleeps on top of the blankets or we both slide between the sheets."

"I'm not sure I'm ready for anything between the sheets."

"Then we'll take it one step at a time."

She glanced at the clock, saw that it was merely getting later. "Would you like some coffee? I have decaf. Or are you ready for bed?"

His lips quirked in a sexy smile, and his brow arched sensually.

She crossed her arms, struggling with a smile of her own. "That's *not* what I meant. I was only asking if you were sleepy."

"In that case, then yes. I started the day at four-thirty, so I'm a little tired. But, again, you're in charge."

Something told her that J.R. Fortune didn't cede control to anyone, so the fact that he was yielding to her must mean something.

"All right," she said, accepting the power position and feeling a bit brazen as a result. "Come on. I'll show you to my room."

J.R. followed her into her bedroom, where the queen-size bed with its green-and-purple spread seemed to take up an incredible amount of space. Then she took him to the bathroom. After giving him a fresh towel, she opened the medicine cabinet and pulled out a new tooth-brush before leaving him to get ready for bed.

In the meantime, she filled the litter box and made sure the kitten had fresh water and food. When she was finished, she decided to leave the lamp on in the living room so Rusty wouldn't be left in the dark.

As the water shut off in the shower, she realized the bathroom would soon be free. So she returned to the bedroom and opened the dresser drawer that held her nightgowns. Before she could choose something especially modest, J.R. entered the room, and she quickly snatched the one on top and turned to face him.

He wore only his pants and carried his boots in his hand, his shirt and jacket draped over one arm. She couldn't help noting the broad expanse of his shoulders, the sprinkle of golden brown hair on his bare chest, the set of well-defined abs that indicated he'd been working out regularly—and that he'd been doing so long before he'd ever moved to the ranch.

"I…uh." She nodded toward the bathroom. "I'll change in there. I'll just be a few minutes."

Once she'd ducked into the privacy of the bathroom, she glanced down at the nightgown she held, a slinky, pale yellow number with spaghetti straps. It was one of her newest, but it was also one her sexiest, and she wished she would have put more thought into the choice.

But it was too late now.

Isabella took a quick shower and returned to the bedroom, where she found J.R. stretched out across the top of the bed, still bare-chested and more attractive than ever. She wondered what he usually wore at night.

Boxers? Briefs? Something told her he might even sleep in the raw. For some crazy reason, she wanted to ask.

She didn't, though. Not when she caught him studying her as though he could see right through her satin gown.

Could he?

Maybe she should have opened the drawer and found something else, something flannel and a whole lot less sexy, but she didn't want to make a big deal out of it.

So she pulled back the covers and slid between the sheets, suddenly realizing that she'd forgotten to turn off the light.

"I'll get it," he said.

The lamp she'd left on in the living room for Rusty provided just enough illumination in the room for them to make each other out. She wondered if that was okay with him. If he preferred sleeping in the dark.

He didn't mention anything, so she didn't ask.

As they lay there, a sense of awkwardness settled around her, and she found herself wanting to push past it. So she turned to her side, facing him. "Thank you for throwing that party for me tonight. You really didn't need to do it, but it was lovely, and I'm glad you did. I hadn't really been wanting or expecting anything special."

He turned onto his side as well. "You're special, Isabella. So it's hard not to want to celebrate your birthday."

"Thank you." She studied him for a while, appreciating how handsome he was, how close.

The walls she'd been building around her heart to shut him out began to crumble, and her hand lifted of its own accord. She cupped his cheek, her thumb brushing against his solid, square-cut jaw. Something surged between them, something hot and blood-stirring.

He took her hand and pulled it to his mouth, placing a kiss on her palm. "I can't think of anything I'd like more than to make love to you, but my intentions are completely honorable. So sleep tight, honey."

The term of endearment, the sweetness of his touch, sent her senses reeling, and her heart pounded with anticipation.

If she kissed him now, there would be no decision to make afterward because, as far as self-control went, she'd be toast.

But what if she didn't kiss him? If she didn't chance taking things to a sexual level?

She rose up on an elbow, leaned forward and pressed a good-night kiss on his cheek.

She could have stopped at that—and she probably should have—but some unseen force took over, pressing her to push beyond the gawky, awkward moment she'd been having and to trail her lips along his cheek until they reached his mouth.

Spearmint-laced breaths mingled, and as the kiss slowly deepened, Isabella closed her eyes, caught in a heady arousal of swirling pheromones, musky cologne and the vibrant and steady beat of two hearts pounding out in need.

She ought to pull back, ought to stop, but it felt too good. It also felt right.

That darn list she'd made no longer mattered. Not now. Not when she wanted to feel his arms around her. Not when she wanted to immerse herself in him.

She was lost in a swirl of heat and hunger. Her fingers threaded through his hair, pulling his lips closer, his tongue deeper.

He moaned into her mouth, and she feared she would melt into a simmering pool in the sheets. For a moment, she forgot where they were. Who they were. All she could think about was the raging desire and the promise of something she'd never experienced before.

But as J.R. ran his hand along the curve of her back, caressing the slope of her derriere, she broke the kiss long enough to catch her breath, to search her heart.

"Now what?" she asked.

J.R. couldn't help chuckling. All of a sudden *he* was in charge? "I'll roll over and go to sleep, if you want me to."

Yeah, right. He might roll over, but he'd be damned if he'd be able to sleep with all the testosterone and adrenaline rushing through him.

"It's your call," he added, repeating what he'd told her before. But he'd meant what he said. She was the one who'd been reluctant to get involved. So when they made love, he didn't want her to have any regrets.

She continued to lie there, the struggle playing in the shadows angling over her face.

Damn, he thought. Her uncertainty was becoming more of a turn-on than it should have.

"What if we're sorry about this in the morning?" she asked.

"*I* won't be."

Her smile nearly knocked him off the bed.

Then, ever so slowly, she reached for him. As she

wrapped her arms around his neck and kissed him, his control faded into the heat-charged air. A hot and heavy rush, the likes of which he'd never known, pulsed through him.

The kiss deepened, and J.R. tasted every moist corner of her mouth. All the while, his hands slid along the curve of her back, the slope of her hips.

She began to throw off the blankets, kicking at them and apparently wanting to shed the cloth barriers between them. J.R. was only too happy to oblige.

Before long, they were lying together—man and woman.

She moved closer, arching toward him and driving him wild with need. The desire to make love to her nearly took his breath away.

Threading her fingers in his hair, she gripped him with sexual desperation. A moan formed low in his throat, and he fumbled to remove her pretty gown, hoping he didn't rip the silky material in the process.

It might be a good idea to pull away long enough to undress, but for the life of him, he couldn't stop. He couldn't seem to get enough of the intoxicating kiss; he couldn't get enough of *her.*

As their tongues continued to taste, to seek, to savor, she tugged at the button on his jeans with one hand, while using the other to skim her fingers across his chest. A shiver of arousal shot through his nerve endings, sparking his pulse and sending his blood racing.

He slipped off his pants, then helped her to remove her nightgown, releasing the most perfect breasts he'd ever seen. He ached to touch them, to caress them.

Taking a nipple in his mouth, he tasted, suckled, and she gasped in pleasure. All the while, he continued to stroke, caress, and then to kiss her senseless.

J.R. had never needed so badly to be inside a woman, to lay claim to her body for the rest of his life. And he couldn't wait another minute. He wanted to make love to Isabella now, to glide in and out, filling her completely, bringing her a satisfaction she'd never find with anyone else.

Then she would be his.

When her fingers brushed against his erection, he shuddered. The time was now.

He stopped long enough to reach for his discarded jeans to remove a foil packet from his pocket. Not that he made a point of carrying them around with him in the years after college, but he'd wanted to be prepared for something like this the moment he'd moved to Red Rock and set his sights on Isabella.

She helped him sheathe himself, and as he hovered over her, she opened for him, arching up to meet him, taking all he had and giving all of herself in return.

He thrust deeply, and her body responded to his, melding, molding, until they both reached a peak. She gripped his back, her nails digging into his skin. Never had he experienced a heat like this, a need that went beyond comprehension.

As Isabella cried out in pleasure, he released with her.

Long after the last spasms of pleasure had eased, he continued to hold her tight, afraid to let go.

J.R. didn't know what tomorrow would bring—he'd never imagined that love would feel like this. But one thing was certain. Tonight, he'd made love to the woman he intended to marry.

As the dawn crept through a crack in the curtains, and the scent of their lovemaking lingered in the morning air, J.R. and Isabella lay amid rumpled sheets, his arm lying protectively across her breasts.

He watched her chest softly rise and fall as she slept and savored the faint fragrance of her perfume.

Last night had been out of this world. If he'd ever questioned whether he could settle down with one woman for the rest of his life, he would never wonder about that possibility again. Isabella had been too good to be true.

They hadn't talked about the future yet. And he wasn't entirely sure when they would get around to it—soon, he hoped, because his mind was set.

He wanted Isabella, and that's all there was to it. He just had to convince her that she felt the same way.

But then again, maybe that wouldn't be so hard to do. She certainly hadn't needed much convincing last night.

He brushed away a strand of her hair and placed a kiss on her bare shoulder. Then he slowly drew his other arm out from under her head. Being careful not to wake her, he slipped out of bed.

After a quick shower, he would go into the kitchen and whip up something to eat. Then he would take her breakfast in bed.

What a great way to start the day and to discuss the future.

He would suggest that they start planning a wedding, the sooner the better. And he'd mention that he wanted a minivan full of kids, little boys and girls who would be the perfect blend of their parents and bear the Fortune name.

Hopefully, after all the two of them had shared last night, Isabella was thinking the same thing—that she wanted it all, too. That she wanted it with *him*. That she wanted them to be friends, teammates, lovers.

Once in the bathroom, he scanned the pale green walls, the ivory-colored shower curtain and the matching fluffy towels that hung on the rack.

He reached into the shower stall, turned on the spigots and waited for the water to get warm. He couldn't help noting all the feminine-scented products that lined the shelf behind the commode—a mango-and-pear shampoo with a matching conditioner, an aloe vera splash for after the bath, a variety of lotions.

A slow grin formed. He couldn't wait to smell each one on her, to choose a favorite.

One inside the steamy shower, he spotted a pink razor he hadn't noticed last night. He'd never felt comfortable with women who left their toiletries behind at his house in California. He'd never wanted to give up his space, his privacy. But Isabella wasn't like any woman he'd ever known before.

Boy, how things had changed.

As the water pounded his back, as he lathered the soap and scrubbed his body, he realized that he was looking forward to having Isabella move into his house. And as soon as she did, he'd happily make room for all her things in his bathroom.

Just as he was making room for her in his heart.

Chapter Ten

As the morning sun peered through the window, and the aroma of fresh-perked coffee filled the air, Isabella arched her back and stretched, then slowly opened her eyes.

Only a portion of the sheet was draped over her naked body; the rest was tangled at her feet. For a woman who'd slept alone for almost every night of the past thirty years, her bed felt incredibly empty right now.

She'd slept soundly in the warmth of J.R.'s arms, and she missed not waking with him by her side.

Their night together had been everything she could ever have hoped for and more. He was an incredible lover—the best.

Yet she still hadn't been able to kick the reservations she had about them having a future together.

Now what? she asked herself. Where would they go from here? Where *should* they go?

She wished the answer was simple, but it wasn't.

To be honest, she truly *wanted* to love J.R., and she wanted him to be the special man in her life. But she just wasn't sure.

There was so much more to life and to love than great sex, although she would have been hard-pressed to argue that point last night. And even as good as their lovemaking had been, she still felt torn about where to go from here.

A part of her wanted more time to think, yet another part wanted to call J.R. back to bed.

She didn't do either.

Her first thought was that the problem was him, that he fell short of what she needed in a mate. Yet as she considered the man she'd gotten to know over the past few weeks and what they'd shared last night, she had to face another possibility, whether she wanted to or not.

The problem just might be her.

She rolled to the side, taking the sheet with her. But her being the problem wasn't something she wanted to ponder right now. She didn't particularly like thinking of herself as a commitment-phobe.

Surely, it wasn't that.

Maybe she was just carrying some excess baggage.

Her parents had shared a passionate relationship before hitting the skids and splitting up. They'd both gone on to other relationships that had appeared lasting.

Her dad had married again and had several kids before losing his wife to cancer. And he'd said they'd been happy.

But while her stepfather had loved her mother, Isabella didn't think they'd been as happy as they should have been.

So was that the problem? Was that holding her back?

The smell of coffee grew stronger, and she found herself craving a cup.

J.R. must be in the kitchen. Should she drag herself out of bed and be a better hostess?

"Good morning." He entered the bedroom with a cup in his hand. "I brought you some coffee."

She offered him a smile, but didn't trust herself to speak. Instead, she studied the handsome man who was only wearing a pair of sky-blue boxers, his hair still damp and mussed from the shower.

Could a man be any sexier than that?

Isabella ought to be craving a lot more than caffeine, and while she was, actually, the sense of awkwardness returned full force.

J.R. took a seat on the edge of the mattress. "I'm not as good in the kitchen as Evie, but I managed to whip up some scrambled eggs and toast for you."

"You didn't need to do that."

"I wanted to."

His efforts were sweet, and while she was touched by his thoughtfulness, he seemed…out of place—and not just in the kitchen or her studio apartment, but in her life.

Still, she managed a smile and tried to shake off the lingering negativity.

What was with her? There had to be a hundred women in the county who'd jump at the chance to wake up in J.R. Fortune's arms.

He set the coffee mug on the nightstand, then picked up a silver-framed photograph of her parents—one of the few she had of them together.

"I recognize Luis," he said. "Is this your mom?"

She nodded. "A friend of theirs took that shot. My dad found it in an old box he had in storage and gave it to me. He knew I'd like having it."

"They look young. But happy."

"I think they were—for a while." Until their differences chilled the passion that had once burned between them. "But the marriage didn't last."

"Young couples face a lot more obstacles than older ones," J.R. said. "Men and women in their thirties and forties usually have a solid sense of direction, as well as a greater ability to weather storms and make things work."

Was he hinting that she shouldn't worry about the two of them facing the same trials and troubles if they chose to walk down the aisle?

She couldn't quite buy it. Isabella's mother had been a little older when she married for the second time, but in order to "weather the storms and make things work," she'd had to give up so much of herself—her family, the people she knew in San Antonio, her heritage.

"Hey, look who's here." J.R. stooped, picked up Rusty and, after cuddling him for a moment, placed him on the bed with Isabella.

She sat up, pulling the sheet up to cover her breasts, and took the kitten in her arms. "Hi, little guy. How was your first night in your new home, huh?"

The kitten purred softly.

Isabella glanced at J.R., who seemed to be studying her intently. "Thanks for getting him for me. I think it's going to be nice having a pet."

"Looks like he's going to be the lucky one."

She grinned, then stroked the kitten again.

"You're obviously an animal lover. Do you like kids, too?"

Uh-oh. Was he hinting at them creating a family? Or was that merely her imagination?

"They're okay," she said, downplaying her hopes for a family of her own.

In truth, she'd love to have children—if it was with the right guy.

But was J.R. that guy?

He seemed so sure of himself, so sure of *them*. She truly wished she could share his confidence.

She had feelings for him—strong ones—but she couldn't quite bring herself to call it love.

Their lovemaking, of course, was out of this world. But could they make a commitment to each other that would bind their hearts and lives forever?

She honestly couldn't say.

What if J.R. got tired of playing cowboy and wanted to go back to California and the successful life he had there?

Isabella wouldn't be happy living anywhere other than San Antonio or Red Rock. And divorce wasn't going to be an option for her, especially if they had children. There was no way she'd do to her kids what her mother had done to her. So what options were left?

"What are your plans for today?" J.R. asked.

"I have some work to do," she said. "So I'm going to the studio."

"Why don't you pack some things and come to the ranch? I can pick you up or send a driver for you."

She'd been a little uneasy at night, but in the light of day, she felt much better. "I'll be okay."

"I'm sure you're probably right." He placed his hand on her hip. "But that doesn't mean I'll feel comfortable until whoever is threatening our families is apprehended."

Okay, so there *was* a real threat out there. But J.R.'s protective streak was just a tad unsettling. Was it a sign that he was controlling, as her stepfather had been?

She couldn't dismiss the possibility.

"Thanks, J.R. I appreciate your concern." She slowly pulled off the sheets, climbed out of bed and put Rusty on the floor. "I'll be careful—*and* I'll keep my eyes open."

Then she headed for the privacy of the bathroom and closed the door, pushing the button that secured the lock.

She certainly hadn't had any reservations about getting romantically involved with him last night.

But now, in the light of day, reality had set in.

Late that afternoon, as Isabella worked on the loom in her studio, the small cowbell on the door chimed, alerting her to someone's arrival.

"I'll be right there," she called, as she slowed the loom to a stop.

It was too bad that Sarah wasn't here to deal with the customers, but she'd asked for some time off to go shopping. Toby was taking her out to dinner this evening, and she'd wanted to find a new outfit to wear.

The girl still had stars in her eyes, and Isabella was happy for her. The two certainly seemed like a good match—in spite of their age.

As Isabella made her way to the front of the studio, she spotted Julie Osterman studying the display near the window. Julie, who worked for the Fortune Foundation, was a teacher and counselor of troubled teens.

"Hello," Isabella said, as she approached.

Julie turned and smiled. "I hope I'm not bothering you."

"Not at all."

The thirtysomething woman with light brown hair and blue eyes was attractive, Isabella decided, but she'd be even prettier if she chose brighter colors and more stylish clothes.

Today she was dressed for comfort in a black top, flowing pants and a pair of clogs. Her jewelry, though, was not only unusual but interesting.

"I really like your necklace," Isabella said. "And those bracelets, too."

"Thanks." Julie lifted her arm, glanced at the bangles. "I found them at an estate sale and thought they were unique."

Isabella wondered why she'd stopped by. "Is there anything I can help you with?"

"As a matter of fact, there is. The Spring Fling is coming up, and Susan Fortune Eldridge and I are in charge of the vendors. We wondered if you'd like to exhibit your blankets and tapestries."

Each May, the Fortune Foundation sponsored the Spring Fling, the proceeds of which funded many of their charity projects. Everyone in Red Rock looked forward to the event, which not only included a dance, but also a carnival and various art exhibits.

"Can we count on you to take part?" Julie asked.

"Of course." Isabella was always happy to be included in a worthy cause. "And I'll donate a portion of my sales to the foundation."

"We certainly appreciate your generosity," Julie said, as she turned back to the tapestry she'd been perusing. "Your work is beautiful. I can understand why Susan would insist that we talk to you."

"Thank you."

Julie looked at several more pieces, then said, "I've got several other stops to make, so I'd better go. Thanks to participating in the Spring Fling—I'll see you there."

Isabella watched the woman leave. She'd just started back to the loom when the telephone rang.

It could be anyone, she supposed. But she had a feeling it was J.R. calling again.

If so, she still didn't know what to tell him. She was torn between wanting to see him again and maintaining her distance.

How would she be able to backpedal on their relationship if they kept getting ever more deeply involved?

J.R. sat in his office, the telephone receiver in his hand as he waited for Isabella to answer. The fact that she still hadn't committed to driving out to the ranch this evening had him a bit perplexed.

He'd been so sure that everything was falling into place that her sudden indecision made him feel off balance. Okay, so she hadn't actually made any real decisions one way or the other. But how could she not want a relationship with him after last night? Didn't their chemistry prove anything?

It made no sense.

The phone rang several times before she said, "Hello, this is Isabella."

"How's it going?" he asked.

She paused for a beat. "All right. How about you?"

He didn't know yet. Not until she gave him the answer he was looking for. He did opt to tell her what he had in store for them this evening. "I've got a quiet dinner for two planned."

"I'm still not sure if I can make it," she said.

The last time they'd talked, she'd told him she had work to do, so he didn't want to push too hard. "You don't have to give me an answer now. Call me later."

"All right."

As J.R. hung up the telephone, he stood with the receiver in his hand for the longest time. Something was wrong. Isabella was pulling away from him, and he couldn't figure out why.

He'd called her twice today, and both times she'd claimed to be busy. He suspected that was true, but he was having a hard time buying it.

"Is something wrong?" Evie asked from the doorway.

He glanced up and managed a smile. "No, everything's fine."

"I've got the table set, and dinner is in the oven. All you need to do is serve it and enjoy."

"Thanks, Evie. When are you leaving?"

"At five. Is that still all right with you?"

"Absolutely. Enjoy the night off."

"I intend to." She glanced around the office floor. "Where's Baron?"

"Snoozing at my feet."

She smiled. "After that close call he had, I want to make sure he doesn't sneak outside without someone looking after him."

They'd nearly lost the dog, which would have been tough. Yet not as tough as losing Isabella.

As the sound of Evie's footsteps disappeared down the hall, J.R. pondered his dilemma. How much effort was he prepared to put into a relationship that still hadn't left the ground? If the woman was anyone other than Isabella, he'd have to say not much. But as it was…

A male voice interrupted his thoughts. "Excuse me, boss."

J.R. looked up to see Frank in the doorway, his hat in his hand. "What's up?"

"We've got a problem with the well in the south pasture. We might need a new pump."

"Why don't you call it a day, Frank. I know you have plans for tonight. I'll deal with the irrigation problem."

Trouble was, the only pressing problem that J.R. wanted to deal with right now was Isabella.

What was holding her back?

And would it be too much for him to overcome?

Two days after the accident, the Red Rock police still had no idea who'd tried to kill Cindy Fortune. But she had her own suspicions.

"Since you have plenty of family in the area," the

nurse said, as she waited for Cindy to sign the discharge papers, "I assume you have a place to stay and someone to look after you while you recover."

Cindy would never ask to stay with family members. And even if one of her kids invited her to, she would decline. She valued her privacy too much.

"I'm going to a hotel," she responded.

"Is someone coming to pick you up?" the nosy nurse asked, as she handed Cindy the papers to sign.

What did it matter?

Cindy picked up the pen, taking care not to exert too much pressure on her sprained finger. After scratching out her name, she pushed the paperwork back to the woman. "I'm not about to bother anyone, so I'm going to take a cab. Will you call one for me?"

"I'll see what I can do."

Ten minutes later, Cindy was seated in the backseat of a taxi and headed for the nearest hotel. But in spite of a headache that continued to come and go, she wasn't eager to check into a room and lie down.

Instead, she would confront the only person who might think he was smart enough to get away with making a murder look like an accident.

As the cab drove through Red Rock, she noticed a black Corvette parked in front of the Blue Bonnet Café, just as pretty as you please.

Well, now. Would you look at that? This must be her lucky day. That had to be Lloyd Fredericks's car.

"Stop!" she ordered the cabbie. "Turn around. I want you to go back to that café. But don't leave. Wait for me."

"I'll need to keep the meter running," he said.

"I realize that." She reached into her purse and pulled out a ten. "I'll give you the rest and a nice tip when I come out. I won't be long."

As Cindy climbed out of the cab, she winced in pain. Damn. Everything hurt like a son of a gun.

She shut the passenger door, then strode into the café. Once inside, she searched each booth and table until she spotted Lloyd seated near the back, reading a newspaper and drinking a mug of coffee.

The handsome man was alone, which would make a confrontation easy.

For the past two days, Cindy had thought long and hard about who could have possibly tampered with her brakes, who might have wanted to see her dead. And, quite frankly, only one person came to mind, and that person was her son-in-law.

He'd never liked her. Never respected the fact that she'd done her best to be a good mother, no matter what some of her ungrateful children might say about that.

And who was he to complain?

No one else might give a turkey's rump about what the man did each day after leaving home. But Cindy knew. Not much got by her.

As she made her way to her son-in-law's table, she studied him carefully. He was fast approaching his fortieth birthday, if he hadn't passed it already. With those soulful eyes, he was still good-looking, Cindy realized. But she'd known the type. He'd been a spoiled, sullen kid who'd evolved into a smooth-talking charmer.

But worse than that, Lloyd Fredericks wasn't a man to be trusted.

Challenging him might undo some of the positive steps she'd made with Frannie the other day. But she couldn't let him get away with what he'd done.

No one messed with Cindy Fortune.

"Well, if it isn't Lloyd Fredericks," Cindy said. "As I live and breathe. I'm in luck."

Lloyd didn't immediately look up from his paper. He clearly recognized her voice, as well as the sarcastic undertone.

"Oh, wait," she said, finally gaining his attention. "I suppose my lucky day was when I survived that little…*accident.*"

Lloyd looked up from his reading long enough to snarl and ask, "Who peed in your stewed prunes?"

She wanted to pinch his little head off. Instead, she crossed her arms, stopping as soon as she remembered how sore her chest was, thanks to the monstrous bruise she'd received from the seat belt and the airbag that had saved her life. As soon as she swallowed her pain, she cleared her throat and narrowed her eyes. "Someone tampered with my brakes, Lloyd. And I have every reason to believe it was you."

He turned to face her, a scowl marring his normally handsome face. "Are you losing it? You're about that age, aren't you?"

She stiffened, ready to claw his eyes out.

He must have sensed her ire, because he softened just a tad and asked, "Why would I do something stupid like that? What would I have to gain? It's not as though you have any insurance policies and made Frannie or me the beneficiary."

"How would you know?" she asked.

He laughed, one of those deep, don't-underestimate-me laughs. "Maybe I checked."

Maybe he had.

"Listen here," Lloyd said. "I'm not saying that anyone would be terribly disappointed to hear about your death, but don't look at me. I didn't do it."

"I *am* looking at you." Cindy wasn't at all sure that she believed him. He'd always been selfish. Would he stoop to murder?

She hadn't thought so, but who knew what motivated a man like Lloyd Fredericks? And just how far did his greed go?

"I'm just about to get everything I've worked for," he added. "So someone else must have it in for you."

She suspected it went much further than that.

Lloyd and his father owned an investment company called Fredericks Financial, which Cindy had learned wasn't all that solvent. As she said, it paid to do a little research and to know these things.

He shrugged. "I'd be a fool to tamper with your brakes. You'll have to keep digging for someone to blame for your near-death experience."

He took a sip of coffee, then picked up his newspaper, shutting her out.

But not for good.

Chapter Eleven

That evening, Isabella stood in front of her closet, trying to find something to wear. J.R. had invited her to have dinner with him in the renovated courtyard of his house, but she couldn't seem to work up the proper enthusiasm for this get-together.

All day she'd thought about calling him and telling him that something unexpected had come up, that she couldn't find time to drive out to the ranch and spend the evening with him after all.

But she hadn't. Deep inside, she desperately wanted to see him, to be with him.

She truly cared about J.R. And she wanted to cling to his kindness, to his strength. Whether she liked it or not, he had claimed a piece of her heart. She just wasn't sure how much.

And that was the problem. J.R. wanted more than a one-on-one commitment. He wanted marriage and babies and the whole nine yards, which frightened her way more than it should. After all, she'd been the first of her friends to make that single-no-more pact. So she ought to be thrilled.

Sure, she felt a definite buzz of excitement whenever she thought about him, but she couldn't fully let go of her apprehension.

She left the closet door open and sat on the edge of bed, where she and J.R. had made love just hours before. She'd washed the sheets this afternoon and put the spread back in place, but even though the room appeared to be in order, it would never be the same again.

And neither would she—no matter what she chose to do tonight.

Still, the questions remained. What did she feel for J.R.? And what did she want from a relationship with him?

Would she be content with an affair?

The answer to that one was easy. It would have to be all or nothing for her. But she feared that "having it all" with J.R. simply wasn't possible.

Isabella exhaled a weary sigh. As often as she'd tossed her dilemma around today, she still had no answer. But she couldn't put it off any longer. She was going to drive out to the ranch after all.

Maybe seeing J.R. again, talking to him, would make things crystal clear in her mind. And if not? She'd come home right after dinner.

So she stood, returned to the open closet and pulled out the new black dress she'd purchased on a recent shopping trip with Jane.

Isabella usually steered clear of dull, mournful colors, but she'd liked the cut of this particular dress, as well as the fit. So she'd bought it, planning to wear fancy jewelry to give it more pizzazz.

But she didn't feel especially decadent right now and decided to leave her jewelry at home.

Besides, the color and somber style seemed appropriate tonight. So she removed it from the hanger and put it on.

Next she applied her makeup, combed out her long tresses and slipped into a pair of heels.

All the while, the battle between her heart and her mind waged on.

Even with the time J.R. had given her to think about the direction she wanted to go, the knot in her tummy continued to twist and turn. And she feared it would do so until she finally decided to run for the hills or to dig in her heels and give a relationship with J.R. a chance.

"I'll let you know about dinner later," she'd told him earlier. So before she headed to the ranch, she picked up the phone to tell him she was on her way.

Evie, her voice more lighthearted than usual, answered.

Had J.R.'s housekeeper/cook been expecting Isabella to call? Or was something going on at the ranch tonight, something J.R. hadn't mentioned?

The man was full of surprises, and she wondered if he'd been plotting something else to charm her, to force her hand.

"It's Isabella," she said. "Is J.R. available?"

"No, he went out to the south pasture and hasn't come in yet."

Isabella wondered if something had come up on his part and hoped that it had. On a scale of one to ten, she was only around a five when it came to the strength of her decision to go to the ranch and let things fall where they may.

"He invited me to dinner," Isabella said, "but if he's busy—"

"Oh, no," Evie said. "He's not too busy. Dinner's in the oven. And the table is already set. He's looking forward to having you here tonight."

Isabella didn't doubt that. And now he had Evie on board and determined to make things work.

"There's a chance I'll be gone before he comes in from the pasture," Evie added. "When we discussed the menu, I told him I'd leave the meal in the oven. But I forgot to mention that I put the salad in the fridge. So will you please let him know that?"

"Where are you going?" Isabella asked. Not that it was any of her business, but Evie lived with J.R. at the ranch. And it would be dark soon. Had J.R. sent Evie off for the night so he and Isabella would be alone in the house?

"Believe it or not," Evie said, "I'm going on a date."

The enthusiasm in her voice was hard to ignore, which indicated that J.R. hadn't had a hand in that.

"How exciting," Isabella said. "Who are you going out with? Anyone I know?"

"Yes. Frank Damon, the foreman."

Isabella couldn't say she was at all surprised. She'd seen the way the man had looked at Evie.

"It's just dinner and a movie," Evie added.

"That sounds like fun."

"Yes, it does. I just hope asking me out was all Frank's idea. J.R. is so good at orchestrating things, and I know that he's really looking forward to being alone with you tonight."

"I'm sure Frank is looking forward to the date, too," she said. Yet she, too, couldn't help wondering if J.R. had been involved. He *was* a master at orchestrating.

"J.R. certainly planned a nice party for me," Isabella said. "And he had very little time to pull it together."

Evie chuckled. "I know. He insisted on everything being perfect for the party, from the guest list to the menu to the music. I have to tell you, when J.R. Fortune sets his mind to doing something, he makes it happen."

And he'd clearly set his mind on having Isabella.

Maybe that's what had been bothering her all along.

A sense of uneasiness settled over her as she thought about the lengths her stepfather had gone to get her mother out of Texas, to keep Isabella from her father.

To make them both forget who they really were.

Last night, J.R. had told Isabella that she was in charge. That she was calling the shots.

But was she?

Had their lovemaking only been part of a carefully planned seduction? One that had convinced her that going to bed with him had been her idea?

A sour taste formed in Isabella's mouth, and she cleared her throat. "Since J.R. can't come to the phone, will you please give him a message?"

"Sure."

"Tell him I'm really sorry, but I won't be able to see him tonight."

"Oh, no," Evie said. "He's going to be terribly disappointed."

Not any more than Isabella would have been if she'd shown up for another carefully orchestrated seduction.

J.R. entered the house and went directly to the courtyard. He wanted to make sure that Evie had followed his instructions to the letter.

As he'd requested, the lights in the alcove were dimmed, and candles sat on the linen-draped table, ready to be lit. Water gurgled in the fountain, and lush green plants and flowers hung from hooks on the walls. All he had to do was hand-pick the music on the stereo, and the setting of tonight's dinner would be perfect.

Before heading for the bathroom to shower, he went to his bedroom to check and make sure everything was just the way he wanted it. And it was.

On the nightstand, near the bed, sat a small black velvet box. He lifted the lid and peered inside, saw the diamond sparkle. It had belonged to his mother. After the day he'd kissed Isabella in the field of wildflowers, he'd known that she was the one who would wear it. So he'd taken it to the jeweler and had it cleaned.

Was it too much?

Was it too soon?

Having second thoughts, he placed it in the drawer, where it would be ready when he decided the time was right.

After taking a shower, he went to the kitchen to check on dinner. He found Evie pulling something from the oven, something that smelled delicious.

"I see everything is ready," he said.

When she turned to face him, he saw that her hair was curled and combed, that she wore lipstick and mascara.

"You look great," he said.

Evie offered him a flustered grin and fingered the side of her hair. "Thanks, J.R. It's been so long since I fixed myself up for a man that I nearly forgot how."

"It must be like riding a bike," he said, "because it certainly came back to you. You're going to knock Frank's socks off."

A happy smile burst across her face. "I sure hope so. But you can't believe how nervous I am. You'd think I'd never gone out on a date before."

"You'll only be nervous for a minute or two. And if it helps, I can assure you that Frank's fretting a bit, too."

She sobered. "Do you think he regrets asking me?"

J.R. chuckled. "Not in the least. It's been a long time for him, too."

"What a pair we're going to be tonight."

Actually, J.R. thought, the two might make a nice pair long after the first date was over.

"By the way," he said, "did you happen to hear from Isabella?"

He hated the idea of calling her again. He wasn't normally the pushy type.

Evie's smile faded. "Yes, I'm afraid so. She isn't going to be able to come tonight."

Disappointment slammed into J.R., but he tried not to let it show. "Did she say why?"

"Just that something came up."

J.R. had never dealt with losing, had never really had

to. But he had to face the truth. He was losing Isabella, and there wasn't much he could do about it.

Hell, he wasn't even sure he should try.

Isabella glanced in the mirror and realized that she was all dressed up with no place to go. Not that she wanted to *go* anywhere.

Maybe she ought to take a long, hot bubble bath. Afterward, she could put on a pair of comfortable sweats and pour herself a glass of wine, then kick back and watch television.

She went to the cupboard, thinking she'd open a bottle of merlot and pour herself a glass. But apparently, she'd opened the last one when she'd hosted a girls' night last fall.

There was a wine shop not too far from here. She could drive there and pick up another, but since she really only wanted a single serving, she'd probably end up tossing the rest down the sink.

She could, she suppose, forgo it completely, but tonight she would really welcome the light buzz a single glass would provide.

"What do you think?" she asked the kitten, who was batting around a little felt mouse. "Should I just stay home and forget it?"

Rusty didn't seem to care one way or the other.

Of course, if she hung out here, she might have to deal with J.R. if he decided to call. Or what if he drove out to talk to her in person? She wouldn't put it past a determined man like him.

Truthfully? She was avoiding him for a reason, and

while she'd eventually have to tell him that she didn't want to see him again, it didn't have to be today.

In the past, whenever she'd needed someone to talk to, she'd always called Jane. But now that Jane was practically living with Jorge, Isabella couldn't possibly pop in on her. So her options were fading fast.

The portable phone rested on the counter, and as she picked it up, she noted a flyer advertising the Trail's End, a new nightclub down the street. She'd set the ad aside to remind herself that she might want to get a few single friends together and check it out sometime.

Since the Trail's End was within walking distance, there was no need to drive.

Feeling somewhat rebellious, she uttered, "Oh, why not? It just might get my mind off J.R."

So she locked up the apartment and walked three blocks to Trail's End, a place that seemed to be hopping with the happy hour set.

As she entered, she noted the music blaring in the background as a laid-back crowd talked and laughed among themselves. Intent upon having that glass of wine and then leaving, she shook off the all-by-herself uneasiness and took a seat at a small table.

Too bad she couldn't just order a glass of wine to go. That way, she could head home, fill up the tub and relax. But she knew better than to ask. They'd never allow her to leave the building.

A shapely blond waitress wearing Daisy Duke shorts and a crop top laid a cocktail napkin on the table. "Hi, there. Can I get you something to drink?"

"Do you have a wine list?"

The woman, who had a name tag that said Sally, handed her a small, sandwich board-type sign from another table and smiled. "If you're a connoisseur, you won't be impressed."

"I'm really just a lightweight, but a glass of wine sounded good tonight." Maybe it would help her sleep.

"I tried to tell the owner that we ought to offer a better selection," Sally said, "but he'd rather offer an extensive beer list."

Isabella glanced at her options. "I'll have the merlot."

"You got it." The woman stopped at another table before heading back to the bar.

"Excuse me," said a man in his late thirties to early forties. "Are you Isabella Mendoza?"

"Yes, why?"

"I thought I recognized you." He grinned, his eyes glimmering. "A man wouldn't forget a pretty gal with hair like yours."

"Have we met?" she asked.

"No, not exactly. But I've seen you from a distance. You hang out a lot in Red Rock—at Red. You're a niece of José and Maria."

"Yes, I am." She scanned his face, trying to remember if she'd ever seen him, but she didn't think she had. He was an attractive man and would have made an impression on her.

"Is that seat taken?" he asked.

Was he hitting on her? It was hard to say. Apparently, he knew her family, so she didn't think it would hurt to share her table with him. Besides, she wouldn't be here that long. "Go ahead and sit down."

He flashed her a charming smile and took the seat across from her. "I've only been in here a time or two, but it's an exciting place. Do you come here often?"

"This is my first time."

He nodded as though making a mental note of it. "Are you meeting someone?"

Should she lie? Tell him that she was waiting for a friend? She was usually pretty careful about what she told strangers, but he seemed like a nice guy. And he knew her family. She was probably being overcautious.

"I'm supposed to meet a friend for dinner," she said, opting to be vague and to at least touch on the truth.

They chatted for a bit, sticking to the basics—the atmosphere at the Trail's End, the service.

"The band is pretty good," he said. "Don't you think?"

She hadn't really been listening, but she supposed it was okay.

The cocktail waitress returned with Isabella's wine, then took the man's order—a gin and tonic.

"Put her wine on my tab." He reached for his credit card and handed it to the waitress. "Thanks, Sally."

Again, he seemed nice enough, she supposed. "I didn't catch your name."

"It's Lloyd."

The name didn't trigger her memory at all, so she was pretty sure she hadn't met him before.

Strange…

His cell phone rang, and he pulled it from the holder on his belt. He glanced down at the lighted display, furrowed his brow, then looked back at her. "I'm sorry, you're going to have to excuse me. I'd let it ring through, but this might be important."

"Of course."

He flipped open the cell and answered without saying hello. "This is a bad time, Josh."

His brow furrowed again, this time deeper. "What? Yes, I cut off your card."

Isabella could only glean one side of the conversation, and she had to strain to hear the man's voice over the din in the bar.

He leaned back in what appeared to be enjoyment. "Because I didn't want you spending your money on that little—" He listened for a moment. "Stop it right there."

His smile faded completely as he straightened. Even in the dim bar she could see him tense in anger. "No, you listen to me, Josh. It's over. You're going to stop seeing—"

His eye twitched, and he frowned, as though the caller may have ended the call before he had a chance to finish. For a moment, he looked absolutely livid. Unbalanced. Then he snapped the phone shut.

He turned to her and forced a smile. "Telemarketers drive me crazy."

That was no telemarketer, Isabella realized. It was someone named Josh. But she didn't want to talk about it anymore than he probably did.

"It sounds like you need to go," she said.

"Not right now. It'll wait."

Sally returned with Lloyd's drink. When she left, he looked across the table at Isabella. "I heard you were doing some work out at J.R. Fortune's ranch."

The fact that he seemed to know so much about her, when she didn't know squat about him, didn't sit right. "Have you met J.R.?"

"Yep. I'm in pretty tight with the Fortunes." He took a sip of his drink. "It's too bad about all the trouble they've been having."

"The trouble?"

"You know. The fire at the Double Crown, Cindy's car accident."

Isabella wasn't comfortable discussing J.R. or his family in public, so she changed the subject.

They made some small talk for a while, and when his drink was empty and hers merely half gone, he motioned to Sally and asked for another round.

Isabella realized that he hadn't actually hit on her—yet, but it sure felt as though he might. And while she wasn't interested, she didn't mind having a momentary diversion.

Maybe the night would turn out better than she'd thought.

After taking a second drink order from the guy at table twelve, Sally returned to the bar.

"Looks like our friend Lloyd is about to score again," Todd, the bartender said.

"I'm sure he's working on it." She blew out a sigh. "I can't stand Lloyd Fredericks. He drives up in that fancy black sports car of his, then parks in back so no one sees it and knows he's here. He's such a jerk. He's always hitting on women and pretending to be single."

"You'd think a woman would be able to see through that," Todd said.

"Yeah, well the one he's with tonight seems nice enough. I hate seeing women fall for guys like that."

"Maybe you should warn her."

"I just might." Sally chuffed. "And I ought to have a little talk with his wife. I'll bet she doesn't know her husband has been here almost every night this week."

"You don't normally get involved," he said.

"I know. Don't worry. I won't call her. She probably already knows."

Todd slowly shook his head. "His wife is related to the Fortunes, isn't she?"

"I think so. At least, that's what I heard. I think her name is Francie or Frannie. Something like that."

"Nice family. Too bad they got stuck with a loser like Lloyd."

"By the way," Sally said, "I'm going to need another merlot plus a gin and tonic."

"You'll have to wait," he said. "I've got a bunch of teetotalers at table seven and I've got six virgin strawberry daiquiris to make."

"I'll wait," she said. "Or better yet, I think I'll take a potty break. I've been holding it for an hour."

"You got it."

Sally headed for the restroom. Once inside, she stopped at the mirror long enough to see that she needed to reapply her lipstick, then she stepped into the nearest stall.

When she came out, she noticed the attractive brunette entering, the woman who'd been sitting with

Lloyd Fredericks. With that gorgeous black dress and the long, flowing hair, she was even prettier in the light.

When the woman smiled, Sally returned it, then bit down on her bottom lip.

Their eyes met a second time, and Sally couldn't hold her tongue any longer. "Excuse me. I make it a point not to butt into things that aren't my business, but you seem like a nice woman. And I figure you probably just met that guy."

The brunette arched a delicate brow. "What are you getting at?"

"Just that you need to watch out for him. He's not only married, but he cheats—*a lot.*"

The brunette was visibly shaken by the news. "Are you kidding?"

"Nope. I'm sorry to be the bearer of bad news. But I'd feel worse if you took him home and I didn't warn you."

"I wasn't going to take him home. But thanks for the heads-up."

Sally nodded, then turned on the faucet and washed her hands. When she finished and activated the automatic dryer on the wall, she glanced around the bathroom.

The brunette was already gone.

While waiting for Isabella to return to his table, Lloyd downed another drink. Damn, but she was beautiful. And a lot more sophisticated than the gals he usually pursued. But he was up for something new tonight. Something exciting.

He flagged Sally, who took her time responding.

The snob. He'd asked her out a time or two, but she was made of ice.

When she finally made her way to the table, she asked, "What can I get you?"

"Another gin and tonic," he said.

As Sally turned her back, Lloyd's cell phone rang.

He glanced at the lighted display, but didn't immediately recognize the number. He thought about letting it go to voice mail, but answered anyway. "Hello?"

His brow furrowed as soon as he heard the familiar voice.

"Why are you calling *me?*" he asked.

"Because I know what you're up to, and it's not going to work."

Lloyd stiffened. "You listen here. I don't know what you've imagined or what you've got up your sleeve, but I don't like threats."

"Not only do I know your big secret, Lloyd, but I'm going to tell the world unless you give me what I want."

Lloyd's blood pressure shot through the roof. No way was he going to lose everything he'd worked for, not when it was within his reach.

And he damn sure wasn't going to let anyone blackmail him, especially tonight. So he ended the call without further comment.

He did, however, have half a notion to leave right now and put a stop to all that crap. But it could wait until tomorrow.

He glanced around the bar.

What the hell was taking Isabella so long?

He glanced around the room. the woman, it seemed had vanished without saying goodbye.

Chapter Twelve

Isabella walked home from the Trail's End at a pretty good clip. By the time she turned down her street, the high heels were causing her feet to ache, but she was so angry and frustrated, she didn't care.

She wouldn't have given Lloyd What's-his-name more than a passing glance, so it's not as though his deceitful charm had hurt her. But somehow, she felt violated on behalf of every woman in the world—married or single.

It sickened her to think that he was hanging out in nightclubs, preying on the lonely. And all the while, Mrs. What's-her-name waited at home, unsuspecting.

Her thoughts drifted to J.R., who waited at the ranch for her. Dinner was in the oven, Evie had said.

A pang of guilt poked at Isabella's chest. She hadn't exactly done the right thing herself today, either. She'd bailed out on J.R.'s invitation, and she hadn't even had the courtesy to tell him herself. Instead, she'd asked Evie to relay the message.

Once back at her apartment, Isabella kicked off her shoes and turned on the radio, trying to do something to still the silence that mocked the compulsion to cry her heart out. But the music didn't help, and she feared that she only had herself to blame.

What had provoked her to chat with a stranger anyway?

Right this moment, she had a decent man who deserved a little heart-to-heart chat with her. Yet she'd chosen to avoid him rather than make a decision or admit what was holding her back.

She'd wanted to blame her hesitancy on the fact that there might be something lacking in him. But now it seemed as though she was the one who'd fallen short.

What was so hard about telling him that she didn't want to cede control to anyone? That she was proud of her heritage and wanted a man who could respect that?

Why couldn't she just admit that she was wildly attracted to him, that she might even love him? That it scared the hell out of her to think of giving in?

She slipped off her clothes and pulled a pair of gray sweats out of the closet. She couldn't wait to get into something loose and comfortable.

She placed her dress on the stack of clothing she was planning to take to the dry cleaners. It wasn't as though it was soiled or couldn't be worn again—she'd only had it on briefly. But she wanted to shuck all reminders of the jerk she'd just met.

If she ever got seriously involved with anyone, he'd

be honorable and trustworthy. A man who would respect his wedding vows and go the distance to make their marriage work.

A man like J.R.? an inner voice asked.

The question hung in the air, and her movements stilled.

To be honest? J.R. certainly hadn't given her any reason to believe he was anything but that kind of man.

His attributes, many of which she'd once down-played, began to flicker on a screen in her mind, one after the other.

His dancing eyes.

That one-dimpled grin.

Those broad shoulders and taut abs.

His lovemaking skills.

But it wasn't just his physical attributes and talents coming to mind, it was his actions, too.

He went out in the fields and worked along with his men each day, getting dirty and sometimes coming home late to dinner.

And what about that birthday party he'd planned for her? It had gone off without a hitch, thanks to his careful planning.

Then there was the beautiful jewelry he'd chosen because it had reminded him of her.

He'd also chased down those kids at Fiesta and gotten Rusty for her, just because he'd sensed that she'd been enamored of the tiny ball of fur. He'd given her a chance to try out having a pet and had even been willing to step in and provide a home for the kitten if she felt she couldn't handle the added responsibility of pet ownership.

Oh, for Pete's sake. She'd also been reluctant to

assume the responsibility of a romantic relationship, without any guarantees that it might last. But wasn't that what it was all about? Loving someone enough to run that risk? To step out in faith and to make it work?

She ran her fingers through her hair and sat on the edge of the bed. She just realized that she had more baggage than she'd thought. What kind of woman would take all that J.R. had offered and throw it back in his face?

Okay, so he hadn't exactly offered her the moon, but she'd clearly known that he was headed in that direction.

What kind of woman *was* she?

Who was she?

She stood and walked to the mirror, where she looked at the image that stared back at her—the waifish eyes, the drab clothes. She might have missed it before, but right now, she could see every little hurt, every little scar that she'd ever had as a child.

Deep inside, she suspected that there might be a little girl, lost and lonely, trying to stand out in the crowd. Trying to pin her heart on someone who wouldn't let her down.

So what made her think that J.R. would let her down?

Just yesterday morning, when she woke to the aroma of the coffee he'd made and the breakfast he'd cooked, she just might have held all she'd ever wanted in the palm of her hand.

But she'd tossed it away.

Or had she?

She wouldn't blame J.R. if he never wanted to see her again. But she had to try to set things to right, even if it was just to share what was in her heart.

Determined to speak to him tonight, she started to

change out of her sweats, but thought better of it. What was she trying to prove with the stylish clothes, the bright colors, the pizzazz…?

She would go to him just as she was. Plain and vulnerable.

Honest.

But she'd better call a cab. No need taking any chances, even if she'd only had a single glass of wine.

While waiting for the driver to pick her up, she packed a few things in an overnight bag, just in case she decided to stay. Then she gathered the pet supplies she would need.

"Rusty?" she called to the kitten.

He poked his head around the doorjamb.

"Come on, little buddy. You're going, too."

She probably ought to worry about how Baron and Rusty would get along. But, in reality, it was only J.R.'s reaction that was on her mind.

J.R. and Toby had managed to jerry-rig that pump and get it going again until they could order a replacement.

He'd seen the old foreman at the Double Crown use the same trick, and it had worked like a charm back then.

It was nice being a part of the solution.

Still, now that he'd gotten home and was getting dinner ready for one instead of two, a cloud of disappointment settled over him. Not just because Isabella was supposedly busy, but because he figured she'd be using that excuse on him time and again.

He also realized that, as good as the sex had been, it apparently hadn't been enough. Isabella was looking for something J.R. couldn't provide.

He heard a vehicle pull into the driveway and wondered who it could be at this hour. Frank and Evie weren't due back for hours. And Toby had driven to San Antonio to meet Sarah's parents.

The doorbell sounded, and he placed the pan on the stove, then set the oven mitts on the counter.

When he answered, he damn near blinked to make sure he wasn't imagining things…

There stood Isabella, her hair a bit windblown, her purse and a canvas tote bag draped over her shoulder. She held a bag of supplies in one hand and the kitten in the other.

In the yard, a cab was backing up and turning around, leaving her on his doorstep, it seemed.

"I'm sure dinner is long over," she said, "but I really need to talk to you. And since I didn't want to ask the cab driver to wait, I was wondering if Rusty and I could spend the night."

"You certainly can if you'd like to." He stepped aside and let her in, yet he refrained from asking which bedroom she wanted to take. Something told him it wouldn't be his.

Dressed in those gray sweats, she looked ready for bed. Had she purposely chosen something that wouldn't arouse him? If so, that was too bad. It hadn't worked. Every cell in his body was buzzing just to have her within arms' length.

Hell, with the way he felt about her, he'd find her sexy dressed in a spacesuit.

"Is Baron around?" she asked. "I'm not sure how he's going to like having the kitten here again."

"He's napping by the fireplace in the great room. And as far as the cat goes, I'm sure there'll be a little hissing and barking, but they'll work it out, as they did when I first brought Rusty home."

At least, he hoped they would. It could end up being a long night. But then again, maybe the cat and dog would work things out before J.R. and Isabella would.

"Can I get you something to drink?" he asked. "A glass of wine maybe?"

"Actually, I'd rather have water. I had a glass of wine earlier, which is why I took a cab."

He didn't ask where she'd been or who she'd had the wine with. At this point, it wasn't his business, even if he'd like it to be.

"Why don't you set up a place for Rusty in the guest room?" he suggested. "We can separate him and Baron if we need to. Then I'll meet you in the courtyard."

"All right. I brought his litter pan and a few of his favorite toys."

As she followed his suggestion, he went to the court-yard, where the table was still set for two. He lit the candles, then turned the music on low. No need to waste the ambience he'd so carefully planned. Of course, depending on what she'd come to say, the ambience might fall flat anyway.

Next, he went into the kitchen, where he took the salad out of the fridge. He removed the plastic wrap and carried the bowl to the table. Then he dished up the hot meal.

Moments later, the table was ready.

"Ooh," she said from the alcove. "It's really beautiful. I hadn't imagined it with candles lit and the lanterns glowing."

She turned, scanning the courtyard, where the water trickled into the fountain.

"It has a completely different feel at night," he said, "doesn't it?"

"You're right. I'm so glad we started the renovations here."

So was he. And no matter what happened this evening, he was glad to finally be able to share the finished product with her.

He pulled out her chair, and she took a seat. Then he joined her.

She looked at her plate, noting the tamales and enchiladas. Then she scanned the courtyard and furrowed her brow. "Is that Tejana music?"

He nodded. "I thought you might like it. Do you want me to turn the sound up a little louder?"

"Yes, but not right now. I'd like to tell you something first."

"Shoot." He sat back in his chair and braced himself for the let's-be-friends talk. Or maybe the it's-not-you-it's-me speech.

"Earlier this year," she said, "I made a detailed list of all the things I wanted in a man. To be honest, when I first met you, I didn't think you fit too many of them."

He wasn't sure where she was going with this, nor whether he was up for hearing why. His ego, which had always been strong, had hit a low point today.

"Even after I got to know you," she said, "I down-played some of your finer qualities, convincing myself that things wouldn't work out between us."

So far, she was right. Things didn't seem to be working out at all, but he bit his tongue and waited her out.

"I have a confession to make, J.R. You were right. The chemistry between us is magic. Making love with you was beyond my wildest dreams."

A smile tugged at his lips. As far as he was concerned, that said a hell of a lot. Any of the other things were negotiable.

"I might even love you," she added.

The heaviness that had been dogging him this evening began to lift. "So what's the problem?"

She sat back in her seat and crossed her arms. "I know that you're an orchestrator. You make things happen. You see what needs to be done, and poof. People do your bidding, and things happen your way."

He didn't see a problem with that. "I'm sorry, Isabella. From my point of view, that should be an asset, not a liability."

"I'm sure you do see it that way. But I don't want to be controlled. I want to call the shots sometimes. And I want to know that my hopes and dreams—past, present and future—will be respected."

He reached across the table and placed his hand on top of hers. "I would never purposely try to steamroll over you or your desires. If I ever get carried away, all you have to do is tell me to back off."

"And you'll promise to do that?"

He cocked his head slightly and slid her a crooked smile. "Back off? Well, I'm not sure. It would depend,

I guess. But I'll always respect your wishes, always temper my opinion based on your advice, your desires. And that *is* a promise."

She didn't respond right away, and he wondered if he'd somehow blown it already. But he wasn't going to let her have free rein and expect him to bow down to her every dictate. In a good relationship, a man and a woman learned to compromise. He'd seen the way it worked in his parents' marriage, and he suspected that was something she'd missed seeing while she was growing up.

"I want you to know that I appreciated the birthday celebration. And I like what you've done here tonight. It's special, and it really touches my heart. But…"

"But what?"

"My stepfather loved my mother, but he called all the shots. She loved him, so she agreed. But I'm not about to live like that, no matter how much I care for a man."

"I wouldn't respect you if you kowtowed to me on everything I said or wanted."

She picked up her glass and took a sip of water.

"For the record," he added, "I've been planning this dinner since the first time I stepped foot in this house. I wanted to see you here, wanted to share it with you."

"You've been planning this dinner that long?"

He nodded. "I think I fell in love with you the very first time we met, Isabella. At Fiesta, with your beautiful tapestries and your incredible eye for color and beauty."

She glanced down at her sweats, picking at the material in the oversize shirt. When she looked up, she smiled. "I used to be uncomfortable when I'd go places with my stepdad and his children because I felt as though I didn't fit in. So I began to counteract that awful feeling by dressing in a way that said, 'Look at me. I'm someone to be respected, to be noticed.'"

"You can rest assured that I'd notice you anywhere and wearing anything. I don't care if you're in a used gunny sack or the latest beaded gown—you're one in a million, Isabella."

She flushed at the pleasure of his compliment. "Thank you, J.R."

While he finished his salad, he realized that he had an admission to make. Because part of what she'd said had been true. He might have wanted to please her with the decorating job, the birthday party, even this dinner. But he'd had ulterior motives. Good ones, to be sure. Still, he'd tried to persuade her to do what he'd wanted her to.

"I have an apology to make," he finally admitted. "I thought that I could get you to see things my way. And I realize that I was wrong."

He glanced across the table, wondering if she would accept his apology.

"How were you wrong?" Isabella asked.

Was he realizing that he'd made a mistake by thinking he cared for her? Had her confession somehow diminished her in his sight?

"I love you, Isabella. And while I suspect that we're both strong-willed, I believe in compromise." He took the hand he'd been covering, turned it over and gave it a gentle squeeze. "More than anything, I'd like for the two of us to make a commitment tonight, but I understand if you're not ready. So I'll step back and let you take things at your own pace."

She'd made a list, but she'd used it to shield herself, to keep her from getting in too deep, from risking her heart. But the only way to freely love, was to open her heart and give love a chance. And that's just what she intended to do.

J.R., she realized, was the man she'd been looking for, the man she'd been hoping for. Her heart filled with so much joy that she thought it would spill over.

"I'd like to make that commitment now," she said.

"Nothing would make me happier."

J.R. stood, took her into his arms and kissed her. She kissed him right back, relishing the love that had been there all along.

When her legs were ready to buckle from his sweet assault of her mouth, he took her hand and led her to the master bedroom. "You wanted to start on the court-yard first, and you were right. It *is* the center of the house. But let's decorate this room next. I want it to reflect us both—our likes, our hopes, our dreams."

"There's nothing I'd like better."

They kissed again, and then he lifted her into his arms and placed her on the bed.

With the windows cracked open, and the background sounds of the ranch at rest, they made love—slowly at first, taking time to cherish the love they'd each declared for the other, the dreams that would take off tonight.

In the afterglow, as they lay wrapped in love, cele-brating the newness of their relationship, J.R. placed a lingering kiss on her brow. Then he slowly got out of bed and stood beside the nightstand.

She watched him open the top drawer, reach inside

and remove something small. When he returned to bed, he held a black, velvet-covered box that fit in his palm.

He handed it to her. "I have something for you."

"What's this?" she asked.

"Why don't you look and see?"

She opened it and saw a diamond ring. It wasn't especially large, but the stone sparkled as if it held all the magic in the world.

"It was my mother's," he said.

"It's beautiful."

"Before she died, she told me to look for my soul mate. She promised I'd find her. And I did. Marry me, Isabella. Be my wife, my best friend and my partner in life."

She didn't know what to say, but not from indecision. That was no longer her problem. Now her biggest struggle was in trying to wrap her heart around all the love flowing inside her.

"I love you, too, J.R. And I can't wait to marry you and start a family. I want a houseful of boys, just as your mother had. And I want them all to be like you."

A smile burst on his face, lighting up his eyes. "I'd like a couple of girls, too. Each one of them as pretty and as talented as their mama."

She withdrew the diamond that had once belonged to Molly Fortune.

"Let me," he said, as he took the ring from her and slipped it on the third finger of her left hand. "I love you, Isabella. And I promise to honor and protect you for the rest of my life. I can't wait to teach our children about their diverse heritage. And I can't wait to start a few new traditions of our own."

In her heart, she knew he would do whatever it took to keep that promise. And so would she. Their children would be unique individuals, yet part of a strong and rich heritage, a chain stretching back through generations.

Just as they sank back on the bed, ready to celebrate the love they'd just declared, the commitment they'd made, her cell phone rang.

She wanted to ignore the call and tell the world to go away, to leave them alone, but then she glanced at the display and recognized her father's number.

"I'd better get this," she said. "It's my dad."

"Uh-oh. Maybe I should have asked for your hand."

She smiled, then placed her index finger over her lips, shushing him. Her father didn't have to know that they'd had their honeymoon before J.R. had formally declared his intentions.

"Hi, Dad." She flashed a smile at J.R.

He made a little small talk at first, checking to see where she was. What she was doing. Then he went on to tell her why he'd called.

"I wanted to give you an update. I just heard through the grapevine that Roberto Mendoza received an urgent message from an anonymous caller, requesting a meeting with him at the Spring Fling and offering information he'd like to know."

Roberto was Isabella's cousin, the eldest son of José and Maria.

"*Mija,*" her father added. "We don't know who's behind the threats that have been made or where they'll strike next. So please be careful."

Isabella looked at J.R., the man she loved. "I'm in good hands, Papa."

And she was.

Neither she nor J.R. knew what tomorrow might bring, but it really didn't matter. Together, they would face whatever the future might hold.

* * * * *

A Fortune Wedding
by
Kristin Hardy

Red Rock, Texas
July 1991

"Come on, boy, come on," Roberto Mendoza muttered, crouching over the withers of Cisco, his big bay gelding, as they raced up the tree-studded grassy slope. The speed was intoxicating. The wind rushed over his skin. A kaleidoscope of sound filled his ears—the thud of hoofbeats, the rush of his own breath.

The silvery sound of laughter ahead of him.

And then they burst up onto the hilltop, the great blue bowl of the sky arching overhead.

"Hah! We beat you!" Frannie Fortune whooped, reining in her little chestnut mare and wheeling around. "Who says the girls can't outdo the boys?" With her short, sunbeam-blond hair and tilted eyes, she looked like a pixie, ready for mischief.

Life, Roberto thought, just didn't get any better than this.

"You girls only won because you took a shortcut," he told her.

"Don't blame us because we're smarter. We just took a faster way."

"Yeah, like straight up the side of the hill."

"Admit it, you're impressed."

He grinned. "I am, but next time you decide to take your shortcut, leave me with a suicide note for your uncle. I'm supposed to be watching out for you."

Her cheeks were still flushed with the excitement of the race. "I keep telling Uncle Ryan I don't need looking after. So I got thrown once. It can happen to anyone. You try staying in the saddle when a killdeer flies up between the feet of that monster you're on," she challenged. "See how you feel when your fanny hits the ground."

Roberto's lips twitched as he slid off Cisco. "I guess you'll have to come to my rescue."

"If you're lucky." She gave him an arch look.

How had he ever thought her standoffish? It hadn't been that, but simple shyness that had kept her quiet and to herself when she'd first arrived at the Double Crown Ranch where he worked. As the weeks had passed, she'd blossomed, quiet diffidence giving way to a sly humor that perpetually hovered around that delicate mouth, the surprisingly bawdy laughter that burst out of her more and more often as the days went by.

Maybe it was just being here, out on the ranch, amid the rolling terrain of Texas hill country. It could make anybody happy, although he might be biased. No matter where his life took him, Roberto thought, no place would ever feel as right as this patch of territory where he knew nearly every tree, bush and bird by name. It was in his blood, as much a part of him as his brown eyes.

Frannie walked over to stand next to him. "You think you'll ever leave here?" she asked, as if she knew what he'd been thinking.

He watched as she bent down to pick a long stalk of grass. "I'd have to have a real good reason. I figure I'll save my money, buy a place of my own someday."

Living and working out on the land, he couldn't imagine anything better. Certainly not sitting all day in a college classroom, no matter how much his father wanted him to. José Mendoza hadn't taken the news of his twenty-year-old son dropping out well. To avoid skull fractures from the two of them butting heads in the family's restaurant, Red, Roberto had come to work at the Double Crown, where his uncle Ruben Mendoza ran operations for the Fortune family.

And where the lovely, coltish Frannie had appeared for a visit just days later.

Too bad she'd somehow gotten snowed into dating Lloyd Fredericks, the original self-important, silver-spoon guy. But she was a Fortune and he was a Fredericks, so maybe they did belong together. It still set Roberto's teeth on edge every time he saw Fredericks drive in to pick her up. The jerk didn't deserve a woman like Frannie.

"So, what are you going to call your ranch?" Frannie interrupted his thoughts. "The Rocking RM? The Double R?"

"I was thinking Red Oaks."

"How about the Slowpoke?" she offered.

His eyes narrowed. "Remind me again who won when we raced last week?"

"That's because you had an unfair advantage," she argued. "Cisco's two hands taller than Peaches. We had to outsmart you."

What she'd done was about stop his heart when he'd seen her tearing up the side of the hill. She might have started out quiet and shy, but she was fearless now.

"You just got lucky this time," he said.

"No, I was prepared," Frannie corrected him, twirling her grass. "Lloyd says that's what luck is, just opportunity meeting preparation."

"That sounds like your boyfriend. Always looking for an angle."

She rolled her eyes. "He's not my boyfriend. We're just going out. Anyway, I don't want to talk about Lloyd. You buy Red Oaks and I'll come to visit." She gave him an impish look. "And Peaches and I will beat you then, too."

He reached out and swiped the blade of grass from her hand.

"Hey," she protested.

"You need to learn some respect for your elders."

"My elders?" She snorted. "You think a fancy new hat makes you all grown-up?" That all-too-delectable mouth of hers curved.

Roberto eyed her. "You got a problem with my hat?"

"I don't know, but maybe you do." And quick as a flash, she swiped the black Stetson and dashed away, squealing.

He sprinted after her. "Oh, you're gonna be sorry."

"Big talk," she scoffed, clapping the hat on top of her

head. She was willow thin and fleet, feinting one direction and dashing the other, making him give chase until both of them were laughing and out of breath, circling the red oak that crowned the top of the hill.

"Give it up," he told her as they faced off on either side of a stand of piñon.

She glanced over to Peaches as though judging her distance. "Not a chance." She faked one way and he mirrored her, faked the other. And then she went just a fraction too far and he whipped around the tree and caught her, snaking an arm around her waist to draw her in.

"That's it, *chica,* you're in for it now," he growled.

"Oh, yeah? What are you going to do to me?" There was humor in those soft blue eyes, and mischief and glee. And under it all, something else, something that started the blood rushing in his veins. He caught a hint of scent that made him think of spring and sunshine. He could feel every breath she took. His pulse thundered in his ears.

She wasn't even out of school yet, he reminded himself. He worked for her uncle. He had no business kissing her. Even as his lips hovered over hers, he made himself release her.

And then Frannie leaned in to press her sweet, warm mouth to his.

SPECIAL MOMENTS™

Single titles coming next month

THE BRAVO BACHELOR
by Christine Rimmer

For Gabe Bravo, sweet-talking young widow Mary into selling her ranch should have been a cinch. But the stubborn mum turned the tables and got him to bargain away his bachelorhood instead!

THE NANNY SOLUTION
by Teresa Hill

Audrey had only been hired to look after Simon's tiny daughter's dog! But Simon was the perfect boss – and now his patience and understanding might just prove impossible for Audrey to resist.

AN IDEAL FATHER
by Elaine Grant

Cimarron is reluctant to become guardian of his orphaned nephew. But headstrong, gorgeous Sarah James knows he'd make a great dad. Can this flawed man become an ideal father?

NOT WITHOUT HER FAMILY
by Beth Andrews

Kelsey is trying to prove her brother's innocence – and creating nothing but trouble for Jack Martin, chief of police. Jack should steer clear, but he's finding Kelsey fascinating…

On sale 19th March 2010

Available at WHSmith, Tesco, ASDA, Eason and all good bookshops.
For full Mills & Boon range including eBooks visit
www.millsandboon.co.uk

MILLS & BOON® ROMANCE

is proud to present

Jewels of the Desert

Deserts, diamonds and destiny!

The Kingdom of Quishari: two rulers, with hearts as
hard as the rugged landscape they reign over,
are in need of Desert Queens…

When they offer convenient proposals, will they
discover doing your duty doesn't have to
mean ignoring your heart?

Sheikh Rashid and his twin brother Sheikh Khalid
are looking for brides in…

ACCIDENTALLY THE SHEIKH'S WIFE

And

MARRYING THE SCARRED SHEIKH

by Barbara McMahon

in April 2010

millsandboon.co.uk Community

Join Us!

The Community is the perfect place to meet and chat to kindred spirits who love books and reading as much as you do, but it's also the place to:

- **Get the inside scoop from authors about their latest books**
- **Learn how to write a romance book with advice from our edito**
- **Help us to continue publishing the best in women's fiction**
- **Share your thoughts on the books we publish**
- **Befriend other users**

Forums: Interact with each other as well as authors, editors and a whole host of other users worldwide.

Blogs: Every registered community member has their own blog to tell the world what they're up to and what's on their mind.

Book Challenge: We're aiming to read 5,000 books and have joined forces with The Reading Agency in our inaugural Book Challenge.

Profile Page: Showcase yourself and keep a record of your recent community activity.

Social Networking: We've added buttons at the end of every post to share via digg, Facebook, Google, Yahoo, technorati and de.licio.us.

www.millsandboon.co.uk

✳ 2 FREE BOOKS
AND A SURPRISE GIFT

We would like to take this opportunity to thank you for reading this Mills & Boon® book by offering you the chance to take TWO more specially selected books from the Special Moments™ series absolutely FREE! We're also making this offer to introduce you to the benefits of the Mills & Boon® Book Club™—

- **FREE home delivery**
- **FREE gifts and competitions**
- **FREE monthly Newsletter**
- **Exclusive Mills & Boon Book Club offers**
- **Books available before they're in the shops**

Accepting these FREE books and gift places you under no obligation to buy, you may cancel at any time, even after receiving your free books. Simply complete your details below and return the entire page to the address below. You don't even need a stamp!

YES Please send me 2 free Special Moments books and a surprise gift. I understand that unless you hear from me, I will receive 5 superb new stories every month, including a 2-in-1 book priced at £4.99 and three single books priced at £3.19 each, postage and packing free. I am under no obligation to purchase any books and may cancel my subscription at any time. The free books and gift will be mine to keep in any case.

Ms/Mrs/Miss/Mr _____ Initials _____

_____

Surname _____

Address _____

_____

_____ Postcode _____

Send this whole page to: Mills & Boon Book Club, Free Book Offer, FREEPOST NAT 10298, Richmond, TW9 1BR